BOUND

A DESICCATED LEGACY BOOK 1

TASHA HAYES

AUSSIE INDIE AUTHORS

Second edition

ISBN: 978-1-7642384-5-8

For anyone who has ever been made to feel less-than.

Keep going, keep fighting.

You are worth it.

MY HUMANITY IS BOUND UP IN YOURS,

FOR WE CAN ONLY BE HUMAN TOGETHER.

- DESMOND TUTU

1

Mila crouched low in the shadows of the corn stalks, her breath tight as she watched her older brother prepare the lesson.

The sun shone bright above them, ever vigilant in the vast expanse of blue. A faint breeze sent the leaves and stalks twitching around them, and Mila swept a tendril of long, dark hair from in front of her eyes. She didn't want to miss a single second of this.

Nasir knelt on folded legs, the tops of his old leather boots flat against the soil. His movements were deliberate, cautious, as if the ground itself might betray them if not treated with the reverence it deserved.

"Watch closely, Mila," Nasir whispered, his concentration already directed to the bare patch of earth before him. "See my breathing? Slow, measured, controlled. This is not just about your intention—it's about controlling what you feel."

Mila nodded, biting back the retort that fluttered at the edge of her mind. She knew all of this. But she also knew better than to interrupt this moment. She picked at the skin around her thumb nail with her forefinger, forcing herself to wait. The breeze fell, and the cornfield was still, silent. The world seemed to be holding its breath. Even the birds and insects knew the risk that lurked in this act.

Nasir stretched out both hands, splayed his fingers and pressed his fingertips into the soil. The contact was tender but firm, like a handshake between partners. Mila leaned forward slightly, her viridian eyes locked on his fingers as they descended into the earth.

Nervousness twisted Mila's stomach, but she pushed it down. This was too important. Within the Satarian community, the knowledge of creomancy flickered like the last embers of a dying fire—fragile, faint and feeble—much to the delight of the government of Ard Aman. Only through rebellious acts like this did they keep the magic alive, and barely. The flame was far too close to being put out forever.

Nasir began to murmur the ancient phrases, his face tightened in concentration, brows drawn together as he focused his eyes on something Mila couldn't yet see.

"Y pemetteray, Gaia, ay dar r'mahiya…"

It was a quiet conversation with the goddess of the earth, Gaia, requesting permission to access her power.

At first, nothing seemed to be happening. Then, suddenly, Mila felt it deep inside the foundation of her being. She took a sharp inhale as the atoms of the universe shifted, sending a thrill up her spine.

The dirt in front of Nasir stirred. It was almost imperceptible at first, then more insistent, and a crack appeared in the soil. From the crack, a delicate sprout emerged into the sunlight, quivering as it grew. It was the purest shade of green, fresh and beautiful as new life always is. It seemed to be yawning and stretching, the way it unfurled into a slender blade that reached towards the sky.

Soon the shoot thickened, leaves unlatched and flopped outwards, and still it grew. Pale tassels began to appear, then hard-looking bulges grew out from between the leaves. After barely twenty seconds, when the tassels turned brown and the bulges looked heavy and thick, Nasir's muttering changed.

"Tyudin velle pariar."

Mila's heart pounded painfully in her chest. She had seen him do this before—had done it before herself—but each time it felt like witnessing a miracle. Something forbidden, yes, but also something so pure and natural that it made the laws against it seem childish and pitiful. How could anyone look at such a marvel and call it a crime? Mila felt a familiar rush of anger at the injustice of it, burning in her gut like molten metal. Why should the Satarian people have to hide their magic? Why should they have to choke down their own heritage, their very essence, for fear of punishment? It wasn't right—but it was pointless thinking like this. There was nothing they could do to change things, no matter how unfair it was.

Mila sighed, letting her quick, fiery burst of boldness drown. She just had to have hope. In time, those in power had to realise that creomancy wasn't the evil they made it out to be.

The soil where Nasir's fingers had connected was now just dust, parched and light, as if the moisture had been completely sucked out of every grain in a radius around his hands. The contrast was stark; two rough circles of pale, deadened granules surrounded by dark, lush earth.

Nasir withdrew his hands, taking deep, calm breaths, then he opened his eyes and looked at Mila. The peacefulness in his gaze was layered with a hint of pride.

"Go on," he said, raising an eyebrow.

Mila stood and examined the new growth, a stalk that stretched taller than her own height, coloured the vibrant green of new life. She grabbed one of the bulges and pried it from its place, then peeled away the crisp husks to reveal kernels in every shade of yellow imaginable. She smiled. It was truly amazing what they could do.

A glint of sunlight caught her eye as Nasir extracted something from inside his tunic; a small shard of metal, honed to sharpness. He took a deep breath and whipped the makeshift blade across his skin, just above the dark birthmark that marred his outer forearm. Blood surged out, seeping down his brown skin to fall in droplets onto the dried soil. As Mila watched, the desiccated dirt devoured the blood and began to darken with renewed vitality. A grimace wrought her face.

"I hate that part," she said, looking down at her brother.

Nasir dropped the blade and wiped at the sheen of sweat that had appeared on his brow, leaving a smear of dirt. "*Pariar* is perhaps the most important aspect of creomancy, Mila. We take from the land, we must give back to the land, one way or another. Otherwise, it will all end up like this." He grabbed a fistful of the dried soil, lifted it and allowed the grains to trickle from his grasp with the breeze. "All dead. And us with it."

Between them, the shoot swayed gently beneath the midday sun, fragile evidence of the strength hidden in the earth—and within them. Their viridian eyes met.

"I'm sick of all this little stuff," Mila said. "Making crops grow, splitting rocks, shifting soil… We've been doing that for weeks. Can we practice something else, something better?"

Nasir eyed her carefully. "I don't think you're ready yet."

"Why not? You know I can do it."

"It's not about your ability, it's about the balance. *Pariar*. You go too fast."

"So?"

"*So*," Nasir countered, a touch of impatience in his voice. "It means you're not connecting properly. You're not in complete control of how the magic will use your body. Until you can access the earth's power without *it* accessing *you*, you're not ready for anything bigger. You risk depleting the earth—or yourself—beyond repair."

Mila scowled, but she didn't push it. She knew Nasir wouldn't budge if there was any danger to her safety, and it was crucial that they went about these lessons the right way, without taking any risks. If the government realised they were using their magic, or if the guards caught them at it... The consequences were too terrible to think about.

Creomancy was deemed illegal centuries ago and, as a result, without the freedom to practice, most of the Satarian community had let their magic wither and die like crops in the winter. It was safer that way, they thought, doing what the Amanese decided was best.

But Mila's family line had not let it die. The intricacies of creomancy were too important to let slip away into dust. This knowledge was their birthright, guarded fiercely and passed down in whispers from generation to generation. Their parents had been taught, just as their parents before them, and now Nasir was teaching her.

Teaching her far too slowly.

"Fine," Mila huffed, and she knelt in the fertile patch of soil, tugging the draping fabric of her grey tunic out of the way with a loud sigh. She tried to settle herself, but she couldn't help it; questions simmered in her mind, distorting her focus. She felt herself scowling, betraying her inner turbulence.

Nasir cocked his head. "Go on then, spit it out."

Mila sighed again. "It's nothing new, Nasir, but... I just don't understand *what* the Amanese are afraid of!" She looked to the sky as the bitterness came bubbling out. "They're so *ignorant*. We could use our magic to help people, to make things better for everyone... Why wouldn't they want that?"

Nasir's expression hardened, shadows deepening in his eyes. "They can't see the good, though, Mila. When you live in fear, you can't begin to trust, and without trust, there can be no understanding."

"But *why* are they afraid? What have we ever done to them? Our magic is for *growth*… and, even so, it's practically all gone!"

"I remember pada said once, fear is good at finding depth to the faintest shadows. We see the fire's light and warmth; they only see its power to burn."

"But—"

"Enough," Nasir cut in. "There's no point going down this path. *Concentrate*. Feel your intention. What do you want to do?"

I want to get answers, Mila thought. What Nasir had said made no sense. Depth to the faintest shadows? If the Satarians were in shadow, it was because the Amanese stood blocking the sun. The people of Ard Aman regarded the Satarians as nothing more than filth clinging to the soles of their shoes… yet that caused the Amanese to fear *them?* Mila wanted to press the matter, wanted to debate the idea with Nasir and come up with an answer. But, she knew, no matter what he said, it wouldn't change anything. The siblings could theorise for days on end, but knowing *why* didn't change the fact that the Amanese held all the power.

She reluctantly let the questions go, at least for the moment.

"I want to grow a corn stalk," Mila said instead, peeking up at him with one eye open, "With even better corn than yours."

Nasir rolled his eyes. "*Concentrate,* Cricket."

Mila stuck her tongue out at him.

Cricket. The nickname had come about one morning when, before heading to the creche, her mother, Sara, had been trying to do her hair— a difficult task at the best of times with her voluminous curls.

"Will you hold still for one minute?" Sara had said, doing her best to twist the elastic tie without pulling her daughter's hair.

"I can't," young Mila whined, bouncing from one foot to the other. She was much better at running and jumping than sitting still, much better at dancing and creating than listening. "My legs are full of energy!"

Her father smiled. "She's like a little cricket, always hopping around, always busy."

"Little Cricket," Sara mused. "That suits her to a tee."

Even as she grew older, and her movements became a little more controlled, exasperated cries of 'wait, *wait*' still followed Mila wherever she went. And so the nickname stayed. It perfectly matched the restless energy she always felt bubbling away just under the surface. She had always hated waiting.

Mila turned her gaze down and cleared her mind of all but the intention: *growth*. Then she pressed her fingers to the soil, feeling the slight coldness, the slight dampness, the promise of energy in every dark grain. As she began to chant, she tried to imagine her veins snaking out and connecting like roots into the soil, the way Nasir had taught her. She searched for the familiar hum of the earth in her heartbeat, an ancient pulse that was always there, waiting for her to reach out.

"Y pemetteray, Gaia, ay dar r'mahiya..."

Then she felt, in the centre of her chest, a sensation of warm golden light. The sunshine feeling, Mila called it, because that was what it felt like; pure and simple and right. She pictured the beginning of the corn stalk in her mind's eye and began to manifest the green shoot pushing up through the earth.

"Breathe deeply, take it slow," Nasir's voice said from a world away. "You are a channel, not a dam. Don't hold onto the power, just let it flow through you."

"Ad tay khiedery, plezht y pemetteray Gaia..."

Pride rippled through her as the seedling formed in the soil before her eyes, the magic filling in reality around her blueprints. The connection with the earth made her very blood feel warmer, made her atoms vibrate at a different frequency. The universe was open to her, full of possibilities and ideas and creation. Mila had to focus on allowing herself to be vulnerable, to allow the magic to flow through as Nasir said. It felt comfortable, natural, freeing… but also scary, to be unbound in such a way. Her instinct was to hold onto the reins of her magic, but she knew she shouldn't. She pushed herself to breathe through it.

Seconds later, as the tassels on the corn ears turned brown, Mila thanked the goddess, Gaia, and allowed the sunshine feeling to fade.

"Nicely ended," Nasir said. He was standing, examining her creation just as she had done his. As he held out the ear of corn to her, he said, "How do you feel?"

"Fine," Mila said. In truth, though, she felt a little lightheaded, and she tried to still her trembling hand as she took the corn from her brother. Inside the crisp green husk glistened plump kernels in golden rows. It was perfect.

Nasir's eyes narrowed with concern. Her tough façade didn't fool him; he always saw straight through her, and he sensed her struggle. Mila dropped her gaze to the soil beneath her hands, surprised and annoyed to see that most of the dirt was still lush and dark, with only faint traces of the same dryness that Nasir had caused. She had really tried to be a conduit this time, to allow the magic to run through her like liquid through a straw. But it made little difference.

With a grunt of frustration, Mila cast around her in the dried soil, looking for the blade that Nasir had dropped earlier.

"Mila," Nasir said gently. "You're not doing the *pariar*."

"I can do it, Nasir. I'm stronger than you think I am."

Her brother's eyes twinkled at her tone. "You're exhausted, Cricket."

"I'm fine! Look at the corn I made—it's flawless this time. I worked hard to control the build, to do it properly. Construct with care, like you said. None of the kernels are missing or shrivelled!"

"It's good," Nasir conceded, "Great, even. But there's no need to spill your blood. The flow is still taking too much of your own energy. You must let the magic move through you freely, and trust that it will do what you want it to. Instead, you've sacrificed too much of your *own* energy trying to control it. The earth was barely involved." He indicated the places where her fingers had dug into the soil. It was only just distinguishable from the surrounding earth.

Mila scowled. "How am I supposed to let the magic move freely when I've never known that feeling myself?"

"I know it's hard," Nasir said. "But you'll get it, don't worry. We can try again in a little bit."

He was already holding the shard of metal, and he reopened his wound from earlier. In silence, they both watched several crimson droplets fall onto the barely dried soil, turning it dark once more.

"I'll work on it, but not today. I'm supposed to go to Haman this afternoon."

Nasir looked at her sharply. "Alone?"

"What's the matter, Nasir? I've been to the bazaar countless times. You don't trust me enough to do something as simple as buying light globes?" Mila raised her eyebrows, pretending to be offended.

Nasir made a face. "It's not about trust, you know that. It's about keeping you safe."

"I'm twenty years old, Nasir. I can take care of myself."

"It doesn't matter how old you are, I'm always going to worry about you. And Haman is a hostile place these days."

It was Mila's turn to roll her eyes. "You're so dramatic! I'll be fine. I'll be back before you know it."

Nasir eyed her for a second longer. Always the big brother.

"Well, you can't go looking like that," he said eventually, indicating her hands where clods of dirt still stuck to her fingers.

"Of course not," Mila said with a dry chuckle. "Can you imagine? *Creo, creo! She's been doing magic!* They'd hang me on the spot. You really wouldn't trust me to shop alone after that." Mila gave a winning smile as she wiped her hands on her dark slacks. The movement did little to remove the dirt trapped under her nails and around her cuticles. "Guess I'd better go scrub up. Are you staying out here?"

"The crops won't harvest themselves," Nasir said, giving her a wink as she began the walk back to camp.

2

A short while later, with her fingers scrubbed raw and all trace of the illicit lessons washed away, Mila pulled a clean tunic over her head. It was the same grey as everything else she owned, the same grey that all Satarians wore. Dreary, drab, unremarkable sameness: the unofficial uniform of Al'Mazraea refugee camp.

Their dwelling followed the same pattern; identical to all the others in the sprawling maze, their canvas shelter was a faded burnt orange colour, the thick material patched many times over the years. But, when one looked closely, furtive signs of her family's individuality were all around. Strips of torn fabric, dyed with the hues of crushed vegetables and plants, fluttered from the awning. Inside, hanging against the far wall, was the tapestry her mother had been working on for as long as Mila could remember, adding threads here and there when they could be scavenged. Beside this hung the small portrait of Mila that her father had drawn with charcoal onto a slip of bark.

A single cabinet made from foraged materials sat near the stove, holding simple crockery and preserved foods on the top shelves. Scattered among these items were a few figures that Nasir had whittled from wood, when it could be spared. Mila's favourite of all his designs were the flowers, and one rose in particular, intricate and meticulously carved. It sat in stark contrast beside a sculpture that a young Mila had made many years ago, from sticks and leaves. No one could remember what the piece of art was supposed to represent, but it was cherished all the same.

The bottom half of the cabinet was divided into drawers, one for each family member's clothing. It was an heirloom of sorts, fashioned—if Mila recalled correctly—by her grandmother's father. Beneath its unassuming exterior lay a clever secret: a false bottom, discreetly designed to keep certain items hidden from the prying eyes of guards during their routine inspections for contraband.

It was this false bottom that Mila now accessed, deftly lifting the hidden panel to reveal the small cache beneath. She went to snatch the black coin purse but, before she could, her attention was caught by the few other treasures nestled there. A brass ring inlayed with a clear stone that Mila had always hoped would fit her skinny fingers one day. A lone metal pendant shaped like a kite, its oxidising silver surface gleaming in the dim light.

Beside these lay the necklace. Mila had asked her parents about it once, about why they kept such a hideous thing. All Mila could gather from their vague explanation was that the necklace was a part of their history, but they didn't seem to know any more than that, and they wouldn't let her touch it. Made of thin straps of leather wrapped around small, yellowed bones, it sent a shiver through Mila every time she saw it, and she quickly averted her eyes to a treasure she *did* like to look at: the map.

The creased parchment was browned with age and split all along the edges, and Mila unfolded it with meticulous care. Her hungry eyes devoured the familiar illustrations; mountains rose in toothy lines, rivers snaked across the land like veins, and vast forests were depicted with tiny clusters of etched trees. Though the ink had faded to a soft charcoal grey, the delicate details remained distinct.

Handwritten glyphs were scattered across the map, their complicated shapes both beautiful and maddeningly unreadable. Like every time before, Mila wished she could unlock their meaning. The Amanese government had worked hard to eradicate every aspect of Satarian culture, and as a result, the written form of the language had been lost to time and memory. The curving symbols meant nothing.

Or—almost nothing.

Mila traced a finger over the emboldened, larger symbols across the top of the map.

Over the years, she was fairly certain she had deciphered what they said: *Stara Zhem*. The old lands.

Mila scowled. Each relic, passed down through countless years, only served to remind her of their long history in the camp. Generation after generation, born and lived and died within these grounds. That was all anyone had ever known, and Mila hated the idea that that was all her life would be too. The idea was depressing and disheartening in a way she could never describe, and there was nothing she could do about it.

She stared at the map for a moment longer, then gave herself a shake. The day was getting on, and she had a long walk ahead of her. Mila gently refolded the map, carefully placing it back in the drawer and grabbed the coin purse before lowering the hidden panel once again.

With the purse tucked into her tunic, Mila slipped out of the tent, blinking as her eyes adjusted to the soft, golden light of the early-afternoon sun. The familiar paths of the camp wound away between the tents, the ground beaten flat by generations of footsteps. The autumn air played with her dark curls, carrying the occasional whiff of smoke from cooking fires. As she headed up the main path, the camp hummed with activity all round. People moved with a subdued pace as they tended to their daily tasks—repairing tents, chopping firewood—their movements routine and steady. Always the same set of tasks, day after day, year after year. Some had grown to find it comforting; Mila found it stifling.

As she neared the north-western edge of the camp, the border fence came into view—a rough structure of wooden posts and crossbars, standing about two meters tall. The top of each post was sharpened to a point, though fist-sized gaps between the slats made it easy to peer through, if one dared to get close enough.

It had been there all her life, that fence—imposing, but familiar, like an old wound that had long since scarred over. And just as any scar acts as an inescapable memento, this one reminded her that her world was a prison, and it always would be.

The hum of the camp faded away behind her as Mila neared Checkpoint B, the more southern of the two checkpoints in the border fence. Mila joined the queue, insides twisting with the familiar dread that came whenever she approached the guards. The scars on her back tingled.

Her gaze drifted through the gaps in the fence, across the expanse that separated her world from the Amanese land beyond. Guards patrolled along the other side, their dark uniforms stark against this stretch of land they called the Salt Strip; a barren section of white pebbles that glittered in the sunlight, deceptively alluring. The crunch of those stones underfoot acted as an alarm and a death sentence for anyone foolish enough to try to cross without approval.

Beyond the Salt Strip lay the city walls of Haman. The vast stone face of perfectly-stacked ancient blocks stretched high above, ending in the rectangular barriers of parapets.

Mila patted the pocket of her tunic, relieved as her palm found the angular outline of her small passbook. It held the details of her life, the acknowledgement that she at least belonged somewhere, as a tenant of Al'Mazraea. She tightened the knot in her belt as the queue of people shifted, and she was able to take a single step forward.

After another twenty minutes, Mila had picked the skin around her thumbs to the point of drawing blood. She tapped her pocket yet again, comforted for a moment to feel the passbook still there, before anxiety swirled anew. She hated waiting.

Finally, the Border Officer wearily called, "Passbook?"

Mila tried to ignore the swilling of her stomach as she approached the desk and slid the precious document over to the man. A crust of sweat and dirt stained the collar of his navy-blue shirt, and a network of tiny purple blood vessels laced his plump cheeks. His dull, hooded eyes looked like he'd rather be anywhere else. It was a sentiment Mila shared.

"What is the purpose of your visit?" the man asked, voice monotonous and bored. He glanced from the passport in his hand to the young woman in front of him. Mila stared hard at the countertop as his cold eyes raked down her body.

"Commerce, *sigiò*," she replied, trying to keep her expression passive.

"You don't have shops in Al'Mazraea?"

Anger flared in her chest. He knew the answer to that. "We need light globes. And netting for the crops."

"They say you can make whatever you want with your magic, yet you happily come over here and take *our* things."

Mila didn't know how to answer this without telling him he was completely wrong, and she couldn't afford to have him think she was being rude. Was he trying to goad her into a fight, to have an excuse to deny her passage into Ard Aman? Her mind whirred with possible acceptable responses. He would know—everyone knew—that Satarians were forbidden from using their power at all, assuming they even knew how. The refugees made their money by selling produce to the Amanese at an exorbitant discount, leaving hardly anything for the refugees themselves. But anything they 'took' from Ard Aman, they paid for. Satarians were not thieves.

Before Mila could speak, thankfully, the guard's beady eyes returned to the faded picture, studying the image of the young woman's full lips, her angular face, her high cheekbones.

"You're too pretty to be a Creo," he growled. "But your hair gives you away. Creo hair."

Mila automatically brought a hand to her voluminous, wavy hair as it splayed over her shoulders and the hollow of her neck, feeling shame burn in her cheeks, as though she had been caught red-handed with a pencil and paper.

"Yes, *sigiò*," she said.

"And your *noterran*?" he demanded. He glanced to her upper arm where a thin armband pinched in the material of her tunic. Mila turned slightly, noticing too late that the band had twisted around so that the symbol—a circle crossed with a vertical line and three horizontal lines—was positioned at her inner arm. Her heart skipped a beat just as the man's thick fingers closed around her wrist, stopping Mila from adjusting the band herself to make the symbol visible. The government had very clear rules about displaying the *noterran*, the sign of creomancy, and it would be up to this guard now to decide if she had broken the law.

"The *noterran* must be exhibited at all times when in Ard Aman," the officer recited, a hint of venom in his voice. "You could be punished for this."

For a moment, Mila thought about telling the man that she wasn't technically in Ard Aman yet, not until she had passed the checkpoint. She still had both feet in Al'Mazraea. And her band wasn't *hidden,* it was merely twisted around. But this repulsive man just wanted another way to make her squirm.

She swallowed her insolence. "I will be more careful, *sigiò*," she said and, after a long moment, he released the pressure on her arm. She hurried to fix the band when she felt a finger hook under her pointed chin.

The guard pulled her green almond-shaped eyes up to meet his, red-rimmed and bloodshot. "Gimme a better look at those eyes, pretty one. Gotta make sure they match the picture," he said, then gave a low whistle. "The greenest eyes I've ever seen. Creo eyes, unfortunately, but they are magnificent. They'd look good staring up at me."

The pit of Mila's stomach lurched, and he held her chin for a fraction longer, making sure she absorbed the meaning of his words, as if she didn't immediately know what he meant. As if the guards didn't do this kind of thing all the time. As if she hadn't been in this position too many times to count. Mila swallowed, the movement painfully noticeable in her stretched throat. Hopefully it would end there, as words rather than actions.

As soon as the man let go, her chin sprang down once more. Mila closed her eyes as the man laughed, a rough sound, then there was a bang as he slammed the *'departed'* stamp on a fresh page of her passbook.

"On your way, Creo. If I see you hiding your *noterran* again, each of the guards will be happy to punish you. *Alizer?*"

The threat, the use of the Satarian word, the lazy pronunciation of it… All of it was laced with condescension and contempt. *I am better than you,* he was saying. *You're clearly too stupid to understand the rules under which you must live, so I will stoop to your level to explain.*

But Mila was used to it. The uncomfortable swirl in her stomach, the fiery anger coursing through her body, the mouth pressed tightly closed to avoid speaking out of turn. This was how the Satarian people had to live.

He held out the booklet, a smug smile playing over his pallid lips. Mila reached for it with trembling fingers but, in one last show of power, he continued to hold onto it as he said, "I'm supposed to advise you that there is a change to the curfew."

Mila waited for him to explain, and when he didn't, her eyebrows raised and she exhaled impatiently.

Watch yourself, her inner voice chided, and she quickly rearranged her features into what she hoped was submissive curiosity. "Please tell me, *sigiò*," she asked, hating the syrupy sweetness in her voice.

"Gates lock at four p.m. now."

"Four?" Mila exclaimed. That was excessively early, even with the changing of the seasons. She cursed herself for leaving her errands this late in the day. The clock behind the guard's thick head showed two o'clock. It would be tight, but she had no choice; she *had* to be on time, back home before the soldiers locked the gates and unslung their eager rifles.

With a complacent smile, she plucked the indigo passbook from the guard's fingers, mottled and rough with callouses and dried cuticles, and tucked it into her tunic. Then without another word, Mila commenced a hurried trot across the wide and blinding Salt Strip, towards the pedestrian gate in the city wall.

Mila hated coming here, hated the way the guards studied her, hated the constant reminders that she didn't belong. Hated that her family, her community, were confined to a small sector of the country, where they were treated like rats in a cage. Most of all, though, she hated that she was expected to be grateful to be allowed to come here at all.

3

Despite the early hour of the afternoon, long shadows already swathed the town of Haman, cast by the mountains that towered above like ancient sentinels: *Uul Serrad*, the Jagged Mountains. Though the days were still warm, the distant tip of the very highest peak, the Dend, was dusted with snow. An early sign of the coming winter.

Mila chewed the inside of her bottom lip as she passed into the thin alleyway between two squat, bricked buildings, tracing a path along the opalescent paving stones toward the main street and the Haman bazaar. There were very few people around, but Mila kept her head resolutely bowed, Nasir's words of warning in her mind: *Don't draw attention to yourself.* He reminded her constantly, and it had become a mantra to her, especially on this side of the border.

She remembered arguing with him once, as a child. "I just *walk*, I don't *do* anything. Why do they even care enough to look at me?"

At that age, Nasir was going through a growth spurt and was a head and shoulders taller than his sister. He had placed his hands on Mila's shoulders and bent over a little to look her in the eye with that half-affectionate, half-exasperated expression he reserved just for her. "*Gaia beht*, Mila. Because we're different."

"If I hid the *noterran* they wouldn't even know what I am…"

"You can't hide it, Mila. Don't even try." His eyes took on a hardness that Mila rarely saw, and it made her second-guess herself. "Not in Ard Aman. It's not worth it."

We're different...

As if she could ever forget that.

Mila's footsteps were loud in the afternoon lull, the echo of her shabby brown boots bouncing around the alley. Here the streets were swept clean, the paving stones pale and even. Though the buildings were worn by time, they were well-maintained and bright—unlike the patched-together shelter she called home. Mila let her left hand trail along the building as she passed, feeling the roughness of the stones catching her skin. She brought her hand up higher, letting her fingers play across the stream of wrinkled, weather-worn posters plastered along the wall. The garish displays towered above her, the same messages she saw everywhere on this side of the border. She didn't even bother to look at them; she knew what they showed by heart.

Golden brown hands, bound at the wrists...

The noterran symbol beneath dark eyes...

And the slogans:

Always Vigilant, Always Here...

Who will protect you? Who will fight for you?

A thousand different combinations of words, a thousand creative images, just to promote a single idea; *us* and *them*.

Mila's fingers noted the change in texture before her eyes were drawn to an unfamiliar dark display. A new poster. She could smell the fresh glue.

On one side of the print clustered children and Amanese landmarks, protected by a figure in a navy uniform. His raised fist, clenched with righteous fury, was poised to strike at demonic figures with green eyes, snarling and fighting behind a chain-link fence, the land behind them black and burned.

Mila's emerald eyes flowed over the inky red script below.

IronHand will keep them contained.

The tightness in her chest grew, but she willed herself to keep walking at the same pace. Anyone could be watching her. Let them think she was compliant, accepting.

Nasir had once told her that the Amanese people got a thrill from making the Satarians feel angry or upset, trying to get a rise out of them. If the Satarian reacted at all, the guards would be called quickly, and their punishment swift.

"We can never let that happen, Mila," Nasir had said, years ago. "We must stay calm, stay small, no matter what."

"Let them call the guards! The Amanese are racist, Nasir. I will show the guards this *khesia*, and then we'll see who is punished!"

Nasir grabbed his young sister's wrist. "*Ny*, Mila. The guards *are* Amanese. At best, they won't care but, probably, they are the ones who put up the posters and distribute the flyers in the first place. If you openly challenge them, I will never see you again."

Mila dragged her gaze from the new poster and compelled herself to continue along the passageway, but its message played on her mind. Is truly that what they thought? That Satarians were demons who deserved to be trapped, for the safety of others?

Keep them contained…

Her heartbeat quickened.

The streets here were far less crowded than the dusty lanes of the camp, yet it was here that she felt crushed, a pressure that hunched her shoulders and constricted her breathing. Stares burned into her as she passed open doorways and seated diners, but Mila kept her eyes forward, beckoned by the scent of spices in the air and the low hum of voices from the market beyond.

Outside the Haman bazaar, unofficial booths were arranged haphazardly, tightly packed together, their weathered wooden frames draped with colourful fabrics that fluttered in the breeze. Vendors called out to passersby promoting their patchwork of wares. Their eyes slipped over Mila, invisible in her outfit the same colour as the stone around. They didn't want her money, and she had none to spare.

The elaborate stone archway of the entrance to the bazaar towered above, its surface adorned with delicate Amanese carvings, faded but still elegant, like the remnants of an ancient story.

As Mila passed into the hallowed hall of the bazaar itself, a million scents and sounds immediately collided with her senses. Here people moved leisurely, bags in hand, chattering with friends or bargaining with shopkeepers. Bright scarves rippled in waves along the stalls, shimmering with exquisite patterns of gold and scarlet and turquoise. Trays of gleaming copperware winked at her, and intricately woven rugs spilled into the walkway.

Mila willed herself to focus as she snaked through the crowd, but distractions tugged at her from every direction. Her eyes flitted over the jewellery and trinkets, silver chains dangling, gems twinkling like tiny constellations. Candles made of marbled wax, dainty jars of spiced jams in hundreds of flavours. Oh, how she would love to contain her wild curls with those ornate hair cuffs. Her *offensive hair*.

Her family couldn't afford these luxuries, and refugees were not permitted to purchase such things even if they could. But looking never hurt anyone, and it was nice, for a moment, to imagine what it might be like to be someone else.

The clatter of coins and haggling voices pressed against her ears, snatches of coarse Satarian words here and there standing out against the more lyrical, official Amanese, forming a pulsing current that added to the river of sound surrounding her.

Mila shook her head, trying to clear it. She didn't have time for this, but there was something mesmerizing about the velvet dresses draped in vibrant shades of blue and indigo, the leather-bound journals that could barely contain the thick stacks of paper within. She could almost see herself with the book laid open before her, sketching on the paper with charcoal rather than in the dirt with a stick. But of all the treasures in the bazaar, that was the most unthinkable. Satarians were forbidden from recording anything, even in Amanese.

Thankfully the store Mila needed was just up ahead. The bell above the door chimed as she entered and, as the door closed behind her, the noise of the bazaar was replaced by a hushed, almost reverent atmosphere. The shopkeeper turned to greet her with a warm smile which immediately cooled as his gaze swept over her hair, her tunic, and the *noterran* armband.

"Can I help you?" His voice was callous, clipped.

Though Mila expected this everywhere she went, it always stung. For a time, she had anticipated that she would one day harden up, that it wouldn't bother her anymore. But it still did, after all this time.

Stay calm, small, no matter what.

Mila kept her gaze low, avoiding the stares from the other patrons who browsed the shelves of multicoloured lamps. They turned briefly, not bothering to hide their curled lips and wrinkled noses as they looked at her.

Mila plastered a fake smile to her face. *"Beht'dyes, sigiò,"* she greeted the man, pretending she didn't see his lips purse at the Satarian words. "I need to buy light globes, please, two."

"For Al'Mazraea connections, I… assume?"

"Yes, *sigiò.*"

The shopkeeper made a face. "They're out the back. I'll have to go and get them. Just wait here. And don't touch anything."

He pushed through a doorway hanging with beads that clinked and shook long after he had vanished. Mila could feel the eyes of the other patrons on her back. She moved towards the opposite wall, fighting to focus on the delicate glass lanterns hanging there, humming with enchanting amber and emerald light. She was almost tempted to ignore the shopkeeper's request, to reach out and run her fingers over the warm, twisted surfaces, but instead her eyes wandered, drawn to the largest lanterns that hung from the ceiling like suspended stars, each casting its own unique glow through the punched metal.

The beads clinked and rustled as the shopkeeper returned.

"Here," he said as he placed the packaged globes on the counter in front of him. He kept a hand resting atop the bundle, trying to look casual, but the meaning behind the gesture was clear. Mila scowled inwardly as she stepped back towards the counter, heart thudding against her ribs.

"I am no thief, sir."

The shopkeeper didn't move his hand. "Twelve liharr," he said, almost like a challenge to her statement.

Mila frowned. She had watched her mother count out the money carefully that morning. "For two globes?"

"Prices have gone up for your kind," he sniffed. "Special tariff. Government orders."

He tapped a long finger to a small sign stuck to the front of the counter. Mila had to step back to read it, slowly decoding the Amanese words.

ATTENTION CUSTOMERS:
IN COMPLIANCE WITH GOVERNMENT REGULATIONS, A SURCHARGE OF FIFTY PERCENT APPLIES TO PURCHASES MADE BY NON-CITIZENS. HAVE A GREAT DAY!

Mila felt a lump rise in her throat but forced it down. Charged more just for existing? The injustice of it made her cheeks flush. But she pulled out the coins, counting them one by one with trembling fingers. She wouldn't have enough for the netting to protect the fledgling crops.

The hostility in the store was palpable, pressing down on her chest like a boot, heavier every second. When the man finally pushed the light globes across the counter to her, Mila grabbed the package and hurried from the store, shaking, determined to lose herself in the torrent of colour and noise before she allowed any tears to fall.

4

The bazaar blurred into a bokeh haze through her tears and Mila moved unseeing through the labyrinth, parting the bustling crowds like soap through water as they caught sight of her grey tunic and the *noterran* adorning her arm. After a few minutes, she stopped, chest heaving and stomach clenched, the package of globes clutched against her chest.

It wasn't fair! Mila swiped the tears from her cheeks. The guards, the shopkeeper, the Amanese people—they all took what they wanted, said what they wanted, and no one stopped them. No one cared. The Satarian people were just expected to stay silent and take it.

No, not to *take it*—they wanted her to *break…* but she couldn't let them get to her. She tried to take a deep breath.

Stay calm, small, no matter what.

But her jaw clenched with bitterness. The anger inside her *wasn't* small, and it wasn't calm.

And there was nothing she could do about it.

In front of her, golden light shone out from an enormous window displaying an array of pastries; glazed, cream-filled, speckled with exotic nuts and pale pink petals. The heavy feeling in her chest pulled down harder and a loud sigh escaped her lips. She had wasted enough precious time wanting these things that were so far out of reach they might as well not exist. It was time to return to Al'Mazraea. Dragging her gaze away from the somnial display, she looked left and right down the strip to get her bearings, catching the faint glimmer of daylight in the distance.

As she took a step towards the exit, something fluttered along the ground and caught against her leg. Looking down, Mila saw a crumpled paper pinned against her boot.

Like attracts like, she thought. Trash caught by trash.

She snagged it with her spare hand, her fingers poised to crumple it further, but bold letters caught her attention. Instead, intrigued, she shook the paper to smooth it out, revealing a stark black-and-white flyer. The heading urged people to *"Take Back Our Rights"* over an image of fists raised in solidarity.

Mila's fingers trembled as she read further. Join the Honourable Draven Lideri to mark a new beginning.

She bit her bottom lip. Lideri. The name was familiar; she had heard it often in the past few months, whispered around the camp like a dark omen, tinged with an undercurrent of fear.

Take back our rights…

Mila's heart began to hammer in her ears. She couldn't believe what she was reading.

Take back *their* rights?

Their rights??

A powerful kind of reckless anger surged through her like wild horses frightened by thunder. Everywhere she looked, the Amanese were enjoying *their* rights. Walking the aisles of the bazaar buying whatever took their fancy without fear of retribution, wearing clothes in every colour fabric and pattern, with money that they earned fairly from jobs they aspired to. These people with all the time in the world, with four walls and a roof, with freedom. What on Gaia's earth did the Amanese have to complain about?

Mila scanned the flyer once more and her mouth went dry; below the image were more details, showing the date and location. The event was happening right now in the Haman town square.

Her better judgment told her to toss the flyer aside and head home. The curfew was ticking down, adding an increasingly uncomfortable layer of urgency to every minute that passed. But thinking of the curfew only fanned the flames of her burning anger. She needed to see the rally, to understand the kind of hate that was growing just across the border from where she and her family curled up each night. She needed to get answers.

Mila strode away from the luminous bakery, winding through the stalls with her jaw set, the colours and chatter now just a haze in her periphery.

When Mila arrived at the square, the crowd was already packed tightly, expectant faces turned up to the steps of the town hall. Ornate sandstone columns framed the landing, awash in navy blue banners that swivelled slightly in the breeze. Each banner bore a striking emblem in silvery-grey: a clenched fist in the centre, framed by the sharp lines of a three-pronged shield. Above, in the façade of the town hall, high, narrow windows looked down on the crowd, reflecting the flickering movement of the city. Above it all, the clock tower stretched into the sky, escaping the afternoon shadow shrouding the square. A glimmer of sunlight caught the golden lion statue perched at the very top of the spire.

Mila edged through the bodies, trying to blend in with the crowd as best she could. She ran her spare hand through her hair, smoothing out the curls a little, then she twisted the armband so that the sigil was against her inner arm once more.

Cheers erupted as a man strode out of the building and began pacing back and forth across the landing. Tall and wiry, he wore chunky black boots and navy pants, held at his narrow waist with a thick black belt. A sleeveless white tank showed off toned muscles flexing beneath his pale skin. White hair, shorn to the scalp, left only a coarse haze across his skull and a rough, purple scar marred the right side of his face. It ran from the centre of his cheek down over his strong jawline and faded away down his neck. This must be Lideri, Mila realised with a jolt. He smiled at members of the crowd, pointing to them and saying things that Mila couldn't hear.

Suddenly Lideri waved his arms, signalling for quiet that fell immediately. He surveyed the gathering below him with eyes sharp as a hawk.

"People of Haman, thank you! Thank you so much!" Lideri's voice cut through the air like a blade. "As we gather today, our country confronts a crisis. For too long, the politicians have stood idly by while foreign invaders take what is rightfully *ours*. Shelter, land, food, money… These *Satarians*—they call themselves refugees, but I tell you now, they are *parasites*, draining resources that should be going to you and your children!"

Mila flinched as the crowd around her suddenly roared.

"Frankly I believe this is the most important political movement in our history. From this day forward, we will not allow ourselves to be taken advantage of any longer. No more handouts, no more compromises. Our power will be reclaimed. Our safety will be restored. The scales of justice will be rebalanced."

Mila's throat tightened as Lideri continued. Every phrase dripped with venom, every pause incited cheers.

"The Creos—they like to pretend they're innocent, they're meek, but it's all an act! That's what they do. They lie and manipulate. Do you like being taken advantage of?"

The crowd screamed, "No!"

He leaned forward, as if sharing a secret, and the crowd leaned in too, eager, hanging on his every word. Mila's stomach twisted. "Long ago, our forefathers—great people, strong people—they accepted the Creos into Ard Aman temporarily, to help them out. That's the kind of people they were—sympathetic, generous. But the Creos used their powers to hoodwink our honourable ancestors. They wheedled access to our lands and our resources. They swindled unlimited funding from *our* citizens. But here's the thing—it's never enough for them! Never! They want more, always more, and they're slowly taking it. I've seen it happening. But we are not going to let them do that anymore, are we?"

The crowd bellowed again, "No!"

"No!" Lideri boomed and he threw his arms wide, open and welcoming, but there was no warmth in his expression. "They're dangerous, these Creos. What they *really* want is to drain us dry. The government has been spending money—*your* hard-earned money—on *them*! Giving them for *free* the clothes and food and everything *you* have to pay for. What *else* will they take if they're given the chance? I see them every day. Every single day. They sneak into Ard Aman, with their dirty rags and their strange language, slowly spreading like black mould, like cancer. They're poisoning the blood of our country! It's happening right in front of us, and nobody else is doing anything! But we see it. We all see it!"

Mila thought Lideri sounded insane. He was rambling, spitting, spouting outright lies… but the crowd was eating up every word, their faces twisted with anger. Mila could almost see their hatred solidifying into something dark and tangible in the air. Their excitement fed off each other like stormfronts colliding, washing away all logic and sense.

"We need to stand up while we still can. There's *nothing* stopping them using their evil powers on us. They could *easily* level this city—in fact they've already attacked villages and cities in wider Ard Aman. Before we know it, Creo gangs will be taking over entire areas of our country. Do you want to be pushed aside, left to scrape for scraps while these intruders grow stronger?"

"No!"

"*No!*" screamed Lideri. He pointed a finger out at the horizon, where the refugee camp lay, beyond the well-kept buildings, clean streets and city walls. "For many years—too many years—this corrupted establishment has allowed the Creos to stay. They have failed to protect the citizens of Ard Aman. The danger grows every day while our people suffer in silence. We've got to send a message: there's no place for these magic-wielding thieves. None. We don't want them here. We can't allow their foreign ways to wipe out everything we care about, or, next thing we know, *we'll* be living in Al'Mazraea and *they'll* be out here!"

Bile rose in Mila's throat as her skin prickled. She wanted to look away, to shout him down, to run… but all she could do was stand there, powerless as always, while his fiery, calculated words stoked the anger of the people surrounding her. He was whipping them into a frenzy, turning their insecurities into a weapon pointed directly at the Satarian people.

"I will not let this happen. As governor, I have no higher responsibility than to defend our city from threats, and that is exactly what I am going to do. The time has come, my friends. The challenges we face are plentiful, but they will be defeated. From this moment on, your suffering is over! Today, I will sign a series of historic executive orders, starting with declaring a national emergency at the border. I will rescue every city and town that has been invaded by this plague. I stand for *you*, the people of Haman city!"

Mila clenched her hands at her sides, nails digging into her palms, trying to fight the panic rising inside. This was more than just an inauguration; it was a promise of violence thinly cloaked by patriotism and pride. The urge to turn and run nearly overwhelmed her, but she steeled herself to stay, to witness this. Her breath quickened as the jeering grew louder and Lideri let his words ferment in the air. He turned his head slowly as he surveyed the masses, the ugly scar stretching as he nodded approval at his followers, their faces filled with fanatical loathing, the square teeming with jeers and fervent fists.

Mila had no doubt these were the same people who spat at her in the streets, who stared at her and who didn't think twice before hurling an insult or a rotten piece of fruit. A chill ran down her spine. Suddenly those experiences seemed trivial compared to what Lideri was proposing.

Then, suddenly, in among the bitter, virulent faces, Mila felt the cold slap of recognition.

Three of her former classmates were huddled near the edge of the square, just out of the thick of the crowd, watching Lideri with rapt attention. These were people she had counted as friends during junior school, before the segregation came into effect. They knew her family, knew her name. They knew how she had been slow to learn the Amanese lettering system and how, whenever they were allowed to play with the toys, Mila always chose to do crafts instead.

Now the three of them stood with their arms crossed, eyes locked on Lideri and filled with a mixture of curiosity and agreement as they nodded along to the poisonous words. They hadn't seen Mila yet. She could still leave, and no one would know she had ever been there.

Mila smoothed her hair once more, then took a deep breath and pushed through the crowd towards them. "Fena? Ylan? Sahte?"

Fena's brown eyes flicked to her briefly, then she did a double-take. "Mila?" Her expression soured immediately. "You shouldn't be here."

The sharpness of her words stabbed into Mila's pounding heart. But she squared her shoulders and held Fena's gaze. "Neither should you," she said. "Why are you listening to him? You don't really believe all this?"

Ylan scoffed and crossed his arms across his green and yellow shirt. "I suppose you're going to tell us he's lying? Lideri's right—our city *is* struggling, but you and your people always seem to have everything you need."

"Everything we need? Have you ever even been to Al'Mazraea?" Mila shot back, incredulous, resentment rising uncontained in her words. "Have you seen the tents and shanties that we call homes? It's squalor. We're barely surviving."

The classmates exchanged a glance, faces twisted in disgust. Sahte shook her head. "Ungrateful, just like Lideri said. You're all just innocent victims."

The other two nodded, as if Sahte had spoken a wise truth.

Mila stared at them, mouth agape. "You can't be serious. You believe those lies? *None* of this makes sense, Sahte!"

Sahte shrugged and looked away. "It makes sense to us."

Mila shook her head in disbelief. "You're letting fear and slurs turn you against people you once called friends."

"We care about our families and our homes," Ylan said. He took a step forward, trying to use his size to intimidate her. "You might've been a friend once, but that doesn't change the facts. We have to look after ourselves first. Lideri's telling it like it is."

"Do you even care what happens to us if he gets what he wants?"

"What he *wants* is to protect us." Fena's brown eyes flashed with something between guilt and defiance. "People are angry, and they have a right to be. If you hate it so much, you should go back to where you came from. Don't steal what we have."

"Back to where we came from?" Mila's voice trembled, but she refused to back down. "I was born in Al'Mazraea. My parents were born in Al'Mazraea, and their parents before them, and before them, and before them." Ylan went to interrupt, but Mila spoke over him. "Where we *came from*, is here, this land. But you don't care about that, do you? It's easier to villainise us than to understand."

The crowd suddenly erupted in another round of cheers as Lideri wrapped up his speech. Mila felt sick, poisoned by the waves of hatred spreading like a noxious gas through the square. She looked back at Fena, Sahte and Ylan, searching their faces for a glimmer of the people she once knew. But all she saw were strangers who had chosen to stand on the side of hate.

"This isn't right," Mila said quietly. "You know it isn't."

Fena's gaze hardened. "We know where we stand, Mila. You should go before someone else notices you. You don't belong here."

The words struck like a sudden blow, making Mila take a step back. She swallowed her arguments painfully, like shards of glass in her throat, terrified by the conviction in their eyes. Without another word, she turned and walked away, her heart sodden with the hate rippling across the seething mass of people.

With the package of light globes still tucked under her arm, Mila navigated carefully out of the crowd, heading for the side streets. Though each step took her further from the rally, the raucous cheering still managed to reach her ears, ears that were ringing with anger.

It was so unfair. She should go back to the square right now, push Lideri out of the way, and tell the crowd the truth. She would make them listen to her and see reason. But, with a sinking feeling, Mila knew that it would be no use. Even if she succeeded in reaching Lideri, the crowd wouldn't hear her, they would just see her offensive Creo hair and the ugly grey tunic, and anything she said would be written off as a lie or used against her somehow, just as it had been with her classmates.

They look at us and only see danger, Mila thought bitterly. They don't see the mothers nursing babies in patched-up shelters, or the families sharing one room, or the kids without shoes and nothing but dust to play in. They don't have to deal with constant outbreaks of disease, not to mention the pervasive depression, anxiety, hopelessness...

They don't have the daily fear that comes with the crime of existing.

Mila's long legs carried her quickly from the square as the sun crawled towards the horizon. How can people be so ready to hate, she wondered. How can they be so scared of us? Every heated word from her former classmates replayed in her mind in a tangle of fear and anger, intertwined with Lideri's hateful speech and a bone-deep sense of betrayal. Tears pricked her eyes for the second time that day, but this time she bit her tongue and refused to let them fall.

Mila continued along the quieter lanes, tracing a path through the side streets back towards the border. Here, she could move largely unseen, just another shadow in the narrow spaces where no one bothered to look—though the spiteful posters plastered above still watched her, as did the mountain peaks. The closest was a smaller mountain, barely five-hundred metres tall and called *Pika* in Satarian: the little one. Mila couldn't remember the Amanese name. Here, the alleys ended in rocky walls, with the buildings nestled into the base of the soaring slope.

From somewhere in the branches of passages came the distant sounds of children playing, their laughter bouncing off the brick walls of the city like music. A small, wistful smile strayed onto Mila's face. The same sounds could be heard in the camp—laughter mixed with shrill cries, the language of lively games. Satarian and Amanese children alike; they found beauty and playfulness in the everyday, regardless of what their life might look like from the outside. Put them together, take away the *noterran* and free them from the boundaries of fences and checkpoints, and Mila knew no one would be able to tell the difference between them. It occurred to her that perhaps that was why the government had segregated the schooling system a decade or so ago—to stop the free from realising that the camp-dwellers were just like them.

As a shriek of laughter reached her, for a moment Mila imagined joining in with the children, out of breath with giggles as they raced up and down the fire escape or playing hide-and-seek in the maze of alleyways. What she wouldn't give to feel that sense of carefree joy again, to have the weight of the world lifted from her shoulders.

But the image shattered as a loud crack rang out, followed by a deep rumble that seemed to emanate from the very depths of the mountain, like an ancient, slumbering beast had awoken and was beginning to stretch its aching bones, preparing to unleash a fury that had lain dormant for millennia. With a second loud crack, a colossal portion of the hillside broke away, plummeting down in a raging river of dirt and rocks. The sound was deafening, thundering, but still she heard the sharp, panicked screams as the slab of land and crashing boulders rushed towards the buildings beneath.

Mila was already running towards the scene as the impact kicked up a surge of red dust that blasted outward, whooshing down the laneways and assaulting her eyes and mouth and nose, making her momentarily blind, coughing and gasping for air. She swiped at her eyes with her sleeves and willed herself to keep running towards the noise. Pulse racing, frantic, she almost lost her footing as she rounded the corner.

What she saw made her cry out loud.

The slab of earth had slammed into a building, completely demolishing one whole side as cleanly as a slice is cut from a cake. Trees had come with the boulders and were lying at odd angles in the debris, flailing with the impact, and bricks were everywhere amid the dust. Wooden planks and glinting shards punctuated the heap, already saturated by streams of water gushing from a ruptured main. And within the wreckage lay small, coloured shapes. People, some unconscious, others pinned and struggling. Their cries pierced the air, joining the gurgle of the spewing water.

5

The air swirled with thick dust as Mila spun around desperately, looking for someone, anyone, who could help… but the alleys were empty. No one came running. Surely not all of the residents were at Lideri's rally? Well, they would be on their way now, drawn by the crashing sounds of the rockfall still rolling through the valley even minutes later.

Mila scanned the site, catching a glimpse of green material maybe two metres up. She could just make out the shape of a boy, screaming, pinned beneath a massive chunk of the stone wall. She started forward, then stopped as Nasir's voice echoed in her mind.

We must stay calm, small, no matter what.

But those people needed help now. How could she possibly walk away and do nothing?

Mila chewed her bottom lip as her eyes flicked over the splintered wood and bricks, the twisted steel, mapping out the safest path across. Her heart thudded painfully, her palms sweaty, mind racing. There was a possible path there—but what if she caused the unstable rubble to collapse further? She might be putting other people in danger, including herself. And what if the mountain threw down more earth? Mila looked up at *Pika*, terrified at what she might see. A deep, rust-coloured laceration now ran across the face of the mountain, ending in a lopsided overhang.

Another scream jolted through her, shattering her hesitation. It didn't matter what might happen—what mattered was that people needed help *now*. The dust was beginning to settle and it seemed stable enough. She would have to risk it. Abandoning the package of light globes on the sidewalk, Mila ran toward the ruins and launched herself onto the closest beam, using it to pull herself up onto the unsteady wreckage. Everything was slippery, wet, and dusty, and she scrambled for balance with her pulse loud in her ears. Every step she took felt like walking on the edge of the world.

"I'm coming!" Mila called to him, not sure he could even hear her, hating the waver of uncertainty in her voice. "I'm going to get you out! Hold on!"

The boy's cries only became more urgent and strangled as she climbed with frustrating slowness.

You can do this. Just stay calm. Focus.

The cries of the trapped people cut through the air, sharp and dire, and each scream stabbed into the walls of her skull, making it impossible to think clearly. Suddenly the whole site quaked and grumbled with the threat of collapse. Mila froze, mid-step, biting her lip to stop herself from crying out. If she moved too suddenly, the whole mismatched pile of fractured stone and concrete might collapse further, trapping her as well. With one foot wedged against a jut of broken rebar and the other barely balanced on a tilting slab, she forced herself to breathe.

She had spent half her life balanced on the brittle limbs of trees, picking fruit to sell to the guards. The branches always seemed one breath from breaking, but she had never fallen. She tried to remember this as the fragments of stone groaned under her weight, threatening at any second to shift and send her crashing down.

Then she jumped forward, throwing both hands onto a wooden panel jutting out from above just as the slab beneath her gave way, clattering to the street below. For a heartbeat, she dangled in mid-air, feet desperately seeking any kind of grip to push against. With her arms screaming, ignoring the stab of splinters into her palms, Mila forced herself up over the lip of the wood.

Just as she got to her feet, water suddenly exploded from somewhere unseen, sending another tremble through the debris. The jolt of it knocked her to her hands and knees on the slick surface.

A sensation of warm golden light swept over her like a heat flash, disorientating like vertigo, and for a moment Mila was certain she was falling further. She threw a hand to her chest, alarmed at the feeling coming from inside. The sunshine feeling? Here, now? It made no sense.

She forced the sensation aside and pushed herself to her feet once more, ignoring her reeling head and instead fixing her eyes on the boy's green t-shirt. She was almost there; his sobs were much louder now, more insistent. Every muscle strained as she continued across, stretching her arms out to steady herself, grabbing whatever she could—slack wires, crumbling brick, or twisted metal, cold and damp. Only a few more steps and she could reach the boy, help him. Everything was slick and slippery with water spraying from the ruptured pipes, every handhold like a bar of soap.

Another tremble rocked her sideways into a splintered shard of glass. It bit into her thigh, tearing both fabric and flesh, pain lancing through her leg as warm blood trickled down her thigh. She sucked in a sharp breath, swiped at the blood with her dirty palm, and forced herself onwards. She would deal with her own injuries later.

Barely a minute later, Mila reached the terrified boy, dropping to her knees beside his head. Tears and dirt stained his pale face, twisted in agony. He was so young, barely ten years old.

"I'm here," she said, breathless. "I'm going to help you."

"Please, it hurts! *Help*!" he groaned, his small hands grabbing at his abdomen, where a metal pole pressed hard against his ribcage, held in place by the enormous chunk of stone. Thankfully it hadn't punctured his skin—yet.

"Hey, hey—It's going to be okay," she said. His dark eyes met hers, terrified but trusting. "What's your name?"

"L—Luca," he stammered.

"I'm Mila," she painted on an assertive smile. "I promise you, I'm going to get you out."

Luca nodded faintly, his breathing laboured.

Mila stood and quickly examined the situation. All around them, water from the broken pipes ran dark and dangerous. It weaved around the boulders and chunks of rock that had fallen from the mountain above, pooling in the crevices and hollows of the wreckage. The hunk of stone holding the boy captive looked heavy, but she had to try to move it. She braced herself against the slab, planting her feet as firmly as she could on the unstable terrain, and pushed—but the stone didn't budge. Beads of sweat trickled down her forehead and into her eyes as she strained, grunting, her muscles trembling with the effort… but still the stone wouldn't move.

Mila stepped back, eyeing the slab with contempt. Then she took a breath and lunged all her weight into it. Her hands slipped and she tumbled forward again, landing hard on her bloodied palms and knees in a sluice of water and red dust. It flowed over her trembling fingertips and turned everything the colour of sun-warmed clay.

As she struggled to push herself up, slipping against the wet, dirty surface, it happened again—the warmth in her chest, and the warmth in her fingers too. The familiar hum of magic quivered in her veins. She didn't understand why it was happening now, but she didn't need to understand. Instinct took over. Something inside her responded, something ancient and untamed, like a call coming through the fabric of the universe. Mila gritted her teeth and drove her palms into the streaming mix of water and red dust running over the ruins, reaching inside herself for the sunshine feeling and the roots of connection. The link came easily, perhaps heightened by her thundering desperation.

She whispered a greeting to the goddess: *"Gaia, ad tay khiedery..."*

But she hesitated. What did she want to do? What was her intention? This was a site of destruction, not a field of fertile soil. She couldn't grow corn here. And Nasir had not taught her how to do much else.

Mila bit her bottom lip. Her wet tunic cloyed at her, Luca's screams mingled with the shouts of the others trapped, while the wreckage shifted and compacted further. All of this was wrong. Panic clawed at the edges of her mind and uncertainty curdled her instincts. She was losing time. The situation threatened to deteriorate at any moment; another chunk of the mountain could descend upon them, and the relentless spray of water was slowly flooding the cavities where people lay trapped...

Frantically, Mila willed herself to focus, pushing through the fog of terror squealing in her mind. Even in the midst of this destruction, there was something deeply, inexorably alive. And, at its core, creomancy was the ability to collaborate with the lifeforce of the earth, and make things grow... develop... intensify...

She scanned the scene before her.

Everything here was born of the earth at one point. The concrete, the stone and brick. The boulders and trees and fragments of the mountain.

And all of it was coated in soil.

It was a long shot... But what if she could manipulate the destruction?

The boy's wide eyes met hers, full of fear. Mila tried to take a deep breath, though her lungs felt tight. As she exhaled, she scrunched her face and pressed her hands harder into the wet dust, at the same time reaching out with her magic, begging Gaia's power to move through her.

Her eyes glazed.

The boy screamed.

"Ad tuy khiedery..." she murmured, as she pictured the cracks in the slab growing, moving inwards, turning into it pieces that would fall away from Luca's fragile body.

"...Y dar r'mahiya..."

The concrete groaned. Mila focused all her energy on directing the fragile bond, trying not to let fear distract her, trying to keep herself open to the flow of the energy. She couldn't afford to let it exhaust her.

Breathe.

Mila was dimly aware that ribbons of steam were rising from her fingers. Was she drawing power from the water as well as the earthy dust that had fallen from the mountain? Nasir had never mentioned this.

For a moment, nothing seemed to be happening, then with a sound like thunder the slab cracked in apart. It fell away like it had never been solid at all, as easily as dry leaves crumbling to dust. And suddenly the boy was free, his grime-stained green t-shirt bright against the monotonous ruins.

He was okay. He was safe.

Relief flooded through her and she thanked Gaia, letting the sunshine feeling in her chest fade away like a slow sunset. Panting, she hurried over to Luca and kneeled to pull him into an embrace, both of them trembling.

"It's okay now. It's okay. You're safe," Mila whispered. For just a moment, she could ignore the screaming of the other trapped people.

As they broke apart, Luca looked at her properly for the first time. His pupils contracted sharply and his expression twisted from gratitude to fear. As if her touch had burned him, he gasped and shoved her hands off, moving back as far as the unstable platform would allow, his eyes locked on the band cinching her arm.

"It's okay!" Mila cried, reaching out for him. "Luca, I'm not going to hurt you!"

"You—you're a Creo," he stammered, eyes wide. "You did that with magic!"

A weight sank into Mila's stomach. "I didn't mean to," she said, reaching out her hand again, but the boy recoiled. "But it was the only way to get you out."

He kept inching backward, trying to put more distance between himself and Mila. His eyes narrowed accusingly. "My dad says people like you are dangerous! He says you do dark magic—stuff that can hurt people!"

"No! I would never. I—Luca, I *saved* you!"

She stared at the terrified child, not knowing what to say or what to do. She hadn't done anything wrong, yet his tear-filled eyes watched her like she was a wild animal about to pounce. The weight of his gaze made her insides churn as the unbalanced structure creaked around them, and a breeze buffeted Mila's wet tunic. She shivered.

From below, ringing through the alleyways, came hurried footsteps and urgent shouts, piercing the uneasy quiet.

"Over here!" a sharp voice called.

Mila's heart and mind began to race with another kind of fear as people began arriving at the scene, looking around, frantically calling for help or loved ones.

"Oh my god, what happened?"

"Tobias? Effe?"

"Get help, someone get help!"

As the Amanese rushed forward to help, Mila remained crouched before the boy. "Please, I'm begging you, Luca—don't say anything about the… the magic," she said quietly, looking up at him from where she remained kneeling. His brown eyes narrowed on her viridian ones. He pursed his lips, silently debating, when suddenly his face lit up at the sound of someone screaming his name.

"Luca! Luca, where are you?"

Mila's heart skipped a beat.

"Dad?" The boy crawled forward to the edge of their little platform, forgetting his fear of Mila. "Dad!"

She glanced down and saw a man, wild-eyed and hysterical, scrambling with reckless speed across the debris.

"Luca!" he cried out again, his voice breaking with relief as he spotted his son.

The man leaped over the broken beams and twisted pipes, barely keeping his footing as he rushed toward them. The second he reached Luca, he dropped to his knees and gathered the boy into his arms. "Oh, thank god. You're okay, you're okay," he murmured, pressing a kiss to Luca's dusty forehead.

The boy clung to his father, sobbing into his shoulder.

As the mass of fragmented bricks and warped steel swayed dangerously, the man eventually looked up, and his eyes locked onto Mila's. For the briefest moment, there was nothing but gratitude in his gaze. Then, just like his son, he focused on her hair, her tunic, her dirt-covered hands. The realisation seemed to hit him with physical force and he moved his body in front of Luca's, shielding him from Mila.

"You did this?" His voice was suddenly sharp and laced with suspicion.

Mila swallowed hard, her mouth suddenly dry. "He was trapped," she said, trying to keep her voice steady. "There was no other way—"

"They're just innocent kids," the man yelled. His expression darkened. "How could you do such a horrible thing?"

"Wait, what?" Mila said, raising her palms in a placating gesture. "No, no, I didn't do *this!* The mountain collapsed, and I was just here to help!"

"Mountains don't collapse on their own," he spat. "Creomancy is illegal! The guards will have your head for this."

A chill run down Mila's spine.

I will never see you again.

The crowd below was growing by the minute.

"This is insane! I didn't cause a rockfall. I wouldn't do that! Creomancy is for *growth* and—and—" she faltered, thrown off by the man's irrational argument, but he wasn't listening anyway. He was already looking to the crowd, waving to gain their attention, his expression twisted with a mix of fear and disgust.

"Help!" he shouted, his voice rising in alarm. "She's one of *them!* Lideri was right, they're attacking our town! She might collapse the rest of this area any minute!"

The animosity emanating from him was overwhelming. Too slowly, Mila took a step away, her whole body starting to shake violently with shock.

"Throw her down!" someone yelled.

"Quick, before she uses any more magic!"

"Someone call the guards!"

Mila felt sick. More people assembled, yelling and shouting expletives. It didn't matter that she had just saved a life. The crowd only saw what they were taught to see: a dangerous outsider who had broken the law.

Without warning there came a shove between her shoulder blades and she went tumbling forward, down the corkscrewed layers of wreckage. She barely had time to scream. Sharp edges snagged her skin, slicing and scratching her legs and arms and torso as she fell. She hit the ground hard. Pain shot through her limbs, but there was no time to think about it. The crowd was closing in.

"Get her!"

"She's dangerous!"

"The guards are on their way!"

Gasping in pain, tasting blood on her tongue, Mila scrambled to her feet. She didn't have time to check if anything was broken. She just had to move. Fear tore at her insides as she cast around wildly for a way out of the alley, but all she saw were snarling mouths and angry fists.

"Creo witch!" a woman hissed, pointing an accusing finger at Mila.

"Someone stop her before she does more damage!"

No.

Mila darted towards the rectangle of open air, slipping on loose stones and the dust-slick pavers.

A man lunged for her, catching the hem of her tunic and yanking her back. With his other hand he grabbed a fistful of her hair, holding tight and tilting her head back, exposing her throat. Certain she was about to feel the slice of a blade, Mila swung blindly at him with both arms, appalled yet satisfied to feel her elbow connect with something and he shrieked and let go, clutching his face while blood spurted from beneath his fingers. "You bitch!"

Terror surged through her as more bodies blocked her way. Someone gave a yell and swung at her with a hunk of wood, but she somehow managed to twist away and it instead struck the wall beside her with a loud thud. Mila raced toward the mouth of the alley, vaguely aware that her leg wasn't moving properly.

"Grab her! Don't let her escape!"

From nowhere, a brick came hurtling through the air and struck its mark. Agony exploded in her back, ripping up her spine and ricocheting down her legs. She screamed as she went down, landing in the gutter as the edges of her vision blackened. Cold, filthy water from the burst pipes streamed all around her, flowing up her nose and pouring into her mouth. Curled and writhing, coughing, Mila watched helplessly as the crowd surged toward her.

She cursed her own complacency, her compassion. How could she have been so foolish? In saving another life, had she forfeited her own? She was certain she was about to die, alone, away from her family and her home. No goodbyes, no hands to hold.

Just pain, and her cold, wet tunic.

Would they beat her to death, she wondered, or hold her down to drown in this gutter of dirty water?

Water.

An unforgivable thought crossed her mind, fuelled by fear and desperation.

Use the water.

These people cared more about hating and hurting her, than rescuing the people trapped in the ruined building. A building they thought *she* had destroyed. They already believed she had done creomancy—why not embrace it fully and turn the very crime she was accused of into her means of salvation?

She had five seconds before they reached her. Less.

Mila concentrated on her thundering heartbeat, on all the places that the water touched her body, on seeking out that connection. The power felt different this time; dangerous and wild, like a cornered beast. It snarled and swiped within her, raring to break free.

She called out ancient phrases, distress making her voice loud, but this time she had no trouble focusing her intention.

"Plezht Gaia, tay orary, biszhessa'y tay fasser seor t'ard!"

Steam began to rise all around her as she drew on the power of the rippling water, using it up and evaporating it away.

Barely a metre from her, a paving stone suddenly cracked.

The advancing group hesitated, the closest man pausing in the act of reaching out to grab her.

The crack snaked outward through the paving stones, a hairline fracture forming a line between her and them, across the dusty alleyway. Within seconds, the surface shattered as the fissure grew deeper.

"Urratoray t'ard! Vazkarr!"

The ground trembled beneath her, a faint shudder that became a violent quake.

The mob screamed.

"She's going to kill us all!" someone shouted as the tremors intensified, knocking people off their feet. The rubble of the ruined building groaned and lurched.

A pulse of energy shot through Mila like lightning, as if the earth itself heard her pain and was moving to protect her. Each tremor matched the beat of her heart and the power flowed in and out through her fingertips as easy as oxygen through her lungs. The ground growled and the force rippled outward, causing more cracks to splinter through the alleyway like shattered glass. The jagged lines grew and deepened as whole paving stones slipped away.

And just as suddenly as it began, the tremors stilled.

The people stood frozen, their faces pale, staring at her as if she were something unnatural; an alien in their midst, something not meant to exist here. As if she were an inferno engulfing the land, wild, unpredictable, powerful. Mila relished the fear rippling through them, because no one said a word, and no one dared to approach her.

Thank you, Gaia, Mila thought.

She wanted to lie there forever, and felt her eyes close for a moment that could have been an eternity, but she willed herself to remain conscious. Every ounce of strength had been siphoned out of her. The anger, the panic, the desperation—it all ebbed away, leaving only cold exhaustion in its place. But the danger had not been removed, only diverted. The people would remember their hateful mission too quickly, and she needed to be long gone by then.

Trembling, her breathing loud in her ears, Mila pushed herself to her feet, fighting the dizziness that pushed in on her vision. Water cascaded from her clothes.

She took a last look at the people across the alley, at the distance separating them.

Then she turned and ran.

6

Her whole body burned.

Mila's breathing came in ragged gasps as she pushed herself to move faster, desperate to reach the border and the safety of the camp. Every step sent a bolt of sharp pain up her injured leg. Her whole body quivered, inside and out, as though her blood was laced with a sickening electricity, making her heart stutter and pound in ways that didn't feel right. The world tilted, her stomach lurched, and she stumbled as another wave of vertigo crashed over her.

The sky grew darker by the minute, the shadows reaching further as the sun dipped low behind the mountains. Everything was the colour of granite, making Mila nearly invisible and, for once, she was grateful for it. If she had to fight again, she wasn't sure she'd survive it. Not her body. Or her mind.

A dried crust of blood felt tight on her upper lip and anxiety clutched like hands around her neck as she sucked in every breath, but Mila urged her weary body to keep going. She couldn't stop. She *had* to get home, *had* to get home… She didn't want to think about what would happen if she didn't.

She scanned her surroundings, searching the shadows. She couldn't shake the uncomfortable prickling feeling that someone was watching her, an invisible threat lurking just beyond her line of sight. After what felt like a marathon, she slipped beneath the arch of the

Haman city gate and the distant white hut of the checkpoint came into view. Its lights flickered to life as she watched, automated by the lowering sun.

The curfew, Mila remembered suddenly, a thought immediately followed by a panicked jolt as she realised she no longer had the package of light globes. The trip to town had been for nothing. Nothing but a costly disaster, in more ways than one.

The stones of the Salt Strip gave an alarmingly loud crunch underfoot, triggering the checkpoint guard to raise his rifle. Even from metres way she saw him flick the safety off as he tracked Mila's limping jog across the white stones. Behind her, high above on the parapets, Mila knew there would be more unfriendly eyes fixed on her.

But she didn't stop running. The movement felt automatic now, as much an unconscious part of her survival as breathing, and just as painful. But she did raise her hands and shout, "I'm Satarian! I live here! Please!"

"These gates are closed," the guard called, his weapon still raised. "It's almost four."

"I'm sorry, *sigiò*," Mila panted. She kept her eyes low as she approached the hut, hoping that he wouldn't ask any questions about where she had been or why she looked like something dragged from a storm drain. One wrong look, one misplaced word, and she would pay for it.

"Where is your passbook?"

Trying to calm her wild breathing, Mila extracted the booklet from her tunic. It was sopping wet but, thankfully, still in one piece. She held it out to the guard. But instead of taking the book, his strong fingers clamped around her wrist.

"I should punish you. You should have been back earlier."

"Am I past curfew?"

The guard's lip curled. "Almost."

Mila waited, letting the guard's words hang in the air. Ultimately, he could punish her regardless of the rules—regardless of anything. It was his prerogative. But she hoped he would recognise, at least in some part of his brain, that she had not in fact done anything wrong.

That he knew of.

The guard scanned her body up and down, still holding her wrist like it was the leash of a disobedient dog. She didn't dare move, didn't let her face betray the disgust she felt, didn't bother to wrap her torn tunic any tighter around her exposed décolletage. This man held the gate between Haman and home, and she had to pay the toll.

"You owe me," he growled. "And I *will* collect."

"Yes, *sigiò*." Relief fluttered in her chest at the same moment as her stomach sank. Yes, he was letting her pass—but she knew what came next. The word came out small, defeated: "Now?"

"No, not *now*," he spat, flinging her arm from his. "You look like shit. You're filthy enough without all this." He waved a hand to indicate the mess of dirt and blood that stained her from head to toe.

"I'm sorry, *sigiò*," she repeated, head down, heart hammering.

The guard snatched her passbook, his nose wrinkling at the lukewarm dampness of the document. "You'll get this back when your debt is paid."

A spark of shock cut through the haze in Mila's mind. Without the passbook, she was bound within the walls of Al'Mazraea. At any other time, that thought would have terrified her. For now though, after everything, the camp was the only place she wanted to be. She didn't protest.

"Hurry back to your hovel, Creo," the guard said.

Mila nodded her gratitude and hurried past the man, past the white hut with its bright Amanese lighting. Silent tears blurred her vision as she cleared the fence.

Safe.

He called to her as she stumbled, limping, onto the familiar dirt path that would lead her home.

"I'll see you again soon enough."

The back of her neck prickled, but Mila forced herself to keep walking until she turned a corner in the path and she felt his gaze finally drop away. Then she broke into a loping run, and she didn't stop running until the ribboned awning of her family's tent came into view. Mila collapsed against the poles propping up the doorway, holding on for dear life as she slowly slid to the ground, crushed beneath the weight of all the fear and exhaustion, the pain and shock. Her vision blackened and her body began to shake. But she was home.

Home.

It was the only thought in her anguished mind.

Home, safe. Home, safe.

For a long time, Mila just sat there, huddled in the doorway. She stared at nothing with her eyes unfocused, while the sky grew inky above her and the night insects began to sing.

Gradually her awareness came back. She brought her hand to her side, her shoulder aching as she raised her arm, and gingerly felt the damage to her ribs. A deep pain swelled beneath the battered surface that was only partly physical.

The world wasn't supposed to be like this. It didn't make sense. When the boulders had crashed into the building, her first instinct had been to help those in need. That was her innate reflex. Was it wrong? Foolish? Was she not supposed to want to help them, because they were

Amanese? The confusion of it gouged at her. Where Mila's first impulse had been to offer aid, theirs was to blame, to strike, to keep her down at any cost. Why? *How?* How could the Amanese people be wired so differently?

All she had ever wanted, all she had waited for her whole life, was to be part of that world. It would shimmer in her mind, a forbidden mirage of endless colours and possibilities and dreams. But today had shown her the truth. The realm beyond the border was feral, malevolent. There was nothing good out there.

But then, what was she supposed to dream of? Her bottom lip shook. It was all a lie. She could never have anything more than this grey existence. There was no hope for a life better than this. She was broken. The *world* was broken. And for the first time a cold realisation settled in her chest; it would never be fixed.

"Mila?" A soft voice drifted out of the darkness.

Mila looked up. It felt like a year since she had heard that voice, rather than just a few hours. Her mother's strong features were wrought with concern as she approached. The sight of her undid something deep within Mila and her face crumpled into tears even before the older woman had crouched at her side. Mila flung herself into her mother's arms, sobbing uncontrollably as Sara held her close, gently smoothing her wild hair while Mila clung to her tunic with shaking fists. But no matter how tight she held on, the fabric of the world continued unravelling. It would never matter what she did, or how much good she tried to bring—the Amanese would always see her as an enemy, a threat to be vanquished. The world beyond the camp was and always would be foreign to her. She was an ignorant child for ever believing otherwise.

Her mother whispered soothing words, stroking Mila's back with her warm cheek pressed against her forehead. "It will be okay, Cricket. Shhh now."

Kindness flowed from her effortlessly, without questions or hesitation, as if nothing else mattered but Mila. Loving her in a loveless world, just as she always had. But her mother's embrace wasn't the safe harbour it usually was. This storm was destroying everything inside her.

After a little while, Sara bundled Mila inside and sat her down on the floor cushions, then went to the small stove in the corner. Mila clutched a cushion to her chest, peeking over it, needing to keep the woman in view. The cushions were the envy of the camp and the pride of her mother, who had made them herself from scraps of clothing, unwanted hay and scavenged thread. Though they were a motley collection, and the straw occasionally poked out through the fabric into the sitter's behind, Mila loved them. To her, they were home: marred and imperfect, but loved all the same.

Plus, it was nicer sitting on these than the plastic floor mat, or the bare ground beneath.

Moments later, Sara settled herself on a cushion beside Mila and held out a mug of tea. The comforting aroma of citrus and ginger wafted up to greet Mila's aching nose. She took a sip, relishing the warmth as it moved down her dry throat.

"I was expecting you home sooner, Cricket," the older woman said tentatively.

Mila nodded dully, absently watching the swirling specks in her tea. Was there any place left in this world where she could truly belong?

"And you're covered in dirt," her mother prodded again; gentle but worried.

"I'm sorry, mahma," Mila sniffed. And then the story was spilling out of her in a torrent; how she had been forced to spend all their money because of the new tariff only for them, the *non-citizens*; how she had gone to the demonstration and heard the hate-filled words spewed by the vile Lideri; that she encountered her old classmates there, and they believed everything he said; and about the rockfall, the sight of the crushed and twisted building.

Her mother listened with her full lips slightly parted, her brows coming closer and closer together with each word.

But when Mila came to the part about rescuing Luca, she couldn't bring herself to admit that she had used creomancy to get the boy out. Instead, with eyes firmly fixed on the steaming tea, she made it sound like she had been strong enough to shift the rubble on her own. She made it sound like her injuries were from clumsiness and the instability of the disaster site. She couldn't tell her mother that she had been beaten and attacked.

And she certainly couldn't say that she had used the magic a *second* time, in full view of dozens of people, in order to escape the crowd. While it had been the only thing she could think of to do at the time, now that the adrenaline had cooled, Mila was intimately aware that she had broken the law. Not broken—shattered, into a million tiny pieces.

"And I—I ran," she finished lamely, still avoiding her mother's gaze. Trying to be casual, she took a sip of the tea and choked, coughing painfully. Mila had never been comfortable with lying.

Sara shook her head. "I don't understand it."

"I don't understand it either, mahma. They were so *angry* at me!"

Her mother sighed and reached out a hand to gently cup Mila's face. Her touch was warm and soft as she ran her thumb over Mila's cheekbone, examining the bruising. "I'm glad you're safe, Cricket. Times are dangerous, and the Amanese people are more fearful than ever. We must all be more careful. The things you heard at that rally are not new ideas; they're the result of a hatred that has been festering for decades. *Promise me* you'll stay away from trouble." She levelled her solemn green eyes at Mila.

Even with keeping the true details to herself, she had still let her mother down, still made her worry. The guilt of it stung, and Mila faltered beneath the weight of her gaze. "I'm sorry, mahma. I…I just acted. I don't even remember thinking about it, I just knew I had to help."

"I know, *dohtamia*. You're too kind for your own good," her mother said. The reality of those words stabbed deep into Mila's darkened heart.

Fool.

"We need to get you cleaned up," Sara added, her eyes roving over Mila's dirty face, her crusted hair.

Mila shook her head, the guilt multiplying. "I already bathed earlier today."

"Don't worry about that, you can have my ration of the water," Sara said. There was a pause while the woman seemed to be struggling with something, then the admission burst out of her. "I am so sorry, Mila. I shouldn't have let you go there, especially not alone. I worried that it would be dangerous. I should have gone to Haman myself." The words were distorted as she brought a hand to her lips, trying to contain a sob.

Mila shook her head and took her mother's hand in her own. She couldn't bear the thought of her beautiful mother suffering the way

Mila was now. "*Ny mahma*. Then *you* would be hurt, and that would be worse for me."

"Would that the people were all like you, *dohtamia*," her mother sighed. "Alas, there are far too many in this world who would love to see us *all* hurting."

Her mother's attention was suddenly drawn by faint movement in the corner of the room. Adrenaline flooded Mila's veins as her head whipped around, imagining for a moment that the Amanese mob had tracked her down... But it was only Nasir, standing in the darkened doorway, his grey tunic and dark pants blending with the shadows. His arms were crossed, his expression unreadable, but his eyes were fixed on Mila.

How long had he been standing there? Long enough to hear the tail end of her story, surely. Her chest fluttered with shame, the sensation so painful she physically moved a hand to steady herself and, when she tried to speak his name, all that came out as a rough croak.

"Maybe I should call you Little Frog instead, Cricket," he joked, eyes twinkling as he came to sit with them. To their mother he said, "Pada said to tell you he'll be in soon. He's just securing the grove."

Sara nodded and stood, her lips pressed into a thin line. As she moved toward the tent door, Sara made to pick up one of the dark lanterns from the shelf, but stopped herself. Without the globes that Mila had been unable to bring back, the lantern was useless. A flicker of disappointment crossed her face, and though she quickly tucked it away, Mila felt as though she had been stabbed in the heart. Silently, Sara moved outside to find her husband and guide him back from the orchards through the near-darkness.

"I'm glad you're okay," Nasir said once she had gone. He placed a hand on Mila's upper arm in a way that felt every bit as heartfelt and comforting as an embrace. "You're not going to Haman alone anymore."

"I'm not going anywhere, alone or not," Mila said bitterly. "The border guard took my passbook."

"What?" Nasir's strong fingers curled into fists. "He can't do that!"

Mila shook her head. She had no fight left in her today, no energy left to be angry. All she wanted to do was curl up on her mattress and sleep. She sighed and shrugged her shoulders, regretting the movement instantly as pain shot through her side. "He did anyway."

"But they can only take it if they suspect you've broken the law," Nasir said with a shake of his head. "Did you?"

"Did I what?"

"Break the law?"

Mila dropped his gaze, and her hesitation was enough to confirm his suspicions. He could always tell when she was hiding something.

"Mila, what really happened over there?"

A flustered, sinking sensation gripped her. "Nasir…You heard what I told mahma, right? I helped that boy and then I came home. That's all."

Nasir surveyed her with the same protective, knowing eyes that had always seen right through her.

Believe me, Mila begged silently. Just let it go. Please.

Nasir tilted his head. "You're my little sister, Mila. I know you. I know when you're scared and when you're hiding something, and right now, you're both." He crooked a finger under her chin, compelling her to look at him. Their eyes met. "You're as pale and blue as a corpse, I don't know how mahma didn't see it."

A fresh wave of guilt stirred in her stomach. Mila could see the consequences of the truth reflected in his eyes—the danger inherent in breaking the laws they were all bound by. But lying to Nasir was impossible.

"It just happened, Nasir, I didn't mean it to," Mila admitted in a rush, her voice trembling. "The boy was trapped, he was being crushed, he was going to *die* and I couldn't move the rubble by myself. I got him out, but then the father—he realised what I am, and he panicked—and he pushed me off the building into the crowd and…Nasir, I really thought they were going to kill me. I had to protect myself."

"So, they saw you? They actually saw you doing magic?"

Mila stared at him, frozen, then slowly she nodded.

Nasir closed his eyes, and, for a moment, the silence was suffocating. When he finally exhaled, it was a long, drawn-out sigh, heavy with the burden of reality. The room seemed to grow colder.

"Mila," he said, his voice low, "You know what this means. You've set something in motion today, and they are not going to let this go."

She closed her eyes at his words. The consequences were too terrifying to fully grasp.

"I didn't mean to, Nasir," she repeated, voice breaking. "I didn't know what else to do."

The pain in his eyes was unbearable. "I know, Mila. But it doesn't matter. The guards won't care, and the Amanese people won't care. If you didn't know that already, surely you learnt it today. I've heard rumours about Draven Lideri, about his followers and their ambitions for us. It would work very well for them to have someone to pin all of their hatred upon. And you've given them just that."

Outside, the sound of their parents' voices grew louder. Nasir leaned in closer and she caught the scent of dirt and grass. "Mila, listen to me carefully," he said, urgency colouring each word. "You *cannot* tell anyone that you were near the accident today. *No one.* Do you understand? You know what happens to the people they suspect of using magic. If anyone finds out that it was you, there's nothing we can do to protect you. They'll come for you. Hell, they'll probably come for all of us."

Mila nodded, tears spilling from her eyes. How could she have put her family in this position? Better to have died in the alleyway than to risk the lives of those she loved. If she could rewind time, she would lie down in the overflowing gutter and let them kill her.

Nasir's face softened as if he knew what she was thinking. He gave her a small, sad smile and reached out to brush away the single tear that slipped down her cheek. "I really am glad you're okay, Cricket." He wrapped his strong arms around her, managing to convey all of his concern and care through the movement.

"I'm sorry, Nasir," she said, her voice muffled by his tunic.

"I know you are. And I'm sorry too, Mila. Maybe one day, things will be different."

7

In semi-darkness, accompanied by the singing of many unseen insects, Mila shed her filthy, torn clothes as a snake sheds its skin. She peeled the thin tunic from where it stuck to her, matted with dried blood and sweat, and dropped the ragged remains of her pants to the ground, and stepped towards the metal pail the nearby families used as a wash basin.

She looked down into the dark, still water, both awed and sickened by the harrowing portrait staring back at her, a halo of mirrored stars around her head. The muted lights of the camp accentuated the shadows under her tired eyes and gaunt cheekbones, making the swelling even more obvious and ghastly. The colours continued down her shoulder blade and ribs, a stripe of purple among the mottle clearly showing where the brick had struck her. The vulnerability etched across her face made her feel sick.

She soaked a washcloth in the cool water, relieved when the ripples distorted her grim reflection. As the rough fabric brushed her skin, she winced, the quick intake of breath sharp against her aching ribs. But she was no stranger to pain, and she pressed the cloth a little harder, her head pounding. She deserved this agony. It was a punishment and a cruel reminder that she had brought this on herself with her naiveté and optimism. It felt like a privilege to feel anything at all, considering the unspeakable alternative that had come far too close…

With deliberate severity, Mila began to cleanse away what traces she could of the encounter. The cloth turned mauve as the water began to dissolve the mess, revealing even more bruising in spectacular colours. Rivulets of water ran down her neck, and she shivered as they trailed over her breasts and rolled in zig-zags down her many scars.

And suddenly she was there again, involuntarily lost in the memory, the moment when she thought it was all over as water gushed into her nose and mouth. She could still taste the grit and filth of it, could hear the gurgling cascade like cruel laughter in her ears…

"No," she murmured aloud, bringing her mind back to the quiet seclusion of the night air. She was here now, safe.

But at what cost? The Amanese mob would be able to identify her by sight, and if the guards came looking for the Satarian girl who had done magic… The idea made her chest constrict. What would they do to her? She had been desperate to escape, but in doing so, she had made everything worse. Her actions had convinced the Amanese that their fears were correct: the Creos *were* the monsters they always knew them to be. The destruction had come to her so easily…

The night air pressed against her damp skin in the same way that the world seemed to press down on her, reminding her that she was trapped. Trapped behind a border fence, trapped in a hierarchy where she shared a tier with earthworms and manure, trapped in the generational cycle of statelessness and poverty. In that moment of vulnerability, beaten and weak, she hated everything about her life.

Mila never allowed herself *that* feeling. Even as it sprang to her consciousness now another part of her mind was already chastising her for it. She should be grateful to have a shelter at all, to have a family and for all of them being in good health. And, by Gaia, she should be grateful to just be alive right now.

But she had held back her emotions too long today, had made herself numb against too much, and now a fury crashed through her as sudden as lightning, striking again and again. She spun around and ripped the bath towel from the clothesline, making the wire twang and snap away from the pole, dumping the rest of the laundry on the dirty ground. *Vafarín!* Could she do anything right? A bark of frustration broke out of her at the unfairness of it all, resentment at *everything*. Though she clamped her jaw tightly against the burning pain of these unchecked emotions, hot tears welled in her eyes and spilled down her rainbowed cheeks.

It was too much. Constantly feeling fundamentally flawed, carrying the weight of just trying to exist day after day after day. Always having to hold her tongue through every slur, every assault. She was exhausted. She just wanted one day where survival was not at the forefront of her mind. To put it down, just for one day, she thought. I just want it to stop for *one* day. Her hands formed fists, the anguish evident in every sinew, her brittle nails digging hard into her palms.

Beneath all the anger and confusion and pain, sickening dread lingered in her gut. The Amanese would not let her violence be forgotten. It was only a matter of time before they would make her pay.

Hours later, Mila lay on her thin mattress, staring up at the stitching in the cloth as shadows danced over the tent. The fabric rustled as a breeze crept through the alleyways, but it did nothing to lessen the sticky heat clinging to her skin.

Sleep was a distant, impossible thing, lost in the whirlwind of guilt and regret churning inside her. The camp seemed alive with nighttime noises—the distant chirp of insects in the fields, the occasional footstep as someone stumbled off to the outhouse. Each noise was magnified in the darkness, keeping her on edge. Her body ached.

On the mattress beside hers, Nasir let out a deep sigh. Was he lying awake too?

Mila slowly turned onto her side, trying to move without disturbing him, or her parents on their adjacent mattress. In their tiny home, they had no luxuries like separate bedrooms or, indeed, a bedroom at all. When the time came for sleep, they moved the scant furniture to the side and unstacked their mattresses, then drifted off one by one. Mila was always a light sleeper, always the last to succumb to the darkness, but tonight that fact was hideously multiplied.

She curled into herself, pulling the thin sheet over her head, but that only created more space for her thoughts to fester. What would her parents think if they knew what she had done? She had risked everything—not just her own safety, but probably theirs as well. Nasir always told her to be careful, to never give anyone a reason to fear them, to keep her head down and stay out of trouble… But she had done the exact opposite. She had thrown gasoline onto a fire that was already burning.

Time slipped away. The more Mila told herself to relax, the tighter her chest grew until she was gasping for air. She pressed her fists against her temples, willing her mind to be still, but the jackhammer rhythm of memories and thoughts only grew louder, more insistent.

The little boy, Luca… His eyes transforming from gratitude to fear.

My dad says people like you are dangerous!

His father's panicked screams. The shove in her back.

It replayed over and over again, burned into her mind.

At some point, the unrelenting memories morphed easily into nightmares in which a dark mass hunted for her. Paving stones melted into a burning hot sludge that oozed over her arms and legs and held her there, trapped, while the darkness came ever closer and, all around her, mountains cracked with deafening volume as rocks rained down from above. Out of sight, children screamed for help, and she frantically ran this way and that, trying to find the source of the sounds before the black mass engulfed them… but the black-eyed children had tricked her into a trap, and they held her arms and legs while the shadow swarmed over her, and everywhere the yells were deafening…

Mila jolted awake. Light streamed in through the pinprick holes of the canvas. Blood pounded in her ears and her heart still drummed a violent rhythm, as it had in the nightmare. She lay still for a moment, staring at the ceiling, feeling the realness of the mattress beneath her, welcoming the prickle of its hay stuffing, breathing hard and willing herself to calm down.

The nightmare tugged at her memory, but the details were slipping away like water through her fingers. All she was left with was a writhing pit in her gut and the insatiable urge to move her legs, to get away. From what, she wasn't sure. Her bedclothes were soaked with sweat and the blanket had wrapped around her torso like ropes, trapping her.

She hurriedly untangled herself and sat up, surprised to see that she was alone in the small space. It must be late in the day. The air in the tent was thick with heat radiating through the canvas from the sun that was surely high above the camp by now.

With the back of her hand, Mila swiped away the slick sweat on her forehead. Heavy exhaustion still clung to her, and yawning only shot pain through her bruised ribs. She slowly got to her feet, groaning aloud as her aching joints and muscles protested each movement. She shuffled to the set of drawers, trying to shake off the churning in her stomach, but it wouldn't go. As if her lies were trapped in there.

Mila desperately wanted to tell her mother the truth about what had happened, but at the same time, fear lingered deep in her gut, eddying like dark clouds on the horizon. In any other storm, Sara was the calm centre. She could make any problem seem manageable. But this… this might be too big. How could Mila dare ask for reassurance when she had been so reckless? To admit the mistake felt like admitting betrayal. Her family had always protected her, shielded her… and she had failed them. Still, every part of her longed to be open and honest, even though the thought of her mother's disappointment was unbearable. But if she told her, she would shatter whatever fragile peace they had left.

She had brought this on herself, and she would have to face the outcome alone.

Mila pried off the cloying bed clothes and changed into a sleeveless tunic, grey of course, and loose pants. The cooler fabric felt good against her sticky skin, but her thoughts were still stifling. What if she was wrong, though? What if staying silent was worse? Like sending her family out into the dark and just hoping they wouldn't stumble straight into the jaws of something waiting to devour them. The lie might eat them all alive.

Mila chewed her lip as Nasir's warning echoed in her mind: You know what happens to the people they suspect of using magic. If anyone finds out that it was you, there's nothing we can do to protect you. The guards would be searching for her soon… They wouldn't care that Mila had acted in self-defence. To them, creomancy was a crime, no matter the reason.

She pulled the soaking strands of dark hair off her neck and tied it all up into a loose bun on top of her head, then draped a scarf of thin slate-coloured material over the top and around her face to try to disguise some of the bruising.

Maybe Mila was the one who should be disappointed in her mother, instead. After all, Sara had been the one who pushed her and Nasir to practice the magic in the first place. It was their birthright, their legacy, she said. Something no one could take away from them, no matter how hard the world tried to erase it. Wasn't this *her* fault then? *Sara* had made Mila learn creomancy. *She* had told Mila to go into town.

Mila shook her head and sighed. There was no part of her that could blame her mother for this. Right now, all she wanted was to be wrapped in Sara's arms and hear her say it was going to be okay. That they'd figure something out, together, the way they always did.

The decision settled over her, heavy but somehow right. Deep down, beneath the guilt and sadness, Mila knew her mother loved her more than any mistake she had made. I have to tell her, she thought, and deal with whatever the consequences might be.

Her mind made up, Mila pushed her way out of the limp tent door into the open air.

8

The wind brought a touch of winter down from the high peaks of the Uul Serrad, prickling goosebumps on Mila's exposed arms. It was an abrupt change from the heat and sweat of inside the tent.

Mila raised a hand to shield her viridian eyes against the midday sun layering the refugee camp in golden light. The camp was alive with the quiet hum of daily activity. Children played near the water pump, creating sculptures from the mud, the dirt like gloves against their skin. The smell of different foods drifted through the air, making Mila's mouth water, and eddies of wind played in the dirt, picking up the debris and spinning it into tiny dust devils between the mismatched tents and small huts.

Here and there, elders, the *soffi*, sat on crates beneath makeshift awnings, watching life carry on around them. Their presence was a quiet miracle, an exception to the rules of life in Al'Mazraea where old age was rare. Diseases surged through the squalor with ruthless regularity, sweeping away many lives at a time. The *soffi* were few, and because of that, they were sacred.

"Ey, Mila," called a voice from nearby, and Mila turned to see the *soffa* Karina waving her over with a wrinkled hand. "The hour is late! You rise with the moon today, ey?"

"*Beht'dyes, soffa*," Mila greeted the elderly woman with a sheepish smile. "It's true. I couldn't get to sleep last night, and when I finally did, it was already morning."

Karina sat with two friends who offered Mila crumpled smiles as she approached. She felt their eyes rove over her bruised face, but thankfully they didn't mention it. They would assume the bruises were a gift from the guards—a donation that was all too common, especially for Satarian women.

The *soffi* were part way through a game of some sort, and Mila looked at the collection of pebbles and sticks with curiosity.

"Who's winning?"

"Olaf, of course," Karina said with playful disgust.

One of the friends, a shrivelled old man, grinned at Mila with his few remaining teeth. "She thinks I cheat, just because I designed the game pieces, and created all the rules."

Mila laughed with the elders, though it sounded fake even to her own ears. Fatigue lingered on the edge of her mind.

"And how are you today, *soffa*?" Mila asked. "Besides losing to Olaf of course."

Karina's eyes sparkled with the easy affection of someone who had known her for almost her whole life. When Mila and Nasir were younger, Karina had run a creche out of her tent, taking care of the young ones while their parents worked. The woman had proudly watched countless Satarian children grow up.

"I'm just enjoying the sunshine, while it lasts," Karina said. "Good for the bones, they say. Though I think my bones are a little beyond the help of the sun."

Mila made a hum of amusement, distracted by the growing nausea in her stomach. She tugged the headscarf tighter around her chin.

The elder woman's brow creased ever so slightly, concerned but smart enough not to draw attention to it in front of the others. "Come by later," she said, "I'll have some tea ready, and we can sit and chat properly."

The invitation sent a spike of anxiety through Mila.

You cannot tell anyone that you were near the accident. No one. Do you understand?

She knew Karina meant well, but the wizened woman was dangerously perceptive. She would surely ask questions that Mila couldn't answer—not without lying. She couldn't let anyone else know about the incident. Nasir was right; the risk was too great.

Mila moulded her bruised face into a reassuring smile. "I'll try," she said quickly, hoping the non-committal answer would satisfy her. "Maybe tomorrow?"

Mila knew Karina wasn't appeased. When she was little, Mila had been sure the woman could read minds. She seemed to instantly sense a child's emotions, whether they were happy or sad, angry or duplicitous. Whatever weight a child was carrying, Karina knew about it and would try to carry it for them, even when they tried to hide it.

Now, the *soffa*'s concern deepened, her brow furrowing further, but she didn't press. "Of course, Mila. Just make sure you're taking care of yourself, *alizer*?"

Mila let out the breath she had been holding. "Yes, *soffa*," she said. She placed a hand on Olaf's shoulder and added with a smile, "Be sure to watch this one closely. I think he's got more rules up his sleeve than playing pieces."

With a playful wink to the spluttering Olaf, she bid the group farewell. As she walked away, she heard the game start up again and Karina's cry of *'It was your turn just before, Olaf!'*

Mila smiled to herself, but it fell away almost instantly. This place—her home, her family, her community—it all felt tainted by the truth that she had betrayed them.

Lost in thought, Mila meandered along the dusty paths that wound through the camp, worn smooth by countless footsteps. Rows of patched and weathered tents lined the path on either side, each of them identical and yet different in small ways that hinted at the personality of the occupants. Gardens of sticks and leaves stuck into the dirt, ochre designs painted on the tent walls, weavings of dried grasses and sculptures of twigs. Humans couldn't help but be creative, Mila reflected as she passed tent after tent. Being able to express oneself was a joy that the Amanese tried to take from them, but never really could.

As she passed the next tent along, her gaze was pulled to a collection of mud sandcastles drying in the sun, complete with parapets of sticks and flags of leaves. With her attention on the art, she didn't see the clothesline until a sopping wet tunic covered her face.

"Watch it!"

Mila ripped the cloth away, crying out a startled apology.

"Mila!"

She turned to see her neighbour, Elaari, shaking her head with a half-smile. The young woman's face was worn with the stress of being a new mother, and it had been a while since Mila had seen the glimmer of amusement now in her eyes. "I should have known."

"*Beht'dyes*, Elaari," Mila said, hurriedly making sure the headscarf was still in place. She reached up to re-hang the wet tunic. "How's the baby?"

Elaari gave a tired smile, wiping her hands before motioning to the small bundle swaddled in a box at her feet. "He's finally sleeping, thank the stars. I wish I could say the same for myself."

"You're still not sleeping?"

"I can't help it. My mind won't stop worrying. If it's not nutrition, it's supplies, and if it's not that, it's everything else…" She glanced down at the baby, a crease forming between her brows. "I keep thinking about what kind of world he's going to grow up in… It's hard to imagine a different future for him. My mind always jumps to the worst, especially these days. You never know what the guards are going to take offense to next, or how they'll dole out their punishment."

Mila felt a sharp pang at the sight of Elaari's concern, and it only deepened her own anxiety. She placed a reassuring hand on Elaari's arm. "He'll be okay. He's loved, that's all that matters," she said. It was feeble, and she wanted to say more, but her mind was too preoccupied to lie today.

Elaari smiled, though the weight in her eyes remained. "I hope you're right." She paused, studying Mila for a moment, seeing her bruised face properly for the first time. "Are *you* okay?"

"Nothing to worry about," Mila managed to smile, trying to keep her tone light. "Just a hazard of being Satarian."

Elaari's eyes narrowed. "The guards did that to you?"

"It's nothing, really."

"What happened? It looks really bad…"

Mila stiffened, then managed a tight, uneasy laugh. "Honestly, it looks worse than it is. I'll be right as rain in a few days."

Elaari examined her for a moment longer, wholly unconvinced by Mila's bravado. "If you say so," she replied finally.

Mila changed the subject. "Have you seen my mother? I slept late today and, well… I need to find her."

"She came past earlier," Elaari nodded, though her expression remained concerned. "Heading towards the lagoon with a cockle bucket, muttering something about your brother."

Mila chuckled. "And what did Nasir do to anger her this time?"

"Not sure, but actually she seemed more worried than angry."

The knot in Mila's stomach returned. Anything that caused her mother to worry was bad enough, the idea that it also involved her brother sent her mind reeling. Was it something to do with Mila's secret? Had he somehow gotten in trouble for her mistake?

Elaari seemed to notice the change in her expression and quickly added, "I'm sure it's nothing serious, Mila. Like I said, mothers worry over anything and everything, especially when it comes to their children. But you should go and find her, before she starts fretting about you too."

"You're probably right," Mila said, trying to sound carefree, but the tightness inside refused to let up. Her mother was resilient, calm under pressure—but when she worried, it was never without reason. With a final glance at the sleeping baby, Mila said, "Take care of yourself, and the little one. He's lucky to have you."

Mila turned and headed down the winding path toward the lagoon, her pace quickening until the camp around her seemed to blur. She felt awful. Elaari's words played around in her mind, and she knew that her own mother would have the same concerns for Mila and Nasir.

It's hard to imagine a different future for him.

What did the future hold for herself, after yesterday? Did she have any future at all? Her fate might already be sealed. How would they reprimand her, she wondered. Over the years she had witnessed many different types of punishment. All of them haunted her, but none more than when the guards had dragged a boy forward—no older than fifteen, frail, his eyes wide with terror and defiance in equal measure. His clothes had hung loosely on his thin frame, his wrists raw and bleeding from the heavy iron shackles. As far as Mila knew, this boy had never practiced creomancy. Like most Satarians, he probably had no idea how to access his magic at all, and he was still a child… But it didn't matter. The punishment for suspected use of magic was always brutal.

The lead guard, a hulking figure with gleaming eyes, had stepped forward and raised a thick whip, its tips embedded with sharp metal shards.

The boy had cried out as the first lash cracked through the air. Mila could almost feel his pain as the lashes continued, each scream louder than the last. She remembered the boy's last shriek ringing in the wind before his voice broke and he slumped, unconscious, hanging limply by his wrists as the guards walked away.

Even now, the memory felt too real, too close, and the scars on her own back prickled. She could still hear the clanking of the chains. Still felt the same knot in her gut as when she watched on helplessly, too frightened to turn away as the child paid for his supposed crime.

The ground crunched with every step as the path led Mila past an open area where children often played. Around the yard, the rare tufts of grass had turned a dull, tired yellow, flattened and thinned from constant use, but clinging stubbornly to life. Eight Satarian children chased a deflated ball across the uneven ground, and the sound of their light, sweet laughter made Mila think of the Amanese children yesterday, playing one minute and trapped the next. Her chest ached as she wondered if all of them had escaped the rubble. Hopefully.

As Mila watched, the children's bare feet kicked up small clouds of dust as the ball slopped around, barely inflated enough to move very far at all… Yet the children hardly noticed, chaotic and carefree, and Mila wondered if they knew any better. Maybe that's just what a 'ball' was to them—barely more than a limp pillow. They were innocent, blissfully unaware of the restrictions placed on their very existence, on their future and dreams. And, in a way, up until yesterday, Mila had been innocent too, with her childish belief in a better world. But she *had* believed in it. That one day the Amanese might hesitate, reconsider the ugliness they were so eager to see, question what they thought they knew.

It dismayed her to find that, even now, a flicker of that hope still lingered. At what point did innocence become ignorance?

Soon the tents gave way to the open sky and rocky, silt shores. The midday sun cast short shadows as she made her way towards the lagoon, where the camp's outer fence met the ocean. Long ago, this fence had kept the refugees away from the sea but, as time passed and the ever-shifting waves slowly eroded both the fence and the shoreline bit by bit, the water was able to sneak through in a way the Satarians never could. The result was an inlet of salty water, barely knee-deep, the perfect habitat for small bivalves and fish. Through the gaps in the tall fence, the distant horizon beckoned.

The air grew cooler the closer Mila came to the water. Tiny waves lapped a gentle rhythm on the crusty shore, accompanied by the faint calls of gulls flying loose on the updrafts. Salty air filled Mila's lungs and blew the scarf around her face, and she tugged the material tighter.

It was easy to spot the pair of guards in their dark uniforms, patrolling along the fence line, lazily scanning for any hint of defiance. At the end of the day, the Satarians would present their gatherings to the guards, who would pay them a pittance in exchange for a large portion of the produce, leaving the refugees with barely enough to sustain themselves. Just another way of reminding them that this land was not theirs; even what they harvested from the earth was not theirs to keep.

Mila spied her mother among a few others, pants rolled up past her knees, lower legs plastered with sea grass and slick leaves from the murky water. She was arched over and digging her hands into the lagoon bed, searching for cockles. Her soft face was lined with peaceful concentration as she worked, seemingly unbothered by the guards nearby. But Mila knew that every now and then, when all eyes were averted, Sara secretly used a touch of creomancy to compel the earth to reveal the shells hiding just below the surface.

Her mother straightened up as Mila approached, using a silt-crusted hand to shield her eyes from the sun. "Mila, there you are," she called, her voice carrying easily over the quiet water. Sara placed a final handful of off-white and brown cockles into the bucket and wiped her hands on her tunic, smearing it with sand and water, then she picked up the bucket and sloshed to the water's edge.

"How's the collection today?" Mila asked as she came closer.

Sara smiled, the kind of smile that always made Mila feel happier just for seeing it. "Better than last week," she said quietly. "With the full moon, there's more power in the water. Gaia is eager to help today. The guards will be happy."

"That's good," Mila said, scowling. "We've got to keep the guards happy."

Sara pursed her lips but didn't argue. "Are you going to come in and help, or just watch me work all day?"

Mila grinned and bent down to roll up her pants, untied her laces and slipped off her socks and boots. Her toes sank into the cool sand. She waded in beside her mother, feeling the smooth current wrap around her legs. There was something soothing about the lagoon—something grounding in the way the water lapped against her skin, embraced by nature herself. When the water was almost up to her knees, Mila bent over and dug with her hands through the silky sand, searching for the hard shells.

After a few minutes, Sara said, "You're quiet today, Cricket. How are you feeling?"

Mila straightened up, and Sara shadowed her movement. Mila shrugged. "Fine. Sore, but fine."

"If you're too sore, please don't feel you have to help me out here. I'd rather you rest and get your strength back."

"Mmm. I'm okay. Besides, I like the quiet out here. It's nice to get away from the noise of the camp, even if it's just for a little while. There's something peaceful about it."

"That's a good way to look at it," Sara said, though her tone belied lingering concern. "For now we just do what we can, and be grateful for what we have. Things could be worse."

Mila started at those words. She had almost forgotten the reason she came to speak with her mother, and now she wondered how she should broach the subject.

Mahma, I lied to you...

Mahma, it's funny you say things could be worse, because...

Mila opened her mouth, but no sound came out. The calming waters had washed it all away.

She swallowed, about to try again, when Sara said, "Do you remember the first time I brought you here?" A playful smirk tugged at her lips. "You must have been only five or six."

Mila smiled faintly. "Was that when we saw the frog? And I tried to catch it?"

Sara laughed, nodding. "Yes! You were so determined. It kept hopping away over the rocks and you just kept on following it."

"And you kept telling me to give up, but I didn't listen, of course. And then it jumped into the lagoon."

"I was terrified! The water was up to your navel, but you didn't care. You just dived right in, a girl on a mission. When you finally caught it, you were so proud. I remember you were talking to it."

Mila thought for a moment, then chuckled as the memory surfaced. "Nasir told me that frogs were enchanted. If I ever caught one, I could tell it my wish and it would hop away to magical frog land, or wherever, and grant my wish." She shook her head with affection for her younger self. "I'm amazed I managed to catch it, really. I remember the little thing swimming so fast!"

Sara cast a subtle glance around, making sure no one was listening, then said softly, "Almost like magic." Her smirk faded into a tender smile.

Mila stared at her mother, realising the meaning behind those words. She replayed the memory in her mind: the tiny frog leaping into the water, speeding toward the other bank. And she remembered, too, the way the water had moved. The frog had suddenly seemed powerless against a non-existent current, pulled backwards into the young girl's hands.

She had never thought about it before…

"I used creomancy?" Mila whispered, bewildered. "At only five years old?"

Her mother nodded, her eyes reflecting the lagoon and shimmering like emeralds. "You didn't mean to, of course," she said gently. "But yes, even then. Your magic has always been there, Mila. It's as much a part of you as anything else."

Mila bent down, fingers in the water once more, but she wasn't trying very hard to find anything. "I had no idea. We never talk about it much. Magic has always felt like a burden, or something that is wrong with us... especially at the moment." She sighed. "I wish I never had the power—I wish none of us did. Then the Amanese wouldn't be afraid of us, and we could live freely."

Her gaze lifted to the tall fence nearby. The thick nails and screws holding it all together glinted in the dazzling sunlight, and the water flowed in and out beneath, as if the ocean were breathing. Mila had never seen the blue expanse without the filter of the fence, never felt the energy of a wave crashing into her legs as she curled her toes in the golden sands of the beach beyond the lagoon. This was as close as she could get. The ocean's freedom was not hers to enjoy.

Sara shook her head. "I understand why you think that, Cricket. Things seem tough and hopeless, especially when you're young. I haven't forgotten. But I have also learned that you must love yourself the way you are, Mila. You must learn to love the life you have. That's the only way to truly feel like you belong. You don't have to accept *things* the way they are—but you do have to accept *yourself* the way *you* are. You are not the problem here, and because of that, changing yourself won't fix anything. It would only make you feel more lost."

Mila gave a small smile. "You sound like pada when you say things like that."

"Mmm, that was a bit deep and philosophical wasn't it." Sara returned the smile. "Speaking of, we should head back. I have had enough sun for the day, and I'm sure we can find a place to stand and chat that doesn't involve wrinkled toes."

9

The calm of the lagoon was quickly left behind as Mila and her mother made their way up the bank and along the narrow, dusty paths leading back to the camp, each carrying their boots and socks in one hand. Shadows from the rows of tents fell in stripes across the ground, and the babbling of voices drifted through the air to meet them.

As they walked, Mila stole glances at her mother. The pressure had returned, making her mouth dry; the pressure to confess, to admit that she had lied. To concede that she had broken the law.

"Mahma…" she began, just as their tent came into view—and so did her father, coming from the opposite direction, his arms bulging with the effort of carrying a bucket filled with water from the pump. He wore a wide strip of the usual grey material around his head, helping to hold his thick, dark hair out of his eyes. His face softened in a smile that crinkled the corners of his eyes.

"There you are! The Medín women, just in time."

"In time for what?" Mila asked, swallowing her confession. She couldn't help smiling back at her father, despite the mayhem in her mind.

"Well, darling *dohtamia*, lucky for you, Nasir has only just finished charring some ears of corn. But five minutes longer and there would be nothing left for either of you," he joked.

Sara raised her eyebrows. "The joke's on you, Andrei. We would then have these delicious, fresh cockles all to ourselves." She held up the bucket to show him.

"Ay, then I am *very* glad you're back in time!" Andrei said. He pushed through the flap into the tent and Mila could hear him chuckling within.

Mila quickly caught Sara's arm and tugged her back before she could follow her husband inside.

"Mila, what…?" Sara's smile faded, a crease forming between her brows as she examined her daughter, eyes flicking over Mila's face. Mila couldn't hold her gaze—she dropped her eyes to the ground, her insides squirming, and words finally began to tumble out in a streaming whisper.

"Mahma, there's something I didn't tell you last night. I didn't tell you the whole story about what happened in Haman yesterday. And it's bad, mahma. I… I did something terrible." Her nerve failed as quickly as it had come, and Mila pretended to be very interested in her wet feet as she toed the dusty ground.

"Out with it, Cricket. Tell me what happened."

Suddenly, the air was torn apart by the shrill scream of a siren, a sound so jarring and loud it seemed to shake the very air in Mila's lungs. The air of the camp felt suddenly electrified, the shock of it like lightning beneath a burst of thunder. Mila slammed her hands over her ears as her mother did the same.

"Quick, inside!" Sara yelled and, wincing against the noise, grabbed Mila roughly, shoving through into the tent where Andrei pulled them both towards him, further into the room. The canvas walls did very little to dull the wailing alarm.

"What's happening?" she yelled, trying to make her voice heard above the din. She looked instinctively for her brother.

Nasir stood by the stove, holding an ear of corn, black and yellow and steaming, with the colour draining from his face. His lip trembled slightly. Their eyes met, and dread sucked the air from her lungs.

They'll come for you...

Between blasts of the siren, confused voices began to shout from nearby tents as people emerged and others took shelter. Andrei peered out through the lifted tent flap, his body coiled like a spring preparing to launch. The fear etched across his face deepened with each passing second. "I don't know what's going on," he said, "But that's the evacuation siren. We should move."

Mila nodded and sat down to pull on her socks and boots, then realised what a bizarrely normal instinct that was. Her father stared at her.

Sara crouched down and pulled Mila close. "Whatever you had to tell me," she put her mouth close to Mila's ear, still barely audible above the siren, "Whatever it was, Mila, *hold onto it*. Don't tell another soul."

Mila swallowed and nodded, her confession drowned out as Sara helped her to her feet once more. The family gathered by the tent flap.

"What do we do, pada?" Nasir asked.

Andrei turned to him, placing a hand on his shoulder. "Take care of your sister. If we get separated, I will find you." He hesitated and turned to Mila, cupped her face in his hand, and she saw true fear in him then. Her stomach twisted painfully. "Follow orders, do *everything* they tell you. Don't give them an excuse to hurt you."

He turned away, his jaw set, and took Sara's hand.

A moment later, Nasir's shaking hand gripped Mila's tight. "Stay close," he said. He raised their clenched hands and kissed Mila's knuckles.

Then they burst out into the blinding daylight.

Mila scrunched her eyes against the pain while the relentless screech of the siren impaled her ears, stabbing again and again. Nasir tugged her forward only to crash into someone that rushed past, sending them spinning away. Nothing felt familiar; it was all sharpened by adrenaline, strange and hostile, looking like an alien land through the haze of dust kicked up by fleeing feet. Even the air smelled different.

Frantic voices blurred together in waves that seemed to be crashing toward her. Mila's insides lurched as she clung to Nasir's hand, his grip never wavering even when she stumbled. In the distance, vehicle engines began to rumble, and still the siren's squeal seemed to shake the very ground.

Deep in her heart, Mila knew; the siren was for her. They we're coming for *her*.

They ran.

The thudding of solid boots followed, uneven and hurried, growing closer, quicker, and Mila's heart thudded with them. Then came the screams.

A Satarian man staggered backwards, covering his face, while a guard held the butt of his rifle up, prepared to strike again. "Don't you *dare* argue with me! Just move! Now!" the guard screamed, spittle flying.

Similar commands were being shouted all around.

Mila stiffened, but Nasir was already wrenching on her arm as the guard struck the man again with a sickening crack.

"Mila, come on!" Nasir cried, pulling her along the dirt path behind many others. Already, their parents had been swept further along the path, and though Mila and Nasir cried out after them, their shouts were drowned by the river of people.

"We'll find them," Nasir panted, "At the border, we'll find them."

The camp became a labyrinth of collapsing tents and fleeing people, and it was becoming harder to find a clear path through the madness. Everywhere, voices rose in a crescendo of confusion, punctuated with violent barbs of insults and thumps landing. Mila's lungs burned and her legs ached as she struggled to stay beside Nasir, but she gripped her brother's hand with all the strength she had as they weaved between bodies. She would not lose him.

As the border came closer, something flicked in Mila's mind and she realised for the first time that, between the blasts of the siren, there were words. In her shock, she hadn't translated the Amanese phrases, but now she heard it:

"This is the National Guard. Gather at the assembly point immediately. If you resist, you will be arrested."

Everywhere Mila looked, chaos reigned, and slowly a line of guards became visible, moving through the camp in tight formation, their uniforms and expressions dark. Some held rifles, others had truncheons at the ready. They progressed systematically, bellowing instructions in Amanese as refugees scattered in their wake.

"Move to the assembly area, now!"

"Leave everything behind! Hurry up!"

A cacophony of shouts and panicked voices reverberated in the open air as the guards pulled people out of their homes and children screamed in fear. Barely metres away, two guards pulled a woman out of her tent and threw her roughly to the ground. Mila opened her mouth to protest, but Nasir yanked her to follow him. "Don't, Mila. Just keep moving, please," he urged, his palm sweaty against hers, holding tight. "Keep your head down, don't look around, just keep moving."

Mila swallowed the shout she had been about to unleash.

"Get up!" the guard yelled. "Fucking stupid Creo! If you don't want to use your legs, I'll break them."

But when the woman tried to get up, another guard kicked her in the back, pushing her back down into the dirt.

It went against everything she believed in, but Mila did as her brother said; she kept her head down, and kept her mouth shut, though she felt like she had swallowed poison. She could feel it burning her insides; any minute now she would vomit it all up.

But she didn't; she kept going. Sticks and pebbles stabbed at Mila's feet through the flimsy soles of her boots as she was herded forwards beneath the siren's endless, deafening wail.

As they neared the top of the path, the border fence came into view, but the torrent of people did not slow. Driven by the tightening circle of guards, they surged toward the assembly area, crashing against each other like waves upon rocks. Hundreds of bodies pressed in from all sides, swirling and tumbling and suddenly Mila was bumped roughly aside, her balance faltering as the crowd pressed against her, and her fingers slipped from Nasir's grip.

No—she couldn't lose him.

A lightning strike of pure panic exploded in her chest. Frantic, she twisted against the tide of flesh and sweat, her hands clawing at empty air. Disorientated, engulfed, Mila stumbled over the uneven ground.

She couldn't lose him.

Panic surged through her as she felt her balance tip, pulled downwards, too fast to catch. If she went down, she would not get up again. She would be trampled to death beneath thousands of feet, and the heaving crowd wouldn't even notice. She planted her feet planted on the churned dirt and shoved her way back up, clawing at the bodies around her, screaming for Nasir.

In an instant he was there, yanking her back to his chest and wrapping a protective arm around her shoulders. She clung to him, her breath coming in ragged sobs. A single tear slid down her cheek.

She couldn't lose him.

Above them, the spiked top of the tall fence stood like fangs against the sky. All around, wide eyes stared back, frantic and worried.

"It's going to be okay," Nasir said, as much to himself as to Mila. He urgently scanned the crowd, still searching for their parents amid the blur of terror and chaos.

Slowly, the movement stilled, and the crowd became a suffocating wall of bodies. Somewhere unseen among the throng, a baby's thin, broken wails cries wavered in and out of the siren's howl. The distraught sound made Mila's heart ache, and the feeling made her think of Elaari and her infant son. Was that his voice, small and terrified, trapped in the stifling crowd? Mila twisted around, straining to peer through the masses, looking for her friend.

At that moment, the siren fell silent, plunging the camp into an eerie stillness.

10

The abrupt end to the noise left Mila's ears ringing. After the onslaught, the silence was strange, and somehow more unnerving. For a brief, suspended moment, time seemed frozen—no more frantic shouts, no more urgent footsteps. Just a heavy, oppressive quiet that settled over the camp like a pall.

Minutes passed. A single cloud crawled across the sky and, drifting in and out of the vapour, a pair of carrion birds carved slow, deliberate circles. Mila tightened her grip on Nasir's arms. Around them, hundreds of pale faces looked around, squinting in the bright light, searching for some sort of answer. The Amanese guards had formed an unbroken ring around the refugees and the compression of the crowd was unbearable, hot and cloying beneath the azure autumn sky. They were penned in like animals with nowhere to go. The faintest breeze slowly stirred the thick air, swilling the scent of many of sweating bodies and carrying shreds of whispered comments. Through the gaps in the fence, the Salt Strip shimmered as if the white stones were crusted with broken glass.

Sudden movement caught Mila's eye as a man climbed onto the roof of the guard hut at the other end of the assembly area. He stood steady on the slanted surface, his tall, pristine black boots braced firmly. The lone figure was dressed in the dark navy uniform of the guards, but with gleaming gold epaulettes on each shoulder, their polished edges catching the sunlight in sharp, almost blinding flashes. Even from fifty meters away, the man's presence exuded coldness and strength as if he were cut from iron.

He raised his fist to his mouth, and with a click the speakers atop the border fence crackled to life. A few people gasped softly in alarm. Tension rippled through the crush.

"Silence, silence!" The acid in his deep voice carried across the sea of terrified faces. "Listen carefully, Creo scum. We are IronHand, and we have taken control of the Al'Mazraea camp and its people under the Integrity Act, article fifty, section eight. Your repellent ways are over. You're finished. We condemn you!"

A cry spilled out from several people in the crowd. Mila listened, every part of her shaking. In the depths of her petrified mind, the voice sounded faintly familiar.

"The people have said *enough*!" the man's voice continued. "Not twenty-four hours ago, the city of Haman came under attack from a deliberate and deadly act, committed by one of *you*."

Confused murmurs moved through the assembly and heads turned this way and that, seeking answers. Mila kept her head down, fighting the churning of her stomach as her palms grew clammy. Nasir gripped her tighter and Mila swallowed hard, teeth pressed tightly together as she tried to steady her breathing.

Just stay calm, she told herself, though her every nerve was screaming in alarm. The guards didn't know it was her—how could they? But if they *did*…

Her pulse thundered in her ears, drowning out the din around her. She glanced at Nasir out of the corner of her eye. He gave the slightest shake of his head, silently begging her to keep quiet, to remain still.

Stay calm, small, no matter what.

The man continued. "Lives were suddenly ended by this evil, absolutely *wicked* act of magic. You people, you *refugees,* you want to frighten us away from our own city with terrible cruelty and mass murder—but, let me tell you, your plan has failed! Finally, the power is back in the hands of the right people! And we will defend our country from more violence. We *will* have the control and obedience of the Creo population!"

A chorus of support burst out from the guards at the periphery of the group. While the Satarians looked around with absolute bewilderment and fear, the man went on, his voice growing louder, more threatening, and Mila suddenly recognised the speaker; Draven Lideri. "Your very presence disturbs the natural order, it threatens the safety of Ard Aman, and it is a risk we no longer have to tolerate."

The announcement ended with a sharp click, leaving a silence that palpitated with terror. For a long moment, no one moved. The threat hung heavy in the air, tension in every breath.

A sudden, harsh voice cut across the space. "Everyone, on your knees, now!"

Panicked yells erupted from the outer edges of the assembly area and a surge of energy swelled through the throng as people tried to move away from whatever was happening there. All Mila could hear was the dull thud of blows landing, at the same time she was pulled to her knees by the movement of the crowd. She was grateful that Nasir kept his protective arms like a halo around her, making sure she could breathe.

Lideri approached the assembly, his scarred face twisted in a snarl of anger and his eyes as cold as winter. He surveyed the sea of faces with mechanical precision.

"That one," he barked, pointing to a woman near the edge of the crowd, and a pair of guards sprang into action. They surged through the kneeling refugees and seized the woman, her eyes wide with terror, hauling her roughly to her feet. She tried to fight them as they wrenched her out of the crowd, but it was futile. The guards were simply too strong. They brought her before Lideri and he looked down at her with ice in his gaze. When he nodded, one guard held the woman tight while the other bound her hands. She was made to stand still, shoulders heaving with uncontrolled sobs, watched by the keen eye of a third guard's rifle.

Lideri prowled further along the perimeter of the assembly area. Refugees recoiled from him like opposing magnets, attempting to keep their distance.

"Her." A slightly older woman was singled out this time. She bucked and thrashed at the thugs who seized her, but she too was removed and had her hands tied.

Lideri continued to pick through the crowd, directing his guards to extract seven more people. With a jolt, Mila realised that they were all women, about her height and build. A cold sweat prickled her skin. Finally, confirmation. He was looking for someone like her.

Mila tried to shrink herself further. But, as she watched the bound and crying women, she also realised that Lideri didn't seem to have much to go on. The same rough tunic, the same worn pants, of course. The same offensive hair. They don't see us as individuals, Mila thought, and for once the idea was comforting, if only slightly. The bland uniformity the Amanese inflicted upon the Satarians might actually protect her.

Lideri seemed to be weighing something in his mind as he faced the line of female prisoners. Then he nodded.

Without a word, the guards pulled something from their belts. The first woman gasped as a rough hessian cloth was yanked over her head and the cord tightened at her neck. When all nine were hooded, the IronHand thugs pushed them in single file toward the border fence, using the butts of their rifles to keep the blinded prisoners moving.

One by one they were shoved through the narrow guard gate into Ard Aman, onto the blinding white stones of the Salt Strip, while still more guards kept their weapons trained on the huddle of refugees in the assembly area. The crowd seemed to shrink. Thousands of staring eyes followed the stumbling march of the hooded prisoners, unable to look away.

The guards steered the prisoners parallel to the fence, slowly parading them for all to see. Then, when they had gone far enough, the women were halted and shoved to their knees. Some of the prisoners tried to resist, but, being still blinded and constrained, they were quickly silenced.

Lideri had clambered back onto the roof of the guard hut, and now he turned to face the crowd, his voice booming through the speakers once more. "This is what happens when you break the laws of our land. We make no distinction between the terrorists who committed this act, and those who harbour them. You are all responsible in our eyes, and you *will* be brought to justice."

He motioned with one hand, and a single guard stepped up to face the women on their knees, his back to the fence and the sea of Satarians. In his hands the guard cradled a weapon; chunky and black, the barrel short and sinister, like the head of a snake waiting to strike.

"You must understand," Lideri said, his voice low but spreading easily across the frozen crowd, "Your magic is a disease, a plague that threatens the very fabric of our world. It is not a gift; it is a curse. And those who wield it are nothing more than poison."

He paused, his gaze sweeping over the scene, his scar twisted in a smirk. "Let this be a lesson to all of you. There will be no mercy for those who defy the laws. There will be no forgiveness."

Lideri raised his arm, then dropped it swiftly.

Whip-cracks sliced along the Salt Strip, each one followed by a sickening thud. The prisoners jerked and spasmed as the bullets hit them, then they slumped forward, lifeless and silent. Just crumpled bodies on the ground.

But the new governor wasn't finished.

"You have one hour to turn over the terrorist who collapsed the mountain yesterday," he bellowed, "Or we will do this again. And again. And again."

The microphone let out a piercing screech of feedback before cutting off abruptly, leaving the air ringing. Mila clung to Nasir's arms still wrapped around her, fighting wave after wave of nausea. The world was spinning.

The unbearable seconds stretched into unbearable minutes.

Fear palpitated around her; she could see it in their eyes, neighbour turned against neighbour, friend against friend. The way people glanced around accusingly, as if they could read each other's minds. They were all hoping that someone would step forward and end this nightmare.

But no one moved. No one spoke up.

Mila was the only person who could.

Among the mosaic were familiar faces; people she had grown up with, who had laughed with her, helped her. The *soffa* Karina trembled like a leaf, barely recognisable from the cheeky old woman who lit up with merriment. The sight of her so fragile and afraid sent a spike of guilt so sharp through Mila's chest, her face crumpled.

They were *all* in danger, and it was because of her.

"Nasir," Mila choked out, fingers gripping his arms like talons.

"No, Mila."

"But—"

"I said *no*." His voice was harder than she had ever heard it. "We'll figure it out."

"How? What are we supposed to do?" she asked. "We can't fight them. We can't even defend ourselves without making it worse."

"I don't know. We just need time."

Time. That was the one thing they didn't have. Lideri's ultimatum hung over them all like a guillotine, and the clock was ticking. Mila shook her head, ignoring the panicked tears that began to swell.

"There isn't any time," she whispered back, trembling. "They're going to hurt more people. They're going to keep punishing us until someone speaks up."

"I'll… I'll think of something," he said. He was hardly looking at her. His eyes raked over the many heads and faces of the refugees, desperately searching for their parents.

"If I could just make them understand…" Mila's shaking hands curled into fists. She could own the fact that she broke the laws when she cracked the pavement trying to escape—but she would not take the blame for the rockslide. "I was there to *help*. I didn't have anything to do with *Pika* crumbling."

Nasir's eyes whipped back to hers. "The very fact that you know which mountain it was will be enough for them. Hell, they don't even need *that* much. Look at what they did to those women, just to make a point…" His voice shook so violently that he stopped speaking. He took a deep breath, and Mila could see how much it was costing him to stay calm. "They know someone did magic. They saw it. Even if you didn't cause the fall, they saw what happened after. They were already convinced that Satarians are dangerous, and now they have a correlation too strong to ignore."

Mila bit her bottom lip. "So the truth doesn't matter?"

"You know that already, Cricket."

She pressed her lips together. Yes, he was right; the truth had never mattered to the Amanese… but it didn't make the fact any easier to bear. The sinking sensation in her gut pulled down, down, into a darker depth than she had ever known. She had caused the executions of nine innocent Satarian women, and if she didn't speak up soon… She knew Lideri's promise was true: more would die.

"I have to turn myself in."

"No, Mila." Her brother shook his head, his hands gripping her painfully. "*No.* If you turn yourself in, they'll kill you. And that might be the kinder of the options."

Mila swallowed hard. She was terrified—more terrified than she had ever been in her life. Terrified of turning herself in, terrified of *not* turning herself in. Of living with this guilt for the rest of her life… or not living at all.

But she couldn't let more people suffer because of her mistake.

She turned her attention to the white hut and took a deep breath. Nasir's grip on her arms tightened further. "I'm not going to let you."

"It's not your responsibility, Nasir."

"It *is*," he said. "You're my sister. I would let a hundred people die if it meant you were safe."

Mila shook her head, "I can't do that."

Suddenly, on the periphery of her vision, Mila noticed movement; a guard running in from the south, probably from Checkpoint B. Though many metres away, his face was clearly pink and flushed. His heavy boots crunched on the uneven ground as he approached the hut. Mila held her breath. A band of guards stepped toward him, drawn by the urgency in his approach, and the scene seemed to move in slow motion. The newcomer paused briefly to speak with them, gesturing wildly and brandishing something in his hand. She saw the meaningful exchange of glances, the subtle nods of acknowledgment, and then the guard hurried toward Lideri, who stood calmly in the door of the small building, smoking a cigarette.

The governor turned as the guard approached, his scarred face unreadable. For a moment, the two men exchanged words, and the guard handed something to Lideri. Even from this distance, Mila could see him flip open the small book. Her stomach dropped.

Then the governor's face broke into a twisted, triumphant smile.

There was little doubt in Mila's mind. That guard was the one who had stopped her last night, the one who had seen her covered head-to-toe in dirt and blood. And he had just given Lideri her passbook, along with, Mila was willing to bet, a detailed description of the young Creo woman who had almost missed curfew.

Mila's mouth became unbearably dry.

Lideri reached for the microphone. The speakers above the crowd clicked to life. Nasir's body tensed around her, as though an electric current was running through him. Mila's breath caught.

There was a screech of feedback, a cry from the crowd, then Lideri purred two words into the silence:

"Mila Medín."

11

"Mila, make yourself known," the scarred man called through the speakers, like she was the winner of some horrific prize. In slow motion, the crowd turned toward her, and thousands of eyes seemed to pierce through her flesh.

Somehow Mila got to her feet, though she was trembling from head to foot. This had to be a nightmare. Her mind hovered outside of herself, like she was watching the scene play out from somewhere very far away to someone who wasn't her. Funny that she had been ready to turn herself in not a minute before, valiant and brave—but now that the choice had been removed, she was a petrified child once more.

She didn't hear the shocked exclamations of the other refugees. She didn't feel Nasir's grip like a vice around her shoulders. She didn't see the guards wading through the crowd. All she saw was, finally, her parents' faces, like pinpricks of light in the dark. Their mouths were open in screams she couldn't hear, both trying to get to her while others blocked the way.

Sudden pain brought her back to her body as the guards wrenched her arms backward and a tied prickly strip of fabric too tight around her wrists.

"Leave her alone!" Nasir shouted and launched himself onto the nearest guard, his hands prying at the man's as he tried to wrestle him away from his sister.

The guards may have been startled for a moment, but it was short lived. One of them swung his rifle with a swift, practiced motion, and a sickening crack rang out as the butt connected with Nasir's face. The impact sent him reeling backward and he fell hard on the people nearby with blood pouring from his nose, spilling down his chin and neck.

Mila screamed his name, struggling against the iron grip of the guard who held her, forcing her forward.

Please let him be okay...

"Stay down!" the guard shrieked to Nasir. He turned his rifle on the crowd, sweeping the barrel across them all. "All of you, stay down! Anyone else who wants to try to be a hero will be shot."

Mila twisted, her heart hammering, desperate to see if Nasir was still moving. And he was, thankfully—but the sight made her stomach drop. Blood smeared his face where the guard had struck him, yet he fought like a man possessed, clawing at the refugees holding him back. It took five of them to pin him down, shouting for him to stop, but he thrashed against them, his eyes wild and locked on her.

A lump rose in her throat. What happened to staying small and quiet? She didn't want him to get hurt any more than he already had. But, of course, that was inevitable now—her fate was sealed, and an aching remorse crept in for the pain he would soon have to live with. The pain that could only come with living.

It was easy to die, she realised. For her, after the fear, there would be no more pain, no more suffering. Just silence and the gentle release of her spirit to Gaia, where she would join the earth, the roots, the stones, her part in the circle of life fulfilled. But to survive, to lose a loved one? The pain of that was indescribable. To survive meant every breath carried the cruel, unbearable weight of absence. To lose someone you loved was to have a piece of yourself ripped away, leaving only jagged edges and an ache that never faded. And Nasir—he would survive. He would have to endure that endless pain, and there was nothing she could do to stop it.

In dying, she was getting the easier end of the bargain.

The guards' rough hands dug into her skin. The crowd seemed to grow quiet, like her ears had been muffed and all she could hear was her hammering heart counting down its final beats.

Her family's pain was her fault. If only she hadn't drawn attention to herself, if only she had stayed hidden… But it was too late for regrets. She had to face the consequences, no matter how terrible they might be. This was the guards' world, and their rules she had broken.

The walk to the border fence felt both interminably long and far too short. Mila closed her eyes, savouring the warmth of the sun's rays on her face; the way the breeze tickled her cheeks and played with her hair; the sharp edges of every pebble that pressed into the thin soles of her boots. But then her eyes snapped open again. If these were her last moments of consciousness, she didn't want to miss a single second.

The sky was so, *so* blue, stretching on forever into lands she had never seen. There were so many things she had never got the chance—or the permission—to do. She had never known what it felt like to be carried by the ocean waves; never indulged in any of the delicacies or wares from the bazaar; had never climbed the Uul Serrad to look out upon the world. She had always wanted to dress up like the Amanese women, draped in fluttering silks the colour of flame and twilight, with their painted lips and nails, walking freely in delicate shoes. And she had always wanted to write—not just in Amanese, but in *Satarian*. To master the curling symbols and leave an inky mark on this world.

These ambitions had always been as distant as the stars, but while she was still breathing, they still shimmered with potential. At least there had been a chance. But now? Now, those stars were being doused with every step she took, and her dreams would never come to pass.

Further in the crowd, Mila noticed a small boy, his head tipped back, watching the birds circling overhead. The sunlight caught the fairer streaks of brown in his curls, and the blue petals of a flower tucked behind his ear. Every pair of eyes that she passed were a different shade and mixture of brown and green. Those cursed Creo eyes, reflecting the horrifying truth: she was walking to her death.

As the guards positioned her in front of Lideri, the entire camp seemed to be holding its breath. Mila's eyes roved the crowd for her parents' faces, but they were lost in the sea once more. Was she about to die without seeing them again? And Nasir... he was still trying to stand, trying to reach her.

A cold hand seized her chin and turned her to face the governor, and her eyes fell on a gilded pin adorning his jacket. It was forged from dark, unpolished iron and shaped like a shield, its surface rough as if it had been hammered straight from the forge. At its centre, a solid fist jutted outward. She had seen it before, on the banners in Haman town square. The IronHand sigil.

With a smirk, Lideri raised the microphone to his lips. "*This* is the Creo that caused the death of twelve Amanese people—men, women, and children. *This* is the Creo who thought she could get away with doing illegal magic."

Each sentence was like a bell tolling her demise.

"*This* is the Creo who allowed us to kill those other woman, who put you all at risk, and caused us to take such drastic measures!"

The microphone clicked off, and Lideri stood in front of her, so close she could smell the sweaty, musky scent of him. So close she could see the keloids in his hideous scars. The wounds seemed to have been stitched roughly; the flesh of them was bright, raised, coarse, and his features distorted slightly where the skin was pulled together. Even now, Mila found herself curious about what had happened to him. How old was he when such a horrible injury occurred?

And—was this the last thing she would ever wonder about? The face of the man that would order her execution?

"You think you're special, don't you, Creo?" he murmured so low that only Mila could hear. "But I know your game. If we kill you, you become a martyr. The scum will turn you into a symbol. A beacon of hope for the hopeless. They'll rally around your memory and fight in your name."

His expression made Mila's blood run cold.

"But I will not give you—nor *them*—that power. No, I am going to make you suffer in a way that will break you. I will shatter your spirit, and leave you with nothing—As you should be."

Mila's heartbeat took over her senses as Lideri straightened up and smiled; a reptilian pulling back of the lips beneath his pitiless eyes. Then he signalled to someone out of Mila's sight. Faint shouts of protest and fear swelled through the refugees as they were shoved aside by guards. And then, through the shifting bodies, Mila saw them—her parents, their faces pale and twisted in fear, hands already bound as guards dragged them forward. Her mother was fighting hard against them, hurling Satarian slurs, but not for long—one of the guards struck her across the face, hard, twice, and Sara fell into line.

"No! Stop it!" Mila cried out, helpless as her voice was swallowed up by the clamour of the crowd. She struggled against the guard behind her, fighting to reach them, to *do something*, but their grip was unyielding.

"Please, no! Leave them alone! They didn't know, they didn't do anything wrong!"

Her parents were shoved to the front and made to stand alongside Mila.

"Mahma!" Mila screamed, "I'm sorry! Pada! Please—" she twisted to face Lideri, "Please, *please* punish me however you want—but leave them alone. They had nothing to do with it!"

The governor watched with cruel satisfaction, his gaze flicking between Mila and her parents. Then he leaned forward and his hot breath against her ear made her freeze. "This *is* how I want to punish you. You will live, knowing it was your actions that led to their deaths."

For a moment, his words didn't make sense. Then she screamed, and she never stopped screaming, fighting with a new strength against those who held her, as tears streamed down her face.

Lideri clicked the microphone once more. "Those who harbour creomancers are just as guilty as the individuals who practice the evil magic. Let this be a lesson to you all! Your magic causes people to die, one way or another," he said, recounting the vitriol of his earlier speech.

Mila's vision blurred, her very soul bursting with utter panic as she struggled with every ounce of strength she had left—but it was no use. The guards held her fast, forcing her to watch as the rough fabric hoods were yanked over her parents' heads.

"Please!" Mila sobbed, her voice breaking, "Please don't do this! I'll do anything, *anything*, just don't hurt them. Please, I'm begging you…"

Her protests and pleas fell on deaf ears. Shouts sprang from some in the crowd, while others turned away, unable to watch what they knew was coming.

Mila couldn't breathe.

A knot twisted inside her and a strange sensation crept outwards from the crown of her head, like an icy cold liquid was oozing down her spine.

"Your Creo poison caused this," Lideri bellowed to the crowd. Then he raised his own gun, pointing it directly at Sara's head. Even Mila's cries of unbridled agony were not loud enough to drown out the gunshot that tore through the air. A heartbeat later, the second shot rang out.

Mila's legs gave out beneath her and she fell limp in the guard's tight grasp, eyes locked on the bodies of her parents crumpled on the ground beside her, their faces hidden by the dark hoods as their Creo blood slowly seeped out to stain the pale stones of the Salt Strip.

12

For a while—maybe minutes, maybe years—there was only a high-pitched ringing in Mila's ears. She might have passed out, though she wasn't sure, because the image of her parents' dead bodies never left her eyes.

Was she breathing?

Did she want to?

A garbled noise reached her, as if someone was speaking from under water. She looked around to see Lideri's scarred mouth moving, but it was like her brain didn't want to process sound anymore.

As she stared at him, understanding slowly startled to trickle back.

"…the Loyalist Act. The fields of Al'Mazraea are now returned to us. You will no longer be permitted to live on our land for free, thinking you are not bound by our laws. Each of you will be required to earn your keep by performing manual labour duties to the satisfaction of the State. And if you cannot work, you will be removed. It is as simple as that."

Through a tunnel of blackened vision, Mila watched Lideri's black boots take a step closer to her face, and suddenly she was being seized roughly beneath both arms and hauled to her feet. A hand seized her jaw, fingers and thumb pinching her tight and forcing her face toward his.

"The previous administration was far too lax with you all. But under *my* leadership," he growled, "You will no longer be able to infiltrate Amanese society. We will always know exactly what you are. And so will you."

Mila caught a glint of metal as Lideri raised his hand to her face and at that moment, searing heat sliced through her forehead. It was pain more intense than Mila could ever have imagined in her worst nightmare. She shrieked and writhed, arching and twisting to escape, but Lideri's hand still clamped around her jaw and the guards held her firmly, forcing her to endure the burning. What were they doing to her? Mila's head spun violently from the intensity of it until she was certain she would vomit or pass out. And still she screamed.

The scent of scorched flesh smothered her, haunting her even as Lideri let go of her chin. Her skin *sizzled*. A moment later she was thrust to the ground as an inconvenient afterthought.

Every nerve in her body was aflame, sending shards shooting through her brain, down her neck and into her shoulders, clawing at her mind and shredding her thoughts. Every second the pain seemed to intensify, deeper, stronger, settling into her bones, and her breaths came in shuddering gasps, sounding far too loud in her own ears. Blackness waded through her consciousness—but still she was aware of Lideri, the way a wounded animal is agonisingly aware of the circling predator. She didn't have the strength to rise, nor the will to face the weight of what had been done to her. Her forehead was molten agony. She just wanted to die.

She stayed sprawled at the governor's feet with the coarse ground biting into her skin, until a raw, blood-curdling sound tore through the heavy air. With effort, Mila managed to open her eyes. Her vision swam, pulsing in time with the relentless pain in her head, but she could still make out the scene before her. Lideri stood poised over a man, holding something to his forehead. He looked to be in his early fifties, his face framed by thick, wavy, dark hair that matched his thick eyebrows. A short, salt-and-pepper beard framed his jawline, now contorted in a piercing scream. A moment later, Lideri released the man and he staggered backwards, managing to take a few faltering steps before he slumped against the border fence and slowly slid to the ground, eyes closed.

On his forehead burned a still-smoking brand. The sight of the white-hot marks and the inflamed red skin around them made her stomach twist, and in that moment she knew what they had done to her.

They had marked her.

Like livestock, like she was nothing more than property.

Like they *owned* her.

Her whole body began to tremble uncontrollably, and not just with shock and pain. Hatred swilled through her insides, black and sickening, filling her until there was no room left for fear. It burned within, fierce and steady, smouldering like the fresh, ugly marks on her skin.

I hate them.

Yet she continued to lie in the dirt where she had been discarded, listening to the screams as the guards made their way through the assembly, listening to the hiss of the brand searing into Satarian flesh. Mila closed her eyes against the sound, but behind her eyelids, she couldn't shake the sickening image of red-hot iron pressing into skin. The stench of it clung to the air, heavy and nauseating, mingling with the coppery tang of spilled blood.

Her parents' blood.

When the assembly area was littered with writhing, branded refugees, all in various stages of shock and despair, the sun was beginning to sink into the west, bleeding hues of crimson and gold across the sky. Wisps of cloud caught the fire of its fading glow, edges kissed with molten light before dusk claimed them.

The unwavering voice of Lideri voice carried above the moans of the newly marked, assaulting Mila's ears after so long listening to screams. "Because I am a kind person, a benevolent person, I will give you until dawn to mourn and bury your dead. But you'd better prepare yourselves. Tomorrow, we begin."

The IronHand group worked quickly, as if they had desired this for a long time. By morning, the border fence had been reinforced with sheets of chain-link wire on the inside, and on the Haman side they lay a four-metre-high wall of cinderblocks, hastily cemented together, not level nor aligned neatly. But its beauty didn't matter; the effect was the same regardless. The Satarian refugees were truly trapped.

The only break in the monotony occurred near Checkpoint A, where a slab of dull, oxidised metal was embedded in the wall. It was wide enough to let vehicles pass through, and topped with curled strings of barbed wire that extended along the entirety of the new wall.

A lone figure sat on the crest that crept up steadily toward the headland. The heavens had whirled overhead as she watched the labourers, and throughout the night the prison wall took shape. The clang of metal and the dull thud of stone locking into place echoed over the distance. With each passing hour, as the bright star of Sirius slipped below the horizon, the wall loomed higher. Soon the ragged line of stone and steel stretched out of sight to the left and right, cutting along the miles that formed the border.

Now, as the ruby-red Antares disappeared and the first blush of dawn coloured the sky, Mila stifled a yawn. Strands of hair clung to her damp cheeks, and her eyes were bloodshot and swollen from the tears that had finally dried up. Her body ached with exhaustion. The brand on her forehead pulsed with a deep, agonising heat that refused to fade. Every time she closed her gritty eyes, she saw her parents' faces, their final moments replaying in an endless, torturous loop broken only by the memory of burying them. Their limp figures had been laid in the ground, along with the other nine women, near where Mila now sat. As she watched, buds of green were already sprouting, spurred on by the energy of the dead returning to Gaia. Very soon, she knew, the blue *felicia* flowers would bloom; a Satarian's final creomancy. Mila tore her eyes from the graves.

The morning air was cold, but Mila hardly noticed. She sat still, numb to everything, until the faint sound of footsteps broke her trance.

Nasir sat down beside her, saying nothing at first. Mila glanced at him, transfixed by the blistering burns that marked his forehead too. It was a symbol, crudely transferred by twisted wires—a circle crossed with three horizontal lines and a vertical line. Their symbol: the *noterran.*

The silence between them stretched out, uncomfortable and heavy, until he finally handed her a small, worn plate holding a meagre portion of bread and half an apple. Mila took the plate without a word, but the food sat untouched in her lap.

"You need to eat something."

Mila looked to the distant wall. "I'm not hungry."

Nasir sighed and tugged his knees up to his chest, tucking his arms around them tightly. "I know. I'm not either."

The silence grew again between them, heavier this time, filled with a million unspoken thoughts. Mila shivered, suddenly feeling the biting cold. Their relationship had never been like this—it felt strained, like a deep chasm had appeared between them. Even when they had argued before, there was always something warm beneath the anger, a thread of love that bound them together. Now that thread felt frayed and hacked. Her throat tightened, trying to form words, but what could she possibly say? What could possibly make any of this alright?

"Nasir—" she started, but he stood abruptly.

"I know, Mila. I know, okay? You didn't mean for it. But that doesn't change what happened. I'm trying—" His voice wavered and he stopped, sucked his teeth. "I'm trying to forgive you. But I don't know if I can."

Those words tore through her like a thousand knives.

"Not yet, anyway," he added softly.

The sun crested the horizon, and, as though activated by the warm light, shrill whistles blasted along the aisles of tents. A monotonous voice came over the loudspeakers and blared across the quiet camp.

"Attention Creos, attention Creos. Report to the assembly area immediately to receive your work assignment. Any attempts to evade or resist will be met with severe consequences."

Nasir had already moved away several steps before turning back, waiting for her. There was reluctance in the movement, like he was merely following what was expected of him as an older brother, not because he genuinely wanted her company. Mila's heart shrivelled further.

"Come on," he called, voice tight with urgency. "We have to go."

She stood slowly as the booming announcement began repeating, and followed him on heavy legs. Her whole body felt like it belonged to someone else. She *wished* it belonged to someone else…

As they walked along the main path through the camp, other refugees emerged from their tents, drifting in the same direction like debris on the tide. Mila could feel their eyes on her back, sneaking glances at her from the side when they thought she wasn't looking. Some were bold enough to stare at her outright, the accusation and hatred plain on their faces. And above every pair of wrathful eyes, twisted burnt flesh in the symbol of the *noterran*.

Without warning, a stocky woman stepped deliberately into Mila's path, forcing her into a collision.

"Watch where you're going, Traitor!" she jeered as she shoved Mila away.

"I—I'm sorry," Mila stammered.

"Sorry? Sorry doesn't fix anything!"

"I know—I'm…" The apology died on her lips.

Another man spat at her feet as she passed him, muttering a single word: "Murderer."

Each hateful glance carved another invisible wound and Mila wished she could shrink into the ground beneath her feet. The weight of their blame pressed against her ribs, suffocating, yet she bore it without protest and kept her head down. They didn't care that she was suffering too, and why should they? They were right; her grief and pain were justice, a burden she deserved to carry for what she had done. She was left to stumble forward alone.

13

The assembly point came into view, the once open area now occupied with another new structure; a cage large enough for hundreds of people. The sight sent a shiver rolling down Mila's spine as the twisting metal glinted in the golden light of early morning. At the edge where Checkpoint A once stood, the cage funnelled in to connect with a solid gate in the border wall. A thick bolt ran across its centre and heavy rivets lined its edges, shiny and freshly pressed, made just for this occasion. On either side of this gate, tied taut against the fence, stretched massive navy and grey banners emblazoned with IronHand's shield and fist sigil.

Around the edges of the cage, both inside and out, armed guards paced like wolves circling the sea of bodies already huddled within. A murmur ran through the crowd as Mila approached and was steered through into the compound. She pulled her tunic tighter around herself, hoping no one noticed the subtle tremor in her hands as she slid further into the crowd, keeping her head low while her heartbeat thumped loudly in her ears. All around, heads turned to watch her. Some glared with open hostility, others with disdain. Even the familiar faces of neighbours and friends were closed off, eyes downcast to avoid her.

Nasir kept a cold and deliberate distance between them, as if he couldn't bear for even his shadow to be close to her. He didn't defend her, didn't put out a hand to steady her, didn't offer any words of comfort. Yesterday he had thrown himself at the guards to stop them taking her from him, and now… Now he might as well be leagues away.

At the far end of the assembly area, near the new gateway, still more guards were gathering, their dark navy uniforms conspicuous against the sea of grey-clad refugees. Dozens upon dozens, more than Mila had ever seen. Over a hundred at least, she estimated. They had to be new recruits… but how had Lideri gained so much support so quickly? Mila thought back to the rally, shocked to realise that had only been forty-eight hours ago. Had his vile words truly inspired so many to volunteer? The thought made her stomach turn.

Mila glanced up at Nasir. His jaw was set tight, eyes locked straight ahead. She wanted to reach out, to say something, anything… but there was only a tightness in her throat and a deep hole in her chest. The darkness yawned wider with every passing moment, pulling at her insides with astonishing strength. Between glances filled with fear and loathing in equal measure, the people were keeping the same wary distance as Nasir, affording her a radius of space as if she were diseased.

Whispers followed her like shadows. *She's the one who did this… It was her magic… She's dangerous…*

Hadn't the little boy, Luca, said the same thing?

My father says you're dangerous…

His father was right.

As the sun cast a golden spotlight onto the new wall, some refugees stared with apprehension, some with a disturbingly defeated expression. But it was the people who stared with anger that scared Mila more than anything. That anger was only a moment away from being turned on her.

"You should be at the front," someone said suddenly, shoving Mila hard in the back.

She stumbled and whirled to face whoever had touched her, but all she found were hard, unforgiving faces staring back. It could have easily been any one of them.

"Get up there, Traitor," a man sneered.

Another hand nudged her, and then another. The hostile crowd parted in front then sealed shut behind, forcing her slowly toward the front of the assembly while their words whipped like dry soil in the summer winds, furious and biting.

"Whatever happens to us today should happen to *you* first," a woman said.

"I didn't—" Mila started, but the woman suddenly lunged at her.

"They killed my sister because of you!" she screamed and she shoved Mila with both hands, hard, through the last of the crowd. With no one to break her fall, Mila landed hard on her back, the breath knocked out of her. A tall guard loomed above, his black boots barely an inch from her face. Slowly, he looked down, his expression twisted with disdain as his eyes met hers, as though he found her no more worthy of his attention than the dirt on which she lay. In an instant, his hand shot out, fingers closing around the front of Mila's tunic like a claw and, in one swift motion, he yanked her up off the ground. An involuntary cry escaped her lips and his sneer deepened, disgust clear on his face as he held her, letting her feel the strength of his control.

"You'll get your turn, Creo bitch," he growled, then he threw her back toward the crowd. She stumbled and barely managed to stay upright, reflexively caught at the last second by refugees who immediately moved away again.

The guards' attention was suddenly drawn by a man approaching the cage. It was not Lideri, but still a high-up official, Mila suspected, judging by the gold glinting on his uniform and his air of self-importance. He sauntered slowly along the other side of the fence, looking at the Satarian cattle through the grille. A patch on his right breast pocket read *Ahriman*.

With exaggerated gusto, the man took the final bite of a pastry then, when he finished chewing and finally swallowed, he made a show of crinkling the paper wrapping then lobbing it over his shoulder toward the distant tents.

Trash attracts trash.

With deliberate slowness, Ahriman unlocked one of the side gates, then entered the cage and locked the gate behind him once more. As he turned, his slicked-back hair and high cheekbones caught the light, throwing shadows that accentuated his severe expression. Every aspect of him seemed considered, as if his very being were crafted to intimidate.

This man held a hand to his mouth and his voice blared over the speakers, high-pitched, like nails on a chalkboard in Mila's overwhelmed mind.

"Good morning, Creos," he called, his tone unnervingly cheerful, reminding Mila of the way the creche teachers would talk to a mischievous young child. The lightness of it made her skin crawl. "What do you think of our new structures, eh?"

There was a pause, while his gaze swept across the crowd, lingering just long enough to make individuals shift uncomfortably.

"Tutt tutt. When I ask you a question, you will reply," Ahriman said with an icy smile drawing his thin lips. "It's beautiful work, beautiful. Finally, a proper wall to keep you all where you belong. And

I love this space," he gestured around him. "Rather like a holding pen for feral animals, wouldn't you agree?"

Another pause. A few terrified people nodded.

"I know, I know. I have been told I shouldn't expect too much from the Creo brain. Slow learners, they say. But you *will* learn to respond when spoken to," he said, barely veiling the hint of a threat. Then he clapped his hands loudly, making Mila and several others jump. His eyes gleamed with predatory satisfaction. "Well, now that you're all *accounted for*, it's time for your work assignments. Time for you to earn your keep!"

Accounted for... Mila thought. Why don't they say what it really is? *Mutilated, disfigured...*

Ahriman began to stroll along the edge of the cage, smirking as refugees shrank away from him. He unhooked his baton and dragged it against the fence as he walked, enjoying the cacophony. "Cheer up, Creos! This is your chance to prove you're useful, to show us that you're worth something. Isn't that all any of you wanted?"

At his signal, four guards strained to heave aside the bolt in the steel gate, allowing it to clank open with a metallic groan, revealing the gleaming Salt Strip and the Haman city walls beyond. The guards began herding the refugees with calculated precision, their barked commands slicing through the air like whips that sent the group stumbling forward; young children clutched at their parents and *soffi* shuffled as fast as their aching joints would allow. The guards worked as a unit, some steering them toward the gate while others flanked the group, waving their batons to close ranks.

Thirty Satarians at a time were ushered forward into groups then corralled through the barricade. Mila's eyes frantically roved over each face, desperate to locate her brother. Amid the movement, she spotted him only a few metres away. She swallowed the surprise and reached out a hand to him, only for a guard to shove her backwards while Nasir was split into a separate group ahead.

She cried out on impulse, "Wait—" but he was already being steered along, following orders without even a backward glance. The thought of facing whatever lay ahead alone made her feel sick. She chewed her lip. It would be alright. It *had* to be alright.

Even as she thought the word, Mila's heart sank. Alright? There was nothing *alright* about any of this. Her life was shattered, broken beneath this crushing present. All she was left with were shards slicing apart her fingers as she tried to hold onto what remained.

As her brother passed out of sight beyond the gate, something in her dimmed. Nothing would ever be alright again.

She clenched her fists, forcing her nails into her palms. Tears burned behind her eyes, but she would not let them fall. She would not let the guards see her cry.

14

The press of bodies carried Mila under the shadow of the wall and through the forbidding gate, toward a line of ancient buses waiting on the Salt Strip. The vehicles were clearly decommissioned and neglected, extracted from the scrap yard to transport the refugees who were deemed just as worthless. With a loud, jarring clank, the door of one bus slammed shut and its engine coughed into action. The bus crunched its way over the white stones, beginning a heavy crawl toward the looming Haman city gates.

So, they were going to Haman. Mila froze. Cold dread fell into the pit of her stomach and her heart began to race, a dull thumping in her ears as dark images rushed in: the screaming, the chaos, the panic of that day. She couldn't go back there. She couldn't face the place that had stolen her peace, her sense of safety… her parents. She couldn't do it.

A rough hand clasped suddenly around the back of her neck and forced Mila to march forward, toward the nearest bus and another guard who stood by the door holding a clipboard, with impatience written all over his face. The first guard pushed down on her neck until she bent, kneeling before them both. The sharp stones of the Salt Strip dug into her knees.

"You will listen when spoken to—or are you too stupid to even do that?" the first guard said, emphasising his words with a final, jarring shove on the back of her head.

Mila kept her eyes firmly on the almost knee-high black boots of the guards. The leather glinted with a perfect, spotless sheen, as if they'd never known a stumble or slip. Mila could never hope to own boots even a fraction as nice as these. What it must be like not to feel the air around your toes with each step, to walk on an uncracked sole. She imagined the life these men must lead; one of certainty and privilege, as unsullied as their boots. What would it be like, to walk with the ease of someone who had never known hunger or fear.

"Apologies, *sigiò*," Mila murmured.

A sudden, brutal, blinding jolt ricocheted through her skull as the guard slammed his fist into the side of Mila's head and she went reeling sideways into the dirt.

"You say, 'yes, *guard*.' None of this 'sid-jaw' crap. You speak Amanese or you don't speak at all."

Reflex tears slipped down her cheeks as Mila righted herself, still on her knees before the guard. A searing streak of fire spread across her cheekbone; the brand on her forehead throbbed and stung anew, and a metallic taste crept onto her tongue. She swallowed hard, fighting to keep her composure.

The waiting guard said, "Might be Ineffective, sir?"

"Up to you, Revaan. But I think we'll keep *this one* around either way," said the first guard before he strode away.

The second guard was silent for long enough that Mila was tempted to look up at him. His thin lips curled into a grimace.

"Ah, the Murderer! Of course. They'd want you to clean up after yourself, at least," he said. "Well. Get up."

"Yes, *guard*," Mila said, climbing shakily to her feet.

He seized her by the arm and hauled her away from the waiting bus. "You know, actually, I don't want you with me, Murderer. You're already too much trouble and we haven't even started yet. And as much as I'd love to shoot you, the High Commander has said you're not to be killed. Not yet anyway."

Mila swallowed hard as he dragged her along to a different bus and a different guard, trying to ignore the throbbing pain of his grip and the even worse pain in her head.

"Cain," Revaan called, "Trade you? The Murderer for one of your weaklings?"

The guard named Cain looked up from his clipboard. His bored expression remained unchanged as his eyes raked over Mila, then he pointed to an elderly gentleman. "Take that one. I was probably going to have to kill him anyway. He looks like he can barely lift his own legs let alone anything we're going to be dealing with. You can save me the trouble."

Revaan released Mila into the supervision of Cain, clamping his hand around the old man's thin arm instead. With a start, Mila recognised Olaf, the game-rigging friend of *soffa* Karina. His wide eyes glazed over her as he was shunted past.

Cain pushed her up into the bus. The air inside tasted immediately of damp mould and rusting metal. Mila quickly found a seat near the back, where the sharp edges of the cracked and peeling leather dug into her thighs. She stared out the stained windows, searching for her brother amid the sea of faces… but he wasn't there. No one sat next to her.

Several guards took up positions along the aisle and the vehicle lurched to life, passing through the city walls with a discord of rattling bolts and the hacking of the struggling engine. Amanese eyes watched the ancient buses pass with curiosity or concern, it was hard to tell which. The bus wound slowly through the paved streets and the familiar sight of *Pika* loomed through the dark grime that covered the windows. Mila swallowed the sickening feeling in her throat.

The silent journey ended abruptly as the bus came to a rocking halt by the mouth of a narrow alleyway and the guards directed them out of the rancid vehicle. Despite the fresh air of Ard Aman, Mila could hardly breathe. She knew exactly where that alley led: to the site of the disaster. To the place where everything changed.

The refugees huddled together, shifting uncertainly until Cain flung out an arm, gesturing for them to move.

As Mila passed into the shadows of the alley, she kept her eyes down, but her heart pounded faster with every step. Across the lane lay thick planks of wood, a makeshift disguise for the cracks that Mila knew ran deep in the pavement.

The sight of the wreckage hit her like another blow to the head. All around, everything was covered in debris; broken bricks, chunks of the mountainside, and shattered stone scattered across the ground. Twisted beams of metal protruded like skeletal bones throughout and, though the damaged water pipes had been turned off, murky pools of oil-slicked liquid lay collected in pockets all around.

Outside the cordoned-off area, bunches of flowers lay in tribute to the people who had died. The people they thought Mila had killed.

Murderer.

Cain pointed at the wreckage. "This is where you'll be working. This site needs to be cleared of rubble before demolition vehicles can enter. You will pile the debris over there. Move fast, and don't put a hair out of line." He tapped his weapon as an unspoken 'or else'.

Mila's legs felt like lead as she stepped forward with the other refugees and began to pick up stones and debris, working silently under the watchful eyes of the guards. With trembling hands, she hefted a hunk of concrete and began to shuffle it away. Being here brought back the chaos of that day—the children trapped beneath the scaffolding, the shouts for help, the fear. Fear in in their voices, fear in the air, fear written on their faces.

And then the magic, *her* magic, that ancient and untamed force inside her that called the earth to respond—and it had, sensing her need for protection against the hatred closing in.

And in that moment, she had ruined everything.

As she worked, Mila felt the quick glances, the stares. Her stomach churned with shame heavier than any of the stones she shifted, but she couldn't escape it. Everywhere she turned, there was a reminder of her crime, of the power she never wanted but couldn't deny.

The hours were marked only by the growing pile of cleared debris and the increasingly desperate need for water while the autumn sun climbed higher in the sky. The guards occasionally barked orders, but mostly they watched in silence, lounging in the shade against the wall of the neighbouring building with their rifles slung across their chests, ready for anyone to step out of line.

Mila moved mechanically. The only way she could steady herself, physically and mentally, was to force herself to be detached. Stone after stone, brick after brick. Blisters formed on her palms, her fingertips, the pads of her thumbs. Her back ached. The burns on her forehead seared as sweat and dust infiltrated the damaged skin. Her knees and hips began to click every time she lowered and raised herself. But she carried on. At the very least, she deserved the pain.

The afternoon wore on without a break nor anything to eat or drink. The guards were testing them, Mila realised, playing with them. They would happily shoot whoever failed first. The notion became more tempting as she bent down yet again, gripped yet another chunk of stone, and heaved it to the side. As she moved, she stole a glance at the others. No one looked back. They hadn't for hours. Their faces were streaked with sweat and dust and grime, their lips swollen from dehydration. Mila thought she would be relieved by the end to their loathsome stares, but the weight of their silent suffering just became a second, separate burden.

She tried to remind herself that her being swapped into this group had probably saved old Olaf's life. There was no way the *soffo* could have kept up this pace, and the guards wouldn't have tolerated such weakness for long. The idea made her feel a fraction better.

As the sun began its descent, casting long shadows over the shattered street, the guards finally called a halt. Mila's back screamed in protest as she straightened up, every atom heavy and sore, every inch of skin covered in sweat-caked dust. Her throat felt full of grit and her tongue thick with thirst. The guards offered them no relief, merely shepherding the prisoners back onto the ancient bus.

Its rusted frame shuddered with every bump as it crawled along the stone road. The silent passengers stared blankly through the grimy windows, white eyes stark against filthy faces, wrapped in the stench of sweat upon sweat. Finally, the city wall arched overhead and the bus shuddered to a halt on the bleak white stones.

Mila stumbled away from the assembly point as the sky became bruised with the deep purple and crimson hues of dusk, drawn towards her home without any conscious thought. She found Nasir sitting alone outside their tent, his face drained and eyes distant in the fading light. He looked up as she approached, and she could see the tear stains down his dirty cheeks as his gaze softened slightly, and in that second her heart leapt with hope.

But he stood and went inside without a word.

15

The passing days could be measured in the little things; bruises turning from deep purple to a sickly yellow, dust settling in the tent where there had once been movement. The brand-mark blistered, bled, then scabbed over several times. Each painful stage was like a chrysalis breaking open, the skin transforming and hardening through cycles of pain and rebirth. After five weeks, only a rose-red mark remained, forever forming the symbol of the *noterran* on her forehead for all to see.

Not long after, cold tendrils of winter began to stretch down from the Uul Serrad, leaving behind a crisp coating of hoar frost each morning. The icy ground crackled beneath Mila's boots as she trudged toward the assembly area.

Mila stared at her palms, the skin raw, blistered, and torn. The sight should have bothered her, but it didn't. It hadn't for weeks. The bitter coldness was not just in the air, it was inside her too; a deep, grey numbness. Any urge to care had long vanished. She believed—no, she *knew*—that she deserved this. It was penance and, no matter how long this torture lasted, it would never be enough to make up for what she had done.

"You're not going through the wall today, Murderer," growled the nearest guard, throwing out a hand to stop her as Mila mechanically followed the others towards the loading area. For a brief, ignorant, shining moment, she thought the work was done, and she paused.

He gestured eastward with a gloved hand, where a grey stream of refugees flowed along the frost-speckled paths. Mila simply stared, unable to muster any initiative to figure out what he meant. The guard grunted and tugged up the fur-lined collar of his thick jacket against the bitter wind. "To the fields, and be quick about it."

The wind stabbed at her skin like a thousand tiny knives as she began to walk, head down, and though she tried to wrap her tunic tighter around herself, it was no use. The thin, worn, crusty material offered no warmth. A thought pricked at the edge of her mind. Why would they be working in the fields, in winter? Nothing would grow in the hard ground without the warming sunlight.

Mila shivered, whether from cold or apprehension, she wasn't sure.

As the ground began to slope gently downward to the valley, she caught a glimpse of the lagoon. The waters were dark and still beneath the winter sky, stretching out toward the horizon that was as distant as it was beautiful. The high tide lapped faintly at the shrubs growing at the edges of the water and, every now and then, there was the tiniest flicker of movement as a crab scurried across the mud, darting in and out of the early morning shadows. The brief sight pulled at her with a spark of yearning. She could still picture Sara there...

She rounded the bend, expecting the wide fields she knew so well, but what she saw instead was jarringly out of place, even in her numb mind. A new, chain-link fence stretched high and wide, adorned with large navy and yellow placards that marked the land as reclaimed property of the State.

These were the same fields where she and Nasir had practiced their magic among the corn stalks, watching their creomancy at work.

It felt like a dream from another lifetime.

Mila kept her distance as she neared the hundred or so workers gathered tensely by the entrance. Time had not eased the hatred her fellow Satarians felt towards her; in fact, it had hardened it. They blamed her for it all, because if not for her, this winter would be like all the others before it; all warm fires and smiling, pink-cheeked faces as neighbours shared stories and songs. Instead, they stood freezing while metal bolts clinked a slow beat in the wind and the wire fence strained against its posts.

Mila sighed, watching the whisp of warm air as it disappeared. Just like their lives, she thought. Warm and real one moment, vanished the next.

With a whistle, a guard got their attention. "Listen up," he barked, his voice cutting through the icy air. "You're here to make the crops grow and survive the winter. Get it done, and get it done right." His eyes narrowed, lingering on a few individuals in the group. Lingering on Mila longer than anyone else. The Murderer. "Of course, you will need to utilise your magic...but we'll be watching closely. Any unauthorised use, any deviation from the approved methods, and you'll be punished severely."

The threat hung in the air, the same intimidation day after day. They knew it all too well by now; anything out of the ordinary, anything out of line, and there would be punishment. The warning would have lost its effect by now if the guards hadn't routinely showed them that it was not an idle phrase.

Mila's frozen fingers curled into fists at her sides. The filthy hypocrites. They didn't seem so scared of the magic when it suited them. The guards were permitting—nay, *forcing*—the Satarians to use creomancy. Didn't they see how absurd this arrangement was?

Her anger quickly gave way to anxiety, gnawing in her stomach alongside hunger. She swallowed hard. The last time she had used magic, she had ruined everything.

As her gaze absently swept over the sea of faces, she froze, and a painful jolt rocketed through her as she noticed Nasir. His head was down, his expression unreadable, but he was there. *Right there.* Had he seen her? Did he even look for her anymore? Did he even care? Mila had barely seen her brother since the day their world had shattered, but she saw his pain everywhere she looked; in the tear-streaks on his vacant pillow each morning, in the absence of snoring when he pretended to be asleep before her. On the rare occasions they had both been in the home together, he avoided looking at her, and only grunted in reply to anything she said. And though he said nothing out loud, Mila felt like he was screaming at her: *you killed them, you destroyed everything that mattered.*

As if she could forget. Her mind relentlessly played and replayed her parents' final moments in a torturous loop; the hessian sacks tied tight at the neck as their bodies jerked and fell, faceless and unseeing. Was it better that way, she asked herself in the depths of the night. Was it better that she hadn't seen the betrayal on their faces? Was it a mercy that they couldn't see the daughter who had put them to death?

She would give anything to trade places with them… but would it be better that way? Would it be better if they were alive to see what had become of Al'Mazraea while grieving the death of their only daughter? Or was it better that the dark inside of a sack was the last thing her beautiful, strong, kind parents ever saw…?

Mila knew she would be left wondering that for the rest of her life—however long that may be. Her world view had been narrowed to each day of existence. Without family, she had nothing to look forward to. She was completely alone.

But now, there he was—Nasir. She missed him so much it hurt.

He shifted slightly, and, for a brief moment, his eyes met hers. Her breath caught, hope flaring like a match in the dark—but before she could even raise a hand in greeting, he had turned away, his face inscrutable once more as he watched the bellowing guard.

So, he knew she was there. Knew, and didn't care. The realisation that her brother—her blood, her only family—wanted nothing to do with her cut deeper than any insult or punishment the guards could inflict. She was truly alone, unworthy of love or redemption. Cavernous despair took hold inside her hollow chest.

He was never going to forgive her.

And how could she expect him to? She was never going to forgive herself either.

The guards unlocked the gate and ushered the workers through. A fog of breath hovered above the group, curling upwards into the cold air from their pale lips, and the chill sank deeper into Mila's bones.

The fields beyond were divided into sections for each type of crop, and bays within those sections. The rows and rows of dead plants were barely distinguishable from the ground; it was all dull, a monotonous sea of browns and pale husks, spattered with frost. All growth had withered with the coming of winter—as it always had, as it should.

The amount of energy that would be required to force new growth from the earth, to persuade forth edible produce… It was unthinkable. Unnatural. The Satarians would never do this of their own accord. Rice, corn and wheat were all warm-weather crops. In winter, the payment required to keep the power in balance was too much. Alarm tightened in Mila's stomach with each step. The guards didn't understand. All they had were prejudices and assumptions and misconceptions about creomancy. They were oblivious to the toll this would take on the land and on the refugees; they didn't understand the process, nor the importance, of balancing the magic with the earth. They risked draining the land dry.

She didn't realise she had stopped walking until a sudden shove in the back moved her forward again. After another few minutes, a whistle signalled them to stop beside a field of dried stalks that stretched away in every direction. The fragments of whatever remained barely reached above their ankles, desiccated and withered and brown. Mila looked around at the other prisoners, but none of them seemed to share her shock at what they were being asked to do. They looked defeated and withered themselves.

"Get to work!" came a voice, muffled slightly by the wintry wind. "Ten Creos per row. Move, now!"

The workers silently split into the rows and sank to their knees, plunging their fingers into the cold, dead soil.

Mila followed slowly, kneeling on the frozen ground, her mind whirring. The land didn't have the energy to support the crops in winter—which meant there was very little, if anything, to draw from the earth to perform creomancy. To achieve any sort of result, the refugees would need to channel their *own* lifeforce into the crops, and when that happened... Mila's head shot up again. She should tell someone. The guards were ignorant, but they weren't stupid. If she could explain that performing this task would result in countless deaths, surely they would reconsider?

Mila looked up and around, craning her neck to spot the nearest guard, then climbed to her feet again, pacing quickly towards him. "Excuse me, *sigiò*—guard," she started, trying her best Amanese. "This plan is not going to work. Creomancy is all about balance, it cannot be used like this—"

Pain erupted in her chest as the butt of the guard's rifle slammed into her sternum. The impact stole her breath in an instant and a sharp, blinding agony radiated outward. She was sure her ribs had cracked under the force. A strangled gasp escaped her lips, her body doubling over as she fought to draw in even a shallow breath.

"How *dare* you, you lazy Creo bitch! Keep back!"

With tears streaming down her face, Mila grit her teeth. "I'm trying…to warn you!" she wheezed, clutching at her chest, her voice barely more than a rasp. "You're making a huge mistake here…This is dangerous!"

"The only dangerous thing here is *you*!" screamed the guard, signalling for backup while he swung his rifle around to point the barrel at her. "If you don't back off, I'll shoot you. You know the rules!"

Mila shook her head, ears ringing. If she could just get him to listen…

The guard flicked the safety switch off.

Mila held up both hands, blistered palms out. "Okay!" she slurred, backing away. Pain laced every breath. "*Kamaar!*"

"Don't you speak your disgusting language at me, you filthy worm," the guard growled, propping the rifle higher in his grip. He looked genuinely afraid of her, and something Nasir had once said swam into her mind.

Fear is good at finding depth to the shadows.

Mila turned and hobbled slowly back to her position in the field, trying to stand upright despite the sickening pain in her guts. The back of her neck prickled and every muscle tensed with the anticipation of receiving a bullet between the shoulder blades at any moment.

But the shot didn't come, and she was almost disappointed.

You're not to be killed. Not yet anyway.

She kneeled again, pulse racing as she fought to keep her composure. She closed her eyes and tried to take a deep breath, willing herself to calm down, to focus. She had no choice. Her fingers seared with the cold as she dug them into the rough ground.

As the workers around her connected with their power, the subtle vibration of magic came as a faint buzz in her ears. Mila searched for that hum in her own heart, imagined her veins connecting like roots into the soil, seeking the pulse of life beneath the surface.

And it was then that Mila felt the absolute nothingness surrounding the woman beside her. There were no threads of connection, no words to Gaia. Mila risked a glance sideways. There was something clumsy and unsure about the way the woman touched the earth, like she didn't know what she was supposed to be doing.

IronHand was already asking for an impossible task, but it hadn't occurred to Mila that the guards would be *this* ignorant. This woman didn't know creomancy.

Centuries past, when creomancy had been stripped from their culture and officially outlawed, those who wanted to practice were forced to rely on scattered knowledge passed on in secret. If they were lucky, they had someone close to them who might still remember the old ways, but as time went on, this became more and more rare. Three hundred years after leaving Stara Zhem, those without proper guidance or resources learned the craft through dangerous trial-and-error—or let it fade away.

Now, as Mila looked around, she saw the signs dotted all over the field. Untrained, unstable creomancers. Most of these people would have never even tried to access their magic before. And if the guards found out…

The woman's eyes lifted to meet hers, wide and brimming with barely contained panic. "I don't know what to do," she said with a whispered sob. "Please, help me."

Mila reached out a hand to comfort the trembling woman, but she froze mid-gesture, hand suspended above the soil.

Help me…

Her chest clenched as she remembered the last time she had stepped in to save someone with the same desperation in their eyes. The last time she had broken the rules to help someone. Everything had fallen apart because of that one gesture, that impulsive, foolish instinct to *help*.

Mila recoiled. She wouldn't do that again.

She swallowed the comfort she had almost given and pushed her fingers back into the dirt instead.

You're too kind for your own good.

Well, not anymore.

The woman stared at her, eyes begging, her whole body trembling like a leaf in the wind. Mila refused to look up and eventually the woman dropped her gaze and pressed her own shaking hands into the dry soil.

Nothing. Not a trace of creomancy.

Mila bit her bottom lip, intimately aware of the guards prowling around, their rifles unslung and fingers itching to pull the trigger.

Perhaps if she worked a bit harder, pushed her creomancy a bit further, she could fool the guards that this woman was working too.

But—no. *No.* She had learnt her lesson. The woman would have to fend for herself.

Though the sun arced through the sky, its rays carried no heat. There was nothing here; nothing left in the soil, nothing to channel, and nothing to connect with. Mila felt the desolation inside and out, growing heavier in her body until her breathing came in heavy sighs through her aching chest.

As the day marched on, a thick, sluggish sound began to chug on the edge of her hearing, like mud forcing its way through a narrow, clogged pipe. It was rhythmic and low, and Mila glanced around, disoriented, trying to locate its source. She was saturated in sweat despite the cold. Dizziness rolled over and over her. The field blurred. All of a sudden, she was certain she was going to be sick. She had barely staggered to her feet before she retched, throwing up something dark over the barren ground. A murky substance that looked horribly like blood. Another heave tore through her and she dropped back to her knees, curls falling limp over her face as she retched again. The taste of copper coated her tongue.

A fist suddenly grabbed her by the hair, and she screamed in pain as a guard hauled back on her neck, forcing her face towards the winter sun.

"What is wrong with you?" he bellowed, spittle flecking onto her face.

"Please, I—I don't know," Mila said.

"For once in your life you're having to actually *work*, you lazy Creo bitch," the guard snarled. His attention was suddenly snagged by the woman beside Mila. She saw his eyes narrow, saw him notice the absence of greenery before her. His spare hand shot out to grip the woman, pulling her backwards as she shrieked. "Another one? Insolent, lazy pieces of shit you all are."

"Please, please *sigiò*, I don't know how—" the woman bawled.

"We've been working for days, *months*," Mila said loudly, hoping to Gaia that the guard hadn't heard the woman's admission. "Without proper food, or rest—"

"That's what you're here for—to work," he growled, "And that's what you'll do until you drop. You're not special. There are plenty more like you who can take your place."

Mila closed her eyes, struggling to remain conscious. The woman sobbed loudly beside her. "There's no power here. There's nothing for us to draw on. Our magic needs energy…Don't you understand?"

"No," the guard said, lips curling. "And why would I want to? I know enough. You've never used your magic for anything *valuable*. You're nothing more than dangerous savages, and if you weren't contained in Al'Mazraea, you would have annihilated our country by now with your *magic*."

How did such ignorance become accepted as fact? Mila groaned. "You're going to need to understand."

The guard's face flushed puce with indignation, and Mila could almost see his mind working. He was weighing his options. To ignore her challenge and risk missing something important, or listen to this woman whom he despised.

"Fine," he grumbled after a moment. "Spin your Creo lies. What exactly do I need to understand?"

Now Mila wondered how much to tell him. "Creomancy needs to draw power from the earth in order to become active, like how a torch needs a battery." She paused, exhausted by the act of speaking, but the guard scowled.

"And?"

"*And*... the power of the earth is not infinite. If the battery is worn-out, the back-up power kicks in."

"You're being purposefully vague," he said, pulling tighter on her hair. Then he rounded on the weeping woman imprisoned by his other hand. "Would you shut up with your noises, or I'll— "

At that moment, another voice rang out from behind.

"You're making a scene, Jormun."

Officer Ahriman approached, his boots crunching on the frosty soil. He considered the tableau with eyes crinkled in amusement. Beside him, notebook in hand, loomed the angular form of Draven Lideri. He wore a long, thick coat over his usual navy uniform, military insignia glinting on the epaulettes and breast pockets. Mila hadn't seen the man since the day he ordered her parents' executions, and the wave of panic that swept over her at seeing him now seemed to stop her heart.

The guard, Jormun, snapped rigidly to attention. In one swift motion, he released Mila; his shoulders squared, his chest puffed out, and he brought his right fist to hover over the centre of his chest.

"My apologies, sir," said Jormun, still gripping the other woman's hair in his left hand.

"Look at this, you're distracting the workers," Ahriman continued, indicating the refugees who had stopped to watch the exchange. They hurriedly returned their attention to their work.

"These *women* were refusing to work, sir. And then this one had the nerve to spin me a story."

Mila cowered beneath their withering stares.

"What story?" Lideri growled, speaking at last.

"Nothing of importance, just lies, obviously, High Commander," Jormun replied.

Lideri's dark eyes flicked to Mila, then back to Jormun. "What did she say?"

Jormun made a dismissive noise. "Something about the earth being a battery, and that if they use all the power there's a back-up source, or—" His brow wrinkled. "—something. Just Creo lies, sir."

"It's *not* lies," Mila murmured, quietly but not quiet enough. Jormun raised a fist to silence her, but Lideri motioned for him to pause. He turned slightly to stand fully in front of the guard and both women.

As if instructing a mutt, Lideri said, "Speak."

Mila somehow swallowed with her throat dry. She couldn't bear to look at him. "Look around you—it's winter. The earth has very little energy to spare."

"The battery's power is all used up, so to speak," Lideri said. His conversational tone made her stomach twist. But maybe... if she could just get him to understand...

She nodded. "Yes. The earth's power isn't limitless."

"And—" the High Commander surveyed the ground where Mila had vomited her black mess. "This has an effect on you, for some reason."

"Yes. The power has to come from somewhere."

"So, if you can't get it from the earth, there must be an alternative," Lideri said. "What is it?"

Mila hesitated, heart pounding in her ears. "It's—it's *our* power. Our life."

"Hmm. That doesn't sound very practical," Lideri mused. "So, you do your magic, your *creomancy*, using up the earth's energy…And then, if you continue, *your* energy gets used?"

A dark edge lingered in his words, sending a chill crawling down Mila's spine. She said nothing, but Lideri took that as confirmation.

"But surely there must be a way to, how would you say it… Recharge the battery?"

Again she said nothing, but the danger felt solid enough that she could taste it. Lideri eyes remained on her; cold, waiting, studying. Finally, she croaked out, "It's a matter of balance. Lifeforce for lifeforce. We call it *pariar*."

The High Commander made an impatient noise. He took a step closer. A flash of silver, and something cold and sharp pressed to the side of her neck. Her breath caught.

"Answer me properly," Lideri said calmly.

Shaking, Mila fought to keep her voice steady. "*Pariar*. Either we repay Gaia willingly, or she takes what she is owed. It's the only way to balance the energy."

Lideri leaned in, unblinking. The point of the blade pressed in harder, biting into the soft skin just below her jaw. She couldn't think— panic drowned everything as he inhaled. His muscles tensed. She closed her eyes.

I'm ready.

"No," he murmured, almost a whisper, so that only she could hear. "Your punishment isn't over yet, Murderer. It's barely begun."

All of a sudden, he whipped the blade away to slice deep across the other woman's throat. Her sobs became a gurgling noise as blood surged down her neck, soaking into her clothes. Jormun released her hair in shock and she crumpled to the ground where her desperate heart pumped crimson into the greedy soil. Her eyes were dark with only the faintest flecks of green, and they remained fixed on Mila as the light behind them quickly faded.

Lideri leant over and wiped his blade on the woman's tunic, then he turned to Ahriman. "Get a message to the other work details. We will use the Ineffectives to make sure this *debt* is paid. Any Ineffectives are now to be treated on-site. They may not be useful in life, but they can at least now be useful in death."

16

"And if there is any more disobedience," Lideri said to Jormun, "Try to use a blade instead. We can waste bullets, but we won't waste blood."

As he turned, his eyes caught Mila's, and a smirk curled the corner of his twisted mouth. "Another notch on your belt, Murderer."

Then he looked down once more and spat on the dead woman before walking slowly away, Ahriman in tow.

The message was clear; you have no power here. And he was right. He decided their worth. The Satarians were all at his mercy.

Mila's gaze lingered on the lifeless body, her insides churning with guilt and shame. She should have done something to help that woman. She could have done more. She could have stopped them…or at least tried. But she hadn't. Mila hadn't done a thing. She had ignored the woman's plea for help; she had allowed her to be bullied, beaten, and slaughtered. Mila was nothing more than a silent bystander, paralysed by fear. Her silence had made her complicit.

But if she had protected her…The cruel fact was that she would be lying alongside the woman, just as dead. Self-preservation couldn't be second anymore. She *should* have focused on self-preservation *that* day. She should have left the children—left Luca—to their fate, just as she left this woman. It was true, she knew, but it made her stomach turn all the same. She could barely recognise herself.

Mila ripped her eyes away from the sickening sight, fighting waves of terror amongst the nausea. How long would it be until *she* was classified as an Ineffective? They already suspected she was more trouble than she was worth. How many others had already been given the unceremonious title and had their life ended?

In the quiet moments that followed, a pervasive dread settled in her heart. In her mind's eye, she could suddenly see all of Satarian history laid out before her like a tapestry, and each thread was a person's life. The tapestry stretched beyond her comprehension, the lives all woven together to form this rich and beautiful art… But then, as she watched, Lideri's blade sliced across the threads with the same ease as he had sliced the woman's neck, and the threads fell away leaving only blackness. Their rich history lain to waste; their beautiful lives cut short.

Their days were numbered, and she was powerless to change it.

The world seemed to spin as another wave of dizziness washed over her. She forced herself to take a deep breath.

Focus.

The dead woman's blood continued to trickle into the soil. In her soul, Mila sensed the vibration of the earth increasing as its energy was refuelled. It was disgusting, vile, horrible… yet Mila couldn't help but also feel a tinge of relief. This woman's life meant that there could now be something for Mila to draw on. The moisture of it brought a hint of bile creeping up her throat as she dug her fingers into the ground, searching. It was barely there, just a whisper of energy. The connection was fragile, like trying to catch smoke with her hands, but slowly it began to flow and a gentle warmth spread from her hands into the soil, and from the soil into her hands.

"Ad tay khiedery, plezht ay pemetter Gaia…"

The hum of magic suddenly became a rumble, and the warmth in her body intensified. The hoarfrost vanished from the ground around her in an instant. It was a wild feeling, fuelled with a wretched, gasping sort of strength. The power within her became more frenzied, like a horse in a lightning storm, bucking and braying, while at the same time she could sense the earth straining as if she were ringing its neck.

Mila's fingers twitched in the blood-soaked dirt, her breath coming faster, as her magic begged to be released unchecked into the ground. The sunshine feeling in her chest felt more like a million summer suns in this frigid winter, so vibrant it was intoxicating. A distant part of her mind knew what the consequences would be if she gave in, but she felt so alive for the first time in days, weeks…

The earth seemed to be begging to be used by her. And for a second, Mila gave in to the temptation. Her fingers curled further into the soil, and the land responded instantly. Immediately, in front of her, saplings burst forth from beneath the ground and they unfurled, elongated, thickened. Leaves stretched like newborns awakening from sleep, reaching outwards and growing taller by the second.

It was thrilling, this raw force pulsing through her. All of her nerve endings were being shocked by an electrical current. Every sensation felt amplified, heightened with a euphoric edge. Beads of sweat punctuated Mila's forehead and slid down her spine.

More.

She wanted *more*.

She wanted to use up every ounce of her power, just to see what would come of it. What was her lifeforce worth, in a world that had already decided she was nothing? And why should she hold back? She was only hurting herself. The other Satarians wouldn't care—if anything, they'd be relieved to watch her waste away. There was no one left to care about what happened to her, if she destroyed herself with magic. She felt the despair rise in her heart, loud and wild and painful. She could throw her life away right now...for the sake of growing a few crops. For nothing. Her actions were meaningless, and so was she—just another thing to be used up and discarded, like the soil beneath her feet.

Sudden awareness rolled through her in a wave of vertigo.

No. This wasn't right.

The memory of the shattered ground in Haman city took over the cracks in her mind.

She couldn't let this happen again.

No matter what, her life was worth something.

She had destroyed enough.

With supreme effort that left her gasping, Mila pried her fingers out of the soil. As the frightening haze faded, she became aware of the erratic thumping of her heart, how her whole body was cold with sweat. The power was still there, a light tingle in the length of her arms and the uncomfortable energy of a compressed spring in every muscle. The world suddenly tilted and her insides lurched, while her pulse thundered like a storm in her ears. She willed herself to breathe, through the spasms wracking her entire body, as the warmth from the earth began to fade...

But the magic was still alive beneath her skin, demanding release. Demanding balance.

Slowly her surroundings sharpened, drawing another gasp and wave of nausea. Mila had expected the radius of dry soil that now surrounded her—but she had not anticipated what had happened to the woman's body. It was suddenly as withered as the winter crops, sucked as dry as the soil. Desiccated, leaving only a brittle husk behind. The woman's skin clung to her like old parchment, stretched thin and cracked over protruding bones. Sunken eyes stared blankly out of her emaciated skull and fragile, claw-like fingers curled inward, stick thin. Mila felt a scream rise within her, but at the last second she swallowed it, forcing the huge lump down. If she didn't know better, Mila would have thought the woman had died years ago, not minutes.

The other workers kept their eyes averted, focused on connecting with the earth and avoiding the wrath of the guards. Occasionally there would be a flutter of green as a single sprout clawed its way through the cold earth, until the creomancer's focus wavered and their meagre control slipped. But in front of Mila, the stalks were thriving—no, more than thriving—they were extraordinary, vibrant and alive in a way that made her swell with pride. It was like nothing she had ever experienced before. For a moment, all the disgust and sorrow and guilt faded, drowned out by the sheer thrill of the power she held in her hands.

Look at what we can do.

If the guards would just take a moment and look at this without fear and prejudice colouring their opinion, Mila was sure they would see the *real* potential in their magic.

But the thought turned sour almost immediately. Her pride twisted into fear as she glanced at the guards lounging near the fence. She had no doubt that they would see these magnificent stalks as a threat. How did one little Creo have the power to do all this? Or else, they would accuse others of laziness and incompetence because *they* were not producing as much as her. Quickly, Mila reached out and, one by one, tore down each of the foot-high stalks. Her hands moved faster, ripping and breaking until nothing was left but a scattered pile of green shards and a cold feeling in her heart. It was better this way. Safer. She couldn't afford pride—not here. Not anymore.

Hours later, when a light frost had gathered around the eyes and mouth of the dead woman's body, the surge of energy had faded and Mila's power had dimmed. Now her head swam as if there was not enough oxygen left in the air; there was not enough energy left in the soil for her magic to breathe. The very force that had once charged her was now draining her. The edges of her vision blurred, darkening, while her heartbeat continued its erratic dance. Fragmented thoughts slipped from her grasp, and she wanted nothing more than to surrender to the heavy pull of unconsciousness. Mila could feel the magic inside sucking away her lifeforce like a parasite, feeding itself at her cost. The world around blurred and twisted while a hammer pummelled inside her head and sweat bloomed on her forehead. Her limbs trembled from the feverish heat, making her skin prickle. Every breath came shallow and ragged.

The others around her barely moved, their faces pale, eyes sunken with exhaustion, their bodies thinning before her eyes as they whispered slurred pleas to Gaia in Satarian.

I must look the same, Mila realised, and somewhere in her exhausted mind, the idea terrified her…Then it slipped away just as quickly as it had come, leaving only a shadow in its place.

By the time the winter sun touched the horizon and the whistle blew for the end of the day, those who could still walk gathered at the fence. Sweat dripped from Mila's upper lip into her open mouth as she dragged the cold air into her lungs and examined the blood-stained soil caked around her nails. She could barely keep her eyes open. Her limbs were steel rods, her knees and fingers numb from being buried in the cold dirt. She brought a hand to her chest, delicately testing her bruised ribs and sternum, at the same time dimly registering that there were far fewer people standing beside her than there had been that morning. Her gaze turned back the way she had come, where many grey lumps dotted the fields. Satarian bodies, collapsed and unmoving. The guards didn't even glance at them. The creomancers had served their purpose, their lifeforce gone, consumed by the crops they had been forced to grow.

A chill ran through her that had nothing to do with the dropping temperature. The magic was killing them. It had taken everything from those who now lay still in the fields, and she knew it was only a matter of time before she would fall herself.

Or before Nasir would fall.

The thought of the power consuming her brother terrified Mila far more than her own bone-deep exhaustion. She didn't care much for her own mortality.

As the prisoners trudged back towards the tent village, Mila's eyes darted through the dim light, searching desperately for her brother among the weary workers. That strange, thick sound crept back into the edge of her hearing; slow, rhythmic, and heavy. The frost-covered ground crunched as she moved along the winding path, the bitter chill of the winter evening biting at her skin, but she realised she was still sweating despite it. Her head gave a particularly painful throb and another wave of dizziness washed over her, making the ground seem to tilt beneath her tattered boots.

Uneasiness threaded through her weary mind. Something was wrong with her. It was more than just exhaustion, more than an illness. She just had to get home. If she could get home, Sara would look after her…

Her ribs felt tight, as though bound by invisible straps, making each breath a laboured effort, and a prickling numbness crept through her fingers and up her arms.

Then she realised—Sara couldn't look after her.

Sara wasn't at home.

Sara was dead.

And Mila was all alone.

Her vision became blurrier with each step and an ache had pulsed deep in her bones by the time she finally stumbled inside the dark tent and found her way towards the first soft thing she could see; the floor cushions. With her head resting on one, she pulled her favourite patchwork cushion to her chest and held it tightly, lying sideways, eyes closed, inhaling the familiar scents. Home. Her safe place. She just needed to calm down and everything would be okay.

Nasir's voice seemed to echo from her memories: *Breathe deeply, take it slow.*

One breath in, one breath out.

Just as Mila began to get some control back, she realised with a sickening lurch that the muddy sound she could hear was her own coagulating blood sludging through her dried-out veins and arteries.

Pariar. The magic. This must be the price of accessing creomancy when the power source was her own body. The guards had forced them to wring out every last skerrick of energy, but she had been able to keep herself separated a little. She hadn't given herself over to it completely. That she had walked away from the field was proof enough of that; those that still lay there were not so lucky.

She clutched the cushion tighter, her fingers brushing against the worn fabric, tracing the uneven stitching her mother had carefully sewn so many years ago. Each irregular patch told its own story, and Mila knew them all. She would sit here with Sara, asking to hear tales about the different pieces. This one—the rough, prickly hessian—came from a sack of flour that Andrei had once stolen from Haman. And this thin, blue patch was from Sara's own school uniform. She had saved it to pass on to Mila, but when the reform came in to segregate the schooling of Satarian and Amanese children, the thin blue dress became simply another source of material. There was a piece from a torn gown, a dense scrap from an old curtain, even a bit from one of her father's shirts. Her mother had woven their lives into these cushions, piecing together memories into something comforting.

A lump formed in Mila's throat as she lay there, feeling the empty space her mother used to fill. She could almost picture her sitting beside her, humming softly as she worked on another project, her hands always busy with something. It had been her mother's way—quietly creating, mending, making things better.

And without her, *everything* felt broken.

Mila curled her body tighter around the cushion. She missed her mother more than she could put into words. She made even the darkest times seem bearable. With her gone, it felt like all the light in the world had vanished, leaving only shadows. What she wouldn't give for her mother's embrace right now… To hear her lilting voice, her reasoning, her laughter. To be held with her unique kindness and understanding. She would know exactly what to say to Nasir, and exactly how to repair this void in her soul.

"I wish you were here," she whispered into the quiet, hating the hollow silence that followed. The ache was unbearable. Her eyes prickled uncomfortably, tears wanting to fall but unable to form, weak as she was. She let out a dry sob, cheated out of even being able to cry properly.

Instead, without Sara to hold her, she tugged a threadbare blanket around her shoulders, trying to calm the storm within. But the darkness around only seemed to grow deeper with every passing second.

17

The following day, kneeling once again on the barren ground, Mila supressed a shudder as the chill soaked through the thin fabric of her pants. Though she mimicked the motions of the others, inside she was holding back. After what had happened yesterday, she couldn't bear the thought of drawing more energy from the land. She hadn't even touched the soil yet, let alone connected with it, and she could already feel the strain of the earth, the dwindling energy, like dark clouds across the sun. Before long, there would be nothing left for anyone or anything. Just as the land was dying, so too would they all die, and soon. Mila was sure of it.

Nasir was only a few rows away, his back to her. It felt like the closest they had been in months, and that thought brought a flutter of lightness to Mila's heavy heart. But the feeling shrivelled just as fast, as a guard began to turn her way and she forced her attention downward.

Frost crunched as she pressed her fingertips through it to the soil below. She closed her eyes and inhaled the sharp, cold air, trying to calm herself while she searched for even the smallest thread of connection. There was so little to work with. The earth felt even worse than yesterday, even more wilted, the soil brittle and lifeless beneath her hands. The hum beneath the surface was softer than a baby's breath.

Without warning, the air beside her shifted as someone moved into her space, far too close. Mila's eyes snapped open, prepared to see a guard or a gun barrel facing her. Instead, a middle-aged Satarian man was kneeling barely an elbow's width away. He had a short beard, the dark hairs speckled with white and grey. The same was true of his thick, wavy hair and the bold lines of his brows. He looked vaguely familiar, but then again so did most people in their small world.

"Keep looking forward," he murmured in Satarian. His voice was barely louder than the wind brushing through the fields. "Pretend we are working."

Mila's breath caught in her throat, but she did as he said and returned her pale fingers to the earth. She didn't try to connect with her magic though; all of her attention was on the man beside her.

"What are you doing?" Mila hissed. "What do you want? Who are you?"

"Quiet," the man said, "And speak in Satarian only."

"Why?" Mila asked, still in Amanese. The guards had beaten her often enough for conversing in her native tongue; she had the scars to prove it. But the man refused to answer. She glanced at the guards to make sure their attention was directed elsewhere, then she murmured, *"Kaefer?"*

"It's simple. The guards are watchful, yes, but we can make them see what we want them to see," the man said. "If you keep your head down and pretend to work, the guards will assume the Satarian we speak is to Gaia, not to each other. They will just think we are working. The guards never bother to learn Satarian. More fool them."

Mila was startled at the brilliance of it. Hiding in plain sight. She kept her eyes on the ground.

"What do you want?"

"I saw what you did yesterday."

Her pulse raced as she tried to keep her expression neutral, keep her movements steady. "And what exactly did I do?"

"You used that woman's blood to fuel your creomancy."

Mila hadn't been expecting this. Her body stiffened and she felt the blood drain from her face. If this man had seen her, then she was in more danger than she had realised. The last thing she needed was for anyone to discover that her magic had absorbed the woman's blood like a sponge and, if this man had seen her, anyone could have.

"I don't know what you're talking about," Mila whispered back, her heartbeat hammering against her ribs.

The man leaned in closer, his voice low but insistent. "I saw you."

Mila fought to keep her composure. "So what? I didn't want to. The guards killed her, not me. Her blood went into the soil, and we need the soil to work."

"You misunderstand me," he said, giving the faintest shake of his head. "I have heard the rumours about what happened that day. The day of the rockslide."

"I didn't cause that disaster," Mila said curtly.

"They say you cracked the earth open, that there is a ravine as deep as the *kor'rizha* in the alleys of Haman."

Mila didn't know that word, but it was easy enough to work out what it meant. Her mind whirred as she sat frozen. She didn't dare look at the man directly, afraid to draw the attention of the guards patrolling nearby.

"What do you want?" Mila asked again, her voice rising. "You want to hurt me, is that it?"

"No, I—"

"You want to make me pay for ruining Al'Mazraea and everything else? Go on then! Go ahead, I deserve it, don't I?"

The man made a small, frustrated noise. "No, that is not what—I am doing this all wrong." He took a breath. "What I mean is, you have done things no one else has done. Things no one else has even considered. And there are others like me, others who understand the implications of the rumours about you."

Mila stiffened, her frozen fingers forgotten in the cold and lifeless ground. "What rumours? What implications?"

"That your magic is immensely powerful. Stronger, perhaps, than anyone else in Al'Mazraea."

There was a pause while Mila waited for the punchline. But nothing came. His expression didn't waver. No flicker of amusement, no hint of mischief, and Mila realised; he was serious.

"That's absurd, I'm not—"

"What if we could use our magic for more than this? For more than growing crops for a corrupt government, or dying while we try? While they starve us, and the earth is bled dry? We want to fight back. We have to fight back. And we need you with us."

This man was insane. He had to be.

"Me?" Mila shook her head. "I can't help you… I don't know what you think I can do, but—"

"I know you have the strength, and, with you, we could all grow stronger," he interrupted. "Together, we could break the chains that bind us here, Mila. We must stand up, or they will keep us down forever."

Mila shot another glance at the guards, terrified that they could be listening. This very conversation was treasonous, reckless, and if they heard… A bullet through her forehead would be a mercy after their punishment.

"You're insane," Mila hissed.

"We are but a product of our circumstances. But, no, on this I am firm. Join us. Work with us, help us fight."

"You keep saying 'us'."

"Ya. There are others."

"Others? How many others?"

"Irrelevant, for now."

Mila paled. The more people involved, the higher the chance of being noticed. Caught. Punished.

"I can't," she snapped. "We shouldn't even be having this conversation. They'll kill me. They'll kill all of us."

"They will kill us anyway," the man murmured. "Better to die fighting than to waste away in these fields."

The words sent a jolt of fear through Mila. She didn't want to be part of this. She couldn't be a part of this. She wasn't a hero; she was a curse, a destroyer of lives. The one with blood on her hands, literally and figuratively. She was useless and cowardly and weak.

"You're mistaken," she finally whispered, her voice trembling. "I can't fight. I'm not strong—I'm not anything. I can't do what you're asking."

But the man didn't back down. "Do you think I came here by accident? I have watched you for days. I see how you keep going when everything in your mind is telling you to stop. I know you are stronger than you think."

His words twisted into Mila like a knife and the corners of her mouth twitched as tears sprang to her eyes, surprising her. His quiet conviction struck something deep inside her, a part that she had buried deep under layers of shame and self-loathing. Somehow, he saw the darkness that haunted her mind and shone a light upon it with his words. She hadn't realised how much she needed to hear it. But, just as quickly, the light faded, and the darkness took over once again.

"Some things are beyond redemption," she murmured.

"You think you are the only one who has made mistakes?" he said. This man was unrelenting. "In life, every choice has a cost. Every single person is paying for something they have done, carrying the weight of something they regret. You can let yourself be crushed beneath it, or you can learn to be strong. The difference is in what you do next."

The words hung in the air and a bitter noise escaped Mila's lips. Couldn't he just leave her alone? He was wasting his time here. *She* was a waste of time.

But the thinly veiled hope in the man's voice remained in her mind, thawing her resolve, and she found herself wondering… What if he was right? What if this was a chance to escape, to fight back?

"You really think we can get out of here?"

The man cast a wary glance at the nearest guard before answering. "What choice do we have? Look around you! Every day, we get weaker. The earth is dying, the people are dying. What is left if we do nothing?"

"You've heard what they call me, haven't you?" she asked, desperate for him to understand. "Yet you think I can save lives?"

The man nodded, and she truly wanted to believe him. "I know you can."

The faintest flicker of hope sparked in her heart and, for a moment, the idea took hold. Mila let herself imagine it. Maybe, just maybe, there was something beyond Al'Mazraea. Her pale lips quivered with the hint of a smile, but almost immediately reality surged back like a wave, dousing the fragile flame. Did this man realise the enormity of what he was asking? He was willing to gamble with the lives of countless Satarians—to gamble with *her* life—on what? A whim that she might actually be useful?

She remembered that young boy, dragged through the camp and mercilessly punished… but if they were caught, this time it would be the whole population, everyone she knew or barely recognised, paraded and taunted and killed. She could feel their blood, warm and sticky on her hands, dripping from her fingers. She could hear it, the wet sound of it plinking into the pool of crimson in which her parents' bodies lay. The corpses twitched. A breath rattled from her mother's throat, or maybe it was her father's. The blood licked at her knees, her thighs, rising higher, and it was in her mouth now, hot and thick on her tongue…

"No!" Mila cried out, forgetting reality, her breath ragged, her hands trembling, expecting to be suffocated by the nightmare.

The man hissed, looking nervously at the guards. *"Be quiet!"*

Mila forced herself to breathe deeply, and slowly the images faded from her mind, but the taste in her mouth and the cold certainty remained. Any rebellion was a suicide mission.

"I can't," she whispered finally, her voice shaking. "I can't be involved in this. I can't do what you're asking."

"I am not giving up on you. I will keep asking. And one day, when you are ready, you will say yes," he murmured. "Just think about it. No more guards, no more fear or rules or punishment… Just us, using our power on our terms. Living on our terms. Does that not tempt you, even a little?"

It did. Of course it did. It was a thought Mila had had constantly, even before IronHand took control of Al'Mazraea. To go wherever she pleased whenever she wanted, to speak her own language without fear of reprisals… To learn to read and write in Satarian, to hold a pen, to be allowed to have dreams and to put stock in them, knowing they had a chance of coming true.

She bit her lip, mind reeling.

The man waited a moment longer. Mila could feel him studying her, but she refused to meet his gaze. "I think you will," the man said, unnervingly confident. Then he stood and moved away as swiftly as he had come, leaving Mila trembling.

She shot furtive glances around her, allowing herself to breathe only when she was sure none of the guards were paying her any mind. Relief was quickly coloured by anger. How could that man put her in danger like that? If he truly thought she was some sort of saviour, why would he risk her safety?

A horrible idea occurred to her. What if the man was a spy? A guard masquerading as a prisoner, entrapping Satarians in treasonous conversations to discover information? Ice flooded her veins at the idea. That made a lot more sense than him believing that she could be of any help to anyone. And maybe that was why the man looked familiar? Had she seen him before in the navy IronHand uniform?

Mila racked her brain, trying to remember where she had seen him, but fear was stopping her thoughts from flowing properly, jammed like rusty cogs. She had better get back to work. Her hands trembled as she pressed them harder into the soil, but still she didn't try to connect. She stared at the person across from her, stared at the dark, raised brand on their forehead.

No more guards, no more fear or rules or punishment…

The man's words repeated in her mind, as uncomfortable as the scars themselves. It didn't matter if what he said was true, there was absolutely no way she could use her magic against the guards.

The power inside her could destroy everything. Again.

The mere idea of it felt like a cruel joke—it was her magic that got them into this horrible situation in the first place, and now, after weeks of isolation and alienation, the people wanted her help? They needed her magic? It was absurd.

And yet… There was a pull to the notion that she couldn't ignore. It was stuck into her like a burr: *Better to die fighting than to waste away in these fields.*

The thought of wielding her magic with purpose, of standing up against the guards and Lideri's cruelty, sparked something deep inside her. For so long, they had been reacting, barely surviving, but what if they *could* do more?

Mila scrunched fistfuls of frost-crusted dust. They certainly couldn't go on like this.

But why did they think *she* was important? Mila tried to imagine how it would look from the outside, tried to see her actions as powerful and inspiring… but she just couldn't. Everything about her was unstable, from her hands to her emotions to her desire to survive. She had no idea what she was doing, and if she made one mistake, she couldn't survive the consequences. She had already caused enough pain.

Still, the idea of being involved in something bigger than herself, the allure of it, wouldn't let go. The power Mila had felt that day in Haman, that surge like lightning coursing through her, still lingered in her mind. If she could harness it, master it, and help others do the same… Could they really fight back?

She felt eyes on her, like a prickle on the back of her neck. A furtive glance showed a guard frowning in her direction, the same one who had hurt her yesterday. Mila quickly dropped her gaze and pushed her hands deeper into the dirt.

"Ay pemetter—"

The phrase had barely left her lips when the guard's shadow loomed over her, and before she could react, his boot slammed into her back, forcing her into the dirt and knocking the air from her lungs.

"Get up, Murderer!" he barked.

Mila clamped her jaw shut against the searing pain radiating through her already-bruised ribs. She wouldn't cry out and give him the satisfaction of knowing how much she was hurting. Instead, she staggered to her feet, struggling to breathe, dragging her eyes up to meet his; furious and dark and full of malice.

"You think you can sit here all day doing nothing?" One gloved hand shot out and clamped around Mila's throat, pulling her face closer to his. The stench of his sweat filled her nostrils, and his steamy breath ghosted across her face. "I'm sick of dealing with lazy Creo scum like you. We have orders for how to manage people who won't work."

"I—I'm trying," Mila choked out.

"Not hard enough." The guard sneered, his hand tightening. Her trapped pulse pounded in her temples.

Mila's hands flew to his wrist, her fingers scrabbling at his iron grip. Just as the corners of her vision began to blacken, he let go. Mila dropped to the ground and managed to cough once before the guard's boot found her again; he drove into her stomach so hard that she flipped over. She could only fold her arms across herself and lay there, heaving with loud, dry sobs, as the other workers kept their eyes averted. No one dared step in, and Mila didn't blame them. Just as she looked on yesterday while the older woman was beaten, now she was the one in need, and no one would come to save her.

There was a crunch as the guard took a step closer. He leaned over her, his voice low and menacing. "Your crying won't save you, little Creo. If you don't start being *effective*," he placed extra emphasis on the word, "I'll make sure you don't get up next time. Now get to work."

It took everything she had to crawl back to her position beside the shrivelled crops. For a long time afterwards, her entire midsection spasmed with intense, searing pain. Bent double, she unlatched her arms and returned her fingers to the soil, allowing the magic to claw its way through her, burning in her veins like acid. It joined in the fiery inferno blistering her from the inside out. But what choice did she have? What choice had she ever had? Her life had always been theirs to command.

18

The night was oppressive without the moon, but Mila hadn't bothered to light the lamp. The turmoil inside her felt comfortable with the darkness.

Mila sat with her back against the tent wall, the man's words from earlier playing over and over again in her mind, urging her to heed his call.

I'm not giving up on you.

Every choice has a cost.

But each repetition, like a hammer striking an anvil, only deepened her unease.

The difference is in what you do next…

No more guards, no more fear or rules or punishment…

Every breath felt heavy with the consequences of the choice that lay before her, and still, the rebel leader's voice echoed.

Living on our terms…

What's left if we do nothing?

His words felt cruel—a reminder of what she should be, and what she wasn't. She wasn't brave. She wasn't strong, or heroic, or powerful. What she was, was alone.

When Nasir entered the tent, he didn't see her at first, sitting quietly in the gloom. He made his way to the kitchen corner and lit their one working lamp. The soft, amber glow fell across his face, carving shadows under his cheekbones and darkening the hollows around his eyes. When he did see her a second later, he immediately averted his gaze, as though the very sight of her burned him.

She couldn't take it anymore.

Mila got unsteadily to her feet and took a step towards him. All of the anger and frustration, loneliness and despair came flooding into her voice as she said, "Nasir, this has gone on long enough!"

He didn't say anything, didn't even look at her.

Her face crumpled, tears already bursting from her eyes. "Talk to me!" Mila cried, "Please! Yell at me, scream at me, but for Gaia's sake Nasir, please don't shut me out anymore!"

He turned away from her, towards the small stovetop, and grabbed an empty pot with his dirt-stained hand. His muscles flexed. For a horrible moment, Mila thought he was about to hit her with it, and she flinched. But he didn't move, just stood there with his back to her, one hand tight on the pot handle and the other on the bench. The silence stretched.

"Say something," Mila finally said, much softer now. "Anything."

"What do you want me to say?" There was something beneath the cold tone, frayed and close to breaking.

"I want you to talk to me. I want you to look at me." She hesitated, then added, "I want you to stop hating me."

At that Nasir slammed the pot down onto the stovetop and spun to face her. His eyes were dark with exhaustion, his jaw clenched so tightly she thought it might snap. "Mila, you got them killed. Our *parents*. How do you expect me to be? How am I supposed to feel?" His voice cracked. He was staring at her with such appal, like she was something unrecognisable.

Mila swallowed against the lump rising in her throat. "I don't know—"

"Of course you don't know. You always rush in without thinking, you never stop and wonder about the consequences, about what anything means. And because of that, they're dead. They're never coming back. Because of *you*."

The words landed with such force it took her breath away, harder than if he had actually hit her.

"You think I don't know that?" she whispered as tears constricted her throat. "You think I don't see it every time I close my eyes? Don't you know I'm thinking of them, every second of every day?"

His broad shoulders shrugged, fury lacing the movement. "Good."

"So that's it?" Mila said, her voice small. Everything she feared was true. He did hate her. She nodded slightly, absorbing this new reality. "You're happy that I'm miserable."

Nasir's face softened slightly, and he looked like he might say something else. But he simply seized the pot once more and moved away towards the entrance of the tent.

"Don't leave!" The plea in Mila's voice was unmistakable, and Nasir faltered.

"I'm going to collect water."

"Can't it wait? You can't leave like this…"

"I'm going to get water," he repeated, "To make us tea. Then we can talk."

Mila could only watch as he left the tent. The tension lingered like smoke. She sniffed and wiped her face, feeling suddenly nervous. What more did he have to say to her? Whatever it was, Mila wasn't sure she wanted to hear it. She was already broken. Whatever he said next could shatter her into a million pieces.

She pressed her hands against her eyes, trying to steady herself with the pressure and the darkness. How was this going to go? They had already started with such fire, and a field is hard to harvest if it's already been set ablaze…

When she opened her eyes again, the shelves in front swam into view. Amid the half-empty jars of preserves sat the carved flowers her brother had once whittled. Her favourite, the rose, was carved with such delicate precision that each petal seemed as smooth as silk. The act of creating them required such patience and care, and that was Nasir through and through, Mila thought. He saw wonders where others saw waste. But that depth came with a cost, and the same skill that shaped beauty with a blade now turned his words sharp, carving her instead. He was hurting deeply, and wanting her to hurt with him.

Mila retreated to the cushions once more, waiting and uncertain. She picked absently at the already-tattered skin around her thumb nails, listening intently, and a few moments later, soft footsteps crunched on the frosty ground outside. Nasir reappeared holding the pot carefully with both hands, which he placed on the small stove without a word. He kept his back to her while he ignited the heat and waited for the icy water to boil. He wasn't going to make this easy for her.

Interminable minutes crept by. What on earth could she say to him? How could she even begin to mend what had broken between them? He was angry—and rightfully so. They had both lost so much. But did he need to be angry at *her*? She hadn't meant for things to spiral out of control like they had. It had been an accident, a terrible mistake. Surely Nasir understood that, deep down? The government of Ard Aman were the ones who doled out the punishment. *They* were the ones who made the laws and policies that had resulted in this situation. And Lideri had pulled the trigger on their parents—not her.

But knowing these facts didn't make things easier. It didn't erase anything. Mila sighed. Was there any point trying to talk to him about it? Would he care how scared she had been, how guilty she felt, how lost she was…? He had made it pretty clear how he felt. He wouldn't understand. Not tonight. Maybe not for a long time.

Maybe not ever.

A bottomless ache pulled at her chest at the thought. She wanted so badly to move forward from this. She couldn't keep going without him.

She had to try, didn't she? Or was the damage already too deep?

The pot began to hiss, and Nasir moved slowly to prepare the two cups of tea. When Nasir handed her the steaming cup and the warmth seeped through her cold fingers, Mila had to stifle a sob. It was a small, simple gesture, but it felt monumental. He was letting her back in. It was the warmest she had felt in a long time.

Nasir sat on a cushion beside her, cradling his own cup with both hands. Though his gaze was fixed across the room, Mila could see the same distance in his eyes that had been there since the day their parents died.

"Thank you," Mila whispered.

His shoulders tensed. "It's just tea."

"It's more than that." They both knew it.

Silence fell again. Nasir blew on the hot drink, and they both watched the tendrils of steam dance away. He had allowed her a crack in his tough façade, but she would have to start this conversation, if they were going to have it. She took a deep breath.

"I know you're angry," she began, "You hate me, and I get it—believe me. I get it. *Gaiabeht,* I hate *myself,* so how could I expect anyone else to feel differently?"

He shifted uncomfortably. "I don't *hate* you, Mila."

She sniffed. "No?"

"I just don't understand why." He looked off to the side, gathering his thoughts, while she waited for him to go on. "You *knew* there would be consequences for creomancy, but you used it anyway. Twice! *Why?* What makes that boy's life worth it?"

Mila opened her mouth to respond, but Nasir wasn't finished. "Mahma and pada and me—we're always telling you; stay small, stay out of the way, keep your head down, don't do anything to make the guards angry… And you just ignored it all. You always think you know better, that the rules can be broken. And now look!"

He was breathing hard, eyes ablaze as he glanced at her.

Mila didn't know what to say. "You're right. You're right! I ruined everything. I've lost *everything*, because of one stupid decision. Because I was too damn *innocent* to see the danger until it was too late. But I'm paying for it, Nasir," Mila said, her voice trembling, "Every day I'm paying for it."

He said nothing.

Mila closed her eyes and whispered a confession, the truth she knew deep in her soul. "It would have been better if they had killed me in the alleyway. They should have. Everything would be better that way."

Suddenly she felt Nasir's warm hand take her own.

Mila opened her eyes, looking at her brother. Despite the distance that had grown between them, despite the hurt and blame, he was still her older brother. And he seemed so much older now. The boyishness was gone from his features, replaced with a hardness that she had never seen before.

"*Ny*, Mila. Don't say that."

"But it's true. You said it yourself. It's my fault. Just look around the camp, listen to what people whisper when I pass. Everyone wants me dead, the way I deserve."

Nasir shook his head. "You can't just stop. You've got to keep going. You've got to survive."

She bit her lip. She would not cry. "Survive for what?" her voice cracked. "Things are getting really bad out there. More and more people fall in the fields every day, drained of their entire lifeforce. Yesterday, the guards killed a woman right in front of me. What's the point of prolonging this suffering when death is waiting anyway?"

Nasir's grip tightened around her hand and a muscle feathered in his clenched jaw. For a moment, it seemed like he was struggling to find the right words.

"The point is life, Mila." he finally said.

"But I've *destroyed* everyone's lives."

"You didn't choose any of this." His gaze flickered, as if he wasn't sure he believed his own words, but he pressed on. "I know what I said before, but I was angry, Mila. The truth is, what happened to mahma and pada… the wall, the work… none of that is your choice."

"It *was* my choice to use creomancy, that day in Haman. My intention doesn't matter; all that matters is what came after. Only the results. And the results are this."

"Have I taught you nothing about creomancy? Your intention is everything. You were just trying to help that boy, in the building. That's who you are. You help people, selflessly. You can't let IronHand take that from you."

Mila sniffed. "IronHand only gained a foothold because of what happened…"

"I don't believe that," Nasir said. "They would have found some reason to do this to us, whether you used magic or not. Their plan didn't start with you. Their hate has been building for years and years."

Mila shook her head, but the guilt clawing at her insides lessened almost imperceptibly. She still let that woman die. She was still responsible for it all. "But if I hadn't been there…" Her words trailed away.

"If this, if that. Mila, you can play that game with anything in life. It never ends." Nasir sighed, releasing her hand to run his fingers through his dark hair. A minute passed in silence, but it was a different silence to earlier, no longer icy and cold.

"I'm scared," Mila admitted quietly. "I'm scared of the guards. I'm scared of Lideri, and Ahriman. I'm scared of what's going to happen if they keep forcing us to use creomancy. They're working us all to death, and I can't—" Her voice cracked. "—I can't lose you too."

Nasir glanced away for a moment, as if the weight of what she said was too much to face head-on. "I don't have all the answers. I don't know how we're supposed to survive this—But we have to. We'll find a way. I won't lose you either."

Mila looked down, blinking back the tears that threatened to spill over. The warmth of his hand lingered. His words weren't enough to make the pain go away completely, but they were a lifeline. Almost at the same moment, they each took a sip from their cups. Coils of steam rose and caressed her face.

They didn't say anything more for a long, comfortable moment. Just the presence of him was enough. Just like her mother's patchwork cushions, Mila's shattered spirit was being stitched together again, piece by fragile piece.

She didn't feel quite so alone anymore.

19

Three days later, the sharp blast of the whistle cut through the pale, misty blue light of morning. As the echoes bounced back off the mountains, the Satarian workers slowly hobbled towards the fields. There, they paused briefly, sharing weary glances laced with dread, before they bent to the ground. To the left, the wheat stalks that they had grown just two days ago were already starting to lose their lurid shine. The question hung in the air with their frigid breath; How many of these people would rise again at the end of the day? How many people would die, only for the crops to droop in a few days' time, as if it had never happened? The injustice of it made Mila's blood boil and she had to dig her cracked fingernails into her palms to keep herself from screaming.

Standing above them, Officer Ahriman clapped three times to get their attention. "Listening up, Creos. Eyes on me! The summer crops cannot grow in winter, we see this now. Well, we live and learn." A lizard-like grin carved his face. "So, the job today is simple: we want carrots, potatoes, turnips. Strong vegetables. Root vegetables. We will focus on these while the cold lasts. When they are grown, you will bring them forward. You will place them in the bins. You will not taste them. You will not hide them. You will not think, even for a moment, that they belong to you." Ahriman raised a gloved hand, finger wagging slowly. "Be warned. You know what happens when you steal."

He let the silence stretch. "Still, the IronHand are generous. As a little reminder that compliance is noticed, whichever group produces the most will get to keep a piece. Each!" As he added the last word, he threw out his arms, highlighting the grandiose and magnanimous gesture. Despite herself, Mila's mouth began to water at the idea of fresh carrot soup, and a burst of relief jolted through her as she noted the rows of muted green fronds sticking out of the frosty ground, barely a few centimetres high. This was good. Root vegetables were suited to colder weather and grew below the surface, meaning the seedlings were still alive, quietly waiting to mature. Far less energy would be needed to encourage something already growing, than to revive a plant that had withered and died.

"Right! You have your instructions, now get on with it!" Ahriman blew another shrill blast from his whistle.

Mila turned her attention to the plot and crouched low, sifting her fingers through the soil, feeling its cool, grainy texture beneath her nails. She was so focused on the earth's scent, so absorbed that she almost didn't notice the shadow that fell beside her or the quiet rustle of footsteps stopping just an arm's length away. The middle-aged man moved deliberately slowly, and he didn't look at Mila as, with a grunt, he knelt to the ground and dug his hands into the soil, mimicking the same monotonous task as the others.

"Curse this frost," he murmured in Satarian. "My knees will never be the same."

Something about the way the man stooped downward triggered a memory. She *had* seen him before; she could picture it clearly now. This man, sinking against the border wall, pale-faced, his forehead freshly marked. She wasn't wholly surprised it had taken her so long to place him—that day, and all the ones after, was something she would rather forget.

"I know you," Mila said.

"Well, I should hope so," the man said. "You are not old enough to be losing your memory just yet."

"No, I mean—I've seen you before. You were the first person to be branded by the guards. After me, I mean."

The man looked at her sharply, piercingly. Then he returned his gaze to the ground. "My fame precedes me then."

Mila straightened for a moment, brushing a strand of hair from her face, and glanced toward Nasir. He was a few meters away, kneeling in an adjacent row of crops, his attention fixed on her and the strange man. His viridian eyes burned with apprehension as he caught her gaze, his branded brow knitted in concern, limbs tensed. Mila lifted a hand at her side—a small, deliberate gesture meant to stay any action he was thinking about taking. She still hadn't told her brother about the rebel leader's proposition, but Nasir was wary enough to suspect that something was wrong.

Somewhere behind them, a guard coughed and Mila hurriedly returned her eyes to the soil, but her awareness was on her surroundings. The IronHand guards stalked the edge of the field like predators, rifles slung over their shoulders, eyes sweeping over the prisoners with bated anticipation.

Mila settled herself on her knees beside the man. The icy cold seeped quickly through her clothing, making her shiver. "So, you're back. What are you doing here?"

"I told you," he murmured, barely moving his lips. He dug his hands deep into the soil, up to the wrists. "I am not giving up on you. Is today the day you will join us?"

She shook her head, her throat tight, before she managed to whisper, "Not yet."

Maybe not ever.

The man was silent, and his disappointment was so clear that Mila felt the need to explain herself. "I can't. I'm sorry, I have to think about my brother. He's all I have left—"

"Til tomorrow, then," the man said, cutting her off firmly. He drew his hands back, grasping a freshly grown carrot in his fist, and slowly raised himself to his feet.

Mila swallowed painfully. The vegetable was a vibrant orange against the muted soil and, though the man dusted off the carrot with an air of nonchalance, Mila immediately recognised the gesture for what it was: a subtle demonstration of power.

This was the strength she could wield, this was the power the rebellion could harness—if only she was brave enough.

As the sun climbed higher, its weak light barely warming the frost-bitten fields, Mila tried to focus on the work in front of her. Her thoughts, though, were miles away, once more debating what the Satarian man had said.

Til tomorrow then.

The tension of it gnawed at her, tugging on her mind minute by minute. Nasir worked across from her in silence, his movements mechanical, his lips pressed tightly as he held back questions.

Mila had so far decided against telling Nasir about the rebel leader, thinking that the glue repairing their relationship was far too fragile to put any weight on it. And she was terrified that he would laugh at the idea that someone—a stranger, no less—had seen worth in her. Or he might think that she actually believed herself deserving of such attention and praise. Her spiralling fears made secrecy feel like safety, at the time. But now, she couldn't shake the fear that by keeping it to herself, she had broken the fragile trust they had started to rebuild. Was he regretting even considering forgiveness? The thought made her stomach twist. She couldn't do anything right. Every move she made felt like another mistake.

Still, she was certain of one thing; nothing else mattered but her brother and the bond between them.

As soon as they could get out of earshot of the guards, she would tell him everything.

Mila pried another small carrot from the soil. It came free with a dull snap, clumps of dirt clinging to its yellowish surface. She stared at it for a moment, feeling both a sense of accomplishment and unease. The magic had worked, but even here in this new plot, the earth was beginning to protest. Each time she pulled life from it, she felt herself draining with the effort, a little more of her own lifeforce slipping away. This was no miracle, no gift, just another sacrifice. Mila wiped her brow, leaving a streak of dirt across the ridges of the *noterran* brand, and slowly willed herself to stand on aching legs.

She squinted against the harsh glare of the winter sun, tracing the countless figures toiling across the barren land, their faces pale as the misty morning fog. Hands shook violently as white-knuckled fingers were forced to stay in the chalky soil that seemed to stretch on endlessly beneath the powder-blue sky. Exhausted murmurs of Satarian phrases clung to the breeze.

Nasir coughed, breaking her from her thoughts. A streak of black snaked from his nose, pouring over his lips and down his chin before dripping onto the soil. The earth drank it up greedily, as if it had never been. He was pushing too hard, straining himself like all the others. Dread sank deep in Mila's heart. How long could they survive like this? How many more would fall before it was enough for IronHand?

At that moment, a faint groan came from a few rows behind, and Mila spun around to see an elderly woman double over, her frail arms wrapping around her middle. Before anyone could react, she crumpled, hitting the ground with a sickening thud. Mila suddenly recognised the woman; her neighbour, Karina.

Not her too…

"*Soffa!*" Mila gasped, rushing over to her. Nasir joined her a second later, kneeling beside the elder. Her eyes were closed and sweat dotted her pallid forehead. Beneath her skin so thin and waxen, thousands of blue blood vessels traced her all over, faintly pulsing with each shallow, uneven breath.

Nasir pressed the back of his hand to Karina's forehead. "She's burning up," he muttered. "Help me get her to some shade."

Along with another worker, they lifted the woman between them with shaking hands. She was so light, her ancient body limp as if all substance had been drained from her. A surge of fear swarmed at the forefront of Mila's mind.

They carefully laid *soffa* Karina beneath the meagre shade between the isolated, leafless trees at the edge of the field. Her breathing remained laboured and her eyes closed.

Mila knelt beside her old friend and reached out with a dirt-stained hand, fighting a wave of nausea as she pressed her trembling fingers to the woman's clammy, paper-thin skin in search of a pulse. Finally, she found it—thready and intermittent, but there. Mila let out a breath.

"Do you think she'll be okay?" Mila whispered as she looked at Nasir, but the reassurance she sought died on her lips as a shadow loomed over them.

"What the hell do you think you're doing?" barked the guard, as his eyes narrowed on the group, face twisted in annoyance. "You're supposed to be working, not playing nurse to this useless old hag."

The words hit like a slap. *Useless?*

Fire surged through Mila's veins as she glared at him, her teeth pressed tightly together. She longed to hurl an insult back at the guard. How *dare* he look at Karina as if she were nothing? The bitter hypocrisy burned. To him, Karina was just another Ineffective, a nameless expendable body to dismiss—while *he* brought nothing but misery and pain into their lives. *He* was the useless one, the worthless one. The one they could do without. But Karina? This sharp-witted, kind woman was far from useless.

Mila remembered Karina's knack for slyly sneaking little flowers—grown with secret creomancy, of course—behind the ears of the children while they weren't looking. "How did that get there? I knew you were growing, but that's not what I meant!" she'd say with a mock innocence that always made them laugh.

Useless? Making someone smile was never useless; it could be the greatest gift one ever received, especially in a place like Al'Mazraea. And Karina did that every day. She added value to someone's life every damn day.

"She collapsed," Nasir said, his voice tight with the same barely suppressed anger. "She needs help."

The guard's nostrils flared. The ground crunched beneath his black boots as he took a step closer. "She's no good to anyone now. Leave her. You've got work to do."

Mila's heart raced as fury bubbled within her. Nasir caught her eye and shook his head; a silent plea for her to stay quiet.

"We'll get back to work," Nasir said carefully. "But we're not leaving her here."

The guard's hand twitched on his rifle, voice dropping to a menacing whisper. "Step away. *Now.*"

For a heartbeat, the silence felt like a drawn blade, tense and sharp. When no one moved, the guard's patience snapped. He lunged forward and grabbed Nasir by the hair, pulling him away from Karina and tossing him to the side with a brutal jerk. The guard flicked off the rifle's safety switch, the action causing the air around them to thicken with tension. This was about to spiral out of control, fast.

Without thinking, Mila moved between the guard and the *soffa.* "Please! We can fix her! You don't have to do this!"

The guard scoffed. "You make it sound like I'm supposed to *want* to save her. I couldn't care less if she dies. No one wants Creos around, you're an infestation on our land. The world will be a better place when there's none of you left."

The guard stepped closer, so close Mila could smell the sour sweat collected in the furs of his winter jacket. He pressed the gun barrel into her breastbone. "*Move.*"

Their eyes locked, and in his Mila saw only fear.

Fear is good at finding depth to the faintest shadows.

The guard's finger tightened on the trigger. Squeezed.

Nasir sprang into action, tackling Mila to the side. She hit the ground hard just as the crack of a gunshot shattered the air, deafening in its suddenness, followed by a wet, horrible thud of impact.

"Nasir!?" Mila shrieked, but it was Karina's body that jerked with the force of the bullet. Dark blood began to seep slowly into the greedy soil around her.

Everything stopped.

Mila became aware that she was screaming, and quickly slammed her dirt-covered hands over her mouth, breathing in sharp gasps.

"Damn," said the guard with a frown. "I was hoping for a two-for-one."

The mark the bullet left in Karina's head was much smaller than Mila expected. She couldn't tear her eyes away.

"Now," the guard said, loading another bullet into the chamber with a clunk. "Are you going to get back to work? Or would you like to help me with some more target practice?"

Mila took a step forward, her body trembling, every inch of her wanting to tear into this disgusting, cruel man, to make him feel the devastation he had just inflicted. Inside she held a violent storm, swirling and crackling with destructive energy and clouding her mind.

But before she could take another step, Nasir's hand shot out, grabbing her forearm. His grip was tight and his voice low, stopping her cold. "Mila, don't."

The guard smirked at them. "Come on, give me a reason," he said. "Not that I need one."

Her jaw clenched, the storm shredding her insides, but she turned away instead, following the steady pull of Nasir's grip on her arm. She wouldn't give the guard the satisfaction. It was all she could do to keep her face composed. With Nasir beside her, Mila strode back to her position in the field without another word, but her mind was sinking faster than she could catch it, weighed down with the bitter truth. Things weren't going to get better. No one was coming for them, no one was out there, coming to help the Satarian people. The Amanese looked the other way, pretending they didn't know what was happening here, giving their support through their silence. And there was no one in the wider world who would be willing to go to war to save them. Fifteen-hundred Satarians weren't worth it. She felt disgusted at her ignorance and naïveté.

Something hardened within her. Shock melted into fury, as cold and hard as a steel blade.

They will pay for this.

For years, she had held onto the belief that someday the Amanese would finally understand that the Satarians were *human*—just like them. But that was never going to happen. Her innocence had become ignorance. There was no end to this. There was no 'enough'. Nothing the Satarians could ever do would convince IronHand that they were worthy of basic rights. IronHand would keep up this endless cycle until they were destroyed, one way or another. Al'Mazraea would consume them, draining any hopes along with their bodies. Just empty shells left to die in the dirt.

Just like Karina—generous, witty Karina, who had done nothing wrong—now crumpled on the ground with a bullet through her head.

Mila's anger sharpened with each laboured breath like a blade against a whetstone. She was done living in fear, done bending under their power.

They will learn what it's like to be afraid.

Every day that passed only fed the guards' cruelty, and her people's suffering deepened. A fierce certainty settled over her. She needed to fight back. She would make them answer for every moment of cruelty, every ounce of pain they had inflicted.

Maybe it was foolish to think they could ever win, but if there was even a small chance they could fight back, didn't they have to try? Life could be more than just waiting for their turn to die.

What if we used our magic for more than this?

A strange sensation swooped in her stomach, terrifying and exhilarating in equal measure, like a baby bird that had finally caught the air beneath its wings after a long, helpless fall. The idea felt reckless, risky, but by the time the guards finally called an end to the day, Mila had made up her mind. She couldn't ignore the pull any longer. She would join the rebel leader, and together they would burn everything in their path.

20

That evening, Mila and Nasir stood either side of their small kitchen space, her by the stovetop and him by the shelves. She had slowly and carefully explained the rebel leader's proposition to her distraught brother, and now he was looking at her with wide eyes.

"But why *you*?"

"I know it sounds insane," she admitted, remembering that she had said that exact same word to the man. *Insane*. "But he seems to think my magic is strong. Stronger than anyone else."

The lamp light flickered, casting trembling shadows over the tent canvas. Mila sliced into a potato, carefully cutting it into eighths, then did the same with a second one.

"And what? He wants you to use your magic against the guards?"

Mila dumped the pieces of potato into the pot on their small single-burner stove, then rested her hands on the bench. "Yes, I think so."

Nasir only stared at her. "They'll kill you, Mila."

"They're going to kill us all anyway, Nasir," Mila said, again echoing what the man had said to her.

Though Nasir's nose had finally stopped bleeding, a dark red crust still covered his upper lip and chin. A pulse of anger flickered through his expression. "We'll find another way," he said though the weariness in his voice only hardened her resolve. "We'll find a way to resist without killing ourselves, and without killing everything around us."

"How? I've been thinking about it all day, and I don't see any other way out of this. And we're running out of time. Don't pretend you can't feel how the earth is struggling. Soon there won't be *any* magic left in Al'Mazraea to draw on, and we will have lost our only advantage."

Nasir was quiet for a long moment while he stared at her, trying to process the idea. Between them, the water began to boil, cooking their miserable dinner. No amount of salt and herbs could make a single potato into a satisfying meal.

Finally, he said, "Do you really think we could do that? Fight back?"

Mila shook her head and shrugged. "I don't know. But we can't keep going like this, Nasir. Look at what it's doing to us." She didn't need to point out the raw, red brands on their foreheads, or their fingernails black and split. Their skin was the same colour as their grey tunics, except where countless bruises bloomed, dark purple fading to sickly yellow-green.

Nasir looked down at his hands, still streaked with dirt. He clenched them into fists. "What if this is all a trap? Using our magic… colluding with others… It's too dangerous, Mila. And not just because of IronHand."

"I know," she said quietly. Her eyes burned as she thought of the dozens of bodies left behind in the fields. Of Karina. Of their parents. "But doing nothing is dangerous too. We can't keep pretending everything will change if we just wait long enough. Right now, IronHand holds all the power, and they're only giving us two options: to die quickly, or to die slowly. But what if there was a third option… What if I could actually make a difference?"

Nasir ran a hand through his dark matted curls. "If the guards catch wind of this…"

"Then I'll die quickly," Mila shrugged. To her, after everything, it felt like an acceptable gamble.

Nasir paced the cramped space of their tent, his jaw tight. "This isn't a game. There's too much at stake for you to be glib about it."

"I know what's a stake, Nasir. I know that all too well. On the first day of the occupation, IronHand executed those nine women, just to uncover the girl who had apparently done magic. Just to find *me*. And then—" her voice caught. She couldn't mention her parents right now. "—you know what happened next. And don't forget all the people in the fields, and all the Ineffectives, dying as a consequence of *my* actions. *My* choices."

Didn't he get it?

"What if it goes wrong? What if things only get worse?"

"I don't see how it can get worse," Mila retorted. "We've already lost everything. What's left to take?"

"Your *life*, Mila! Isn't that worth anything to you anymore?"

Mila swallowed, and Nasir saw the answer in her hesitation.

"You don't care, do you?" he whispered, shaking his head. "You've already given up."

"It's not like that," Mila said. Her voice trembled, but she managed to continue. "IronHand is here because of *me*. I got us into this, and I'm *going* to get us out."

Nasir stopped pacing and glared at her. Mila held his gaze, steady, even as she saw the flash of pain in her brother's eyes. "You're being a martyr."

"Better a martyr than a nameless no-one. I'd rather die fighting for something, not as a withered corpse among the crops."

"Mila—"

"You always told me to stay calm and small, no matter what, so for as long as I can remember, I've tried to do that, hoping that one day things would change. But it's never going to happen, Nasir. They don't see us. We're not human to them. They don't care if we break, or if we bleed, or if we don't make it through the day. We're bound to Al'Mazraea by the wall, by their rules, by their fears, and by the fact that we've never known anything else. They're counting on the fact that we'd never dare to dream of a different life. They don't *care* that we've been stuck in Al'Mazraea for three hundred years, or if we stay here for three hundred more. We have nothing that's truly ours; not the land, not our bodies, not our lives… Nothing but creomancy! It's the *only* thing in the whole of Satarian culture that they can't completely control. If we don't do something—if we don't use our magic—we're going to wither away. Like the crops. Like the earth. Death is coming for us, Nasir. The only question is when. Do we resign ourselves to it… or do we fight?"

She was breathing heavily by the time she finished, one hand in a fist to emphasise her point.

Nasir made a face, his eyes crinkled with a mix of affection and exasperation. "That was quite a speech, Cricket."

"Yeah, well… Did it work?"

"No amount of fancy words is going to make me okay with the idea of you risking your life, Mila." Nasir was quiet for a long moment, battling internal demons. Finally, he looked at her, his eyes dark with worry. "If we do this, we need to be really, really careful."

"We…?"

"Of course *we*. We're in this together."

Mila bit back the protest she had been about to make. She couldn't in one breath convince Nasir of the importance of the rebellion, then tell him it was too dangerous for him to join. He was a part of this world, and by that very fact he was involved, no matter how strongly she hated the idea. Instead, she took a steadying breath.

"I'll let the rebel leader know he has two new recruits."

21

Twenty-four hours later, inside their cramped, dimly lit tent, Mila and Nasir listened in tense silence. They both stood, too nervous to remain seated, their ears pricking at any sound. Darkness was closing in fast.

The rebel leader had contacted her again that day, as the morning's cool light softened into silvery afternoon glare, and she had told him one word: *yes*.

A satisfied half-smile had escaped onto his lined face. "*Beht.* I will come to you tonight, as Altair rises," he had murmured.

Now, as the bright star appeared above the distant hills, the man should arrive at any moment. Mila felt sick, the thumping in her chest so forceful that she wondered if Nasir could hear it. She glanced at him, but his gaze was fixed on the entrance.

Suddenly, the tent flap stirred, making Nasir and Mila flinch. The middle-aged man with his salt-and-pepper hair stepped swiftly inside. He acknowledged them with a small incline of his head, and the movement was so reminiscent of her father that Mila momentarily forgot where she was. Emotion constricted her breathing as quickly and powerfully as if a hand was there, strangling her.

"*Beht'erev, sigià,*" he greeted her, his voice deep and comforting. He nodded to Nasir. "*Et sigiò.*"

Mila choked out a noise of acknowledgement as the voice sent another wave of emotion through her. She hated hearing it, she loved hearing it, she never wanted to hear it again and she wanted to run into the sound like it were her father's arms.

Mila stared as the man walked past her, then realised a second person had followed him into the tent; a woman Mila had never seen before—tall, muscular, her dark hair cropped short above hawk-like eyes that scanned the tent in one swift movement. She looked entirely unbothered by the defensive tension that greeted her.

"I didn't realise you'd be bringing someone else," Mila said. This man felt unpredictable, and she didn't like it. A meeting of treasonous rebels was not the kind of situation where she welcomed surprises.

"She is with me," the man said simply, his deep voice washing over her.

"Right," Mila said. "And who *are* you? I don't yet know your name."

"There is no need for that. If we get caught, well, it becomes harder to be turned in."

"But you know *my* name. You could turn me in. I would rather this be a situation of equals…"

"With respect, *sigià*, everyone knows your name."

Mila Medín. The Murderer.

Her cheeks burned with embarrassment that slowly turned into resentment. Here she was, risking her life to join a cause that could save her people—yet she was still being dismissed, overlooked, and blamed.

No.

Mila straightened, forcing herself to meet his eyes. "That's right. Everyone knows my name. They know what I've done. And you came to me because of that. But I will not work with someone who refuses to trust me enough to even tell me his name," she said.

Nasir folded his arms, silently backing her up.

There was a pause while the man considered it. The woman watched him cautiously.

When he finally said: *Muharram*, Mila recognised it for the admission of fealty it was.

"And this is Thani," Muharram added, waving a calloused hand towards the woman.

Thani gave an exasperated huff. "So much for secrecy," she said, and her lips pursed in disagreement. "*Beht*, let's get to business. Our plan has two parts; the training, and the escaping."

"We've scouted the fence," Muharram said. "The only way out is through it—or under it. Obviously, even if we did manage to get through it, we would then have to contend with the Haman city walls and everything that entails. A tunnel seems like the better option, though it brings a different kind of difficulty."

"A tunnel?" Nasir asked. "But we have no tools…"

Thani looked at him with open disdain. "You have earth magic. You don't need any tool besides that. We will dig from here, using creomancy, and we will need to work only at night."

Mila tugged on a strand of her long hair, feeling like a child among adults once more. "How long will it take?"

"A month, maybe more," Thani said. "If we can get more people to help, it may take less."

"And what of the others? The Satarians without working magic?" Nasir asked.

"They can't help us dig, but we're not leaving them behind, don't worry. We take everyone with us."

"Everyone?" Mila blanched. "That's over a thousand people…"

"I did warn you about her penchant for stating the obvious," Muharram said to Thani, with an eye roll.

Thani grimaced. "You would rather leave people behind?"

"Of course not, don't twist my words. I just mean, the more people involved, the more likely we are to get caught."

"The risk sits heavily on all of us—but it's a chance we have to take."

A beat of silence followed.

"And what do you need my sister for?" Nasir asked. "Why her?"

"Well, let me ask you," Thani said, turning to fix her narrowed eyes on Mila. "What did you do in Haman that day?"

Mila stiffened, at the same time as insecurity rolled through her. She hadn't *done* anything. She hadn't done *anything*. Moments passed as the scene replayed through her mind, a waking nightmare. Thani and Muharram didn't seem perturbed by her hesitation; they waited, watching Mila pick anxiously at her fingernails.

"I didn't cause the rockslide," she said finally, mouth dry.

Muharram nodded, prompting her to keep going.

"But… I did split the earth."

Something like victory flickered across Thani's intense gaze. "Perfect."

"No, *not* perfect!" Mila said shortly. "I don't know how I did it! I've only ever worked on small things before… splitting rocks, transferring soil. I didn't mean to tear open the ground, and I don't know if I can do it again."

But that half-smirk hadn't left Thani's face. "You can. You've done more than any of us ever have. Not only do you have the brightest power—the brightest eyes—I've ever seen, but you've been honing your skills in secret."

"Illegally, might I add," Muharram said with a touch of reverence. "Bold."

But something icy slithered into the pit of Mila's stomach. They didn't understand. They thought she had *meant* to do it.

"Bold? Bold?! There's nothing *bold* about it! It was a stupid mistake that cost me *everything*! I wasn't being brave, or subversive, or even smart—I didn't know *what* I was doing. It was a complete fluke! I don't even remember *trying* to use creomancy, it just kind of happened."

Thani turned to Muharram, eyebrows raised. "She's a little too humble for my liking."

Muharram nodded in agreement.

"Would you two stop it!?" Mila cut in. "You don't understand what it was like. You're standing there looking at me like I'm some sort of magical prodigy, but I can tell you I most certainly am not. And I'm not being humble!" Mila turned, pacing around the small space, her voice rising with each word. "It just… *happened*. I was about a minute away from being murdered that day, in Haman, and all of a sudden…" Her voice fell as the memory washed over her. "…I felt that surge, that pull of magic, and the next moment, the ground was splitting open, like the magic was acting of its own accord. It was like trying to tame a wild animal, but the wild animal was me. I *wasn't* in control."

Thani sighed, but it was a noise of frustration rather than resignation. "You're the one who doesn't understand, Mila. You *were* in control."

Mila balled her fists. "You're delusional."

"That may be," Thani said dryly. "But it doesn't change the facts."

"I keep telling you—"

"Then maybe you should hold your tongue and listen for a minute, instead," Muharram said. He didn't raise his voice, he just said it clearly and calmly, such a contrast to the atmosphere of the room that Mila stopped pacing in her tracks.

"Mila, please do not misunderstand us. We know that your life has been completely turned upside down since that day in Haman, and we also know that you did not mean for any of it. Accepting that you have the power does not imply you meant to use it, or that you planned any of it."

"I didn't," Mila said in a small voice. Muharram had hit on a nail of truth and it pierced her painfully.

"And yet, I am willing to bet that if you think back to that day—if you are completely honest with yourself—you know you had control. Not entirely, perhaps, but more than you have been letting on. You needed a way to escape those who were attacking you. No one can fault you for wanting to stay alive, Mila. It is human nature."

Mila stared at him, gripping her own arms tightly, knuckles white. Not for the first time, she was struck by the idea that this man seemed to know what was in her heart. He looked at her, patiently waiting, and his dark green eyes held not an ounce of judgement.

She took a breath and allowed herself to think back to that day in Haman.

She remembered that unforgivable thought, to use their fear to her advantage…

And the water touching her body, the way she had yelled to Gaia.

Urratoray t'ard! Vazkarr!

Break the earth, quickly.

She remembered the mob hesitating as a paving stone suddenly cracked, tremors and fractures reaching out in all directions. The feeling that the earth was rising to protect her.

And the feeling of savage pleasure as alarm rippled through the crowd.

Mila dropped Muharram's gaze. He was right, and she couldn't deny it anymore. Yes, the power had felt dangerous, desperate and wild, but she had encouraged it, allowing it to break free.

She felt Nasir's stare burning into her, and guilt writhed in her gut. She couldn't look at him, couldn't bear to see the surprise and disgust there.

"That's what you want in a leader?" Mila said, her voice small with shame. "Someone who can't stop herself from tearing the world apart?"

"The world is *already* torn apart, Mila. It is a festering wound, utterly broken—"

"Yeah, because of me!"

"No, because of the Amanese," Muharram said, his whispered Satarian flowing like a hiss of steam. "Because of their prejudices and racism, because of their belief in the idea that some people are better than others, and that they are entitled to control our lives and our freedom. For centuries, they have relentlessly squashed Satarian culture until it no longer exists in the open. The system is meant to break us down. They have made it so that nothing we do means anything." The older man paused, letting his words crash like stormy waves. "They say that's just how life is. But I'm saying no. No more."

Thani nodded in agreement. "The world was broken a long time ago, Mila, and we have all learned to live with its twisted, crooked pieces, told that this is how it's supposed to be. But, just like a fractured bone that heals crooked, we must break it all over again to set it right."

Mila said nothing, her eyes on the ground.

"You're starting to make me question if you've got the guts for this," Thani said.

Mila's head shot up as she bristled. This woman had no idea what she had the guts for.

Nasir changed the topic before Mila could argue. "You said the plan had two parts. The escaping, and the training. We'll be training others?"

Mila closed her mouth again, but her eyes stayed locked on Thani with fiery intensity.

"Yes," replied Muharram. "Other Satarians with the old magic strong in their veins."

"And what are we training them to do, exactly?"

"To use their creomancy for better, bolder purposes."

Nasir raised a palm. "That kind of activity will draw the guards' attention like flies on shit. One wrong move and they'll kill us."

Thani exchanged a glance with Muharram, and the older man rolled his eyes. "Obviously."

"So why risk it?"

Thani said, "You could think of it like cooking, I suppose."

"Cooking," Mila repeated weakly. She had never been very good at that either.

"Yes," Thani continued. "Anyone with the ingredients can throw them together and make something technically edible, right? But it takes time, practice, and skill to become a great cook, creating delicious meals. It's the same with creomancy. Anyone with magic can connect with the earth, but only those who train and develop their skills can truly harness that power and achieve remarkable things."

It seemed simple enough, but Mila's stomach writhed like a pit of snakes. This felt less like rebellion and more like stepping into a noose. She tucked her trembling fingers under her arms.

Concern wrought Nasir's face too. "How can anyone move around the camp at night without being caught? What about the guards?"

The rebel leader leaned in. "We have been watching for a few weeks now, tracking their movements, learning their habits. It became clear quite quickly that the night guards follow a routine. They each have an area to check, and they zig-zag along each row of tents, then once around the perimeter. They follow this same pattern, night after night."

"Every night?"

"Like clockwork. It is embarrassingly predictable, but their stupidity works in our favour. We will have scouts positioned at key points around the camp, ready to signal when a guard passes their checkpoint. Anyone needing to move around the camp will be guided by that signal."

For some reason, Thani shot Muharram a resentful look at these words, but Mila finally felt a faint flicker of confidence. Though it felt hastily composed to Mila's fresh ears, the more they explained, it became clear that they been developing this plan for a while now.

Nasir spoke suddenly. "You said we'd dig a tunnel from here. Did you mean here as in our *tent*?"

Thani nodded. "Yes. Strategically, logically, it makes the most sense. You're close to the fence, but not close enough that the guards would hear anything. You have the power, and the space, to make it work."

The space, because it was only the two of them now. Mila saw Nasir's lips quiver, and knew the same heartbreaking thought had crossed his mind.

Muharram looked around the space, analysing it for the first time. "You'll dig down about nine metres, and then westward for nine-hundred metres. The tunnel will need to pivot then, north-west, for around another eleven-hundred metres… Then up again to the surface."

"That's a really long way…" Nasir murmured. "The tunnel will be at high risk of collapse, not to mention the amount of power it's going to take to move that much earth…"

No one bothered to acknowledge what he said. He was right.

With extremely limited knowledge of the area beyond Al'Mazraea, Mila couldn't predict the endpoint. "Where are we aiming to come up?"

"On the other side of Haman, past the city walls," Thani said.

The weight of those words settled like a boulder on Mila's shoulders. No Satarian that she knew of had ever been past Haman—it was forbidden, of course. The idea of digging beneath the enemy city and into the unknown was terrifying. "How do you know what's out there? How do you know we'll be safe past the walls?"

"We don't," Muharram answered, "Not for certain. But we have solid information that leads us to believe that it is our best chance."

"Where are you getting this information from?" Nasir asked. "How do you know it's trustworthy?"

"We don't," Muharram said again.

"But we have to try, don't we," Mila murmured, saying aloud the words Muharram had not. Muharram's gaze softened with a hint of respect.

Mila turned away from him, her eyes on the ground, imagining a tunnel snaking away in the dirt beneath. It was audacious, dangerous, bold, but—hadn't they used that word to describe her, moments ago? Bold?

Nasir ran a hand through his dark hair. His face was pale and his voice tight. "We'll need more than creomancy to make it out of here. The earth's energy will be depleted in one night. Don't you think it will be painfully obvious to the guards, ignorant though they may be, that something is afoot when the soil around our tent has turned to dust?"

"We did think of that," Muharram said, looking to Thani.

"Yes," she agreed. "Each morning, several people will come past your tent and release their lifeblood into the soil here. Those who can't help us with their limited magic, will help us this way. Everyone has a part to play."

Mila's eyes narrowed. It's true that the bloodletting process was necessary to ensure the balance with the earth's power. Lifeforce for lifeforce. But Mila felt a little queasy at the thought of the soil beneath her feet moist with the blood of her community. Still, it was the only way. She nodded, her mouth dry.

No one spoke as they all digested the distasteful information. The plan had merit, but there was also so much that could go wrong. In Al'Mazraea, their whole lives had been built on the understanding that survival depended on caution. From childhood, they had learned to second-guess promises, to expect cruelty in place of mercy. And that idea had only grown since IronHand took hold. Even now, in the dim light of their hidden gathering, Mila could feel it in the way they spoke; measured and guarded.

And yet, they were about to risk everything on nothing more than blind trust. Not just trust in the plan, but trust in each other. It felt as foolish as running her palm through a flame and hoping to not get burned. Yet… wasn't this what people were meant to have? Trust? Mila thought of Elaari's baby, how he turned toward his mother's voice instinctively, secure in the knowledge that she would be there. That innocence, that feeling of safety, had been taken from them, carved out of their culture over generations. Something in her soul ached for it. They had to do this, not just to strike back at the system that had hollowed them out, but because trust was something worth reclaiming.

The evening winds swept through the alleys of tents, rustling the canvas. Somewhere in the distance, a baby cried.

Then, suddenly, a heavy footstep outside made them all freeze. Mila's heart leaped into her throat. Every muscle in her body stiffened, her eyes wide, ears straining. For a moment, time seemed to stretch, the silence unbearable. A bead of sweat slipped down her neck.

Muharram moved toward the entrance to the tent, deftly slipping a dagger from inside his tunic. Mila had a split second to be surprised at the sight of the slightly curved obsidian blade as it glinted in the amber light, before her attention snapped back to the unmistakable crunch of bulky boots on the frosted path just outside.

Were they waiting? Listening?

Her heartbeat was surely thudding loud enough to give them all away.

Then, slowly, the footsteps continued on, slow but regular, passing by their tent and gradually fading away. Mila let out the breath she had been holding.

It was a few minutes before Muharram slipped the weapon back into the folds of his tunic. "We've lingered here too long," he said. He pulled back the tent flap a fraction of an inch, his eyes scanning the night sky. "This was supposed to be a short conversation. We meet again tomorrow night, as Altair rises, just as we did tonight."

"But—wait a minute—" Mila looked from Muharram to Thani. This whole thing had moved at a frightening speed, hurtling forward with the momentum of an avalanche. She needed a moment to catch her breath. There still seemed so many things they needed to discuss.

"Canopus approaches the horizon," he said to Thani, who gave a final glance over the space, her expression unreadable.

"Tomorrow evening," Thani said. "Eastern quarter. Look for the red ribbon."

And suddenly, the visitors were gone.

Nasir sat heavily on one of their mother's patchwork cushions, tucked his knees up under his elbows, and rested his chin on his arms. He gave her a shaky ghost of a smile, his face reflecting the same fear-filled hope she felt in her heart. Her whole body was quivering slightly with adrenaline, her mind whirring at the enormity of the plan.

Their plan.

It was daring, yet horribly fragile. If one thing went wrong—if the guards even suspected something was happening—there would be more punishment, more executions. And it would all be her fault.

Again.

22

The following day, Mila worked the soil mechanically, her fingers digging into the dirt like they always did, but her mind was elsewhere. For the first time in months, she wasn't weighed down by dread. The fear was still there, biting at her in the background, but something else had pushed it back. Something stronger.

Hope.

They were doing something. They were subverting the guards, undermining the very people who thought they had taken total control. A small smile tugged at her lips, though she kept her head down, pretending to focus on the crops. The guards could never catch even a hint that something was happening, or it would all come undone.

Mila felt like an alien trying to pretend to be human, second-guessing every little movement she made, wondering if that was how an innocent person would conduct themselves. Did she usually breathe like this? Where would she look, if she had nothing to hide—around her, or down at the ground? Could the guards sense her increasing heart rate, could they see the beads of nervy sweat punctuating her brow? And what on earth did she usually do with her hands? Surely, the navy-clad guards would notice how odd she was acting and become suspicious, and they would kill her and everyone around her. The demise of the Satarian race might come down to the way she scratched her nose. *Should* she scratch her nose? What would an innocent person do?

She glanced at Nasir from the corner of her eye, watching him work in the adjacent section. His face was tense, jaw tight as he concentrated on the task. She knew he was still worried—rightfully so—but Mila couldn't help feeling that this was the first time in a long while that they weren't completely powerless.

That *she* wasn't completely powerless.

For so long, even before IronHand, they had been trapped and forced to scrape by. Their spines had been bent to the will of the guards, and their lives were an endless cycle of exhaustion and fear. But now… now there was a plan. A way out.

The more she thought about it, Mila felt a strange kind of energy building inside her. It wasn't the blooming sunshine feeling of her magic, nor the wild feeling of unleashed creomancy. This was different. This was purpose. She had a direction, something beyond the dull day-to-day survival that had previously consumed her. The idea of escaping, of digging a tunnel beneath IronHand's feet, thrilled her in a way she hadn't expected.

She knew the risks, of course. They lurked in her mind like beasts prowling for prey, a constant reminder of what could happen if they were caught. But somehow, the fear was easier to bear now. She had Nasir by her side, and they had Muharram and Thani. There was a group of people willing to fight, to escape IronHand and the walls of Al'Mazraea. She was a part of something bigger than her guilt now.

The feeling grounded her, stirring something she hadn't felt since childhood.

One bluebird day, when she was a tiny girl of five years old, Nasir had come home from school to find her curled up outside the door of their small tent, tracing patterns in the dirt. Her eyes stung with the frustration of a child who couldn't put her feelings into words. She didn't fit in with the other children in the camp. They never seemed to enjoy playing with her, and that day she had heard them whispering about her bright green eyes. One kid had even called her names. She was different; she knew it and they knew it. Her young heart felt heavy as a deep sadness crept in, but she didn't want to cry. She wanted to be strong instead, like mahma always said to be.

And to be strong, she thought, meant she didn't need anyone else.

Her lanky ten-year-old brother knelt beside her. "What's wrong, Cricket?"

She had continued to look down at her drawings in the dirt, embarrassed, then muttered, "Go away, Nasir. I'm better off alone."

Nasir frowned. "What are you talking about?"

She looked up at him and whispered, "Everyone stares at me. They don't let me play."

Nasir's face softened. "Is that why you've been sneaking off on your own?"

Mila flushed defiantly. "Mahma says I'm different, and different is good, but… it doesn't feel good. In here." She touched a hand to her belly button, where a deep ache had settled.

Nasir's response hadn't been what she expected. He laughed. Not a mean laugh, but the kind that said she had missed something obvious. "Of course you're different, Mila."

She sniffled and blinked at him, confused. "You agree with them?"

Nasir smiled then, that affectionate glint in his eyes. "Being different doesn't mean you have to be lonely, you know."

Young Mila wrinkled her nose, her head tilted. She didn't understand.

"Come with me, Cricket," he said, holding out his hand. "I want to show you something."

Mila had followed him, her curiosity overpowering her sadness. She could always trust her big brother. He led her through the camp, holding her hand tight along the familiar paths, weaving past clusters of Satarians gathered around fires or bent over their laundry. He led her to the very edge of the tent city, where the ground began to slope away. Nearby, a group of people were building a long channel to improve the camp's drainage system.

Nasir had then described each person in the group to Mila.

"See Amara, there, with the long hair?" He pointed to a lady with a plaited rope winding around her middle.

Mila nodded, then a second later gasped as she realised the rope was, in fact, the woman's hair.

"Wow," she breathed.

Then Nasir indicated an elderly man, his thin arms taut with muscle as he worked. "And *soffo* Giani? He can do sums in his head using numbers that are bigger than any numbers I know."

Mila turned her wide eyes to the old man, amazed. Numbers bigger than even Nasir knew? That was incredible, because Nasir knew everything.

"That man there? He has no front teeth! He loves to tell scary stories because his toothless grin makes them extra spooky."

Mila stared curiously at the man, still holding onto her brother's hand with both of hers. As Nasir's hand twisted against hers, the dark birthmark on his forearm came into the light. The other children liked to tease him about the paint-like smear of mauve. It was his own irregularity.

"Each of these people is different, Cricket, see?"

"But they're all part of something. Look, they're working together to build the pipes," Mila said stubbornly. "No one wants *me* to be part of their group."

Nasir's eyes had narrowed and his lips scrunched together as he thought of how best to explain it to his young sister. "You know mahma's cushions?" he asked suddenly.

"Yeah?"

"Well, she makes them from all random sorts of material, right?" Mila nodded.

"And each piece feels different, different sizes and shapes, right?" Mila nodded again. "Some bits are fuzzy and some are smooth and they're all different colours."

"So, the world is like that. We're all a little different. Different skills, different minds, different dreams. And together, we make Al'Mazraea."

"So Al'Mazraea… is like a cushion?"

Nasir smiled. "Yep! Everyone's piece is important—and we need that little Mila piece, otherwise Al'Mazraea would have a big hole in it."

Mila still remembered how the weight had lifted from her chest as his words settled in. That night, as she cuddled one of the cushions and drifted off to sleep, for the first time, Mila had felt like she belonged.

Now, years later, kneeling on the frosted ground, that same feeling was warming her once more. It was the same feeling of camaraderie; but this time, the stakes were infinitely higher. This time, it was about existence. Freedom. Their quiet rebellion filled her with that same sense of wonderment she had felt walking around the camp at five years old. This time, though, it was a shared hope among those who had been stripped of everything.

And the more she thought about it, the more she became certain they would succeed. They would light the match that would spark a wildfire.

It would be difficult, of course. The tunnel would be dangerous, the guards vigilant, and there were a hundred ways this plan could go wrong. Training others, letting them in on this greatest of secrets, added a layer of refraction that made Mila's gut twist unpleasantly.

But the alternative was to keep living like this, merely subsisting until the day when they would be too weak, too drained, to resist at all. If it came to it, she would rather die fighting than live as a slave to IronHand and their cruelty.

Her fingers curled tighter into the soil. Whatever it took, she was going to see this through. The guards thought they held all the power, but they had no idea what was coming. The magic in her veins pulsed faintly as she eked power from the blood-stained soil, and for the first time, her magic didn't feel like a burden. It felt like a weapon.

In the dead of night, as Altair crawled into view overhead, Mila and Nasir scurried towards the eastern quarter, shadows among shadows. Nasir was nothing more than a dark silhouette ten metres ahead of her, and Mila watched his shape carefully from where she crouched between two tents. The cold glow of moonlight rinsed away all colour, blanching the ochre tents to grey and darkest blue.

Somewhere in the distance, the faint warble of a native bird echoed—a signal, not a song, urging her and Nasir to keep moving. A guard had just passed by one of the scouts.

As Nasir moved off again, so too did Mila, ducking into the alcove where Nasir had been moments before. The slow way of moving frustrated her, and she was thankful that Nasir was with her to maintain this cautious pace. Without him, she probably would have rushed ahead by now, into the waiting arms of an IronHand guard.

The thought sent a shudder down her spine and she forced herself to focus. Nasir moved ahead again and disappeared inside a tent further up the alley. On one of its support poles, a ribbon fluttered, still the faintest shade of red despite the leeching light.

Mila tried to force herself to count to ten before moving off again. At eight, she crept forward, eyes locked on her goal. She seized the tent flap, and flitted through into the thick, warm air within. She let out the breath she had been holding, her heart beating fast in excitement and nervousness.

The tent was spacious, the fabric extending further than her own dwelling. For the first time Mila wondered whether this was Muharram's tent, or Thani's. Or both, perhaps. A family must live here, for the tent to be this size.

Seven or so silhouettes huddled together in the dim glow of a single lamp. Flickering shadows played over sunken cheekbones, anxious eyes and clenched hands. The air was ripe with the mingled scent of unwashed bodies and nervous sweat.

The tent flap stirred again and a tall, wiry woman slipped through to stand beside Mila, blinking in the sudden lamp light. Her dark hair was pulled back into a tight braid, though several trademark Satarian curls still managed to escape. Her light brown complexion looked weathered, deepened and lined with hardship, making her age elusive. Fine wrinkles gathered around her eyes and mouth, but her gaze held a fiery intensity.

"Beht'erev, sigii," Muharram's deep voice resonated through the near darkness, greeting the women.

The air shifted once more behind her and Mila turned to see a dirty young man—very young, maybe not even a man yet—carefully lowering the tent flap. He swiped his messy dark hair out of his eyes. The motion revealed his brand, oddly asymmetrical above unruly eyebrows. His skin was pale despite the outdoor labour, and his thin legs were lined with lean muscle. He wore a ragged coat several sizes too big for him, the dirty sleeves rolled up unevenly, the fabric hanging awkwardly off his slim body.

Surely this teenager wasn't one of the trainees. He was too young to be involved in something so risky.

But he was involved regardless, wasn't he? The guards had made sure of that. Children, adults and elderly alike were trapped in the walls of Al'Mazraea, labouring until they couldn't anymore. Why *shouldn't* a teenager be included in the fight?

"Welcome," Muharram greeted the newcomer. "Please, everyone, take a seat."

Mila scanned the faces. In addition to Nasir and the two people who just arrived, there were another three women and three men, all of varying ages. She didn't seem to recognise anyone, until she peered closer at the oldest in the group.

"Olaf?" Mila said, with a sudden spasm of familiarity.

The *soffo* looked up at her from the depths of an enormous, prickly-looking cloak. Though his weathered face was etched with weariness, and his eyes barely held a shadow of the sharpness she remembered, he immediately cracked into a smile that showed his many missing teeth. A sharp pang of guilt twisted within her—she should have sought him out sooner. *Soffa* Karina was his friend, and he would be mourning her loss just as deeply.

Mila settled on the earthen ground beside the old man. "Oh, Olaf! It's so good to see you."

Before the elder could respond, Muharram gave a soft clap of his hands and said, "*Dasbeht,* everyone is here."

"This is it?" Mila said before she could stop herself. She had only counted twelve people including herself and Nasir.

"For now," Muharram said calmly. "We will gather more, as time goes on."

"Why is *she* here?" a voice said, ringing with disappointment. It was the same woman who had arrived just after Mila. The woman's high cheekbones and thin, almost gaunt face gave her an air of sharpness, and her lips returned to a tight line after her short phrase.

"We need everyone we can get," Thani spoke up. Mila hadn't seen her in the corner, sitting furthest from the lamp's glow.

"Still, the Murderer? She doesn't exactly have a good reputation."

Nasir gripped Mila's arm and she swallowed a wave of indignation.

"Everyone has a role to play if this plan is going to be successful, Lina." Thani replied.

The woman named Lina didn't miss a beat. "I'm just saying, you can count on some people easier than others, *Thani.* And I don't even know *these* people. Who are *you?*" She turned to the teenager seated to her left.

A scowl creased his brow at being put in the spotlight and his messy hair fell into his eyes again, hiding his skewed brand. Mila couldn't help but wonder about it. Had the boy fought against the guards that day, while they brought the red-hot instrument to his face? Or had they merely become lazy as the hours had passed?

"I'm Khalen," he said, eyes down as he picked at the dirt around his nails. Then his voice suddenly picked up volume. "You're probably wondering why *I'm* here too—but I am *not* a child. I'm sixteen, and I can do just as much as any of you. More, probably." His eyes flitted over Lina's wrinkled face and Nasir's swollen nose.

They went around the group, introducing themselves one after the other. It reminded Mila of the first day in school each year, when they would have to say a little about themselves to the class. And just like back then, the introductions blurred together. Too many names, too quickly. She tore at the skin around her nails.

"Great, well, now that we're all *acquainted*," Thani said with a look at Lina, "Let's get to business. So—"

But a woman with high cheekbones and strong jawline interrupted this time, looking at Mila. Her name was Mahgda. "I want to know, is it true? What the guards accused you of—the creomancy in Haman?" Her voice was scratchy, as though lined with the dirt they had been working in, but there was no malice there, only curiosity.

Mila sighed. Would she ever escape this reputation? "It's true that I split the earth, but I did *not* cause the rockfall. I would never do that. I would *never* hurt someone on purpose. Our power is supposed to be used for good."

"They would have deserved it though, if you had, you know," Lina said.

"That's a horrible thing to say," Mila said, taken aback. "You think a building full of people—men and women and children, just going about their day—that they deserve to be hurt? Why, because they're Amanese?"

"Why not? That's what they think about us," Khalen jumped in, his eyes dark. "If we returned the favour and *they* had to live for even a minute in our shoes, maybe they'd stop treating us like shit."

"Wrong does not fix wrong," Muharram growled from the corner of the space. "We are not teaching you to hone your skills so that you can hurt people."

"What do you think is going to happen when we enact our plan?" Lina said with a shake of her head. The long plait snaked side to side. "People are going to get hurt—on both sides—and that's just a fact." Her long fingers, slender and scarred, twitched with impatience.

"I have learnt in my life that it's true: wrong doesn't fix wrong," Olaf repeated quietly, "But neither does kindness and complacency."

A stocky man, a few years older than Nasir, with kind eyes and a broad face, cleared his throat. "If our goal is to fix the wrong, well, I'm sorry, but that's never going to happen. We can't force empathy, and the IronHand guards have none for us. They don't think they have imprisoned real people—they think they have merely fenced in the basest of animals. We are their property to slaughter or utilise as they see fit. This is a prison, and we must learn to truly harness the full power of the earth to escape, while we still can."

"Exactly," Mila said, grateful to have someone on her side. Arviz, she thought his name was. "To *escape*. Your intention matters so much when you're performing creomancy. To escape, to survive—that's noble, necessary. I doubt Gaia would permit it if your intention was to harm others. She, at least, knows that everyone deserves to live."

Khalen gave a sharp, humourless laugh and looked away. There was something guarded in the defiant gesture, a pain deeper than the sense of injustice he had already voiced.

"Enough talking," Thani said firmly. "You're here to practice and learn. You already know how to access the power to grow and maintain crops. Tonight, we are going to work on shifting soil. This is difficult, and you must have a greater focus on your intention, because there's no physical thing to pour your energy into. There's no seedling to grow, no withered husk to bring back to vitality."

"So, what do we focus on, then?" asked a slim man, thoughtful and intense.

"Focus on the movement that you want to make," Thani replied. She got to her feet and walked to the centre of the group where she knelt on the bare ground. "I want to relocate the soil from here—" she used a finger to draw a circle in front of her, then another to the right, just within arm's reach "—to here." She looked up, scanning the faces before her with her fox-like eyes. "I'm going to manifest the flow of energy moving through the soil to push it aside, like waves moving sand in the ocean."

With that, she dropped her focus from the curious, dubious stares and whispered, "*Plezht y pemetteray, Gaia, ay dar r'mahiya…*"

It really was magical; to watch the grains of dirt moving on their own, flowing like water from one spot to the other. When a small pile had gathered and an equally small hole was left in front of her, Thani thanked Gaia. Muharram handed her a shard of metal and she made a small cut in the flesh near the crook of her arm. Pearly droplets of blood dripped downward and the grateful earth became darker once more.

Thani addressed the group again through heavy breaths. "Do you understand?"

There were various murmurs of agreement. Lina rolled her eyes and was the first to stand. She stalked to a bare patch of earth, in the opposite direction to Mila, but for all her gusto, she didn't seem to do much once she was there.

Mila drifted toward the teenager, Khalen, instead. Something about the young boy called out for support, though she suspected he would never ask for it. He was murmuring under his breath, repeating something that sounded like 'waves', and his eyes darted around with a restless energy. Sensing his unease, Mila ventured, "Remember to breathe and be calm, Khalen. If you're agitated, so is your magic, and you won't have as much control as you need."

The boy scowled, but he took a deep breath, and then another. His shoulders squared and he straightened slightly. "Okay," he said quietly, and he knelt just as Thani had moments earlier, burrowing the tips of his trembling fingers into the hardened earth. He murmured the words of greeting and request with his jaw tight, green eyes scrunched in concentration as he willed the soil to shift before him.

At first, nothing happened. Sweat beaded on his brow, seeping into his mop of dark hair, but he didn't withdraw. He pushed harder, fingers pressing in as if trying to force the magic from the earth. Suddenly, a plume of dirt erupted in front of him, shooting up to touch the canvas roof. Soil scattered in clumps and dust floated all around, catching the dim light of the lamp. It was nowhere near the graceful, controlled movement Thani had demonstrated.

Still, it was something. Khalen's chest rose and fell heavily as he looked up, panting and defensive, daring anyone to criticise him. But Mila nodded her approval, and Arviz whooped from his spot nearby. Khalen had done it—albeit clumsily, and with far more force than necessary—but he had moved the earth.

He stood, wiping away the sweat with his forearm. A gleam of excitement lit up his formerly cold expression and he smiled at Mila, a big toothy grin. She was smiling just as much. It was the look of someone who had seen a flicker of the power they could wield, and the change they could spark. This was the start of something. The plan was in motion.

23

As the minutes leaked into hours, the trainees became more confident, even gaining a bit of finesse. Thani and Muharram roved among the group, watching and giving tips, while Nasir seemed to gravitate towards Irani, a young woman with sad, almond-shaped eyes beneath long lashes.

Olaf was in good hands working with kind and patient Arviz. Mila made sure to check on the old man every now and then, but she found her eyes drawn to Mahgda with intense curiosity, captivated by her deliberate movements and effortlessly formidable presence. Mila longed to inspire such respect just by existing. Was it even possible for *her* to emulate that measured grace and confidence?

Khalen showed the most progress of all. Though his style remained forceful and crude, he began to channel his power more effectively. Mila could see the raw potential in Khalen. His youth might be an asset to the cause, rather than a hindrance.

Lina, on the other hand, was overconfident and hasty with her power. Her fingers brushed the soil without engaging a deep connection, and the earth was resistant to respond. She became frustrated quickly, and Mila overheard Thani explaining—with limited patience—that creomancy was a joint effort, a collaboration with the earth. There had to be a give-and-take, and Lina couldn't just demand that the soil followed her instructions. The sharpness in the woman's face deepened at this, and Mila could see her struggling to think of the earth as a partner.

By the end of the session, Mila was tired but optimistic. The trainees had each shown improvement, albeit in different ways. It all pointed to a future where they might truly harness their abilities—not just to move the earth, but to change their fate.

While Thani straightened up and rearranged her meagre possessions and Nasir helped Mila re-fasten the thin winter cloak around her shoulders, the recruits slipped out of the tent like bats into the night. Only Olaf remained, seated on a low stool fashioned from a tree stump. She turned to wish the *soffo* good night, but the sight of his tear-streaked face stopped her cold.

She went to him, kneeling in front of him. "*Soffo*, are you okay?" she asked softly. She knew he wasn't, of course—how could he be?—but she wanted him to know that she cared.

"All my life has come to this." His shoulders sagged, and he took a long, steadying breath. His wispy white hair barely obscured the puckered, purpled skin of his *noterran* brand. "I'm too old for this. I'm useless. I can barely work the magic, and my hands are old and stiff… It's only a matter of time before the guards notice and—and—"

He couldn't finish the sentence, but he didn't need to.

And kill me.

Nasir said, "We won't let that happen, *soffo*."

Mila took Olaf's trembling hand. It was cold to the touch.

Olaf looked at Mila, tears swimming in his sunken eyes. "It shouldn't be like this. Our people didn't leave Stara Zhem for our story to end like *this*."

Mila drew in a sharp breath. Stara Zhem. The name made her think of the ancient, brittle map concealed in the secret bottom drawer of their shelves. The ancient symbols twisted through her mind. Stara Zhem. Mila had learnt at a young age not to bother asking about the old lands. No one spoke of it, and questions led nowhere. Between the low life expectancy and the laws against Satarians recording anything, no one seemed to know very much about the fall of Stara Zhem, only that the original Satarians had been forced to abandon their homeland. The knowledge of why, or even how, had passed out of all memory. Or so they thought. Mila and Nasir exchanged a glance. In the corner of her eye, Mila saw Thani become very still, listening intently.

"What do you know, *soffo*?" Mila asked, trying to control the curiosity from making her voice jump. "Why did our people leave Stara Zhem? What would make them choose the fences of Al'Mazraea over the homeland?"

Olaf shook his head, and Mila sighed inwardly, thinking he wouldn't—or couldn't—continue. But then, he said, "My own *soffamia* told me stories, a long, *long* time ago."

His voice trailed away as his gaze shifted, called back into memory. Mila and Nasir hardly dared to breathe.

"She said there was *us'ikhaerishik*..." He paused, the old word heavy in the air. "A plague. A great famine. A wasting that claimed millions of lives... So the survivors fled the dying lands. They became refugees."

"And they came here..." Nasir prompted.

Olaf nodded. "*Soffamia* said it was the Old Crone who got them out. I remember she called it a final miracle, performed by the most powerful creomancer who ever lived. The last true Satarians were able to cross the Erulean Ocean and take refuge here, in Ard Aman." The old man sighed heavily. "Only, the details of it never sounded much like a miracle to me, even as a young boy."

"Why? If the Old Crone saved the people…?"

"*Saved?*" Olaf said, suddenly agitated, and Mila's skin prickled. "It was Dark, what the Crone did. Horribly dark. It was a siphoning of blood and bone, fed by the lives of those sacrificed for the so-called greater good. It was a curse, not a miracle, and we're paying the price now. *Pariar.* Soon we will all be nothing more than dust; our bones, our culture, and our history. Gone."

Mila wanted to ask more, but her curiosity was eclipsed by concern for the old man. His face had flushed a deep crimson and his lips trembled as sweat dotted his brow beneath the brand. They needed to get Olaf home.

Mila took one of Olaf's arms and Nasir took the other and together they helped him to his feet. As the three of them moved toward the tent flap, the old man suddenly turned to Mila with urgency. "I did rig the game, you know," he said.

Mila's confusion must have shown on her face because he added, "On that day? You remember… The last good day? You saw us, playing together, the game of Sticks."

The memory clicked in Mila's mind.

I think he's got more rules up his sleeve than playing pieces.

"I hardly think that matters now, Olaf," Mila replied gently.

But Olaf continued as if Mila hadn't spoken. "Karina, she always knew I was cheating, and she just let it go, because it wasn't about the game or the winner and losers… It was about being together, smiling, laughing. She always knew that."

"She always did manage to see the fun," Mila agreed.

"Ay, Karina," Olaf said, shaking his head, and his voice carried the jarring sadness of loss after decades of friendship. When he spoke again, though, nostalgia laced every syllable. "I will never forget this one summer storm when we were young. Have you heard this story, Mila?"

Mila cast a glance at Nasir, who shrugged. Olaf seemed to only have eyes for her now. Mila shook her head, "No?"

"Ay! I must have been barely your age, I think, and Karina a few years older. Ay, Mila, she was *so* beautiful."

Mila's eyebrows shot into her hair. "Did you two…?"

Olaf chuckled, "*Ny, ny*. She was beautiful—always was—but I was never one for the women."

Mila made a small noise of amusement, but she suddenly found the whole thing incredibly sad. All these stories, all this history, gone without a trace. A person was essentially the sum of their stories—their laughter, their love, the dreams they dared to whisper, and the fears they kept buried. And if those stories couldn't be shared, or if they were forgotten, it was like that person had never existed at all. People were never meant to live in fear and isolation; life was meant to be enjoyed and shared. She felt a pang of loss for all the Satarians who had come before her, their memories, their struggles, their small, quiet joys. Without someone to carry them forward, all of it vanished, leaving only a hollow emptiness. Did a person exist at all if no one remembered them?

"…The storm clouds rolled in thick and fast," Olaf was saying, "And all of a sudden we were caught in a deluge! And all I can remember is Karina laughing so hard, spinning around in the rain while the rest of us yelled and fussed and tried to find shelter. You know what she said to me later, Mila? She said, *life is about learning to dance in the rain*. She was always full of little things like that," Olaf added quietly.

But the beautiful *soffa* isn't here to dance anymore, Mila thought to herself. And this is one storm no one can dance in. This storm threatened to wash away everything, to extinguish all Satarian history as if they had never been here at all.

The bright star of Canopus sank below the distant peak of the Dend as Mila and Nasir finally slipped back into their own tent. Mila lit the lamp in the darkness, then turned to her brother with an exhilarated grin. From across the room, he returned the smile, though it didn't quite reach his eyes.

"What's wrong?" she asked, folding her arms. "I thought that went really well."

"Are you going to be able to work now, Cricket?" he asked. As he spoke, he rubbed his temples with both hands. "You look exhausted."

"Gee, thanks."

Nasir tilted his head, vaguely amused. "You know what I mean. Maybe we should get some sleep."

In truth, Mila had been so focused on the training session that she had forgotten about the task they now had to do. She swallowed. Nasir was right; she was exhausted. But nothing worthwhile was ever achieved without hard work.

"I'll sleep when I'm dead," she said with a shrug.

Nasir came closer and put his finger under her chin, forcing her to look up at him. He looked from eye to eye, scrutinising. "I know that look," he said.

"What *look*?"

"The petulant toddler look."

"*Excuse* me?"

"You look like a young child who's just been told to take a nap."

Mila raised her eyebrows. "Are you serious?"

"The scowl?" Nasir gestured, and Mila quickly relaxed her face.

"I am not—"

"The folded arms. Just stomp your foot and shriek 'I'm not tired'." He smirked with affection, knowing how he was riling her up. "I'll grab you some warm milk."

"I am not a child," Mila said, reminding herself of Khalen. The scowl was back. "I can do this, Nasir. We're in a fight for our lives. The time for childish things like *naps* is long gone."

"You're still a child to me," her brother murmured quietly. "And I'm never going to stop protecting you."

Mila sighed. "You can't protect me from this."

Nasir shook his head sadly. "No, I suppose you're right."

"But I'm glad you want to," Mila said, looking up at him with wide, appreciative eyes—the way only a little sister could.

Nasir exhaled, conceding defeat, then swung his arm around her neck and used his other hand to ruffle her curly hair. "Ay, Cricket," he said. "Fine. But the second you start to look like you're using *your* lifeforce and not the earth's, I'm pulling the plug."

Mila rolled her eyes, just to solidify the role of brazen little sister, but she was secretly grateful for Nasir's imperious presence. It was nice, for a moment, to feel like she had a parent again.

24

Mila stood in the centre of the tent, her forefinger absently picking at the skin around her thumb nail as she stared at the three mattresses at the edge of the space.

Hers. Nasir's. And the one that had belonged to their parents.

"It's a good idea," Nasir said, his voice rough. He didn't sound wholly convinced.

Mila nodded, but the gesture did nothing to ease the tightening in her chest. They had decided to dig the tunnel underneath the unused mattress, using it like a trapdoor to hide their work during the day. It had sounded simple, genius even, when Mila had suggested it half an hour ago.

But now that the time came to actually move it, it felt horribly wrong, like they were disturbing something sacred. If they moved the mattress, the imprints of their parents would be gone forever, and there would be nothing left of them.

Nasir placed his hand on the mattress and stiffened. Mila could see the conflict etched throughout his body, his shoulders tense and a muscle feathering in his jaw as he fought within himself. She knelt beside him, reaching out and placing her hand next to his. If it had to be done, they would do it together.

For a moment, they just sat there, hands resting on the mattress, neither speaking. Midnight was approaching fast. The thick fabric of the tent muffled the soft chirping of insects and the occasional footsteps of the night watchmen haunting the alleys.

Mila knew her mother would have told her to be strong, that it was okay to do this. But the thought of lifting the mattress felt like prying open a deep wound. If they did this, all the anguish she had locked away would spill into the open air and she would surely bleed out.

The fabric beneath her hands was the last mark of their lives. It was the faint memory of wide eyes as pada spun a bedtime story and she drifted off to sleep to the sound of his voice. This mattress had held the four of them on chilly mornings, two little bodies burrowed between two big ones, safe and sleepy. It was mahma's fingers squeezing hers during the frightening sounds of the night. It was her and Nasir, sitting atop the pile of mattresses and other belongings during that big storm, while rain gushed through the fabric and their parents tried to stop streams of water reaching them. It was her father's rhythmic, comforting snoring shuddering the silence.

Mila bit her bottom lip. Their voices had faded from her mind, and almost every physical trace of their existence had disappeared. It frightened Mila how quickly a person could become reduced only to memories, and holding on to those fragile moments in her mind still might not be enough. They too would someday slip away, leaving nothing behind. One day, it would be as if her parents had never existed at all.

For a moment all she wanted to do was lay in the imprints of her parents and inhale their scent, wrap herself in their thin blanket and go to sleep like she used to do as a young child. Everything in her ached for that time.

But she had to be stronger now.

"I guess we should just… lift it up," she said eventually.

Nasir nodded, his eyes dark but resolute.

"On three, then. One… two…"

A deep breath. Goodbye, mahma, she thought. Goodbye pada.

"Three."

The imprints faded immediately as, together, she and Nasir tipped the mattress up against the tent wall and the straw inside shifted. The flimsy thing was so light in her hands, yet the action held the weight of a future they would never have. Their parents would never see the lives they would have, they would never know what great and wonderful things their children went on to do.

Mila pressed a hand to her mouth, fighting down a swell of emotion.

A moment later, they pulled back the plastic mat, revealing the bare earth beneath. It was strange to see it, to know that this was where their escape would begin, in the very place their parents had once rested.

The act of digging a tunnel with creomancy required them to compact the soil away from a central point, hardening it all as they did so. It was much more difficult than the movement lesson they had given the trainees earlier, but it also meant there would be no tell-tale pile of extracted dirt to give them away.

"It's not too late to back out," Nasir said suddenly.

"Nasir," Mila said, quiet but firm. "You know that's not true. There was never a chance to back out, not really. We were born into this. It has always been too late for us."

Neither of them moved for a long moment, then Nasir exhaled slowly, bending down to press his fingertips into the soil. "Let's get to work."

Mila knelt beside him, placed her own fingers down, feeling the earth's lifeforce reach out to faintly caress her own. Kneeling here, in this particular spot, she felt her parents' presence more than any other time. It felt like they were making sure Mila and Nasir followed through with the plan. Like making a promise. A promise to survive, no matter the risks. No matter how many times they were beaten or knocked down.

No matter what it cost them.

The thought twisted inside her like a knife. Tears suddenly pricked the corners of her eyes. Would they be proud of her for what she was doing? Or were they disgusted by the way she had betrayed them?

Mila pushed the thought aside. There was no room for doubt now. This was their only way out. Her only way to redemption.

Time passes differently at night, when the world is mostly silent and the shadows could hold miracles or menace. It felt like an eternity that Mila and Nasir had been digging in the amber hush, though it had only been an hour.

The only sounds came from the rhythmic scraping of fingers and the soft sound of soil shifting. Mila's every muscle screamed in protest and her burning limbs felt as if they were tied down with weights. Her eyelids drooped with exhaustion, but she pushed through, knowing that every litre of soil they compacted was another inch closer to freedom. But the earth's energy was drying up, the magic scraping through her veins like sandpaper. If she didn't stop now, her own lifeforce would be tapped into and drained to keep the creomancy going.

Mila stared down into the narrow, shallow pit, the compact dirt walls barely two meters deep, suddenly unable to breathe. A flood of dismay rose within her, drowning her with the thought of digging even deeper, night after night. It wasn't just the physical effort—it was the psychological toll. As the dirt opened up before her, inch by inch, she was pulled further into an abyss with no guarantee of success. Nine meters down—that was what they needed to reach, and it felt impossible. Soon they would be into the hard earth, the layers of rock and mineral, and their progress would be slowed to an excruciating crawl. The sheer enormity of the effort pressed on Mila as though she had piled the dirt upon herself instead, digging what could be her own grave.

Her fingers, caked in grime, trembled slightly as she brushed the dirt from her knees. Her back throbbed with each breath. She had been certain Nasir would call it quits before she wanted to, but now she glanced with half-lidded eyes at her brother, his face set in a grimace of determination and exhaustion, and murmured two words: "I can't."

Nasir nodded and exhaled a noisy sigh, sitting back on the edge of the hole. "We've done good, Cricket. It's a start."

Nasir helped her up and, without a word, they carefully moved their parents' mattress back in place, covering the site. It sagged slightly as the unsupported section bowed inward, but that would go unnoticed by all but the keenest observers. Nasir threw some of the floor cushions on top to disguise it further.

Finally, Mila and Nasir collapsed onto their own mattresses, each staring absently at where the hole was hidden, invisible.

"How can we possibly do this day after day on end?" Mila murmured. "It's going to take so long… What if we run out of energy or… what if we run out of time?"

"I don't know," Nasir croaked. "But there's no other option. We have to do it, so we will."

Of course he was right; they had said those words often enough over the past few days.

No other option.

No choice.

Mila closed her eyes, leaving Nasir to extinguish the lamp. Her body ached, her mind was numb, but for the first time in months, she drifted into a deep, dreamless sleep.

25

Gunshots echoed across the field. Mila counted them, each one sending a little jolt through her body.

One, two, three…

Between each shot came the sound of another bullet being painstakingly ratcheted into the chamber.

Eight, nine, ten…

She refused to look anywhere but at the ground, but in her mind she could see the scene clearly. A long line of Ineffectives, their branded foreheads hooded and their wrists bound, standing on the edge of a ditch. They may have been forced to dig it themselves, or perhaps other Satarians had dug the trench and now had to listen to the thuds as body after body toppled in.

Fifteen, sixteen, seventeen.

Something about the pause between each shot made the whole thing even worse, if that were possible. In those seconds, the IronHand guard had to intentionally choose to load a new bullet. They made the conscious decision to murder the next person, and the next.

Twenty-one, twenty-two.

Silence.

Twenty-two Satarians were no longer worth keeping alive. Maybe, to IronHand, they never had been. Someone had just lost a friend or family member—maybe their last one in this cruel world. Maybe an entire bloodline that had survived for hundreds and thousands of years had just been ended with a single bullet. Now, as their bodies toppled into the pit and the clods were dumped over them, their blood steeped into the parched soil and their essence was returned to Gaia—far too soon, but where they ultimately belonged. It was the smallest blessing. Others were not so lucky; they stayed alive through their punishment. Young women and men, girls and boys…Those taken to the guard station never returned the same—if they returned at all.

A month had passed since Mila and Nasir had begun digging the tunnel. The days had stretched into weeks, each one as indiscernible as grains in a mound of sand. The full moon had come and gone, and now the peak of the Dend was hidden inside low-hanging cloud. Winter winds occasionally brought flakes of snow down from the Uul Serrad to dance wickedly before their stinging eyes. The tunnel occupied Mila's every waking thought and snaked like a labyrinth through her dreams. She couldn't escape it. It was both a lifeline and a grave, either a path to freedom or a crypt that might bury them all. Only time would tell which.

Each morning at sunrise, a fresh smattering of dark blood was deposited around their tent by unseen Satarian comrades, and greedily soaked up by the desperate earth. They had reached a depth of nine metres after the third night, and had since carved nearly two hundred meters along through rock and soil, pressing forward night after night.

Now, a month later, Mila no longer felt sick as she touched the tacky, soaked soil in the evenings. She only felt persistent, crushing pressure. Pressure from the rebels, pressure from herself. Pressure of an unbroken line of Satarians ancestors begging her not to let their legacy die. If she and Nasir failed, it wasn't only the escape that would be forsaken—the entirety of Satarian culture would cease to exist. That thought pulled Mila down, forcing her to dig deeper, to press harder, to succeed at any cost.

Any cost.

Mila sighed, inhaling the scent of damp soil. That scent. It clung to her skin, to her clothes, it seemed to be inside her very nose and lungs even when she tried to sleep. That scent meant she was both alive, and imprisoned; it grounded her, and smothered her.

At that moment, a sharp clang rang out. It was the sound of something dull striking metal, and across the field the Satarians paused, momentarily lifting their eyes from their work. It was Muharram. He had thrown a potato at the collection bin, deliberately missing to create the noise. His usual grave expression was carved deeper by the harsh light, but it was the red ribbon tied around his forearm that seized Mila's attention.

It happened every few days, though with unpredictable frequency. Muharram or Thani would be seen wearing the faded red ribbon, a clear message for the rebels: a training session would happen tonight.

A flutter of anticipation began to beat in the pit of her stomach, the familiar mix of fear and exhilaration she always felt before they gathered.

"Apologies, *sigiò*," Muharram said to the guard. "My aim is not what it once was."

"Be more careful, you idiot. Your creo shit is only good while it's edible. The moment it rots, so do you."

Muharram bowed his head in submission and shuffled back to his place in the rows, but as he did, he caught Mila's eye with the shadow of a wink. The audacity of it almost made Mila smile, but it wasn't worth the risk. She would save such insubordination for tonight, instead.

The training sessions were as capricious as they were vital.

Each recruit brought their own unique presence to the dimly lit space, and the volatile mixture of personalities determined how the session was going to go. Sometimes the dream of freedom felt closer than ever, and other times, like tonight, the session was full of tension and doubt.

They were working in groups, taking turns to raise a mound of earth into a barrier. It sounded simple enough, but the earth's resistance was a constant reminder of its power.

Arviz gritted his teeth, eyes narrowed in concentration, and the earth beneath his hands began to rise steadily. Sweat trickled down his temple as he forced it upward, to ankle height, then knee height. Maghda's eyebrow cocked, the only hint at how impressed she was. Suddenly, Arviz pulled his hands from the ground, panting and pale.

"There," he gasped, attempting to give a triumphant smirk that looked more like a grimace.

"You are trying too hard," Maghda remarked in her smoky voice.

"I'm doing better than she is," Arviz said, pointing to Béa's small mound as it swayed and collapsed.

The round-faced woman exhaled in amusement, unfazed by his insult.

"Maybe," Maghda said. "But she is not half-killing herself every time. You need a better connection."

Arviz scowled. His trembling hands rested on his knees as he doubled over. "And who's the expert on that? You?"

The elegant lady flashed Arviz a confident smile, then raised a dome-like mound in front of her with ease.

"You can hardly call that a wall though, can you?" Béa chuckled.

Mahgda narrowed her deep-set eyes and drew herself up to her full height. "I was learning creomancy before either of you were even conceived, *pika homme*. I don't need *your* approval. You should focus on yourselves."

The older woman ran a finger along Arviz's wall, and it instantly crumbled to dust, leaving the man agape.

On the other side of the tent, Olaf and Nasir watched as the softly-spoken Irani raised a wall slowly in front of her.

"Very good, Irani," Nasir gushed, his cheeks flushing the faintest pink as she faced him.

She beamed, then turned to Olaf. "Your turn, *soffo*."

Olaf regarded Irani's creation with a mixture of awe and frustration. He sighed, and his knees clicked loudly as he lowered himself to the ground. With an encouraging nod from Irani, he began muttering the Satarian greetings, and the soil stirred like ripples in murky water. However, a few moments later, he withdrew his gnarled fingers and placed his head in his hands. A small pile sat in front of him, barely an inch high.

"It's no good," he said, his thin shoulders slumped. "Experience should count for something but this? This seems beyond me."

"It's not just you, *soffo*," Arviz muttered, his hands grasping the ruins of his wall. "Why is this so difficult? Are we ever going to get this right?"

"You will," Muharram said sternly. "You *all* will. Now is not the time to give in. This is not the hardest thing you have done or will ever do—so try again. And again and again."

The mood in the training tent was low, and Mila felt herself being pulled under with it until she caught sight of Khalen. His creation was almost perfect, and he gave Mila a grin that she couldn't help returning.

"*Behtyer'im,* Khalen," Mila exclaimed as she stepped closer. Her eyes roved over the dirt barrier and she rested her hands on top, eyeing him. "You seem calmer lately."

He jerked his head to shake the unruly dark hair from his eyes. "I'm just focused."

Mila considered him. "No, it's more than that. I see it—you've been trying really hard."

The teenager shrugged and said nothing, guarded once more.

"You're allowed to be proud," Mila said gently.

"Pride is useless," he said brusquely. "All that matters is actions. I've got to get better at this. I *need* to."

She waited for him to go on. When he didn't, she said, "Well, keep taking on feedback like you have been, and you'll keep improving. In the meantime, *I'll* be proud of you."

Even in the dim light, Mila saw his cheeks redden. He gave a tight smile and returned his attention to the earth. Mila studied him a little longer, but didn't press. Everyone was entitled to hide their pain.

Lina, however, made sure that everyone saw her pain and paid for it. The woman was constantly complaining and reluctant to listen to anything anyone had to say, Mila least of all. Earlier in the evening, Mila had given Lina a few reminders and prompts, and Lina had received each one with a sneer or a sigh.

Now, Mila looked up from fastening her cloak to see if was just the two of them left in the quiet tent. Thani and Nasir had escorted the poor *soffo* home, and the others had dispersed into the night. But Lina was still here, pulling on her own cloak far too slowly.

Their eyes met, and Lina's flashed with unmistakable disdain.

Mila lifted her chin, folded her arms. "If you have something to say, now's your chance, while no one's around."

It barely took a second for Lina to let loose. "I'm sick of you acting like you're better than me," she spat. "You need to back off."

Mila's face flushed. "I'm just trying to help you."

"I don't need a *child* telling me how to do it, Mila. Children are nothing but trouble."

"You're trouble all by yourself!" Mila said, fighting and failing to keep the frustration from her voice. "It's the same thing every week with you, Lina! You can't *tell* the earth what to do, like you're its master. You treat the earth like it owes you something, but the connection is a partnership. You need to *ask*, to *listen*."

"I do listen to the earth—I just don't listen to *you*. And you can't handle it. Ever since Muharram brought you here like our miraculous saviour, you expect everyone to worship you, to bow to your wisdom. But I don't see what the big fuss is about you. You're no more talented than anyone else here, and definitely not as strong."

Mila seethed inside, but somehow managed to reply, "You waste all your energy complaining and hating on everyone, Lina, but you're the one who's yet to show *any* talent or strength."

Lina crossed her arms, the line of her mouth tightening further. "I'm trying, okay? It's only the fourth lesson, and I've got more important things on my mind."

"No, it's *already* the fourth lesson. How much time do you really think we have? And—more important things on your mind? What could possibly be as important as this?"

Lina hesitated. She straightened her cloak before returning her gaze to Mila, sharp and dismissive. "I'm trying," she repeated, flicking her long plait back over her shoulder. "I just don't understand. My creomancy was fine until I started coming here."

"Well, what is it about here, do you think? Maybe you're finding it difficult to work with others?" Mila said, hands curling into fists in an effort to keep her voice steady.

"Or maybe I just don't like working with *you*."

Not for the first time, Mila found herself thinking that Lina acted more like a teenager than Khalen, the actual teenager.

"I'm trying to help you, Lina. We're all trying to help each other. We're a team, and we're only as strong as our weakest link."

Lina scoffed. "You think *I'm* the weak link here? No, no way. The *soffo* can barely move, Irani can't keep her eyes off your brother, and the great leader graces us with his presence even less than Béa's skills do."

Mila shook her head. She couldn't believe the audacity of this woman. To insult her fellow rebels, to imply Muharram didn't care? She opened her mouth to interrupt, but Lina continued over her. "I *know* what I'm doing. Creomancy has been passed down through us Alberti women, year after year, on and on. If you don't mind, I think I'll trust the advice of my grandsires over *you*, the selfish *idiot* whose ill-use of magic got us into this whole situation. What the hell do you know about the right way to do *anything*?"

A heavy silence fell between them and Mila felt her cheeks flush. But she raised her chin. Lina's words hurt, but it wasn't enough to cripple her anymore. She held the woman's furious gaze and took a steadying breath.

"Lina, don't you get it? If we don't work together, there may not *be* any more Alberti women for you to pass your legacy to. There may not be *anyone* to pass our legacy to!"

Lina moved her arms across her body. "That sounds like a threat."

"It is, but not from me. IronHand want us all dead, or have you not realised that yet?"

"Not all of us," Lina murmured, and she stepped around Mila toward the tent flap.

For a beat, Mila wasn't sure she heard her right. At the last second, she snagged Lina's arm. "What?"

"I said, not all of us. I've got it figured out. I am *not* the weak link—I'm a survivor, Mila."

Lina's words were quiet and calm, almost casual, but Mila felt the ripple of something darker lurking beneath. Her stomach twisted. "We're all trying to survive, Lina, that's the point of what we're doing here. That's why I'm trying to help you."

"I don't need your help. I don't need anyone's help. There are other ways to get by, if you're willing to work for it."

"Willing to work for it? How much harder can we possibly work?"

Lina's eyes met hers defiantly and the implication of her words became clearer. Mila tried to swallow the lump in her throat. "You're working *with* them?"

"No, Mila, I would never do that. The only traitor here is *you*. But if you're looking for a bit of overtime, so to speak, it's there, and IronHand has ways of rewarding that."

Mila couldn't find the words to respond. Her mind was whirring, trying to understand. Her eyes drifted over Lina's figure, piecing together the unsettling details, and Mila couldn't believe she hadn't noticed before; while everyone else had begun to look like shadows of themselves, with each rib visible beneath stretched skin and their eyes hollowed out from hunger and exhaustion, Lina's face had fullness to it. There was a softness to her cheeks, a hint of roundness that defied the anguish around her, and her skin was more pink than yellow. Mila's breath caught as the realisation hit her like a punch to the gut; Lina wasn't starving like the rest of them.

For a long moment, they stared each other down, tension crackling between them. Mila swallowed hard, her mouth dry. "Useful or not, none of us are safe as long as IronHand controls this camp."

Lina tore her arm from Mila's grasp, looking suddenly pale. She placed a hand on her stomach. "Don't worry about it, Mila. Just keep playing your little games in the dirt. It must be nice to have your choices be so clear-cut. Now, will you leave me alone? I'm not feeling well, and I'm going home."

She turned her back on Mila then and, when the warbling signal came seconds later, the wiry woman disappeared into the cold night.

26

Mila jolted awake as the shriek of the siren split the morning air, followed by shrill whistles and shouted orders. She would never get used to that sound.

Nasir was already sitting with his back resting against the shelving unit and a warm mug of tea cradled in his blackened hands. He wordlessly held out a second mug for her. With a groan, Mila struggled to her feet, joints creaking like old branches hollowed out by mites. They had both fallen asleep in their dirt-stained clothes of the day before, and now changing seemed pointless—they would be covered in grime again soon enough.

"Thanks," she said as she nestled herself beside him and took the proffered mug, taking a deep inhale of the ginger scent before dissolving into a yawn. She leant her head back against the wood and closed her eyes. "I hope there's no training tonight, or tomorrow. I could use a little break…"

"Mmm, me too. And you and Lina could use some time apart."

Mila sat forward, eyes open suddenly. "Yes! I don't know why she's having so much difficulty with it… She was working with Khalen and he had built this perfect structure, and she just couldn't get it at all. And then she acts like everything is everyone *else's* fault!"

"You can't have a rose without a thorn, I suppose," Nasir said. He retrieved a hunk of bread from the rations pack and pulled it into two, handing one part to Mila.

"Is Khalen the rose in this scenario? I'm not sure he would like that," Mila smiled as she bit into the stale, cold chunk.

"Lina would be happy as a thorn though. She enjoys getting a jab in wherever she can, and she's definitely prickly to handle," Nasir said through his mouthful. "That's probably why she lives alone—she can't stand the idea of answering to someone else. She's fierce, and independent. Maybe you've finally encountered someone more stubborn than you are."

His eyes filled with affection and Mila tried to smile, but Nasir's words scraped at something in her mind. She bit her bottom lip, trying to puzzle it out.

"Hey," Nasir said, brow furrowed, "I was only joking. Well, half joking. It'll be okay, Cricket, Lina will come around. I know this is important to her. She's with us, even if she can be a prick about it."

"You didn't hear her last night though…" Mila hesitated. "I'm honestly starting to wonder about that. I know we want to have as many creomancers with us as possible but… well, it doesn't feel like she *is* with us, you know?"

"What are you talking about?"

Mila choked down the stale bread and recounted the murmured argument of the night before. When she had finished, Nasir's face was contorted with confusion and anger.

"You think she's trading sexual favours for extra rations of food?"

"She didn't say it out loud but, yes, that's what it sounded like."

The idea seemed repulsive to Mila, after everything she had seen the guards do. But a small part of her couldn't fault Lina for doing what she thought she needed to do to survive. Isn't that exactly what Mila had done, that fateful day in Haman? What she needed to do to survive?

Nasir ran a hand through his dark hair, biting his bottom lip. A mix of disbelief and worry clouding his face. "Muharram needs to know…"

Muharram. Lina's mocking remark about their leader's disappearances echoed in her head, and Mila's thoughts wandered. Where *did* Muharram withdraw to in the darkness? Mila didn't want to doubt him. *Couldn't* doubt him. She had placed too much trust and hope in him, in his idea. If it cracked, then so would she. The very fact that *Lina* had planted the question made it even worse.

Mila sighed. "We need to find him, as soon as possible. He'll know what to do."

At that moment, the siren blew again; time to go. As they stepped outside, Mila reached up to the fabric strips decorating the awning of their tent and quickly untied a piece the same bloodied colour as the sun rising behind them.

"What are you doing?" hissed Nasir, already a few steps ahead.

"We need to get Muharram's attention, and everything else we have is grey-grey-grey," Mila said. She tied it in a single knot around her unruly curls. The fabric was so worn, it resembled an ancient strip of bark.

"It seems like forever ago that they told us about that, the red ribbon," Nasir said quietly. "The whole thing felt so hopeful back then. I remember thinking we would have to work hard of course, but also that we'd be out before we knew it. Now it just feels like a never-ending game, and we're losing."

As the sky began to pale, they fell in line with the other refugees, their movements automatic as they trudged toward the fields down the familiar frosted paths, along the slight bend that offered a glimpse of the lagoon. The surface lay still, smooth as glass, catching the pale hues from above. The salty scent of the distant ocean teased her senses.

Mila scanned the heads around her, desperate to see that familiar salt-and-pepper wave of Muharram's hair. A few metres ahead, Nasir was doing the same. But the rebel leader was nowhere to be seen. Mila began to feel more than a little uneasy.

The hours slipped past. Each time Mila or Nasir pried a rare creation from the ground to the collection bin, they took the opportunity to surreptitiously change positions in the field, moving through the rows of workers. But there was still no sign of Muharram anywhere. Unease became anxiety, and anxiety became fear. What if something had happened to the rebel leader?

For once, the day went too fast. The guards' whistles cut through the early evening chill and the surviving Satarians were herded toward the gates at the edge of the field. As Nasir approached from the opposite direction to Mila, their eyes met across the flow of bodies. The distress in his eyes only made Mila's heart beat faster.

Then Mila saw her. Lina. Slipping furtively out of the guard hut near the field fence and sliding into place amongst the workers.

Mila swore under her breath. While she had been working—while Satarians had been *dying*—Lina had been with the guards. The tunic she wore clung tighter than usual, drawn across her chest in a way that felt deliberate, provocative. Mila couldn't believe the overtness of it.

She hasn't been able to grow or build anything this past month, Mila thought with her teeth clenched as she noted Lina's rounded stomach, but she's definitely growing in *other* ways. How many rations was she allowed in exchange for her favours? Bitterness rose in her throat. She hardly noticed the long walk home, hardly felt the clammy press of the bodies releasing as they peeled off into their tents and shanties. Again, something nagged at her mind, but the thought drifted just out of reach, refusing to take shape.

Nasir arrived in the tent just after her, his viridian eyes disturbed.

"Where is he, Nasir?" Mila asked, barely managing to contain her hysteria to a whisper.

"I'm sure we would have heard about it if something happened to him, Mila."

"That's flimsy at best…"

"He's probably just been put on a different work detail today."

Mila paused, biting her lip. That could make sense… A different work detail. In the western quarter, or even across the border. That's why they didn't see him, and that's why he didn't respond to the red ribbon. Though she had been toiling there for weeks on end, field work was not the only laborious task IronHand forced them to do.

Relief pushed away the fear, until she remembered why they needed to find Muharram in the first place. "But, Lina…"

"One night won't make a difference," Nasir said quietly.

He was probably right. What could happen overnight in a prison camp where every movement was watched? Well, *almost* every movement. So far Muharram's scouts had expertly monitored and reported on the guards' rounds, and the system had been faultless. But IronHand maintained constant surveillance during work time. It was lucky for Lina that she had the guards on-side, given her poor creomancy skills lately.

My creomancy was fine until I started coming here.

More like, until she started selling her body to the enemy, Mila thought.

As though that thought was the key, she suddenly saw how the pieces fit together. Her stomach dropped.

"Her creomancy…" Mila said aloud, slowly fixing her eyes on Nasir. This couldn't be right. Comments about feeling unwell, her unique failure to perform creomancy, moodiness. And her body… What if the changes weren't just from additional food. Could it be? The realisation burned and her heart beat faster by the second. "Nasir, I didn't realise before…"

He looked at her, and a crease appeared between his brows. "What? What is it?"

"It's—oh Gaia—the tunic and—she's always so tired—she can't do magic," she said in a rush, her words making no sense as they tripped over each other to get out.

Nasir tilted his head. "Do *you* even know what you're trying to say?"

Mila ran her hands over her face. There was little doubt in her mind; the idea was heavy as bedrock and just as crushing. "Lina said that she was able to do creomancy just fine before joining the training sessions, and she was blaming me but—Nasir, it's been more than a month. What if she can't grow anything outside of herself because she's growing something *within* her?"

Nasir blinked, brows furrowed as he tried to catch up.

"Nasir, I think… I think Lina's pregnant."

The impact of these words rippled outward with quiet force, like a stone dropped in still water.

"*Pregnant?*" Nasir swore. "*Gaiabeht.* Well, that would at least explain why she's going behind our backs to get extra food. And why she seems irritated all the time. Good for her, I guess."

But Mila was shaking her head. "Nasir… she lives alone."

Shock flashed across his face as he comprehended her meaning, and his eyes widened. "You think she's pregnant with one of *their* children?"

Mila nodded, feeling a strange, sinking dread in her chest. "I think so. Maybe. Oh *Gaiabeht*, Nasir, I don't know. It could all be nothing! She might not be pregnant at all, or it could be a Satarian child, but… What she said the other night? She's got *more important things to worry about…*"

He shook his head. "All we have are suspicions. You of all people know that a rumour can be very far from the truth."

Mila glared at him. As if she needed reminding of her infamy right now. "There's more at stake here than just Lina's reputation, Nasir. This is bigger than any of us. If I'm right, and Lina is pregnant with a guard's baby… It could compromise everything."

27

Mila wore the blood-red ribbon in her hair again. They had to find Muharram today.

The dark grey water of the lagoon churned restlessly through the wooden fence as the tide slipped in. Faint movement on the silty sand caught her eye, and Mila watched a crab in its quick, deliberate scuttle toward a cluster of grey rocks half-obscured by shrubs, before it vanished from view. A throb of weariness pulsed through her aching muscles, and the full weight of exhaustion settled back in as the lagoon slipped from sight.

As they reached the barren work field, Mila cast another furtive glance around before dropping to her knees. A cough, a shuffle, the clang of metal... Every sound made her flinch as she worked the dry soil with trembling hands. Sweat dripped down her back, but it was the cold sweat of fear, not exertion, as she dug into the arid earth. The urgency of their situation gripped like a hand around her throat. *Where was Muharram?*

She tried to concentrate her fretfulness into creomancy, releasing a burst of anger into the soil. A wave of dizziness tugged at her as she snatched the resulting potato from the ground. It was smaller than she had expected, not even the length of her thumb, but she knew her powers were dwindling and her hope fading with it. Each time she connected with the earth, whether it was in the fields or in the tent, it took more out of her and out of the earth. As a result, progress was slowing in the tunnel. Each movement felt heavier, each night felt longer, yet they advanced only half as far as when they started. And that smell, the smell of the blood-soaked earth…

Mila carried the small potato toward the collection bin, walking as slowly as she dared. The guards loitered all around, some pacing along the rows and the edges of the field, while others leaned lazily against the field's fence, rifles slung about their necks like elegant furs, talking amongst themselves and casting occasional glances at the prisoners. Beside these men, the IronHand banner hung straight and tight against the fence. The underlying chain-link wire pressed a diamond pattern into the navy and grey shield and fist sigil.

The collection bin was barely a quarter full, even this late in the morning. By midday, the guards would notice the shortfall, and there would be consequences. But there was nothing the Satarians could do about it; the soil yielded less and less with each passing day, just as their bodies grew weaker under the guards' relentless demands.

Muharram waited until Mila had returned to the far end of the rows of crops which they were to work on today. Careful not to draw the guards' attention, the rebel leader knelt a metre to Mila's right, and the scene reminded her strongly of the very first meeting, when Muharram had tried to recruit her. His hair had collected far more grey strands since then, and stress had carved a permanent line between his thick eyebrows.

In Satarian, he said, "What's wrong? Is it the tunnel?"

"*Ny*," Mila replied, "The tunnel is fine. It's Lina."

"Lina?"

Mila hesitated, wondering how best to phrase what she wanted to say next. Muharram waited for her to continue. "We know that she has been…working… with the guards, to get extra food rations—"

"What?" Muharram snapped, his head flicking towards her momentarily before he schooled himself. "How did you find that out? When?"

"The other night. She told me."

"And you waited to tell me?"

"I tried to find you…"

"There are other ways to get messages to me, Mila." He frowned. "This is highly troubling. Lina knows too many details of our plan…"

Mila swallowed, realising perhaps for the first time how dire the situation was. Her stomach churned like the ocean beyond the lagoon. "That's not all."

"*Gaiabeht*… what else?"

"There are signs that she… I think she might be pregnant. With an IronHand baby."

Muharram swore once, twice. After a moment, he let out a heavy sigh. "I will investigate," he murmured. "Don't do anything until you hear from me. No training, no digging. The guards will be watching and, if they *have* been informed, we may have already done enough to make them suspicious. If there's any risk, any at all, we will need to act quickly. This could unravel everything."

Mila nodded as a chill settled over her.

They said nothing further, and a short while later, Muharram tugged a tiny potato from the earth, walking away to deposit it in the collection bin. Mila felt sick. She should have told someone the moment Lina mentioned it. She should have held the woman back and made her tell Muharram or Thani herself. But she hadn't grasped the full implications of it at the time. When Lina implied she was trading sex for food, Mila had been too shocked to think any further. Lina said she wasn't a traitor, and Mila believed her.

Once again, her naiveté might ruin everything.

Muharram was right; if Lina had divulged anything about the resistance group to the guards, and if they were watching, it was better that Muharram was nowhere near her.

The day dragged on in relentless monotony, each hour blurring into the next. Around noon, the word 'Ineffective' drifted across the cold grounds as the guards dragged several of the weaker Satarians away, and someone in her eyeline slumped to the soil, their life force depleted by creomancy. Such death was no longer shocking. Instead, it was just another mark against her name, another failure.

At the end of the day, as Mila trudged back toward the tents, her gaze drifted to the lagoon once more. The fading light cast a pale glow over the water, turning it dull and jaundiced. The surface was still now, broken only by the occasional ripple as insects landed. Nestled in the brush by the water's edge was the same grey shape she had dismissed as a cluster of rocks that morning. But now, the dull contours shifted in the fading light, and the truth of its form became horribly clear. The sinking sun cast long shadows across the landscape, and Mila's gut twisted as she realised what she was looking at.

A body.

The grey-clad figure lay crumpled and partially concealed in the mud and brush, but it was unmistakably a body.

Icy prickles crawled up her spine and before she could stop herself, Mila lurched into action. Whoever it was, she had to help them. Her legs propelled her forward, taking rapid, uneven steps down the slope toward the body, the ground beneath her feet slick with the evening dew, when a sharp voice sliced through the quiet.

"Stop right there, or I'll shoot!"

The unmistakable sound of a rifle being cocked rolled down the hill.

Mila froze mid-step, her pulse roaring in her ears. She raised her hands into the air as she shouted, "There's someone down there!"

Two guards started down the bank toward her. She braced herself, certain they would drag her back by force, but they continued past, their attention fixed on the figure as they moved quickly toward the lagoon's edge.

"You there!" one of them yelled at the figure. "Don't move!"

By now, the flow of refugees had slowed, and many were either staring at Mila or looking further down the bank, their eyes drawn by the unusual lump in the gathering gloom. Mila watched on, oblivious to the mosquitoes leeching from her skin, every second stretching painfully.

"Get moving!" called the guards, droving the line of refugees along. "Back to your hovels. Hurry up!"

Mila moved back up the bank, going as slow as she dared with her eyes still glued to the scene at the lagoon.

At some point the IronHand guards must have realised the person wasn't a threat, and they hauled the figure out from the bushes, dumping it on its back on the sludgy bank. The ghostly skin gleamed in the fading light, stark against the dark water and shadows that surrounded it, and the body was draped in the same faded grey that all refugees wore, now mud-streaked and tattered, blending so easily into the earth that it was no wonder Mila hadn't recognised it at dawn. If they had been passing this way even ten minutes later, she wouldn't have seen it in the dusky light either.

It was a woman, and even from this distance, Mila knew the woman was dead. She could see her staring eyes, could see the unnatural rigidity of her limbs, twisted unnervingly in the gloom. She could see dark stain over the lower abdomen. And she could see the long, dark plait trailing from her head.

The guards walked back up the slope, leaving Lina's useless body abandoned in the mud.

A hand suddenly grabbed Mila's shoulders, and she spun around expecting to see the cruel face of a guard, but it was Nasir.

"Come on, Cricket," he said in a low, forceful voice. "There's nothing we can do for her."

Her voice quivered as she struggled to keep herself composed. "They killed her, Nasir." The sight of the woman wasted like that was too much.

"Shh," Nasir's grip tightened as he urged her forward, "Please, just hold on until we're inside. Please, Mila."

Mila nodded numbly and allowed him to pull her gently but firmly, all the way back to their tent. As soon as they stepped inside, Nasir pulled her into his arms. Mila thought she had no tears left to shed, no shock left for any of this, but at that moment she cried so hard and for so long that she began to wonder if her skin might erode away like sandstone beneath a river. She couldn't shake the image of the body—*Lina's* body—lifeless and discarded like trash.

Darkness began to creep along the alleys of the camp and the light in the tent faded before Mila had calmed enough to ask, "What do you think this means, Nasir?" Her voice came out hoarse, barely above a whisper.

He didn't answer for a long moment, and Mila began to wonder if he had even heard her, or if her voice was muffled by his shirt. She pulled back and was about to ask again when he spoke.

"I think it means our concerns are valid. You saw where they stabbed her… I think they also found out she was pregnant, and they didn't like it. I just wonder how much she told them to try to get them to spare her life. I think we can assume her loyalties weren't to us, at the end."

A chill so raw slipped down the back of Mila's neck and wrapped itself around her ribs, squeezing until she could barely breathe. "No… No, she wouldn't…You think she told them about us, about the rebellion?"

Nasir nodded, and another primal pulse of terror shot through her veins.

At that moment, the tent flap ripped aside. Nasir whirled around, pulling Mila behind him, but he relaxed as he realised it was Muharram. The rebel leader charged in, followed closely by Thani and Mahgda, their faces grim and panicked.

"What's going on?" Nasir said, tensing once more.

"I just received word from one of my little birds," Muharram said. "The guards know. They are coming. If we don't go now, we'll be dead within the hour."

28

Mila stared at Muharram in horror.

"But the tunnel isn't finished yet!" she croaked, thoughts spilling out of her as quickly as they came to mind. "We can't go now—we'd have to dig as we go—it will be slow and—oh Gaia, even if we did, there's not enough time. We'll never get everyone out before the guards find the tunnel!"

"The tunnel is short?" Muharram exclaimed sharply.

Nasir looked away, jaw clenched. "We're about a hundred-and-fifty metres short of the western wall."

"We will excavate as we go. If we leave now, if we seal the entrance behind us—"

"No!" Mila felt like she was going to be sick, her mind whirling. "I will not leave them all behind!"

"Mila, the tunnel isn't finished," Thani said. "We couldn't get a mass of people out even if we wanted to. It will have to just be us."

Muharram's jaw stiffened, and he couldn't meet Mila's eye. "We always knew we could not save everyone... and some is better than none."

"But this isn't *some*, Muharram—this is five people! Out of over a thousand!"

The rebel leader's eyes flashed. "And we can't fight back if we're *all* dead. At least this way, there's a chance."

At that moment, the tent flap flipped aside and Khalen bolted into the tent. She swallowed a rush of affection for the skinny teen, wearing his ill-fitting, shabby coat with the sleeves rolled up. A small blue *felicia* flower sat tucked through one of the buttonholes. Mila stared at it for a moment, the bizarreness of its beauty in a world that was falling into ruin.

Nasir swept into action. Without a word, he yanked their parents' mattress away from the tunnel entrance. Dust swirled like smoke in the dim light, revealing the hole in the ground like a conjuror's trick.

"You first, Cricket," he said.

She shoved his hands away as he reached for her. "I won't leave without trying to save as many as I can. I will be last or not at all."

In the tense silence that followed, Nasir grabbed Khalen, his hands on the boy's shoulders. "You need to finish the tunnel," Nasir said.

Khalen blanched. "I—I can't. I don't have enough control."

Nasir squeezed Khalen's shoulders. "That's what I'm counting on."

"What? I—I could make the whole thing collapse!"

"One solid blast will lift the paving stones and foundations in Haman. You can do that."

"If we come up in the city, the chances of us making it out of Haman alive…" Muharram didn't need to finish the sentence. They all knew. The older man's throat bobbed as he swallowed. "Do it, Khalen. We'll take care of the rest. Just give us a way out."

He ushered Khalen toward the tunnel. Khalen's face crumbled momentarily, his eyes wide with fear. He really is just a boy, Mila thought, vulnerable and terrified, thrust into a role far too heavy for his sixteen years.

"You'll come after me, right?" Khalen said, eyes flicking from Mila to Nasir. "You'll be there?"

Nasir nodded, and Khalen's shoulders relaxed slightly. Let the boy have hope, she thought. But she knew there was a strong chance they would never see him again, one way or another. She had to be strong.

Mila put a hand on his shoulder. "Go, Khalen, now. Remember, focus on your intention," she urged, her voice somehow steady despite the panic rising inside.

Khalen nodded, suddenly determined. "If mahma could see me now," he murmured, so softly that only Mila heard him. He began to descend into the darkness, his long legs and wiry arms grasping at the dug-out holds. Mila gave him one last smile before the boy disappeared completely into the dark.

Mila spun back to the others, urgency making her yell. "We need to go out there. All of us. Find the other rebels and gather as many Satarians as we can, and tell them we're evacuating. Bring them here, as fast and as many as we can. Let's go!"

She started towards the exit, expecting to be followed, but no one else moved. Mila shook her head. "I can't believe you. The whole point of this group was to fight—but did you ever stopped to question what we were fighting *for*? Is it freedom, or do you just want to save yourselves? Well, I guarantee you, if you don't do everything you can to get more people out, you will *never* feel free. It's a prison all of its own, when you survive at another's expense."

Suddenly Muharram was holding her by the front of her tunic, his lined face inches from hers. His calm, comforting demeanour had vanished, replaced by something darker. "You think you know everything about loss?" he growled.

"Hey! Muharram, let her go!" Nasir yelled, but he had as much impact as a raindrop in a desert.

Muharram glared at her. "Children are supposed to bury their parents, even if it is too soon. You haven't seen the true depth of grief. You have barely begun to wade into its depths."

Mila struggled against him for a moment before he opened his fist and let her go. He turned away from her, but he didn't move any closer to the tunnel.

Mahgda took a step towards Mila. "Are you alright?"

"I'm fine," she said dismissively. "Please, Mahgda, get the others. Hurry."

The woman nodded and swept from the tent. After an appraising glance at the rebel leader, Thani followed.

Mila placed a gentle hand on his back. His shoulders softened under her touch. "Muharram, I don't know what you've been through, but I do know this; Our survival means nothing without the others. Satarian culture *is* its people. Why have we clung to it so fiercely all this time, if we're just going to throw it away now?"

He turned slowly, his eyes hard but searching. "You would really risk it all?"

Mila nodded.

Muharram shook his head without looking at her. He cursed in Satarian, then said quietly, "On your head, then. I'll do my best."

The rebel leader disappeared into the night as Mila rounded on her brother.

"Come on!" she yelled, but Nasir grabbed her arm again.

"Not you," he said. "Mila, please—You need to head down the tunnel with Khalen."

"Didn't you hear me? I'm not leaving until we've got every last person!"

"You're too important, Mila—"

She cut him off. "Nasir, I'm no more important than anyone else in Al'Mazraea. It's my fault this is happening. I have to at least try…"

At that moment, the piercing sound of the camp siren tore through the night.

Nasir applied pressure to her arm. "We don't have long."

"I know," Mila said. "So go. Find Olaf! Please, Nasir."

Nasir looked at her with a sad reverence in his eyes, then he let go of her arm. "Five minutes. That's it, okay?"

"Yes, fine! Come on!"

They burst out of the tent into the cold evening air, turning in different directions. The rumble of vehicle engines came over the hills like the calls of distant predators, hunting them. They had maybe ten minutes before the guards descended upon the camp and began tearing the place apart, searching for the resistance.

For the tunnel.

For her.

The siren screamed through her thoughts as Mila ran, pulse pounding in her temples and her breath coming shallow and ragged. She tore along alley after alley, ripping open tent doors, barely stopping to register the surprised faces as she shouted at them to flee.

"Go, quick! The tent with the fabric ribbons, you'll be safe there. Now! IronHand is coming!"

Some sprang into action immediately, grabbing what they could, gathering their children. Others stood frozen, stunned by the sheer terror of the moment. But Mila didn't—couldn't—wait for them to act. She ran to the next tent, and the next, and for the first time in her life she felt overwhelmed at the sheer size of Al'Mazraea, knowing that she couldn't reach everyone in time.

Mila pushed through clusters of frightened faces that loomed out of the darkness like ghosts. Tent ropes and thick electrical wires threatened to trip her, but she kept running, her voice hoarse as she yelled for anyone and everyone to head to the tunnel. She cut through another row of tents. Shadows seemed to creep closer, the dread weighing heavier with each passing second.

Her gut lurched as she spotted a familiar figure huddled between the tents with her baby held tightly to her bosom. The woman was a shadow of herself, frail, her face ashen in the fading light.

"*Elaari*!" Mila rushed over.

The woman glanced up at her, eyes glassy with confusion. "What's happening, Mila?"

Mila shook her head. There was no time to explain. "Come with me," she begged. She didn't wait for a reply before she slid her arm around her friend's clammy shoulders to support her. Mila tightened her grip, pulling her along with more force than she intended, but they were running out of time and Elaari was moving so slowly.

The ground vibrated beneath them as the unmistakable rumble of engines grew louder. Doubts stabbed at Mila's mind: could Elaari make it down into the tunnel, especially with the baby?

"I'm not leaving you," Mila whispered fiercely, more to herself than her friend.

As the roar of noise intensified, something occurred to Mila that made her feel sick to the stomach. The baby wasn't crying. He hadn't made a sound.

Mila quickened her pace, nearly dragging Elaari along. Both women gasped for breath, legs trembling, their determination fuelling each shaky step.

Suddenly there was a bright amber glow in the distance, and Mila's first thought was that she had mistaken the time, that she was watching the setting sun. It took her tired mind a moment to register that it was an hour too late for that.

The light wavered unevenly, casting flickering shadows that danced along the lines of tents, highlighting the silhouettes of people moving this way and that. The more she stared, the more unnatural it became. The light danced with wicked ferocity. It was no longer soft like sundown; it was too harsh.

Fire.

A rush of adrenaline tore through her as, far too quickly, tongues of flame lashed at the air, casting a dark orange tint between shadows that stretched and warped, leaping and licking. This whole camp would go up in minutes. Almost everything was made of either wood or hay.

Tents melted in on themselves, consumed by the advancing flames, and dark tendrils of smoke curled upward to pollute her nose and mouth, her eyes already streaming. It choked the air and blocked out the stars with an eerie orange canopy, and the ground itself seemed to shimmer.

Urgent shouts and screams were carried on the wind amid the acrid smell of burning plastic. Mila stumbled on the uneven ground as Elaari began to cough, her already snail-like pace slowing to a halt so that she could wrap the bundle in her arms more tightly.

"There, there, shhhh," she cooed to the silent child.

Mila pulled at her friend's arm again, voice tight as she urged, "Come on, Elaari, we're almost there, just keep going." She scanned the camp for more people; people who needed help, people who wanted to harm them. She tugged harder on Elaari's frail form, guiding her along the dirt path. Sparks flew all around like angry spittle, and the very air seemed to burn Mila's lungs from within. Clothing and other belongings lay strewn across the paths, trampled into the ground by thousands of fleeing feet.

When they finally reached their tent, Mila all but shoved the woman ahead of her, overwhelmed with swirling dread, her pulse racing.

Inside the tent, chaos reigned. There was hardly room to move. Everywhere, people jostled and shoved as they tried to reach the narrow tunnel entrance, pleading to escape before the guards arrived. Muharram stood by the pit, turning this way and that to hold people back as he yelled for order, but his words made little difference. People surged around him, rushing toward the tunnel mouth with feral desperation, and clambering down without any care for who might be below them. A man grabbed wildly at the uneven edge, his fingers scraping the dirt as he struggled to keep from falling while a foot stomped him downward. The situation was quickly falling apart, and the guards were getting closer by the minute.

Mila's eyes searched, finding and counting the rebels—Ishak, Irani, Mahgda—when hands suddenly grabbed her shoulders. "There you are!" Nasir yelled, mad with urgency. "For Gaia's sake, Mila!"

"Did you find Olaf?" she called.

Nasir nodded and momentary relief punctuated her panic. "He's already in the tunnel."

"How many have gone down?" she asked, eyes sweeping the space. There were too many people here, and not enough.

"I'm not sure, but we're out of time. If we don't leave now, we won't leave. They've set the camp on fire."

To Mila's faint relief, the refugees moved into the tunnel quickly. Within a minute, the line had thinned, leaving just the last few people crowded around the pit entrance. Irani went down. Then Mahgda. The other trainees were already gone.

Suddenly finding themselves with room to move, a splinter of doubt dug in. Maybe they *could* get more people out? But smoke had begun to infiltrate the air inside the tent, seeping through every seam and stitch. The canvas walls were growing brighter, the air hotter, as the sinister, flickering light came closer.

"We have to go," Thani said, one leg already in the hole. "There's nothing more we can do here."

Muharram nodded and Thani slipped away. As he neared the pit himself, Muharram glanced back to see that Mila and Nasir were following, then the older man's face hardened and he too disappeared into the passage.

Mila and Nasir locked eyes. "It's time."

They were the last ones left now.

"I know," her voice cracked. "But there's still so many out there— "

A sudden, sharp voice ripped out of the darkness; so loud and clear it must have come from only metres away.

"Find them! Tear this place apart. Leave no hovel intact!"

Mila's bottom lip began to tremble. No time. No second chances. If they were found, it was all over.

Nasir suddenly darted to the set of shelves, dropping to his knees as he scrambled for the hidden compartment and ripping out the false bottom. No time to be gentle. He shovelled the treasures into a tattered bag—the kind they would have otherwise used for garbage—then swept the few items off the top shelf too. He tied the bag tight as he ran back to Mila's side at the tunnel mouth.

Breathing heavily, he pressed the bundle of artefacts into her hands and demanded, "Here, take these, now. Keep them safe."

With trembling hands, Mila tucked the precious bundle inside the top of her tunic, then looked down into the tunnel, just as she had done every night before they descended to dig further. But this time, the darkness wasn't just before her—it was within her very soul, a gaping maw of despair that threatened to consume her. She imagined the families left behind, terrified, running out of their tents only to come face-to-face with IronHand guards…

"Go!" Nasir demanded, begging her to begin the descent. "Now, quickly."

Mila lowered herself over the edge, then paused. Something about his expression made her hesitate. "You'll be right behind me?" Mila asked, but Nasir's hands gripped her shoulders, urging her to continue down.

"I'll be right behind you," he repeated. "Go, Cricket. Please."

It was the *please* that made her realise how much Nasir needed her to be okay. He didn't care about the others; all he cared about was her. She closed her eyes for a moment, fighting the weight of all the lives she couldn't save. All the lives she had ruined.

Then, heart aching, she began the descent. The tips of her tattered fingers gripped onto the shallow holds carved in the walls. Through the haste and concentration, Mila found a moment to be proud of what they had achieved here, that their magic had created such a solid structure. Despite the hundreds of people climbing frantically, carelessly downwards, the compacted soil had held up.

The temperature immediately dropped, and the thin wedge of light faded as she quickly descended. Faint voices echoed up out of the darkness as people moved away along the tunnel, unseen beneath her.

"Okay, Nasir, you can start climbing now," she called up.

When no boots appeared swinging into the hole above her, Mila called again.

"Nasir?"

Then, suddenly, there came a heavy *thwump* of air as the mattress slammed back into place over the hole, and darkness swallowed her.

29

A few heartbeats passed, then a few more, each one growing heavier, pulling down against the hope trying to remain afloat in her chest.

The silence stretched.

In a minute, Mila told herself, Nasir would appear beside her. He would be here. She could still feel his grip on her shoulders as her mind replayed his insistence that she leave first.

Why wasn't he following?

"Nasir?" she called again, but the earth swallowed her voice. It was the most complete darkness Mila had ever known, and panic washed over her with such force that it separated her consciousness from her body like oil from water. The moment seemed to last a lifetime and a millisecond all at once. A sense of weightlessness took over. For a moment she was unsure where her body ended and the soil began. Was she falling, or floating? Climbing, or swimming?

Maybe this was death? Maybe she hadn't actually made it into the tunnel—had she been shot by the guards, or burned alive in the encroaching fire? Was this instead the darkness and listlessness of death?

Then something—the earth? Or maybe Gaia herself?—called out to her. *Keep going*, it said, and Mila somehow knew where the footholds were, where to place her fingers. The magic inside her roiled in a sense of euphoria at being surrounded by nothing but the pristine, crystalline purity of the earth. The cold, damp air reached out to give her skin the gentlest kisses while the earth called to her, beckoning every atom in her body… and she wanted to let go.

A deep shout booming above snapped Mila back to the present with a fear so paralysing that she almost let go.

"No!" The word came bursting out of her, "No, no, no, *no*. Nasir!"

Up. She needed to go back up. Mila scrambled to find the hand-holds again, though her arms felt too weak to support her weight.

"Nasir!"

Her breath came fast, the walls of the tunnel suddenly closing around her.

"Nasir!" she screamed again. Why wasn't he answering?

Just as Mila felt the top of her head bump the soft mattress above her, the ground trembled. The recess beneath her right hand suddenly disappeared. A low rumble echoed along the tunnel as if she were inside the jaws of some enormous beast, and she sensed the soil lurch and crack all around her. Amid the deafening pounding of her own heart, a wave of horror washed over her as she realised what was happening. The tunnel was collapsing. Debris poured down into her eyes and purely by reflex Mila's hands flew up to her face. A sharp "oh" of surprise escaped her lips, and then she was falling, racing the gushing dirt down to the bottom of the tunnel.

She landed hard on her hip and shoulder, the impact jolting through her bones while still more dirt spilled from above, coating her arms, her legs, her face, and filling her lungs with every panicked breath. The earth shuddered violently.

"*Ny!*" Mila screamed, pressing on the collapsing walls with all her might—but the earth was being controlled by something stronger, and her fingers only slipped through the loose dirt.

She begged the earth with her whole heart, pushing her magic out into the foundation of the tunnel, desperate to hold on as wave after wave of soil crashed down on her.

"*Gaia! Ny, Gaia, plezht! Kardan! Kardanay orua tenes!*"

She was drowning in it, the weight pressing down, sealing her in darkness. "Please, no!"

But it was too late. The shaft was folding. Through the terror, somewhere in her mind she knew she couldn't stay here. She couldn't let herself be trapped. Blind in the pitch-blackness, Mila pulled herself free of the smothering soil, hands outstretched.

The earth shook and a loud crack shook the air. There was no time to think.

She ran along the pitch-black tunnel as fast as she could, her hands pressed into the sides to guide her, the vibrations of the collapsing trench shaking the ground beneath her feet. The earth was pulling her forward again, the pulse of life beneath the soil pushing her away from the danger. Though the darkness never moved, the sounds eventually became lesser, and finally Mila could slow down.

Her mind was blank, numb, as if her thoughts had floated away into the ether that surrounded her. Every sense was overwhelmed with the pure darkness and the rich scent of the soil. Each step felt like dragging herself through eternity. The walls of the tunnel seemed to close in on her, the rough edges scraping her outstretched hands as she moved. Her eyes were wide, straining to see anything at all. But there was nothing to see. She was alone; completely alone.

Nasir.

Mila was certain; the tunnel would only cave in if it was compelled.

Nasir had *made* that happen…

He had asked Gaia to collapse the tunnel, with him on the other side.

Mila couldn't fully process it. What he had done, what it meant… How could he do that to her?

She wanted to stop walking. Just for a moment. To ignore the silent song of the earth beckoning her onwards. To crouch in the darkness and let the grief wash over her, to scream and cry and thrash around… For her brother, for herself, for those left behind.

For all of it.

But there was no time for that. She had to keep moving. One foot in front of the other. There were people waiting for her at the tunnel exit. People who needed her to be strong.

And what would they do now? Where would they go? They hadn't yet organised this part of the plan with Muharram and Thani.

They had always thought they would have more time.

Mila bit down on her bottom lip, hard, savouring the physical distraction from her emotional pain.

Everyone always thinks they have more time. But you never know when time is up. Life can end in the blink of an eye.

Time had run out for her parents.

It had run out for the hundreds of Satarians who worked themselves to death in the fields.

Had time run out for Nasir?

All because of her choice that day… the choice to save that little boy.

Why should she, Mila, be alive now? Why should *she* be allowed more time? And, what was the point of having it? She couldn't do what she *wanted* to do. What she *longed* to do… To spend hours with her head resting in her mother's lap, looking up at her as they talked, watching the sun rise over the distant Erulean Ocean. To kiss her father's forehead and feel his curls tickling her nose. To gossip with Karina. To watch Elaari's son grow up. To laugh and play around with her brother.

What was the point of having all this extra time if she couldn't spend it with the people she loved the most?

It was all so far away now, unreachable, and not because she was nine metres down in the depths of the earth.

She would never have any of that again.

Through dust-veiled eyes, Mila finally noticed the suffocating darkness begin to lift, and she could make out the faint outline of her fingers scraping against the wall. But instead of hurrying towards the hazy circle of light at the end of the passage, Mila stopped altogether, her breathing loud in the darkness.

She curled her fingers into fists, jamming her nails into her palms in a sharp burst of pain. Thoughts tore through her mind like shards of glass, each one cutting deeper than the last.

The Amanese had been right about her all along; she was dangerous, even to those she wanted to protect. Her entire family had paid the price for her recklessness.

She couldn't leave. It was a certainty, as clear as the constellations on a cloudless night, and she didn't try to fight it as her legs gave out from under her and it crushed her to the ground.

Did she really want to live in a world that could be so cruel? She should stay here, away from the light of day, buried in the earth where she belonged. She deserved to be *here*, entombed in the earth, claimed by the darkness of her own doing. Let the clods fall upon her face and her bones turn to dust. Everyone would be safer that way. Everything would be better.

Then she wouldn't have to deal with this agony and despair tearing her apart from the inside out.

She wouldn't have to feel anything.

It hurt to breathe. Her insides ached and tears came finally, carving hot streaks down her dirty face. She couldn't bear to keep going. The thought of taking another breath, another step. It was too much. Living was pain. Living was torture.

But dying… No, she didn't want to die. She just wanted the pain to stop. *Needed* the pain to stop. And death seemed to be the only way that would happen.

Mila curled her arms to her chest, surprised to feel the lumpy bag hidden in her tunic. In the rush to descend and the chaos that followed, she had forgotten all about it. She lay still a moment longer, feeling nothing but her pulse, lost between the deep darkness inside and out. Then, relying solely on her sense of touch, she carefully extracted the bundle. The old fabric carried the faintest scent of the herbs her mother used to freshen their laundry, and the scent hit Mila like a phantom embrace. She pressed it to her face, inhaling deeply, using it to collect her tears and muffle her sobs as if it were Sara herself.

Slowly, her distress began to ebb, and her fingers fumbled over the items, identifying them by touch alone; the cold, circular metal of the ring, the lumpy surface of the pendant. Mila traced over something solid and small, smooth and light… Realisation stabbed through her. She was feeling the soft ridges of the petals Nasir had painstakingly whittled. Her favourite, the rose. A painful lump formed in her throat.

Nasir.

Maybe if she waited here long enough, he would make his way through the dirt to get to her?

Her fingers returned to their blind search. A leathery string came to hand, and she followed it until she brushed against something worn smooth: the bone necklace. At that exact moment, a sharp jolt shot through Mila's hand as though a viper had struck, sending red lightning streaking up her forearm. She gasped and jerked involuntarily, spilling the relics from her lap. It wasn't just pain—it was something alive, coursing through her veins with a heat that seared and electrified.

With her heart thumping, Mila sat frozen, the world around her still pitch-black. A rush of exhilarating unease filled her. Had that come from the necklace? The idea sent a shiver down her spine. At the same time, a sound slipped into her awareness, low and eerie. The bones in her lap were *humming*. What magic was this?

The hum grew stronger and, despite the foreboding in her gut, Mila felt a sudden overwhelming urge to touch it again. To put the necklace on. Her mother had always told her never to touch it, but her mother wasn't here anymore. Mila had to make her own way now.

Mila lifted the string and brought the necklace gently to her throat. The moment the bones settled against her skin, the scorching heat surged once more, rushing through her chest and down to her fingertips like wildfire on the wind, like the most intense concentration of the sunshine feeling—then, just as quickly, it stilled. Her hand hovered, wondering if touching it would set the lightning off again. Her skin tingled. She swallowed.

The bones were cool to the touch now, as though the burst of fiery energy had never happened. But it *had* happened. How? And *why*? Why hadn't this happened before?

Mila racked her brain, trying to think whether she had ever touched the bones before… She had definitely wanted to, and she had even held it up by the leather straps once, but Mila vividly remembered her mother screaming at her to put it down. Sara never screamed…

A deep breath in and out, and Mila placed her hands to the ground. The curved nodules of the bones stroked her clavicle, vibrating against her with a pulse that didn't quite match her own, as though each one had a heartbeat of its own.

Repulsion made her twitch, and as she moved, her fingers brushed against an unmistakable papery texture that drew her complete focus. The map. This parchment that had survived century after century, all the way from the old lands, and had ended up here, buried in the dark with her. Though she couldn't see it in the gloom, she could picture the inked illustrations; the mountains and towns and the irregular lines of rivers, the curving symbols of written Satarian.

It was more than just ink and parchment. It was proof; proof of a thriving land, of a past woven with millions of lives. But, just like Satarian culture itself, time had eaten it away, piece by piece, until only this fraying relic remained. Faded lines, illegible names, forgotten places.

Now, centuries later, the same thing was happening again. They risked perishing altogether. All of Satarian culture had come to this moment.

This is bigger than any of us.

This map needed to be seen again. These lines were drawn to be remembered.

With the bones still ringing her neck, Mila returned the other items into the limp fabric, bundling it all up again and shoving it inside her tunic. She couldn't allow herself any more fear and pain and despair right now.

She had a job to do.

30

With a deep breath, Mila slowly unfurled and willed herself to stand on shaking legs, urging her feet to move the last few metres to the end of the tunnel. She stood in the faint circle of light shining down from above, and looked up. She would not let the darkness claim her. If she truly believed that she had caused this, then she also had a duty to put it right. She had to see it through to the end, to live and fight. For Nasir, and for everyone still trapped in Al'Mazraea.

For now, she was still alive—and that was a gift, not a burden.

Her fingers gripped the crude ridges hacked out of the walls and she began pulling, feet pushing, mechanically climbing toward the light. Khalen had done a rough job of blasting out of the unfinished tunnel into open air, and the shaft grew wider the higher she scaled. Her laboured breaths bounced back off the earth surrounding her, until she scrambled over the edge of the tunnel mouth and peered around. She blinked, waiting for her eyes to adjust to the ambient light, slowly discerning onyx from obsidian, sable from slate. The space must have been quite large from the way the echoes of many quiet murmurs moved in the air.

Her first thought was that Khalen's creomancy had caused a disaster. Far above, the ceiling appeared to be buckling in places, the textured concrete slabs cracked and broken with streaks of exposed wiring and rusted beams dangling down. Fragments of faded stone tiles lay scattered across the floor, half-hidden beneath layers of grime and dust. In the far back, Mila could just discern a collapsed stairwell beneath a yawning hole that led upward. On the adjacent wall, a large, cracked mirror reflected haggard silhouettes in angular fragments.

Where there should have been a fourth wall, there was only the night and hazy lights from houses beyond. The bricks that had once made the wall were scattered all around like crumbled cornbread, allowing the frigid breeze to snake through. It felt too open after the earth's snug embrace.

In the dim light, the hundred or so refugees were little more than phantoms, blending in with the grey concrete as they drifted around, crying, holding loved ones. A sudden bite of envy swooped over Mila as she stared at a woman nearby, wrapped in the arms of another. They had lost a lot, there was no denying that... But they had not quite lost *everything*.

Mila would give anything to be held like that just one more time...

In the sea of worried faces, here and there a familiar few stood out; neighbours and friends dotted the assembly, alongside the determined faces of the rebels. Khalen sat with Ishak by the gaping hole that led into the night, their grim faces lit by the faint glow of the streetlights beyond, scanning for signs of the inevitable approaching threat. Olaf hunched on the floor with another *soffo*, the man's head resting on Olaf's shoulder. Off to the right, Arviz scooped up a young girl in his arms as she threw her thin arms around his neck. The girl peeked out over his stocky shoulder, looking like a baby possum in a tree, her wide eyes innocent and frightened beneath the *noterran* brand. Her eyes locked with Mila's and, in that moment of connection, envy curled in Mila's gut once more. She quickly looked away, bitter and ashamed.

To be held like that just one more time...

Mila became aware of someone speaking close by. With great difficulty, she pulled her attention back to see Muharram at her side, extending a hand to pull her away from the tunnel mouth. His grip tightened as he steadied her, then he turned expectantly back to the tunnel.

There was a beat; a moment of sickening anticipation.

"Where's Nasir?" the rebel leader asked.

Mila froze, unable to meet his eyes. The lump in her throat made it impossible to speak and though her lips parted, no sound came out. She just shook her head. She couldn't say it. If she said it out loud, that would make it true—and it couldn't be true. She couldn't be alone in this world. What was the point of anything if Nasir wasn't here?

Her silence hung in the air in the moment before the weight of it sunk in and the realisation dawned on Muharram's face. Mila felt his devastation in her soul.

Thani hurried over. "Are you the last one?"

Mila nodded.

The last one.

"We have to seal the tunnel," Thani continued, callous but practical.

"The entrance, it—" Mila croaked. "It's already sealed."

No one can follow.

"Good, but we should do the same from this end too."

"No!" Mila said, shocked. If they sealed the tunnel from this end, Nasir wouldn't know where to come out when he eventually dug through again. "Nasir is coming! He still has a chance to make it. He's strong. He'll clear the soil at the entrance and find the rest of the tunnel. You'll see."

Thani tutted. "It won't take long for the guards to suspect we tunnelled out, and their first thought will be that we're in Haman. When they inevitably start to search, we don't want them knowing where we came out. It could give us a head start. A small one, but still."

"No. No. Nasir is coming," Mila repeated. "We need to leave this end open so that he has a way out."

Thani's voice cut through her hope like a blade. "I'm sorry about your brother, Mila, but we need to think about what's best for everyone now." Her tone was sharp, rational, her expression closed as she glanced toward the tunnel. "The longer that tunnel stays open, the more danger we're all in. If the guards get through—"

"You don't understand," Mila spat. "I won't leave him."

Thani crossed her arms. "Then stay here. But you stay alone."

"He's coming. He'll be here. I know it," Mila said, her eyes blazing with tear-streaked determination even as her voice crackled with doubt. How could they propose that she would abandon him? Her mind was a frantic blur. If the tunnel was sealed, it meant accepting he wasn't coming. Accepting that he was gone.

But if it stayed open, there was still hope. He could still find her.

Thani's expression didn't change. She stood firm, unflinching.

Muharram placed a hand on Thani's arm, shaking his head slightly, then he turned to Mila. His eyes were full of sorrow and understanding, and somehow Mila hated that more than Thani's ruthlessness. "We can leave it a little longer," he said softly. "But only a little. Not forever, Mila. You know that."

Mila nodded.

For once she was completely comfortable with lying.

She stepped back toward the pit, staring down into the darkness, waiting, picking at the skin around her thumbnails until they were red and raw and bleeding. This pain was better, better than thinking about the painful truth beneath Thani's words.

Mahgda's raspy voice lilted through the others, drawing Mila's attention briefly before her gaze returned down the pit. Somehow the woman still managed to look elegant and put-together, despite her torn tunic and the dusting of soil in her hair.

"What's the plan?" Mahgda asked.

"We don't yet have one," Muharram said. "Everything happened too quickly. The tunnel wasn't even completed before we were forced to use it. If not for Khalen's power…"

"You must have had some sort of idea though?" Mahgda said, her tone patient, the way one might coax a struggling child to solve a problem on their own.

"All we know for certain is that we cannot stay here," Muharram said.

Mila scowled. The conversation was pulling her concentration away from the tunnel exit, and she resented the distraction. Any minute now, the top of Nasir's head would come into the circle of light deep down below.

Mahgda huffed. "You know more than you're saying," she said curtly.

"*Beht*, okay, we have some idea," Muharram admitted.

A rustle of paper.

"Where did you get that?" Mahgda breathed, and something about her tone made Mila look over despite herself. Thani was in the process of slowly unfurling a tattered, stained roll of paper which she spread on the dusty ground. She smoothed it with one hand, but Mila couldn't make out any detail. To see more, she would have to move away from the tunnel mouth.

At the thought, it felt as if a giant, taloned hand seized her heart, its sharp claws pressing deep. It would only be for a moment, she told herself. She would step away, look, then immediately return and wait for Nasir. A minute or two would be okay.

Mila bit down on her inner cheek, hard, and stepped toward the small group of rebels with her eyes locked on the paper in front of Thani. Faint, inky lines twisted across the scrap of torn parchment, stirring a pang of recognition so sharp that her hand flew to her torso, grasping for the relics that should still be tucked inside her tunic. Relief eased her pounding heart as she felt the bundle. Her map was safe, so… what was this? Concern turned to curiosity and she leaned in closer.

Details came into focus: tiny markings, symbols clustered around certain spots, sharp triangles and a deep blue expanse. And labels, legible in Amanese. Mila's breath caught as she realised what she was looking at.

A map of Ard Aman.

She had never seen cartography of the land on which they lived. Satarians were forbidden from possessing or even seeing such things. Mila's pulse quickened, her shoulders tensed, knowing she would be punished just for looking at the illicit illustrations. She automatically braced for the sharp bark of a guard's voice or the force of a blow… until she remembered where she was. How long would the rules of Al'Mazraea remain in her mind?

With her pulse settling slowly, her eyes traced the size and scale of the drawings. All she had ever known was Al'Mazraea and the easternmost district of Haman but now, seeing this, Mila was astounded—the world was so, so much bigger than she ever knew. This was proof that the continent stretched vast and sublime beyond her, each mountain and river etched on the map an inherent reminder of how small she was—and how much more there was to reach for. It was humbling and empowering all at once.

A section of the paper had been torn clean away, and the remaining edges were worn thin, with small rips at the corners and deep fold lines. Though stains and smudges blurred some areas into obscurity, most lines and features remained clear. Thani must have stolen it from Haman months ago, before the wall went up and they were trapped in Al'Mazraea. Back when the fence was merely made of wood, and they could leave its confines for a few hours. Mila never imagined she would miss that constrained sort of freedom with every fibre of her being.

"We are here," Thani jabbed a finger at a symbol labelled *Haman*. "Unfortunately."

Mila scanned the page, finding Al'Mazraea, and the cuneal lines of the mountain ranges—the Uul Serrad to the north and west, and the Uul Arkhaa to the south.

"This path here," Thani continued, tracing a finger north-west, "Leads through the Serrad. It will be rough, especially without food or supplies, but if we make it, we'll reach here—" She tapped an area that looked on the map to be made out of thousands of tiny circles.

"What is that?" Mila murmured.

Thani looked up at her, eyes bright. "It's a forest."

Arviz leaned in, brow furrowed. "Through the mountains? That's got to be at least a day's walk—probably more—just to reach the foothills."

Thani didn't flinch. "IronHand won't follow us into the open ground."

"You don't know that," Mila shook her head.

"They know enough about creomancy now to know that there's too much power out there for us to draw on. They're ignorant fools, yes, but I don't think they are *that* stupid. They can't win out there."

"You don't *know* that," Mila repeated through gritted teeth. "We can't underestimate IronHand, Thani. They've gone so far beyond the realms of predictability... Who knows what they'll do."

"Look," Muharram interrupted, "It's not ideal, but we knew this wouldn't be easy. We have to go through the mountains. That forest is our best chance for survival."

"But we must get out of Haman first..." Mahgda murmured.

Thani pointed to the map again. "We will move through the city in small groups, that way we're less likely to draw attention. And if, Gaia forbid, someone is caught—well, at least then it's only a few of us."

No one responded. The same grim expression contorted each person's face.

Thani continued, "So, we aim for the north-western corner of the wall. Everyone will meet up here, where the battlements join the mountainside. Once we're through, we cross this wide field," Her finger traced across a barren space and landed on what looked like a gap between the taller mountains, through the low hills. "Toward this passage in the foothills of the Dend. There we can regroup and figure out the next step with whoever has made it that far."

The silence that followed her words was heavy, awash with the enormity of the trek ahead. Mila stared at the map while her mind drifted back to the tunnel. She would fill Nasir in on the plan when he got here. Her fingers twitched, aching to dig back into the earth, to feel some kind of power amid this chaos.

"How do we get out of Haman?" Arviz asked. "Are we going to keep tunnelling?"

"No, that will take too long," Thani said. "We don't have that sort of time."

"How, then?"

"That one's easy. We tear the wall down."

Silence followed these words. Mahgda shook her head. "That will surely get IronHand's attention, if we haven't already by then…"

"The time for being small is over," Thani said. "We need to go at this with so much power that they're caught off-guard. That's the only way we'll have any sort of advantage."

Mila thought about it, her mind racing through every alternative. An untold number of Satarians would die… but, thought she hated to admit it, Thani was right. No matter how hard she tried, she couldn't think of any other way out of Haman that would be fast enough. The risk was enormous, and the cost sickeningly high, but time was slipping through their fingers, and the only escape lay down this perilous path.

Her gaze flicked to Thani. "When do we leave?" she asked.

Thani stood, gently folding the map and tucking back into her tunic pocket.

"We leave now."

31

Thani stalked away across the debris-strewn floor. Nearby, a heap of concrete and bricks lay in an angular cascade, wedged mid-collapse like a waterfall turned to stone. Thani climbed up to stand high on the pile and, when she could be seen above the crowd, she put two fingers in her mouth and blew. Her sharp whistle cut through the scattered murmurings and the noise in the room fell quickly as all eyes shifted toward her, desperate for guidance. She scanned the group, her expression steely, authoritative.

"Alright everyone, listen up!" she called in Satarian. The tension was thick, each heartbeat suspended in the stillness. Thani raised her chin. "It wasn't supposed to be like this. We were supposed to have more time. Time to plan, to prepare. But, of course, they took *that* from us too. They forced us out of our homes with no warning, no mercy… Yet here we are, still standing."

She paused, letting her words sink in.

"I know you're scared. I know you're tired. But look at what we've already done. We've escaped. We've outrun them—at least for now. And that's because we are *more* than they think we are. We always have been. We've been surviving, day after day, in that camp, and we've learned to adapt. That's what we do—we endure. We're resilient. And now, more than ever, that resilience is going to keep us alive."

Thani took a step higher, her fox-like eyes sweeping over the group.

"Our next step isn't going to be easy. We cannot stay here, but we cannot all leave at once, either. We will move through the city in small groups. Keep along the back alleys, and stick close to the mountains. We'll move through the wall together, then follow the open plains towards the western arm of the Uul Serrad. It's our path to freedom. We can do this. We will show them just how wrong they were about us."

The silence that followed her words was heavy.

A voice suddenly called from the crowd, "What about the others? My aunty, she's still in Al'Mazraea!"

A flurry of many voices picked up, echoing the concern, and Mila fought down a wave of nausea.

We can't save them all.

"I hear you," Thani called, quieter now but with no less intensity. "Every one of you has someone left behind. We *will* go back for them, and we *will* get them out—in time. It can't happen right now but, I swear to you, we are not done fighting. We will go back. Once we've reached safety, once we've built a secure base, we'll return for every last one of them." Her eyes flicked to Mila as she smacked a fist into her palm.

We will go back.

As the refugees headed towards the gaping hole in the building's side, where Ishak and Khalen prepared them to move out into the night, Mila wandered back to the pit. She stood on the very edge without any fear of it crumbling, for she could sense that Khalen had focused all of his strength into making the ground stable. They had taught him well, and he had come a long way in the weeks they had been training.

Khalen was much more than the defensive teen he had first seemed to be. His anger had fuelled his focus, and this had become strength.

Just like Thani said, Mila reflected. *We are more than they think we are.* We are *always* more than *anyone* thinks we are. Humans have the need to categorise, classify and label. It's part of our nature, as an outdated survival instinct. We trim them to the most limited of categories; good or bad. But despite what IronHand thought, no one could be defined by a single quality. It's the layers that make us human. Everybody holds both light and shadow. And right now, Mila's fierce determination made her cling to a stubborn hope.

She willed for Nasir to appear. More than anything she had ever wanted in her whole life, she wanted her brother. She could almost picture it; his strong hands would appear first, then his eyes, alight with affection and that playful annoyance. Strong, protective, unwavering. She dug the toe of her boot into the parched soil, kicking a stream of dust downwards, and tears welled in her eyes as she followed the grey swirl until it was lost to the blackness.

A hand settled on her shoulder.

"It's time, Mila. We need to block the tunnel," said Muharram.

She shook her head. "Just five more minutes."

"Mila—"

She turned to him with tears in her eyes. "Do I know enough about loss now, Muharram?"

A shadow crossed his face, then he sighed. "He will not come, Mila. You know that. Somewhere in there—" he touched her back, over where her heart would be "—you know that."

The truth twisted like a knife in her gut, before she forced the pain down behind her inner shield of numbness.

"If you could get them back," she murmured, "Wouldn't you risk it? Wouldn't you risk everything?"

He was silent for a moment. "This is not your decision to make," he said softly.

Mila whirled away from Muharram and stomped away across the space, dodging refugees and debris, not sure where she was going or what she was doing. She just knew she couldn't watch the tunnel cave in.

When she came up against the far wall, opposite the open air, Mila rested her forehead against the coldness of the bricks and wrapped her arms around herself, trying to hold her insides together even though it felt like a blade had sliced her open from clavicle to hip.

She sensed it rather than saw it; the warmth of the crowd slowly fading, as the steady stream of people moved like mice out into the night. Mila didn't care. Why should she? She stayed there, head against the wall, arms trying to hold herself together. She didn't look around, didn't even move when she felt the ground shudder beneath her feet, but the knowledge that the tunnel had been blocked seemed to choke off her own throat.

Nasir wasn't coming. She knew that. Of course she knew that. She'd known it from the first moment that soil began tumbling down in the tunnel entrance.

She expected to cry, to be paralysed, or unconscionably angry. She expected to be overcome by thoughts and memories of Nasir. But that didn't happen.

There was only one clear thought, and it slammed into her with near-physical force that dropped her to her knees on the cold, dust-covered concrete.

No one would call her *Cricket* ever again.

Only her family called her that. And her family was gone.

There was no one left who knew her as a child, when that nickname came to be. There was no one who knew her, no one who loved her.

Who was she now? Without anyone to share memories with, did those memories even matter?

She was no longer Cricket.

No longer a daughter, or a little sister. No longer part of a family.

No one could protect her or keep her safe from what was to come.

Mila's heart hardened as she crouched there, the searing pain in her soul gradually giving way to something colder, fiercer. Her breath came in short, shaky bursts, but her mind had sharpened with a terrifying clarity. She didn't know how, she didn't know when, but she would make them pay. She would make them all pay. Every guard who had raised a hand against her, every person who stood by while her family was torn apart—they would pay for what they had done.

For what they had taken from her.

Muharram bent down, his strong arms gently gathering Mila up from where she crumbled. She barely registered it at first, this man's presence so like her father that she wanted to crawl inside the comfort he brought and never emerge again.

"Mila," he murmured, his voice low and urgent. "It is time. We must leave, now."

She blinked, dazed, and followed him towards the open wall. All around, the cold shadows seemed to close in. The refugees had been released into the night, already on their way towards the city wall, with the rebel trainees dotted among them.

Only Khalen remained at his post, watching the alleyway with narrowed eyes.

"Can you do this?" Muharram said, not unkindly.

Mila looked at him. It took a beat to realise he was asking her, and a beat longer to bristle at the insinuation. Her parents hadn't given their lives for her to give up this easily. And Nasir hadn't sacrificed himself for her to only wither and break. He had sealed the tunnel to save them all, to give her a chance to fight another day. Another hour. She owed him every minute now.

She refused to be seen as weak. She clenched her jaw, pursed her lips, took a deep, rattling breath and steeled herself to stop trembling. "Of course I can," she said. "This is the easy part."

Mila straightened her shoulders, lifting her chin, then she stepped out and began to climb down toward the alley, moving with maximum caution. The wintery night air made her shiver and goosebumps prickled on her exposed forearms. In the depths of her numb mind, something tugged at her memory. But it took all of her focus not to fall as her hands and boots slipped on the steep decline. She kept moving, down, down.

As she reached the ground, Mila looked for Thani. The short-haired woman had already moved away, her profile a shadow at the end of the alley. Again something tugged at Mila's memory, and at the same time movement caught the corner of her eye, something flickering in the darkness. Her breath hitched. Not the guards already?

She spun to face the danger, only to see a strip of twisted plastic flapping in the wind, its once-bright colour faded. Bold black letters, hard to read in this light, spelled out CAUTION. Mila froze; it hit her like a punch to the gut and her hands curled into fists as she realised where they were.

The ruins. The building from months ago. The rockslide.

Her wide eyes took in the partially collapsed structure that haunted her dreams and her bottom lip began to tremble as Khalen made his way down the escarpment of brick and concrete, splintered wood and twisting metal.

Mila rounded on the teenager, her voice cracking with emotion. "Khalen? How could you—*why* would you bring me here?"

This was where it had all started. The moment that changed everything. The place where her life—where all their lives—had been condemned.

Khalen flinched at her tone, guilt flashing across his face in the shadows, but there was defiance there too, in the way he squared his shoulders.

"The tunnel wasn't finished, Mila," he said quietly, "I had to find us somewhere safe to come up, from nine metres below the surface, and I very little to go on. I had no guidance, no plan… so I followed the earth, and it pulled me here."

"To *this* place?" Mila's voice wavered. She stared at him, horrified, the past crashing over her in waves. This place was a graveyard of memories, the very ground soaked in pain and fear. And now they had returned, as if Gaia herself had chosen to stab her in the back.

"It seems like a perfect place to me. Abandoned, out of the way." Khalen shrugged, and the juvenile response sent a flash of fire through Mila's gut.

"A *perfect place*?" she hissed, just as Muharram reached them.

"Keep moving!" he said.

But Mila stood her ground. "Do you even understand what this place is? What happened here?"

"We haven't got time for this," Muharram cut her off, his weathered features tight with frustration. "We're in the open. Whatever you're arguing about can wait."

Khalen glowered at her, then he took off at a jog, chasing after the others. Muharram pushed Mila on the upper arm, forcing her to turn around, then pushed her again in the back.

"*Go*," he growled. When she didn't move right away, he pushed her a third time. "You're stronger than this place, Mila. Stronger than the past. All we need to focus on is the present, here and now. Don't look back."

He gave Mila one more push, and it seemed to kick-start her.

She swallowed hard, willing her legs to move, and began jogging down the alley. The air felt cold and uncomfortable, as though the memories were clammy fingers clinging to her skin, but she pulled away from them. Muharram's words echoed in her mind.

Stronger than this place.

Stronger than the past.

Mila turned sharply at the end of the alley, already short of breath, and found herself on a wider, darker street. The empty husks of unlit streetlights hung over the path. The hair on the back of her neck prickled, knowing that every darkened doorway could be hiding something—a concerned citizen, or worse, a lurking guard. Her pulse quickened, instincts screaming at her to stay alert. From the upper windows of the stone houses hung banners showing the IronHand sigil. Every now and then, the wind would stir up the fabric, making it flap like the wings of a bat in the night sky.

Ahead, she caught a glimpse of movement. Khalen's lanky form, barely visible a dozen metres ahead, dipped in and out of the solid shadows. Mila pushed harder, forcing herself to keep up, her eyes darting around as she ran. The silence was deafening, broken only by the occasional rustle of something unseen.

Don't look back.

She couldn't shake that uncomfortable sensation that someone was watching her. Even so, it took Mila a moment to realise that Khalen's silhouette had frozen up ahead. Instinctively, she froze too. Khalen melted into the shadows of a narrow space between buildings and Mila did the same, taking refuge in a recessed doorway. Only her eyes peeked out, glued on the place where Khalen had disappeared. The scrunch of boots and chatter of Amanese words echoed out of the night and three people appeared, walking casually along the road, perhaps heading home from the tavern. Mila relaxed, but only a fraction. They may not be IronHand guards, but these people were still dangerous.

Their footsteps seemed to be slowing, and then they stopped altogether. Mila risked another glance, and saw just the back of one of them heading away. Where were the other two?

Mila didn't know what to do. Had they seen one of the refugees? Had they seen Khalen? Why else would they have stopped walking? But there were no cries and noises to indicate that they had been exposed... Yet.

Heat surged through her body. What should she do? What *could* she do? They hadn't discussed anything about the journey, about what they should do if they were discovered, and now it was too late. She took a deep breath, held it, and ducked back out into the street, keeping low. At that moment, a muffled thud came from further along, followed by a low grunt. Then another sound, higher pitched, and a scuffling noise. The sounds of a struggle.

Khalen.

Mila didn't think about it, she just straightened up and launched herself towards the noise. Her hurried footsteps were almost soundless on the paving stones, her breath sharp in her lungs. She didn't think about what she'd find; all she knew was that Khalen was in trouble.

She tore around the corner of the alley. A figure lay slumped against the wall, unconscious, his body crumpled like a broken puppet. A metre away, Khalen was locked in a brawl with the second man, their bodies tangled as they grappled and twisted. Khalen's face was contorted in concentration, his grip slipping as the man tried to get his hands towards the boy's neck. Any second now the man would succeed in pinning Khalen down.

Mila ran towards them. The man heard her when she was still a few steps away, and he started to turn towards her. Wild terror flared in her gut—she hadn't thought this through, and she had no idea what to do now. But Khalen saw the man's attention waver and seized the opportunity; he pushed up against him, using the man's momentum to his advantage. Mila saw the man's dark eyes widen as he realised he was outnumbered, but there was nothing he could do. Mila leapt forward, crashing into him with all her force, knocking him sideways and off Khalen. And then she was on him, trying to hold the man down, but he was far too strong for her.

He shoved her hard, knocking all the wind out, and he twisted free. But Khalen was there, holding what looked like a fractured brick, and he raised his arms high, then brought the stone rushing down towards the man's head. The man managed to bring his own arm up to deflect the blow, and the brick slammed into his flesh instead. He let out a sharp cry of pain, clutching his arm, but the sound was quickly silenced as Khalen brought the brick down again. There was a terrible, dull crunching noise, like an overripe apple hitting the ground; a sickly, fleshy smack that lingered in the air. The man's eyes rolled into the back of his head and he dropped to the ground, unmoving.

There was a second where Mila expected him to get back up again, but there was no way he could. His skull was no longer whole. Thick blood oozed from his head like treacle.

His torso lay across her legs, heavy and motionless, and she had to fight down the revulsion as she struggled frantically to wiggle out from under him. Adrenaline and strength faded quickly, replaced with the intense desire to scream as she stood, looking down at the two bodies strewn across the paving stones like trash. The second man's leg twitched as his nerves died.

Her hands began to tremble. A storm of feelings erupted inside her; anger, confusion, relief, disgust.

"What did you do, Khalen?" she whispered.

"I didn't… they just…" his incoherent words shook. He looked at her with wide eyes, no longer the self-sufficient young man, but a lost and terrified child.

Mila wrapped her arms around him in a mechanical hug, while her eyes remained locked on the bodies. "It's okay," she said, trying to believe her own lie. "It's okay."

His thin frame trembled violently, like a brittle reed bending in a storm, each shudder threatening to snap him in two.

More footsteps echoed from the street behind them and she felt Khalen freeze. Still half-hugging, staring down the dark alley, their breaths became shallow. Someone was coming.

Mila pulled away from Khalen, her body tensing, ready for the worst.

But then, out of the darkness, Muharram's familiar figure emerged, his face set in urgency. Relief broke over her like a cold sweat, but the sick feeling in her gut remained. This was a disaster. They had barely made it ten minutes from the tunnel exit and bodies were already piling up.

"What happened here?" Muharram said, voice quiet and low.

Mila looked at Khalen. His head was down. "It happened so quickly," he said. His voice sounded heavy, dead. "I saw the people coming—no, I heard them first. Then I saw them. So I froze and I thought they would just keep moving on but then they were coming towards me. And I was close to this alley so I moved in here to hide." He swallowed thickly. "I thought for sure they'd seen me, but they were just chatting, and I moved to the back of the alley trying to, you know, hide. That one—" he pointed to the body with the crushed skull "—started to take a piss against the wall but the other one decided to walk in further and, well, he saw me."

He suddenly retched and vomited.

Mila looked away and Muharram winced. The older man put a hand on the boy's back, steadying him. "Okay, okay," he said, thinking aloud. "It's dark, not yet the middle of the night. The chances of someone discovering the bodies before dawn is low. We potentially have hours, maybe longer."

"What about the woman? She'll know they're missing."

Muharram glanced at Mila sharply. "Woman? What woman?"

"There was a woman with them. I don't know where she went."

Muharram's eye twitched. "Keep going," he said urgently. "Follow the plan and I will find you."

Then without another word, the older man hurried out onto the street, disappearing quickly around the corner.

Mila and Khalen, the boy still catching his breath, watched him go. They didn't discuss where Muharram had gone, but Mila had little doubt that the woman would live to see the sunrise.

And she was okay with that.

32

The stone building that housed the Haman bazaar was unrecognisable at night, a ghost of the vibrant and bustling market it had been the last time Mila saw it. The pale moonlight drained everything of colour, leaving the outer stalls like skeletons cloaked in tarps, while the internal sections of the sprawling business district were secured behind closed gates of black iron wrought into a diamond pattern. Beyond the bars, the shadows seemed deeper, the stalls behind them locked away like bad memories. The smell of spices lingered.

Mila and Khalen slowed their pace, exchanging glances filled with tension. The wintry wind whisked across the vast emptiness of the open concrete mall, snatching up litter and dirt. Mila chewed her lip as she scanned the perimeter. The sensation pressed at her from the outside in with increasing pressure; they were being hunted. With their branded foreheads and grey tunics, they were a deadly animal to be flushed out, found, and killed.

Thin electrical wires criss-crossed overhead, reminding Mila of spider web strings glistening in the moonlight. The distant tip of the Dend could just be seen above the buildings, silhouetted against the stars.

"Can you see anything…" Mila whispered, eyes flicking between the shadows.

Khalen had been silent the entire walk, shrunken in on himself, already haunted by the souls of the men he had killed. He shook his head.

When Mila was satisfied there were no guards prowling in the recesses of the bazaar, they moved on. The western city wall was still far, and they needed to keep moving. Every minute they delayed was another minute trapped inside.

As they wove further and further through the tight alleyways, the buildings suddenly dropped away, leaving the towering wall rising just meters ahead. Mila's mouth went dry as she took in the sheer size of it, feeling like an insect at the base of a mountain. Cracks and crevices etched across the rough, ancient stonework, streaked with dark moss and weathered by centuries of storms and wind. The nearby houses and shops leaned in, casting their own warped shadows against the wall, and the structure appeared to shift slightly in the uneven light cast by spotlights mounted at intervals along the parapet. As her eyes adjusted, Mila could just make out the soft silhouettes of people clustered in the crook between the wall and where it collided with the mountains, keeping away from the watchful lights as they too scrutinised studied this final, formidable obstacle.

So close and yet so far from free.

That had always been true.

Mila had been a prisoner from the moment she was born. Yes, the border fence had been smaller then, the restraints more bureaucratic, the prejudices more subtle. But the message had been there all her life; she had to be suppressed, caged, bound. She was not a real person, and never had been.

As a very young child, Mila had never conceived of a world without wire fences, where one's house had solid walls and a straight roof, with running water and privacy. As a child you don't know any better, until you're exposed to a reality different from the one you live in. You can't make comparisons if you have no context, and she had none until it was shoved in her face.

Mila wondered; if her mahma had never taken her into town, if she had never laid eyes on the brick buildings and paving stones and the colours of the bazaar, with all its forbidden treasures, would she still live in ignorant bliss thinking conditions in the camp were standard? Was it possible to never want for more?

No, she didn't think so. A captive animal always knows it is caged, even if it has never smelled the fresh air of the outside, even if it has never basked in the sunshine beneath a clear blue sky. A living being always feels the call of nature, of freedom. It's innate, and there's a darkness that comes with being restricted from the wider world. The Satarians had become so stunted in their segregation from nature, from their magic, their true power. Restricted magic can never grow, just as a caged being can never thrive.

And the Amanese knew that. That's what they wanted; subdued, disappearing magic. Disappearing people.

For three hundred years, the Satarians had been wardens of the state, bound to the same fate as the generation before. Doomed to live and die in the dusty grounds of Al'Mazraea.

But now freedom seemed closer than ever, just on the other side of this wall.

Mila and Khalen slowed, every movement cautious. Her fingers traced along the ragged rocks of the mountainside as they approached the Satarians. Her palms tingled with anticipation, her magic simmering just beneath her skin, aching to be used. Khalen was just in front of her, his hand also touching the mountain, eyes fixed on the wall ahead.

Irani pushed through the waiting throng, and her small smile fell. "Is Muharram not with you?" she asked.

Mila shook her head. "I thought he would be here, with you. We got separated…"

Khalen made a noise part way between a groan and a cough. Irani glanced with concern at Khalen and opened her mouth to ask, but Mila shook her head. They didn't need to relive it. Not now.

Mila looked back, raking the black and grey for any sign of movement, dread coiling in her stomach with the awareness that if there *was* movement, it might not be Muharram. She chewed her lower lip.

A smoky cough alerted them to Mahgda's presence. Shadows clung to her high cheekbones and strong jawline. The elegant woman didn't waste words asking; she could see the rebel leader was missing, and her expression hardened. "Should we wait?" was all her deep, gravelly voice said.

She looked to Mila, as did the others. When had they come to see her as a leader? Why? Mila didn't want to have to make this decision.

Quick footsteps sounded in the distance, echoing down the streets. Two sets. Without a word, the four of them faded into the shadows of the nearby building, leaving the clustered the refugees near the wall. Would the four rebels be enough to overpower the approaching figures before they could sound the alarm?

Through the gap in the buildings, Mila saw two indistinct silhouettes creep through the darkness, fluid and silent, moving closer to the mountain. It was as though the air itself thickened, pressing down on Mila. She couldn't keep going like this; stress after stress. Was this the sound of death coming towards her? Or would she have to bring death down upon another person? She slipped around the corner, intending to come up behind the hunters. And what then? Mila swallowed.

Then Thani moved into the moonlight, closely followed by Muharram.

"Oh Gaia," Mila exhaled, causing them both to whirl around. They hadn't heard her coming.

Muharram was covered in blood from shoulder to waist. Thick globules of it caught the light, glistening. Mila's eyes widened and she hurried towards him, grabbing Muharram forcefully and patting him down, looking for the injury. There was no way he could be okay with that much blood.

But he shoved her away. "It's not mine," he said, corners of his mouth tight.

"Who…" The question faded away. She knew who.

His dark green eyes focussed on her. "She had to die, Mila. If she had realised her friends weren't following, she would have alerted the guards right away and they would come looking for us—for *all* of us. I don't think they expected us to come into Haman, and that's the only thing working for us right now."

Mila didn't answer. She hated herself for the wave of relief that came at Muharram's words, but she knew he was right. They were in the clear now with all three possible witnesses taken care of. It was good.

Thani's face was pale, her movements stiff, like she was holding herself together by sheer will. Muharram gripped her shoulder, a silent gesture. "Are we all here?"

Mahgda and Irani nodded.

"Good. Let's go."

The others followed as he led the way through the crowd of people huddled in the shadows at the foot of the Uul Serrad. Wary eyes watched them, not yet daring to hope that this plan might succeed.

When they reached the wall, Mila looked up. The structure loomed above them. Muharram moved close beside her and rested his hand briefly on her shoulder.

"We can do this," he said, then he knelt and pressed one hand to the ground, and the other against the stone wall.

The others followed, and Mila crouched with them. She closed her eyes for a moment, focusing on the power thrumming beneath her hand. This wall, however massive, would bend for them.

"Ad tay khiedery r'mahiya, plezht y pemetteray Gaia..." Mila whispered, in unison with the rebels. These ancient words that had been passed from the free people of Stara Zhem to the oppressed people of Al'Mazraea, that had only survived in hushed tones by people too bold to be crushed completely.

The sunshine feeling swirled to life in her chest, and it felt to Mila as though its pure warmth and happiness shined a light on all the dark, broken spaces within her soul. Tears spilled down her cheeks, startling her, and she forced herself to take a deep breath. Just this one last barrier, and they would be free.

Voices joined hers and Mila felt the surge of power as the group united, each drawing from the raw, ancient strength of the mountain. From the ancient strength of her people. The earth's power was mightier than anything that man could build.

She pressed her palm harder against the stone, drawing energy from it and pouring energy through it. The corner of the wall began to crack. The Satarian whispers turned into a low, thrumming chant, and the ground began to quake. The foundations trembled as the magic reached deep within the wall. With a sudden, sharp noise like thunder, a crack appeared directly above Mila, branching out like lightning frozen in time. The wall shuddered violently as the individual stones ground against one another with shrieks and groans. Dust puffed out from the fissures like ancient souls set free.

Within minutes, crumbled rock cascaded to the ground, bringing a billow of dust that stung Mila's eyes. Rumbling thuds rolled away through the alleys and a reverent hush fell over the assembly. Mila knew the guards would have felt the disturbance, but she found that she *wanted* them to know. The city *should* feel the power of the magic it feared. Their creomancy had stirred the stone like a warning bell, and now it was a dire race between predator and prey.

As the dust began to settle, Mila could see the breach—narrow, imperfect, but enough. She moved forward to help refugees clamber over the crumbled stones and squeeze through the narrow opening in twos and threes, as frantic as rats escaping a flood.

With his daughter clinging to his back, Arviz stumbled across, helping to guide the Satarians on the other side. As the last few slipped through, Mila paused, glancing back at the city, thinking of the shadows and death that lay on the other side, back in Al'Mazraea.

Her parents' bodies were there.

Nasir too. He should have been beside her now.

Tears pricked her eyes as she pressed her hands to the cold stone, preparing to climb up and through to the other side.

I'll come back for you, she silently promised him. *I won't let you rot in there.*

With one last look back, she slipped through the gap, her promise mingling with the dust in the darkness.

33

There were very few houses on this side of the wall; simple dwellings, older and more weathered. Property boundaries were far between and marked with lines of wire.

The land seemed to stretch on forever and ever. So much space, so much room to share—yet the Amanese confined them to a tiny area, then said they were being selfish in wanting more.

Mila let her gaze drift to the stars shimmering above the grassy plane. It was hard to get truly angry about that now, looking at the expanse above. She felt suddenly very small, standing there looking out across the dark land, beneath those ancient lights. The problems of humans were but a blip in time, less noticeable than a blink of the eye. What did the stars care for all of this? The heavens didn't care if she was alone. They didn't care if she lost everything that was dear to her, even if that included her life itself. It would all keep going, twisting, expanding, whether she was around or not—just as it had done for billions of years, and would continue to do for billions more.

Never before had she felt so untethered, never had she had nothing to hold her to earth. Like her very molecules of existence could float away at any moment, scattered like the grass pollen upon the westerly breeze that was caressing her face. It was deeply unsettling.

Her parents…

Her brother…

Her home…

She couldn't run to the familiarity of any of those now.

All she had was herself.

The constellations made slow progress overhead, mirroring the crawl of her thoughts as her heart seemed to beat in time with the thud of her boots. The moon threw out silver light onto the knee-high grasses, creating stark shadows beneath, and the blades whipped at the exposed skin of her ankles and legs. She shivered as sweat trickled down her brow and neck and disappeared into her tattered tunic.

She glanced beside her to Khalen, his eyes forward but distant, as he too was swallowed by his thoughts.

As Mila's eyes adjusted to the moonlight, the petechiae of silhouettes across the plain became visible. Tears pricked her eyes at the surreal sight; the refugees, free, beckoned by the open sky and the unmarked path, the mountainous horizon promising a life no longer dictated by walls, but by their own choices and dreams. Closest, Mila could just make out the faint figures of Muharram and Thani, maybe fifty metres away. The sight of their familiar shapes brought her a small, fragile sense of comfort, but they weren't the man and woman she truly longed to see.

As they pressed onward, the scattered groups drew closer to each other, the distance between them narrowing, and with that closeness something began to stir. It started with a soft hum, barely audible over the vastness of the plains and the swish of feet moving through tall grass. Mila didn't notice it at first. Her thoughts were too consumed by the ache deep inside her. But the sound grew like the rising of a distant rain shower, tickling her senses, soft and familiar.

A melody, she realised.

The people were singing.

Mila felt a deep unease at the sound. They shouldn't be making this much noise. Not now. Not out here where the danger was still so close, where anyone could hear. This might be the closest they had come to freedom in a lifetime, but they weren't there yet.

The Satarian words sparkled through the night air:

How vast the distance lain before me
How high the peaks I could not tame
In my need, I turned to nature
And to the winds whispered her name

The refugees drew closer together as if magnetised, and the song grew louder, the voices around her stronger.

Then through the darkness, humbling power
Shook the shadows in my soul
Work of life, unfolding flower
Gaia's land, my living home

From beside her, Khalen's voice gave Mila a start. She glanced at him, eyebrows raised, as his steady tone matched the rhythm of their steps. He was weary, his features crumpled and drawn, but as he sang something about him seemed lighter, more peaceful than ever before.

The pull of the music was irresistible. It tugged at her, softening the edges of her grief, coaxing something loose that she had buried deep inside for months. Years. The song washed over her, filling the corners of the void inside, lifting her up. Slowly, hesitantly, her throat loosened, and Mila began to hum. Her sound was almost lost in the night, but it was there, fragile and uncertain, joining with the others.

In hours darkest, lost, unknown
Who could quell when we are one
Through the rivers, sands and stone,
Mother Earth's daughters and sons

The melody roused a distant memory, and Mila remembered learning this tune as a young girl, around the cooking fire with neighbours and friends. Now the dormant words awoke after all these years, as though they had been awaiting this moment. Tears welled in her eyes, spilled down her cheeks, but she didn't brush them away. Not just tears of grief, of loss and anger, no—there was something else there too, something she hadn't allowed herself in a long time.

Hope.

Mila's heart surged with sudden defiance. For once, let them hear us, she thought. For too long we have whispered our words in the shadows, for fear of being heard. Let them hear what they tried to silence! Her lips parted, and she sang in earnest.

The power is ours to share together
Expanse of greatness that I roam
Beautiful Mother, yours forever
Gaia's land, my living home

Muharram was within reach now, and he slipped his arm around her shoulders, beaming between syllables.

"We did it, Mila."

The hymn began again and the refugees, all together now, began to sing louder, their voices no longer whispers but full and vibrant. The song drifted across the plains, carried by the wintry wind, a song of gratitude and survival for whoever might hear it.

Above, the towering peaks watched over them, cutting toothed shapes into the satin sky, their snowy tops silver in the moonlight. A cold wind rushed down to bite at the Satarians' faces, whipping their tattered grey clothes. It carried the unmistakable scent of ice and stone but, despite the chill, there was something invigorating about it. Clean and unsullied. A promise of the freedom that lay just ahead.

Mila leaned forward, hands pressing into her legs to keep going as the ground began to slope upward. Her eyes traced the massive silhouette of the Dend, its broad form dark against the stars, guiding them to the passage they needed to take. She could picture the map in her mind: just beyond this passage, over the foothills and past the formidable presence of the Dend, lay the forest of the Verd.

As the song swelled, Mila glanced over at Khalen again. He caught her gaze, and a small smile tugged at the corner of his lips. Mila smiled back, though it was bitter-sweet. They were alive.

So many weren't—but *they* were.

And for the first time, they were moving forward.

Mila sang with everything she had, her voice joining the others in a powerful cry. She threw her arms out to her sides, palms and face up, then spun slowly around and around as she walked, enjoying the space and the feeling of it. So much space!

But then something caught her eye—movement beyond the last of the refugees, emerging from the distant vestiges of the Haman city walls. She squinted, trying to make sense of it across the distance and the dim light, as her stomach plummeted with dread.

Three separate disturbances, headlights muted but unmistakable.

Trucks, hurtling across the plain with the speed of a starving cheetah, kicking up clouds of dust in their wake.

They were gaining fast. Too fast. The wind had worked in their favour, blowing the sounds of the trucks away from the refugees. Mila had never heard them coming.

Panic surged through her, quick and cold.

"Run!" Mila shrieked. Khalen lifted his head. The singing faltered. In an instant, the choir dissolved into a chaotic stampede as people began to run. Shouts and screams surged in a swirl of hysteria, crashing together like thunder in an approaching storm. Mila grabbed Khalen's arm and dragged him forward into a staggering run.

"Move! Over the hills!" Muharram's voice boomed from somewhere to her right, his figure just barely visible through the darkness. He urged the others forward, rushing them toward the distant mountains that beckoned with the promise of safety. "Stay low!"

Bodies slammed into Mila like the winds of a hurricane, buffeting, pounding against her, and suddenly Khalen was swallowed up as if he had been pulled beneath a wave.

A hand snatched at her shirt and she ripped herself away, the momentum throwing her into someone else. Sweating bodies crashed into each other, knocking her off balance, and she went down, screaming. A knee collided heavily with her shoulder, and still more people stepped on her, tripping themselves and pushing her into the dirt.

At the same time, the ground began to vibrate with a low, ominous rumble and the revving of engines grew louder. The trucks closed the distance with every breath like vultures following a scent.

Terror threatened to root her to the spot, but Mila clenched her jaw, forcing herself to crawl forward. They should have known. Had they really been naïve enough to think they were in the clear? It was foolish to allow herself the joyful, hopeful feeling of moments ago. A foot caught her in the stomach, knocking her breathless. Mila cursed herself for relaxing, for joining in with the celebration when she should have been urging them all to move faster.

Was she really foolish enough to believe the guards would let them go?

She cried out in pain as her fingers were crushed beneath another darting foot, and the earth pulsed with power that took away what little breath she had. It was so much stronger than anything she had experienced back in the camp. Even the richest soil of Al'Mazraea seemed weak and drained compared to this, out here, in the uncultivated wilderness. It was like comparing the light of a lamp to the blaze of the sun. The feeling of it coursed through her fingertips and up her arms, filling her with an electrifying force.

This; the power that only the Satarians had access to, that the earth goddess shared with them and them alone. The power that the Amanese feared and hated. The power they had had the whole time, though they were taught to feel powerless.

Mila knew in that moment that the guards were never going to stop. Even if the refugees managed to outrun the speeding trucks now, the guards would never let them go. They would chase them, through the mountain ranges, through every forest, until there was nowhere left to go. Running meant living in fear for the rest of their lives. The guards would hunt them down, every last one of them, from the smallest child to the weakest elder. They would massacre them all.

And why? Because they wanted to live?

The unfairness of it all burned behind Mila's eyes as her fingers tightened around the tussocks, knuckles white. None of them would survive unless something changed. They couldn't outrun IronHand's hatred. They had to fight it, fight the future the Amanese had bound them to.

No more crying. No more feeling inferior. No more running away. This was their chance.

This was *her* chance to make it all right.

The last time she had used creomancy to defend herself, things had gone horribly wrong. The destruction she had caused, the lives that were ruined—it haunted her, every second of every day. But now? Now she had no choice. Without creomancy, they would all die.

Her pulse quickened with a new kind of determination. She pushed her chest up, seeing the refugees scattering as fear drove them in every direction.

"I can stop them," she whispered. On her knees now, she turned to face the trucks once more. They were closing in, barely a kilometre away, the moonlight glinting off their hard metal chassis. Bright headlights seared through the gloom and cast long shadows with the grasses.

"I *will* stop them."

As she gouged her fingers into the dirt, Mila was surprised to feel the fear that had gnawed at her gut a moment ago vanish. The earth responded to her touch immediately, warm and alive beneath her fingers. The power of it took her breath away. This was raw, primal, free. Already the connection consumed her; already the pulse quickened and flowed through her veins.

Behind her, the refugees stopped running, sensing the call of the earth.

Mila closed her eyes.

The ground beneath her hands began to stir, trembling as if awakening from a deep slumber. She envisioned the earth splitting, opening wide to swallow the trucks, to stop them in their tracks. She poured every ounce of her fear, her grief, and her rage into that vision.

The earth groaned in response.

Her whole body vibrated with the power coursing through her as the energy responded to her will, and she dug her hands deeper into the dirt, feeling the rocks shift. The soil trembled.

Suddenly, with a sound like a great beast roaring to life, the ground began to crack. A fissure, narrow at first, snaked its way across the plain, growing wider and deeper with every second. Clouds of dirt billowed up as it stretched out, forming a ravine between the refugees and the approaching guards and completely cutting off the advance.

The trucks screeched to a halt at the edge. Dust swirled and twisted in the headlights. Panting, Mila pried her hands free from the earth, staring at the crevice she had created. It stretched on for what seemed like miles, a great scar across the land.

But it wasn't enough. IronHand was still there, still a threat.

For a moment, the refugees held their collective breath.

Then, one of the truck doors creaked open.

A man stepped out, his tall frame illuminated by the headlights of the vehicle behind him. He strolled forward casually, slowly, his boots crunching on the rocky ground. It was only as he stepped towards the edge of the ravine that Mila saw his face clearly.

Lideri.

34

The sight of him standing barely fifty metres away sent Mila spiralling. One moment, she was crouched in the grass, the night torn apart by the truck headlights—the next, she was back in Al'Mazraea, the restraints biting into her wrists, the air thick with the stench of gunpowder and copper. Her breath came in shallow gasps, as though an invisible hand had clamped around her throat, cutting off any sound she might have made. She couldn't breathe. She couldn't move. Time seemed to stop and her vision swam. All she could think, all she could see, was Lideri's twisted scar as he ordered her parents to be shot. Over and over again their blood pooled before her eyes. The sound of gunfire echoed through her mind in time with her racing heartbeat.

The governor's face was calm, almost bored, as he inspected the changed earth. Mila pushed to her feet, muscles trembling and heart hammering like a caged bird against her ribs. Every instinct told her to prepare, to defend. The ground beneath her still hummed with power, but she could also feel its weariness now. The debt needed to be paid.

Lideri paused with the abyss yawning in front of him.

"And you wonder why we feel the need to control you," he said. He looked down, almost curiously, then, with a casual kick of his boot, he sent a loose stone tumbling into the shadows below.

Silence followed as it fell, and he finally looked at Mila. His dark eyes bored into hers and a dreadful, glacial sensation crawled down from the crown of her head. Those eyes were a window to his soul, and what Mila saw inside chilled her to the core; a suffocating darkness, a rotting pit of hatred, cruelty, and ruthless ambition. Icy spiders skittered in her veins at the sight. He gestured dismissively at the fissure, as though it were nothing more than an inconvenience, something they had conjured in a fit of childish defiance.

"You think this will save you?" he continued, his rising voice carrying easily across the plain. "You think hiding behind your tricks will keep you safe?" He sneered. "It won't. You have nowhere to run, nowhere to hide. And this—" he waved his hand at the broken earth "—this is just delaying the inevitable."

Though he gave the impression of composure, a muscle spasmed in his clenched jaw, betraying the anger that boiled just beneath his cold exterior. His hands twitched like he was itching to grab the insolent Creo in front of him.

"Give yourselves in now, and I will show you mercy," he cried.

Behind Mila, other refugees stirred uneasily, murmurs passing through them like wind in the treetops. But no one moved. No one dared. Mila's eyes narrowed.

"You'll be allowed to continue working, and we will permit your return to Al'Mazraea." Lideri spoke as if he truly believed he was offering them a gift. "But, if you continue this ridiculous charade, we will shoot you all where you stand. And no one will bury you—we will burn the bodies and use the ashes for concrete. You will *never* return to the earth."

A long, heavy silence fell over the plain.

The guards behind Lideri readied their rifles; the mechanical sound of shells being slid into chambers punctuated the stillness. Mila struggled to see the possibilities through a tide of rising panic. From all around her, the refugees' doubts and fears coalesced with her own.

Lideri crossed his arms and tilted his head, his steely gaze locked on Mila. "I'll give you five minutes to confer with your *people*," he spat the word, as though it tasted foul in his mouth. "Tell them yourself what you've decided—whether you will surrender, or be sentenced to death." He leaned back, waiting. "The clock is ticking."

Without acknowledging him, Mila turned her back on Lideri. A hundred pale, terrified faces looked back at her, scattered across the tableland. Only a hundred, when there should have been fifteen times that.

She felt Lideri's words like a gun to her head, and for a moment— one insane moment—the thought of surrendering crossed her mind. But she would not return to Al'Mazraea as a slave. That hollow life was not *life*. It would just be a slow demise, dying one by one like candles burning down to the quick, as IronHand worked them to the very end.

Khalen came to her, followed by Muharram, Thani and the other rebels.

"I won't go back to the camps," Béa said, shaking her head. Her face was pale, no mirth in her eyes now. "I'd rather die."

"You might get your wish," Ishak muttered. "Lideri's men are just waiting for an excuse to slaughter us all."

"We're outnumbered and exhausted... He knows we can't fight him."

"There has to be another way," Arviz said. He was standing just outside the conversation, slowly rocking from foot to foot as he held his daughter to him, leaning his head against hers that was buried in the crook of his neck. What kind of future would this girl have, if Lideri got his way?

Mahgda's lips pursed. "Lideri is a monster. He won't stop until we're crushed."

Mila shook her head. She didn't know what to do.

Nasir's words whispered in her mind; *Stay calm, small, no matter what.*

But life cannot be lived by being small, Mila thought. We are *people*. We are allowed to take up space. To own who we are and what our future holds. We are allowed to have an identity.

She could feel the anger building, feeding off every ounce of pain, every loss, every night spent wondering if tomorrow would come. She would not be small anymore, and she wouldn't be calm; not for him, not for anyone. Not after everything.

Mila glanced at the others, knowing what she had to do, but she couldn't do it alone. It would take the full force of the Satarian magic to stop this once and for all.

Khalen's voice broke through her thoughts. Mila looked up. He back with eyes ablaze, perhaps sensing the fire within her. He plucked the rumpled blue flower from his buttonhole and handed it to her. "We're with you, Mila."

She shook her head, needing him to understand. She couldn't ask this of him. "He'll kill us all, Khalen."

"Maybe he will. We risk being destroyed either way but..." he said, voice low and firm. "If we fight, at least we die free. Free because of *you*."

The words hit her like a sudden sunbeam. She had triggered it all. Countless deaths, punishment, months of misery; it was all her fault. But as she looked at the people around her, each burning with the desire for something more, something began to shift inside her. She was still responsible for their lives, but it was no longer a burden or a constant reminder of her mistakes. It was an honour. The heavy knot of guilt began to melt away. What she did had set things in motion. She had unleashed a power, power that for so long she had thought was a curse but… She could finally see it all for what it truly was: the path out.

Maybe she wasn't the reason they were all in danger… Maybe she was the reason they would be free. Maybe she had been the spark they needed to ignite a revolution.

Slowly, one by one, each of the refugees came closer, gathering around. They formed a half-circle, shoulder to shoulder, bound not by fear, but by a purpose larger than any one of them alone. They were ready.

Mila swallowed hard, pushing every ounce of conviction and strength into her voice. "They'll hunt us forever if we run," Mila called. "We're stronger than they know. We've trained for this. We can stop them—but only if we stand together."

Would they listen to her, the Murderer? Could they follow her, after what she had done?

Their eyes met hers: searching, questioning, fearful. But there was something else there too. The song of freedom had ignited a long-dormant hope, and it still flickered in their eyes. They didn't turn away.

"For so long they have told us where we can go and what we can do. They've told us who we are; evil, useless, worthless. But they're wrong! They don't see your desires or your dreams, they don't hear the song in your soul. But the time has come for them to finally hear us! We will shatter the silence that bound us, and they will feel the force of the words they fear. Let the ground quake with the fury of all we've kept buried!"

"Nos unisar!" came a single voice from the crowd. To Mila's surprise, others echoed the cry.

"Nos unisar!"

"Nos unisar!"

She turned to Khalen, speaking in a low voice. "Get them ready. As many as you can. Tell them to keep as close to the ground as possible and, on my signal, start the creomancy."

"What are you going to do, Mila?"

"I'll do my best to stop the guards, but I'll need all the help I can get."

Khalen looked like he wanted to say something else, but with a solemn nod, he moved away. She watched him for a moment; this teenager who had become a warrior, then she turned back to face Lideri and stalked carefully to the edge of the ravine, drawing his attention from the group behind her.

"So, what will it be?" the governor asked, "Surrender, or die?"

"Let me ask you something," she called in reply. "Why do you hate us so much? What did we ever do to deserve this?"

The question seemed to catch him off guard. Even from this distance Mila saw his eyebrows flicker upwards, as if he hadn't ever considered it before. The guards behind him stiffened, but Lideri waved a hand, signalling them to lower their weapons.

"The riverbank doesn't get to question the flood," he growled. "It is simply overrun."

"But when the waters recede, the riverbank remains," Mila replied, trying to keep her voice steady. "Go on, explain it to me. All we've ever done is try to live. We work, we grow, we have no luxuries—we barely have enough to survive. What's the reason for all this?" Her hand gestured to the guards, the trucks, the rifles pointed at them.

Lideri's jaw tightened as he looked at her, as though even acknowledging her was beneath him. He gestured to the scar at his feet in return. "Do you really need to ask that?" he spat. There was a pause, before the torrent of vitriol spilled out of him. "Your *people*… You came here—illegally—and you took our land. You don't want to learn our ways or follow our customs, but you're happy to take our money and our resources for yourselves. All the while, you have the power to ruin the earth, and to kill as you see fit. You're parasites!"

His venomous voice was almost drowned out by the anger ringing in her ears. Mila fought to keep control of her actions.

Stay calm.

She couldn't jump the gun. They needed more time. She had to stall, keep Lideri's attention on her.

"We didn't ask for this," Mila yelled. "The people you're talking about came to Ard Aman three *hundred* years ago, yet you've kept us fenced in for generation after generation. We—all of us—we were born in the camp. We were born stateless, with nothing to call our own. We didn't *take* anything. Your people kept us away."

"And good thing we did!" Lideri yelled. "If we hadn't kept you under control, who knows what would have happened. The way you manipulate the earth, imposing your will where it doesn't belong. It's dangerous. *You're* dangerous. The Satarians are nothing more than a disease. A plague!"

The words echoed in Mila's mind, stirring a distant memory.

"Your magic is a disease, a pestilence that threatens the very fabric of our world. It is not a gift; it is a curse. And those who wield it are nothing more than poison."

Mila shook her head. "You never cared to find out what really happened that day, with the rockfall in Haman. You never gave us a chance, you just decided we're evil and condemned us to captivity. You don't care about the truth!"

"The rockfall," Lideri said, and something gleeful crossed his face. "That worked out better than even I could have planned it! You dug your own grave that day. I never dreamed there would be an actual Creo on-site, and one dumb enough to use her magic, at that. When that guard showed me your passbook and told me one of you was *actually* involved… Well, I had all the support I needed."

Mila's blood ran cold as Lideri's words sank in. He planned this? She opened her mouth to speak, but words wouldn't come. She had unwittingly become a pawn in his malignant plot, and her suffering was merely a bonus. Deep, black rage seeped into the edges of her vision and thundered in her ears. She wanted to *kill* him, to end him, to dig her fingers into his flesh, rip his limbs from his torso and spill his innards all over the thirsty soil.

Stay calm.

"So that's what this is?" She somehow found her voice, though it sounded like it was coming from somewhere else. She had to keep him talking. "You're so afraid of us that you had to set us up? Some might call that cheating, Lideri."

The words hung in the air as a challenge, and for a split second, Lideri's face twitched—barely perceptible, but enough. "This conversation is over," he snapped.

"Let the Satarians go to the forest," Mila insisted. "Leave us the Verd and you'll never have to hear from us again. We'll gather the people still stuck in Al'Mazraea, and you can take back those lands you seem to want so much. It's win-win."

Lideri gave a mirthless chuckle. "Oh, *thank you* for allowing us to have *our* land back," he said, sarcasm dripping from every syllable. "That's so kind of you. Did you hear that, men?" He turned his head to call over his shoulder. "They're going to *let us* have Al'Mazraea back—as long as we let them take the Verd." His black eyes returned to hers. "That's still our land, you Creo thief. You're in no position to negotiate."

Mila braced herself to hold his gaze even though she felt his poison seeping into her. He needed to die. It was a truth so deep and raw, and the longer she stood there, the harder it became to keep the rage from consuming her completely.

Stay calm.

"We're not negotiating, we're begging—and all we're begging you for is freedom. The freedom to live in peace. But you can't see that, can you? You can't imagine that we are *people* just like you. People, with feelings and dreams and rights! Not animals to work for you, caged until you next need us. Not a disease infecting your lands. *People*."

Cheers reached her ears. The refugees were cheering… cheering for *her*.

"You have no rights," spat Lideri. "Our constitution doesn't recognise you. You're not even mentioned. As far as we're concerned, you're *not* people."

"But we are," Mila said, tipping her chin up. Her voice rose above the wind. "And we're not going back. We deserve to be free."

The guards behind him raised their guns higher. Their fingers slipped onto the triggers, awaiting the order.

"Then you'll die, like the vermin you are." A cruel smile curled his lips, and Mila knew; this was the answer he had been hoping for.

The earth seemed to hold its breath, the tension between them stretching taut like a garotte.

Mila's heart raced, but she didn't flinch. She stood tall, looking Lideri straight in his black eyes. Lideri's smirk vanished, his eyes narrowed, and he turned his back on her, walking to a safe place behind his men.

When he turned back, Mila could barely see his face for the headlights blinding her.

"Last chance," he called.

"No."

The word hung in the air, heavy and final.

Mila saw the hand raise, and she threw herself to the ground once more.

Time seemed to slow as the guards' fingers squeezed their triggers.

As the first bullet fired, the earth beneath her roared to life.

35

Mila drank in the surge of power like it was water in the desert. The magic was undeniable. With the strength of a hundred Satarians fuelling her, the connection had a physical heat, radiating through her as she accessed a power that had been theirs for hundreds and thousands of years. The Amanese would *not* be their keepers anymore.

Mila closed her eyes, blocking out everything else—the light, the gunfire, the screams. She thought only of justice.

They deserved to feel what she felt. The fear. The helplessness. The pain.

As her fingers dug in further, the ground responded to her rage, ripping further apart. Mila fixed her gaze on the nearest truck, still idling, too close to the edge of the ravine. It was so easy, so effortless to call on Gaia again.

Urratoray t'ard.

The Amanese soldiers beside the truck stopped firing and looked down with confusion as the ground beneath their feet began to quake. Then, with a mighty lurch, the land started to crumble away, pulling the closest truck toward the ravine that *she* had created. The men started shouting, panicked and scrambling to get out of the way as the vehicle slid forward onto the collapsing ground. The front tires slipped over the edge, and the truck began to slowly tilt into the gaping hole.

"Shoot her!" Lideri yelled. The men fumbled with their weapons. A bullet whizzed past her cheek.

Mila's breath quickened, and the truck tipped further. With a final surge, the chunk of earth fell away, taking the truck tumbling down with it. Savage satisfaction wrought a smile on Mila's face as the vehicle disappeared into the darkness, swallowed by the earth.

Her earth.

The power inside screeched like a magnificent beast sending wildfire through her veins. She pushed harder, pulled in more energy. The ground trembled violently with anticipation, and moments later, the second truck teetered upon the disintegrating edge before it too toppled into the expanding abyss with a deafening crash.

Mila gasped, trembling from the effort, her breath coming in ragged bursts as her eyes fixed on Lideri. Every muscle quivered and ached from the exertion, but beneath it all, something euphoric spread through her like a golden light; a hunger, a craving that pulsed in time with her heartbeat, wrapping around her like a lover's embrace promising something dangerously close to bliss. It was intoxicating, a high she never wanted to come down from. She needed more.

In a dim portion of her mind Mila was aware of a burning sensation against her neck and collarbone. Without thinking, her hands pressed harder into the dirt. The earth shivered beneath her touch; waiting and eager as sparks of red lightning laced her arms.

She held the power of life and death in her hands. Why should she let *any* of them live? Her awareness flicked to the guards. They had murdered her parents, hunted her, slaughtered thousands of Satarians… all without hesitation.

Mila's eyes narrowed. She would pull them into the earth. Crush them all and end it, right here, right now. She would tear down the people who had destroyed everything she loved. She would change everything.

She focused on the two closest guards and time seemed to freeze as one of them looked at her, his eyes wide and fearful. She saw his lips form an O, and she thought he might have been saying *no*.

No?

Her lip curled. How *dare* he say that word to her, when the Satarians never had the option to say it themselves. All the times in her life that she was assaulted, all the times of brutality and coercion, the forced acts and beatings and labour… If she had ever said no, it only made things worse.

Do you feel that, she thought to the men. Feel that fear? You only have it for a moment, yet you made us feel it every minute of every day. She directed the earth's magic toward them.

I will make it that you'll never feel anything again.

The earth ripped apart like fabric at the seam, and each guard let out a strangled cry as gravity took hold—they disappeared in the blink of an eye, their screams swallowed as easily as their bodies as they plummeted into the silence of the ravine.

That was only two people. Two of them versus the *hundreds* of dead Satarians. The score was not even close to settled.

"Shoot her!" Lideri yelled again, but the men were no longer listening to orders. Rifles slipped from their hands, thudding uselessly to the ground as they turned and sprinted away from the ever-expanding chasm, too concerned with their own survival to obey Lideri.

The High Commander screamed after them, but it was no use. He seemed to realise this, and his shoulders dropped for a fraction of a second. Then he stooped and snagged one of the dropped rifles, ducking behind the remaining vehicle.

Despite the demise of the other two trucks, Lideri had the confidence to believe he could be safe there. He had the audacity to think he could be safe anywhere.

But Mila was a force of nature—powerful, unrelenting, untamed. She had come to learn that only those with power know safety, and *she* had the power now.

The crevasse snaked along, chasing down the other guards, black smears amid the tall grasses. She focused on them.

Three, four, five, six.

It was so easy and so quick to end these lives.

The earth cracked and groaned as the fissure grew, expanding and stretching across the valley like a grotesque smile that opened toward the final truck and, quickly, it too nosedived into the darkness below.

Exposed now with the vanishing of the truck, Lideri stood facing her, his grip steady as he cocked the rifle, leveling it at her.

The savage power arced through Mila like a viper, coiled and ready to strike once more.

Lideri.

He had set her up, made her life a living nightmare. He thought himself a god, imposing his will over all their lives, believing he had the right to decide who lived and who died. But he was not a god—he was pure evil. Every lie he had ever said about the Satarian people was truth when it came to him. *He* was a curse. *He* was poison. *He* was the wicked purveyor of terrible violence and mass murder.

Pure, black hatred tore through her, bursting like window glass blowing out in an explosion. She would not allow this man to survive. He deserved to die. No, he deserved worse. Each life he had taken should be experienced by him as torture and pain worse than anything she could dream of. He was not a god.

She was the god, and she would show him as much. She would show him what true power looked like.

The shot rang out, louder than even the earthquakes.

Mila barely flinched as the bullet sliced through the air, kicking up a trail of soil a metre to her left as she willed the earth to twist and crack beneath him. The ravine reached for him with greedy hands.

Another shot.

She felt nothing. Not the sharp sting of metal grazing flesh, not the warmth of blood slipping down her arm. Her focus was only on him— on his desperate, scrambling movements as he hurled the rifle away and turned to flee.

No.

The canyon crumbled with violent shockwaves that rippled outward, rolling across the land all the way back to Haman city. The distant buildings juddered as their foundations quaked, glass windows splintered, and the streetlights flickered once, twice—then the night claimed the streets entirely. The ravine stretched wider, chasing Lideri with unrelenting force. His footing faltered. His arms flailed. And then, the ground beneath him gave way.

Thick plumes of dust and debris shot skyward, momentarily obscuring the stars. For a moment, his gaze met hers, wide with the realisation of his fate. Then he was gone, pulled down into the darkness where he belonged.

Only then did she exhale.

Mila smiled to herself with savage pleasure. Lideri was gone, swallowed by the earth.

Her earth.

But it was not enough. Not yet. The red energy thrummed in her trembling limbs as she willed the creomancy to continue. Why stop there? She could crumble the whole town of Haman, make the people feel the devastation of having their home turn against them. She should shake the earth until every building ceased to stand, until every town in the whole of Ard Aman was nothing but stone and dust and carnage.

They all must pay.

Her fingers curled in the soil.

Suddenly she had her arms wrenched from the earth.

Pain ricocheted through her as if her very soul had been torn in two, as her fingers lost contact with the earth and the raw connection she had been feeding on was ripped away.

Mila let out a savage scream, fury and agony merging into a primal sound that tore from her throat as she ripped herself away from the interference. Her world spun, and she lost her balance, disoriented, crashing hard onto her side. The breath knocked from her lungs as she hit the ground. Immediately, a heavy weight landed on her, trying to hold her down as she bucked against it, writhing in rage. Mila would not be held.

"Get off!" she screeched.

"What the hell are you doing!" Muharram bellowed. He pinned her arms out by her sides. "You can't attack Haman!"

"Why shouldn't I?" Mila spat. "They deserve it. They deserve worse!"

"They're just people!"

"They're not! They *supported him.* They *wanted* this!"

Muharram shook his head, doubling down the pressure on her arms. "It's not going to make it right—it just confirms all their prejudices about us. Everything they ever feared about us just came true when you killed those men!"

"Let it be true! Let them fear us for a *real* reason. They made us into this!"

"No!" He yelled. "We don't have to be what they think we are. We don't have to be monsters. You said that yourself once, didn't you? They have told us what we are, our whole lives. *They* created this identity. Why would you give into it?"

"Because!" Mila yelled, twisting against him. "Because! That's all they've left me with. If they want a monster, I'll show them one."

The older man shook his head. "This won't make you happy, Mila. This won't bring your family back."

The words hit her, cold and sharp. She blinked. For a second, her breath caught, but the fire in her heart still smouldered.

"I know that!" she shouted, voice trembling with fury and something else, something she didn't want to admit. "But what else is there, Muharram? What else can I do?" She suddenly felt like a child, hopelessly lost in a world that had taken everything from her. Everything except this burning anger, and she clung to it desperately. "Tell me, please, what else I can do! This ravine doesn't go on forever, and IronHand still exists. They will find a way around, and they will come after us."

Muharram's grip softened slightly, though he didn't let go. His eyes, filled with sorrow and weariness, searched her face. "You're talking about killing them all, Mila."

Angry, hot tears streamed down her face. "We *can't* just let them get away with it. There *has* to be some justice! It can't just be for nothing. It *can't*."

He let silence hang over her for a moment before continuing quietly. "You want to know what we can do, Mila? We can *survive*. We can protect what's left. Killing them isn't right, and it isn't going to help."

She shook her head, the sting of his words piercing her defences. It *should* make it right. She had to somehow make it right… But as she looked into his eyes, the thunderous fury inside her began to weaken, like a wave retreating after crashing against a cliff.

"Is this it, then?" she whispered, more to herself than to Muharram. "We run… and hope we're hidden well enough, forever?"

"We live," Muharram corrected softly. "We live, Mila. We're free, right now."

"*For* now."

"*Now*," he said. "That's all we ever have."

Mila closed her eyes. The ferocity within her continued to ebb, replaced by a cold, hollow ache. She cast one last glance at the ravine, at the destruction she had caused, and turned her head away.

Muharram gently released her arms and got to his feet, offering a dirt-stained hand to help her up. She looked at it for a moment, then glanced from his hand to his face, seeing the steady resolve in his eyes. She didn't need his help. She could stand on her own. She didn't want to be coddled or forgiven.

She wanted to unleash this anger inside her somehow.

She wanted to be free of the pain it caused as it burned her up inside, charring her soul.

With a deep breath, Mila swallowed her stubbornness, reached out, and took his hand. His grip was firm and warm, pulling her up from the ground like a lifebuoy, pulling her back to the surface. Her fingers came away smeared with blood. Her blood.

She stared, finally registering the sting in her shoulder, but the ache was nothing compared to what she felt inside.

In silence, Mila's eyes drifted over the fallen Satarian bodies lying silent among the tufts of long grass. She couldn't bring herself to count them. Thankfully, there were many more moving toward the mountains in a stream of grey.

"We live, Mila," Muharram repeated. "We live."

36

Slowly, step after step, the gibbous moon faded into the brightening azure.

Mila could feel Muharram's eyes on her back as they passed steadily through the foothill passage, but she refused to look at him. Shame and defiance battled in her mind. How could anyone say she was unjustified in taking the lives of the IronHand guards? They were not innocent, guiltless, harmless…

But then, neither was she.

Where did the desire for vengeance end? When did one finally believe things were even?

Mila thought about what Lideri had said. He truly believed that the Satarians had committed crimes in the past and that they were deserving of everything IronHand had done. He had felt justified in it all.

The idea picked at Mila's mind. No one was ever justified in hurting someone else, yet it would never be allowed to be that simple. She felt justified in hurting the guards… The guards felt justified in hurting the Satarians… The Amanese would want payback for the creomancy Mila had just done. Where did it end? All she knew was it couldn't end yet, not while hundreds of Satarians were still imprisoned in the camp.

Maybe it would never be over.

There was a crisp bite to every breath of thin air that filled her lungs. The earth's call pulled her forward, vibrating softly through her veins and whispering in her mind. The promise of freedom.

Still, questions and doubts tugged at her. What if the Verd was just another trick, another place they would be hunted down and enslaved, just like before? What if it was just another illusion, another false promise that would leave them with nothing but more broken dreams?

Ahead, the foremost refugees crested a hill that looked much the same as all the others around, but suddenly loud gasps rolled down to meet her. A woman clutched the arm of the man beside her. Hands flew to mouths or stomachs. Some sank to their knees, overwhelmed by whatever they saw beyond the ridge, while others stood in stunned silence. A child, half-starved and hollow-eyed, let out a sound somewhere between a sob and a laugh.

Mila paused, watching and wondering what could stir such a reaction in people who had lost everything. Slowly, an ember of joy ignited within her, warming the grey numbness soaking her mind, and she allowed herself the thought: What if this was everything they'd ever dreamed of?

As Mila reached the hilltop beside Muharram, she paused, unable to breathe. Before them, in the valley below, was the forest of the Verd. It stretched out like a vast, endless sea, its treetops thick and dense. Every leaf seemed to shimmer with gold under the light of the rising sun. The forest was aglow with an ethereal beauty that seemed untouched by the suffering they had left behind.

Tears stung Mila's eyes and she gripped Muharram's arm to hold herself upright. The sheer beauty of it made her legs weak.

With wide eyes, the refugees moved down the slopes and into the trees, and Mila's heart swelled as she watched them. They had fought, they had endured, and now they stood on the brink of a new beginning.

"It's like a dream," Muharram murmured, as if afraid that speaking too loudly would shatter the magic of the moment. He tore his eyes away to look at Mila. "Should we go down?"

Mila nodded, and her worn boots carried her forward in a trance, one hand absently clutching the necklace at her throat. Ancient, towering trunks, all silver and bronze, reached out with branches that stretched toward the sky. Soft grasses enveloped her ragged boots, and soon she found she was jogging, then running, running towards the glen, tumbling through the colours all around. So many colours! Deep emeralds, shimmering golds, and bunches of wildflowers that bloomed in splashes of colour trailing away into the depths of the forest. A babbling trickle played in her ears, and she peered around the trees to see a stream shimmering with all the shades of apatite.

All of a sudden, Mila drew in a deep breath, overcome by a wave of emotions she wasn't prepared for. She wanted to scream, to laugh, to cry and collapse all at once. Overwhelming gratitude filled her, flowing out in tears that rolled unchecked down her cheeks, carving tracks through the dirt. It was more beautiful than anything she could have imagined, more vibrant than any dream. She breathed in deeply, hungrily, like she had been drowning every day of her life until this moment.

The air here was different, too—the wind that swept down from the mountains lost its harsh edge, swirling the rich scent of pine and earth, mixed with the delicate perfume of wildflowers. It was cleaner, fresher. Richer.

Magic called to her from every blade of grass, every tree trunk, every grain of dirt. It was pure, untainted and ancient. This was a place where the earth's power thrived unchallenged by the cruelty of men. A place of life, of growth, of harmony. A force so strong it made her tremble.

The thrill of survival became mixed with a peculiar feeling and, as she watched the light dance over the leaves and settle on the dewdrops, she tried to figure it out. It was a pleasant swelling in her chest, a warmth… like a hug, but from inside.

Joy. She was feeling joy, for the first time in a very long time.

She couldn't stop the smile that broke across her face, wide and unrestrained. It had been waiting to emerge for years.

But as much as the sight of the forest filled her with a sense of victory, there was something else that lingered beneath it all. A small, nagging whisper that wouldn't leave her alone. The magic humming beneath her feet wasn't just life and beauty; it was power. It had given her the strength to fight back, to defend her people, to take vengeance. And that power was still there, coursing through her like a dark undercurrent, waiting to be called on again.

Her job wasn't done.

Three days later, Khalen found her, sitting with her back cradled by the thick roots of a tree. She was watching the leaves above dance slowly in the breeze, squinting every now and then as the sunlight filtered through. Her gaze flicked to him only briefly before she was drawn back to the leaves as though hypnotised. She was certain that she could spend the rest of her life watching this shifting dance and never grow bored of it.

"I never imagined it would be like this," Khalen said. He leaned against the silvery bark, looking down at her.

"Mmm. Even with knowing two languages, I can't find the words for all these shades of green," Mila said dreamily.

"It's so beautiful. There are creations here I didn't even know existed."

"It shows how our imagination limits our world, I suppose. We'd never heard of flowers like this, so how could we imagine it?"

"You're in a philosophical mood," Khalen said.

"Just pondering our understanding of the world," Mila replied with a chuckle. "That's all."

A comfortable silence fell between them before Khalen spoke again. "It feels like we're meant to *be here*." He paused, then added. "I don't ever want to leave."

There was something in his voice that made Mila sit up and look at him properly. His eyes darted around, never resting for long on any one spot, as though he was searching for something unseen. The shadows still haunted him, like they haunted her, even here in this golden place.

She debated letting him in on her plan. He needed it, she decided. And it might even make it easier.

"Will you walk with me?" Mila said, taking him by the hand.

He nodded and followed her.

All around, the gnarled trees stood like columns in an ancient temple, some covered in mosses and climbing vines that twisted along the branches like serpents. Bronze leaves loosed themselves from high above to float dreamily downwards. As they walked, Mila trailed her fingertips through the delicate fronds of rich, feathery ferns, shimmering with droplets of dew. Soft sunbeams sliced through the branches, spilling across the ground in pools of frolicking light as the two survivors silently traced a path out of the trees, towards the mountains.

"I need to go back for the others," Mila said presently. "Muharram will come with me."

If Khalen was surprised, it didn't show; his voice was firm and fierce when he said, "I'll come too."

Mila shook her head. "No, you need to stay here."

"I'm brave, Mila. I know I said I don't want to leave here, but—"

"You *are* brave, Khalen. More brave than anyone had a right to expect. But that's not why you can't come with us."

"Why then?"

"Someone needs to stay here, to protect the people. To be a leader. Someone with the power to protect them if something goes wrong."

"What could go wrong?" Khalen stopped walking, tugging on Mila's hand so that she turned to face him. "What do you mean?"

It was the only way, but she couldn't bring herself to say it.

"Mila…?"

"IronHand will come again, Khalen, you know that."

"But Lideri is dead, I—I saw."

Mila shook her head. "IronHand is bigger than Lideri. It's an idea, an evil idea, that has taken root in the Amanese people. You heard what he said. He planned this. They *will* come for us. They will cross the foothills as easy as we did; easier, probably, with their trucks and technology."

"Lideri may have planned IronHand's take over, but he didn't plan on us getting out. He didn't plan on us using our power against them. He didn't plan on *you*." Khalen's chin lifted stubbornly. He still carried innocence somehow. But innocence could quickly become ignorance, and a blindfold an execution hood. "Besides, they'd have to cross the ravine to get to us, and they can't. It's too wide. We're safe."

Mila shook her head. "The ravine will slow them down, but it's not enough. You know that."

He didn't argue; of course he knew it. It was written all over his face.

Khalen's throat bobbed as he swallowed. Beneath the *noterran* brand, his viridian eyes fixed on her with a new sadness. "I can't stop you going, can I?"

Mila shook her head. "No. Our people deserve to be free—*all* our people. I need to go back. I need to know…" She trailed off.

Khalen nodded, biting his bottom lip. "You need to know if Nasir is really gone."

"And if he is, I need to make sure he is buried properly. I couldn't—" Her voice cracked. She balled her hands into fists. "—I couldn't do that for so many. I have to do it for him."

Khalen's brow furrowed suddenly, and he looked unsure. "How are you going to get back in? And how are you going to get out again?"

Mila picked absently at the skin around her thumb nail as her eyes traced along the zig zag line of the mountain tops. Eventually she said, "Don't worry about that now. We'll find a way."

"But you are coming back, right?"

Mila tried to give a comforting smile, but her face felt like clay, thick and unworkable. She gave up and sighed. "I can't lie to you Khalen. We barely made it out once…"

"Then stay here. You don't need to go. Stay here, *please*."

The despair in his voice cracked Mila's heart. She looked away. "I have to."

"You *don't* have to. You've done enough!" he snapped, trembling with anger. "You're trying to save everybody, when for all you know they're already dead. You could be walking straight into a trap!" The boy stood with fists clenched at his sides, glaring at Mila with burning intensity.

She thought about yelling at him. Thought about telling him that he couldn't possibly understand the depths of guilt and responsibility she felt. How, if everybody was already dead as he had said, then she deserved the same fate. She let out a long sigh, shoulders slumping slightly at the weight settled there. "They deserve a chance. They deserve to be free."

"But so do you!" Khalen yelled. Several small birds erupted from a nearby tree, taking flight into the clear blue. Mila was surprised to see tears in the boy's eyes.

She placed a steadying hand on his upper arm and shook her head slowly. "Come here," Mila said, and pulled him toward a grassy area at the base of the hills. "Sit with me."

He sat, knees tucked up under his folded arms—just the way Nasir used to sit, Mila thought. She sucked her bottom lip, mentally searching for the words. She had to explain this to him before he shut down completely. But she also had to go carefully.

"You had a *felicia* flower with you last night," Mila said gently. "Who were you visiting, Khalen?"

The blue flowers only bloomed on the graves of Satarians, where their energy had returned to Gaia.

Khalen placed his forehead on his arms, hiding his face, and said nothing. But Mila remembered what he had whispered as he had climbed into the escape tunnel.

If mahma could see me now…

"How old were you when she passed?"

With his face still buried, Khalen murmured, "Ten."

Mila's heart ached for him. Before she could say anything else, Khalen lifted his head.

"It was the guards' fault. It's always their fault, even before IronHand came along."

"What happened?" Mila asked, steeling herself for the answer.

Khalen drew in a deep breath. "She was sick. Really sick. Pada and me, we tried to get help for her, but the border guards wouldn't let her cross. They didn't want her sickness on Amanese soil, they said. The last time, my father fought with them, tooth and nail—and I haven't seen him since. Mahma died just a few days later. So, yeah, I picked a *felicia*. I always pick one every time I visit her..." His voice trailed away.

"You lost them both..." Mila couldn't believe what she was hearing. A wave of sadness and understanding flooding over her. Of course he'd built walls around himself, always determined to do more—he'd been so young, too young, to carry that kind of loss. It made what she was trying to do that much harder. She swallowed. "How did you feel when your mahma was sick, when you realised she wasn't going to get better?"

There was silence for a long moment, and Mila worried that she had gone too far. Then Khalen grunted one word: "Useless."

"You wished you could change it, right? Wished you could do something about it?"

The boy looked over to the right, away from Mila. His dark hair fell into his eyes. "Yeah," he said quietly.

"And if you knew there *was* a chance you could save her, wouldn't you take it?"

"Of course, but—"

"Well, that's what this is for me. There's a chance—a reasonable chance—that Muharram and I can save many of the people still stuck in Al'Mazraea. If I don't take this chance, how could I live with myself?" She added quietly, "It's already hard enough."

Khalen shook his head. "There's a chance I can save *you*, Mila. How can you ask me not to take it?"

"Because it's not up to you to save me," she said quietly. "I'm living on borrowed time, Khalen. I have been ever since that day in Haman. If I had died that day, maybe none of this would have happened… and I don't know if that's good or bad. But I didn't die, and it did happen, and now I need to do this last thing. Either we'll come back, or I'll die trying, but I will have made it right."

The boy shot to his feet. "There's *nothing* you can say to make me believe that you dying is the right thing." Without waiting for a reply, he turned and stormed off.

Mila sat frozen for a moment. Her lips pressed together as she blinked back tears at the sting of his words. He wasn't supposed to care this much. Mila sighed as she got to her feet.

She walked slowly back to the tree line and leant against one of the thick, dark trunks. Flakes of old bark crumbled away at her touch. A few metres into the forest, a group was working together to fashion a kind of shelter from fallen branches and large slabs of moss. The first team passed the long branches up to others who were nestled in the trees, and these people did their best to secure the wood by tying strands of the dark green vines around and around. It was impressive work, but it did little to soothe Mila's soul. She was restless. She needed to get away from here. Every moment she stayed was a moment that someone else was trapped, tortured, or worse…

Mila turned away, leaning her back and head against the tree. Once again, her eyes traced the distance to the tall peaks of the Uul Serrad. She was doing the right thing, wasn't she? Going back for more survivors, for Nasir… it was incredibly dangerous, but it *wasn't* pointless.

The Satarians finally had a place to call their own, after three hundred years of being bound by Amanese walls and Amanese rules. They belonged here.

They were safe.

For now.

Epilogue

Seven days had passed since the Satarians trickled into the Verd. The evening air was chilly, but fires scattered throughout the camp kept the warmth alive. Around the fires, laughter echoed through the night air. True laughter, loud and unrestricted, full of joy and merriment. Groups of friends sat close together, faces glowing in the warm, dancing light. Some leaned back on their elbows, gazing up at the stars, and every so often, someone would burst into a carefree tune that would be picked up in a chorus of mismatched voices. There was an ease in the way they moved and talked, their smiles wide and unburdened. The magic-born flames flickered with ease, lighting up the trees around.

Mila watched from a distance, her mind swirling with a mix of emotions. Could she truly let it go? Could she walk away from this beautiful forest and back to everything they had just escaped?

Yet again, she scanned the faces illuminated by the firelight, searching for Khalen. She understood his anger; he wanted to her to stay, to enjoy the freedom they had finally achieved. But she needed him to understand that she just couldn't do that.

Not yet.

"He'll come around," Muharram murmured, reading her like he always could. He adjusted his boot laces, glancing toward the horizon.

"He's avoiding me," Mila replied, scowling so the older man wouldn't see her sadness. "But we need to go now, otherwise we'll be getting to Haman in daylight…"

"I know," Muharram said. "Have faith. He will show up."

"And if he doesn't, I'll kick his ass," Thani said. Her sharp features were made even more dramatic by the firelight.

Mila looked around her at the downcast, determined faces of the rebels, knowing it might be for the last time. They were fewer now. Of the eleven who had once trained in creomancy with her, one, maybe two, would never be with them again. And the others? Since arriving at the Verd, freedom had softened their edges; the urgency that once bound them had unravelled in this wonderland. Only three stood by her in the gloom; Muharram, Thani, and Mahgda, with their branded foreheads and scarred, mottled skin evidence of everything they had survived. They had been abused and assaulted, silenced and starved and stripped. But they were not finished, not yet. Still they stood, with the strength of the earth in their veins and its memory in their bones. They stood for those who couldn't, for those still caged, for the fallen ones and the ones who had escaped.

The shadows stirred and a lanky figure appeared, momentarily silhouetted by the firelight. Khalen stepped toward them, his scowl deepening as he neared, and he crossed his scarred arms tight across his chest. "You're really going to do this?"

Mila met his gaze, eyes pleading. "I have to."

He looked like he was about to argue. He opened his mouth but, at the last second, closed it and shook his head, eyes full of hurt beneath his dark hair. "I know."

Mila squeezed his hand, but there was nothing she could say. In her other hand, concealed in her pocket, she clenched the whittled rose.

The firelight flickered. The moment had come.

"Take care of each other," Mila said quietly, her voice cracking. She looked at each of them in turn, wanting to say so much more, but the words were impossible to form.

Khalen avoided Mila's gaze, but she could see what it was costing him. A muscle feathered in his jaw and his entire frame shook as he fought to keep his anguish contained. Muharram pressed a kiss to Thani's forehead, nodding to Mahgda in silent farewell. Then he turned and marched away towards the foothills.

Mila shot one last, desperate look at Khalen, but he kept his eyes down, leaving the scarce goodbye to linger like a ghost.

The air felt colder as they left the canopy and the fires behind, the wind biting as they neared the foothills once more. Before long, they were climbing steadily, away from the peace of the Verd. Muharram led the way, steady and determined as always. Mila followed in silence, fingers picking at her thumbnails, her thoughts on the mission ahead. She just hoped they would get there in time.

It wasn't until they had reached the crest of the foothills that they stopped, turning back almost simultaneously to look at the paradise below.

"Do you think we'll come back?" Mila asked him, eyes on the distant fires, ears straining to catch the faintest of joyful songs.

Muharram didn't answer for a long moment. When he did, it wasn't the platitude Mila had been expecting.

"I think either way, whether we return to the forest or to the earth, we'll finally find peace."

A little while later, the landscape steadily flattened before them. Remnants of the battle were everywhere, etched into the ground; dried pools of darkened blood, scattered bullets and clawed soil. The fallen bodies had already been claimed by the earth, marked by the blue of the *felicia* flowers that already dotted the dusty, red-stained plains. With every step, the bone necklace bounced against her collarbone and she inhaled the metallic tang lacing the air.

Stretching off into the haze on either side, the jagged scar of Mila's creomancy cut across the valley, a boundary separating one world from another. Seeing it with fresh eyes, a mix of shame and pride tightened her throat. She had done this. She had the power to ruin the world.

The wind howled through the hollows in a low, haunting echo that reverberated off the stone walls. Immediately around the rift, the soil was pale and parched. Brittle, ashen residue swirled in the wind but, thankfully, the desolation didn't extend too far.

Not visibly, anyway.

A shiver crawled through Mila and raised bumps on her arms.

"This is it," Muharram said, breaking the silence. His eyes scanned the mountains, then came to rest on Mila, the enormity of what they were about to do evident in his tense muscles and steely eyes.

"Are you ready?"

Acknowledgements
and Author's Notes

Hi there!

Thank you **so** much for picking up my book. I can't believe it's out in the world now, and that someone is holding my words in their hands right now. Words that came to my mind, that I agonised over, and read hundreds of times. *My* words.

I have always wanted to write a book, but for most of my life I didn't believe I had anything worth saying, let alone the time and space to put it all down on paper. The process of learning that my voice is valuable has been a long and difficult one, but, thanks to some beautiful people (too many to list, but your initials are at the end!), I made it through. Still, I felt terribly exposed in writing the rawness of the mental health struggles that Mila goes through… but it's my hope that, in reading this, even one person out there will feel seen, and then every vulnerable word will have been worth it.

To my incredible friend, Ash, who was the very first to read Bound from beginning to end. You didn't just read the words, you really saw it for the message I'm trying to share. Your honest, thoughtful feedback made this book stronger in ways I couldn't have managed alone, and you did it with such care, patience, and enthusiasm. Your belief in both me and this story gave me the courage to keep going when doubt crept in. I'm endlessly grateful for your insight, your support, and the gift of meeting you on that staircase. Thank you.

To my booksta besties: Jazzy, Kerrie, Courtney and Balls. Thank you for proving that real friendship can bloom in the most unexpected places. Your encouragement, excitement, and genuine kindness have made this journey brighter at every turn. Whether it was cheering me on during the hard days, celebrating small victories, or simply checking in, you've each played a part in getting me to this moment. I'm so grateful for you!

The dream of writing a meaningful story would not have come about without my senior high school English teacher, Mrs Hutton. Her passion and dedication inspired both my career in teaching (though I went with primary school instead) and my penchant for symbolism. She taught me that there is always more than meets the eye, and that there are people in your corner even when you might not think so.

Along those lines, any Aussies who studied the unit *Into the Wild* in the 2000's will surely recognise the influence that unit had on this story, hopefully without having HSC flashbacks. In these pages, the magic of the earth is a reminder of what we stand to lose if we fail to honour it, and the power we can have if we reconnect with nature. It was an important message then, and it's an important message now: we must remember that the ground beneath our feet is alive and take better care of this beautiful planet.

Jeffery Deaver deserves recognition for his kindness towards teenage me, a budding author who once dabbled in Law & Order fan-fiction (yes, it still exists on the internet somewhere). Back in 2005, I had the audacity to send my writing to Mister Deaver and, to my shock, he actually replied, along with notes that proved he had actually read what I'm now embarrassed to say I wrote. Fast-forward about five years, and Deaver is in Sydney for a book tour. He signed each of the eight books I brought with me (one-book etiquette, what?), then I recounted my teenage audacity and nervously asked if he remembered me. Not only did he say yes, but he described details of that fan-fic story I'd sent him. I was blown away and, because of that, he has a lifelong fan and now an eternally grateful baby author in his debt.

To my darling husband, Mitch. When we first met, I hadn't read a book in years and years—not because I didn't want to, but because my mental health simply wouldn't allow it. I was so overwhelmed by stress and anxiety to clear my mind enough to read and, if ever I sat down to try, I would quite literally fall asleep within two pages. But thanks to you, I began to clear my head and could therefore return to something that I always considered part of my identity; because of you I could begin to be myself again. And then, I could start writing. Bound wouldn't have happened without your love and support, without us bouncing ideas around, without you bringing me tea and snacks and a kiss on the head. Thank you, forever-ever.

Lastly, but most importantly: this story is imagined, but its roots grow from very real events. It is shaped by the echoes of the war in Afghanistan, the ongoing persecution of the Rohingya people, the current devastation in Gaza, the civil war in Sudan, the genocide in Rwanda, and the displacement and violence of the Nakba. These events, and countless others like them, have left deep scars on real people. It makes me sick, the way humans can treat each other. My hope is that this book honours the resilience of those who have endured such atrocities, and serves as a reminder that their stories must never be forgotten, and the events must never be repeated. Human rights are supposed to be universal and irretractable; currently they are just privileges enjoyed and allowed by those in power.

〜

Because of you: KB, SEB(P), KRB, SK, KW(B), MR, GR, AB(S), A(T)R, JER, JBR, MMH.

Endnote: It's not complicated.

All human beings are born free and equal in dignity and rights.

Everyone is entitled to all the rights and freedoms set forth in this Declaration, without distinction of any kind, such as race, colour, sex, language, religion, political or other opinion, national or social origin, property, birth or other status.

Everyone has the right to life, liberty and security of person.

No one shall be held in slavery or servitude; slavery and the slave trade shall be prohibited in all their forms.

No one shall be subjected to torture or to cruel, inhuman or degrading treatment or punishment.

Everyone has the right to recognition everywhere as a person before the law.

All are entitled to equal protection against any discrimination in violation of this Declaration and against any incitement to such discrimination.

Everyone has the right to an effective remedy by the competent national tribunals for acts violating the fundamental rights granted him by the constitution or by law.

No one shall be subjected to arbitrary arrest, detention or exile.

Everyone has the right to a nationality.

Marriage shall be entered into only with the free and full consent of the intending spouses.

No one shall be arbitrarily deprived of their property.

Everyone has the right to freedom of thought, conscience and religion.

Everyone has the right to freedom of peaceful assembly and association.

Everyone has the right to a standard of living adequate for the health and well-being of himself and of his family, including food, clothing, housing and medical care.

Everyone has the right to education.

Everyone.

Extracted from The Universal Declaration of Human Rights UN General Assembly, Resolution 217A (III), Universal Declaration of Human Rights, A/RES/217(III) (December 10, 1948)

Tasha is an Australian author based in Sydney, where she lives a wonderfully chaotic life with her husband and four cats. A primary school teacher for over fifteen years, one of her greatest passions is using literature to spark critical thinking and reflection in her students. Her debut novel, *Bound*, is part 1 in *A Desiccated Legacy*, a trilogy which focuses on human rights and respect for the environment.

tasha.hayes.author@gmail.com

@t.hayes.author